William Dalton

**Phaulcon the Adventurer, or, the Europeans in the East**

A romantic biography

William Dalton

**Phaulcon the Adventurer, or, the Europeans in the East**
*A romantic biography*

ISBN/EAN: 9783337048921

Printed in Europe, USA, Canada, Australia, Japan

Cover: Foto ©Andreas Hilbeck / pixelio.de

More available books at **www.hansebooks.com**

# PHAULCON THE ADVENTURER;

## OR,

# THE EUROPEANS IN THE EAST.

LONDON:
PRINTED BY R. CLAY, SON, AND TAYLOR,
BREAD STREET HILL.

Yours very Sincerely

William Dalton

TO

CAPTAIN

THE HONOURABLE HEDWORTH LIDDELL.

My dear Captain Liddell,

Whatever the merit of a book, its dedication is ever
intended as a compliment. Thus to you I inscribe this
work; less, however, in admiration of your great talents
in a very different walk of Art, than in remembrance of
your warm-heartedness, and in sincere regard for one
whom I must ever esteem a valued friend, and the companion of some of the most pleasant and intellectual hours
of my life.

WILLIAM DALTON.

London, *September,* 1862.

# PREFACE.

The very kind reception given by the "Press" and the Public to "Will Adams, the first Englishman in Japan," induced me to try my hand upon another worthy, whose remarkable career appeared especially adapted for the purposes of historic fiction.

For the notion I am indebted to the Jesuit Fathers, D'Orléans, * and Tachard, † from whose works I have gleaned the outline or rather basis of my narrative. My chief object being, as in "Will Adams," to amuse, I have made free use of the materials; at the same time, as it was to Phaulcon's exertions in the cause of Christianity that he mainly owed both his rise and fall, I have, at every opportunity, endeavoured to illustrate the doings of his French contemporaries, who, at the earnest desire of Louis the Fourteenth, were struggling to raise the Cross and establish Empire in the East, an attempt, however, in which, like their predecessors in Japan some few years earlier, they signally failed.

WILLIAM DALTON.

* Histoire de M. Constance, par Pierre Joseph d'Orléans, Paris, 1692.
† Voyage de Siam des Pères Jésuites, par Guy Tachard, Amsterdam, 1689.

# INDEX TO COLOURED ILLUSTRATIONS.

# CONTENTS.

CONTENTS.

## CHAPTER V.

PAGE

## CHAPTER VI.

## CHAPTER VII.

## CHAPTER VIII.

## CHAPTER IX.

## CHAPTER X.

## CHAPTER XI.

## CHAPTER XXI.

## CHAPTER XXII.

## CHAPTER XXIII.

## CHAPTER XXIV.

## CHAPTER XXV.

## CHAPTER XXVI.

## CHAPTER XXVII.

## CHAPTER XXVIII.

## CHAPTER XXIX.

## CHAPTER XXX.

FRAULON

# PHAULCON.

## CHAPTER I.

THE YOUNG GREEK, THE JESUIT, AND THE MALAY.

ONE evening in July, 1660, a youth stood upon the rugged shores of Cephalonia—at that time, like the other six of the Ionian Islands, a dependency of the mighty republic of Venice. One arm, or rather elbow, was resting upon a fragment of rock fallen from the cliffs which towered a hundred feet above him; while with his right hand he was shading his eyes from the setting sun whose rays had changed the glassy surface of the Mediterranean into a sea of living gold.

It was an hour in which to ponder over the past, and to peer into the future, a scene to fill the senses of the happy, and to warm the hearts of even the wretched with hope, and a foreshadowing of some coming good; above, beneath, all around, was singularly sensuous. The deep blue of the serene sky was varied by the rays of the declining orb of day, the air was filled with the last faint warblings of the birds, and perfumed by the golden limes and fragrant orange with the sweetness of "Araby the blest."

B

But that surrounding of enchantment was as nothing to the lonely boy; for his heart was overflowing with grief, disappointment, and ambitious aspirations for a future that might obliterate the past. Not upon the glorious vision of the sun as it sets in those seas was he earnestly gazing, but upon two large vessels in the roadstead, respectively flying the English and French flags. It was to the latter his attention seemed chiefly directed, as if in doubt as to her right to the ensign which floated from her mast. As for the other, he knew she had touched at Cephalonia for water, and to barter for currants, oil, and wine, products for which that isle was then, as now, famous. But while he is thus engaged, let me endeavour to describe his personal appearance, for that youth' was Constantine Phaulcon, the hero of the following narrative.

His finely chiselled features, pale high broad forehead, swarthy skin, dark fiery eyes, and long black hair, which fell from beneath a small Greek cap over his bared neck, bespoke the two classic races of Greece and Rome from which his mother and father derived their origin. The latter, a Venetian, had married a Greek lady. His dress exhibited to the best advantage his tall slender figure; a small cap of crimson embroidered with gold and with blue silk tassels, sat jauntily upon his head, giving relief to his long black hair. From the hips, an ample skirt of snowy Indian cotton reached to the knees; his legs were gaitered, and his feet enclosed in red morocco shoes; a loose fitting vest of blue silk, embraced a silk shirt, the collars of which were laid over the spencer or jacket, so as to expose his throat. The latter was of crimson cloth, and like the vest embroidered with gold, and ornamented with loops, fringes, spangles, and buttons of the same precious metal. The sleeves were slashed, but fastened at the wrists. To complete the picture, I must add, that from a silken girdle or sash which was bound around his waist, was suspended a richly mounted dagger. The whole costume, indeed, strongly resembled that of the Greek corsairs, since become traditional with poets and dramatists.

Although at that time Phaulcon possessed the thoughtful brow and gait of a man determining upon, or rather longing for, the opportunity of performing great deeds, and the form of a youth of twenty, he had not quite completed his fifteenth year; but that you may not believe I am making my hero a prodigy, I will quote the words of the Père d'Orléans, a French Jesuit, who knew Phaulcon intimately, and learned his history from his own lips.

"He was scarcely," says the Father, "ten years old when he became aware of his destitute condition, and felt it keenly. He did not, however, lose time in lamentations, but with a courage above his years, formed the resolution of endeavouring to raise himself in the world, and that no time might be lost, he determined to leave his native land, where he foresaw that he should meet with many obstacles to his advancement."

While the lad stood in deep meditation, a man in the sombre garb of the Society of Jesus was descending the rough pathway cut from the rock to the beach below. Still so absorbed was the lad's attention, that he knew not another was near him until the priest, tapping him upon the arm, said,

"Peace be with you, my son."

"*You*, my father!" replied the startled lad, reverently baring his head; adding, as he seized the ecclesiastic by the hands,

"But truly our holy mother hath sent thee to counsel me in my sore distress."

"Distress!" exclaimed the priest with surprise; "why, what

can have happened that the young, the gifted, and the nobly-born Constantine Phaulcon can talk thus? Nay, nay, son," he added, " cheer thee up, doubtless it is but some vexatious disappointment, magnified by thine imagination into a mountain of sorrow, but which, nevertheless, will disappear with the night's sleep."

"Father," replied the youth seriously, almost sternly, "being of the holy priesthood, it would ill become me to address thee profanely ; moreover, thou hast been my tutor and guide ; yet must I call it cruel for one so learned and experienced in the world to scoff at the sorrow even of a boy. But then, *thou* art without kith or kin, and comprehend not the feelings of one like myself."

" Nay, nay," replied the Jesuit ; "I meant not to offend, neither would I grieve thee ;" adding, as he led the youth to a small pile of rocky stone, " but come, come, sit thee here, tell me thy troubles, and mark *how* earnestly I will give my attention, and if need be, counsel."

"Thanks, Father Thomas ;" then seating himself by the side of the priest, he said, " It is now six months since my father sailed for Venice."

" And was lost at sea," interrupted the priest. "Truly, it is a great calamity for one so young to lose so dear a relative ; still, my son, it is sinful to repine at the providence of God ; faith in the wisdom of *His* dispensations is a balm that healeth every sorrow ; even thy trouble is at least soothed by the ample provision it pleased heaven to enable thy lost parent to leave to thee and thy mother."

" Father," replied the youth mournfully, "my parent's death by shipwreck, and the wealth he left behind, were currently reported

lately in the possession of my father. He also brought a letter
from my uncle, who tells us 'That my unhappy parent, finding it
no longer possible to keep secret his delinquencies, made the
voyage to Venice to entreat his aid. The vessel, as was reported,
went down in the Gulf, and, save *one*, all on board perished;
that one was my father, who, by means of a raft, succeeded in
reaching the shore. Going to the house of my uncle, who is a
member of the Council of Ten, my father confessed his weakness—crime, if you will—and prayed his brother to use his influence in obtaining him time to make up his deficiencies, if only
to save the family from disgrace.'"

"Surely this was not refused?" said the priest.

"It was not; but, alas! by some mysterious means my father's
presence in Venice, as well as the purpose of his visit, had become
known to an enemy; for my uncle having obtained an interview
with the Doge, his Highness placed in his hands a paper which
had been dropped into the Mouth of the Lion of St. Mark. This
proclaimed my father's presence in the great city, and charged
him with having defrauded the State of a portion of its revenues.
The charge having been formally made, it was impossible even for
the Doge to do otherwise than comply with the laws : my father
was, therefore, speedily seized and conveyed to the dungeons. Still
my uncle hoped that the disgrace might be kept secret; but the
same enemy who made the accusation caused it to be spread abroad
that a member of my proud relative's house was then lying in
prison charged with defrauding the State. This public disgrace
has so enraged, galled my uncle, that he has determined that my
father, as an atonement, shall be dealt with as if he were the
meanest gondolier who plies upon the Adriatic; thus has he sent
officers to Argostoli, to take possession of our property, and

henceforth we—at least, I—am a beggar. No," he added, almost fiercely, "not a beggar, for beg I will not of living man; but penniless—Constantine the Penniless."

"This is a sad story, my son, but .thine uncle is rich, powerful in the State, and will look to thy welfare till this cloud has passed over."

"Nay, he will not; but even so, I would accept nought from one who writes so sternly, cruelly, of my unfortunate father."

"My son, this pride is unwise, it is unjust, as it may be injurious to thy mother, it is sinful; nay, too sensitive to remain among thy former friends in Argostoli, what canst thou, so young, so gently nurtured, do alone in the world?"

"*What* can I do?" replied the proud boy, evidently stung by the smile and words of the priest.

"Aye, what? my son."

"Help myself, father. Work, and that, too, without the useless lamentations of a craven heart. Nay," he added, starting to his feet, "even now I am sore ashamed at the hours I have wasted in foolish regret for the past."

"*Thou* work? *Thou* help thyself?" was the incredulous reply. "*How*, my son?"

"By my hands—by my brains—by entering upon a track that has led many to fame and fortune, and perseveringly pursuing its course till I have gained—well, nothing, or the end I seek."

"Alas! my son, of the thousands who, at the outset of life, have made the same resolutions, how few have found within themselves the sustaining powers to help them to their goal? How many have been struck down upon the very threshold of their career?"

"Then, father, *I* will remember the few, and forget the many. The pages of history point out the small beginnings from which hosts of the great have arisen, why, then, should I not profit by the teaching? Have you not yourself told me that when the butcher, the father of English Wolsey, laughed deridingly at his son's declaration that he would some day make himself a cardinal, the boy replied that, at least, he would strive so hard that even should he fail in reaching the hat, it would go hard with him if he did not grasp a fragment of the mantle? In short, father, I am penniless; for one with health, strength, and will, to remain so, would, in itself, be a greater disgrace than that which is now driving me forth into the world. Nay, even the heathens had a saying, 'that the gods help those who help themselves,' and wherefore should I be worse than a heathen?"

"But even now, my son, you have not pointed out the track by which you propose to enter upon this career."

"The ocean, my father; the vast pathway which Marco Polo traversed, and whose winds have wafted all her wealth and greatness to the gorgeous Queen of the Adriatic." Pointing to one of the vessels, from which his attention had been drawn by the father, he continued, "I would seek service with yon Englishman, for I have learned the language, and, from what I know of them, like the people."

"They are heretics, my son," replied the priest, with scowling brow.

"They are brave, they are generous, and, from what I have heard from their sea-captains at my father's table, enterprising, and determined to obtain the mastery of the seas," replied Constantine, warmly; but, perceiving he was angering his companion, he added, "But pardon me, father, I had forgotten that you were a Spaniard, and cannot forgive the English for having plucked the island of Jamaica from thy sovereign's crown."

"It was taken not in chivalrous war, but by the aid of buccaneers, pirates, sea-robbers."

" By the great English admiral Penn," said the boy.

"A man who was worthy to be the servant of Cromwell, the regicide chief, of a regicide people."

" Ah, father! that Cromwell was one of the great men whose brain and muscle raised him from low beginnings to power and command," replied Constantine, with an enthusiasm that swelled the blue veins in his forehead. " That man," he added, musingly " was indeed great. Who that dwells upon his career could falter in his determination to raise himself?"

" Son," cried the father, angrily, " the arch-heretic, Cromwell, was the mere creature of chance, one piece of the lava thrown up by the volcano of rebellion above his fellows—the brigand leader of a nation of pirates. But," he added, " do you seek sea service, my son, in what nobler direction could you find it than in the navy of Spain, upon whose mighty dominions the sun never sets, and whose ships float in every sea?"

" Ah, father! you are laughing in your sleeve at me. The service of the Catholic King would be more befitting one brought up in our holy church. But Spanish ships rarely enter our harbour," replied Constantine, I am afraid with some cunning purpose, for, as he spoke, he gave a quick glance at the French flag flying at the mast of one of the ships in the roadstead.

" Then you would prefer the service of the Catholic King to that of the English heretics?" asked the father, inquiringly.

" Surely it is a useless question; but why ask me when I may not have the choice?" was the evasive reply.

" My son," replied the priest, earnestly, " you may choose, for yonder floats one of each nation," and he pointed to the before-mentioned ships.

"Nay, father," replied Constantine, in real or affected ignorance, "the one ship flies the *French* flag."

"True, but nevertheless it floats above a Spanish vessel and crew, good reason has her captain for flying that flag, for the English are at peace with France."

"Are they at war with Spain?"

"Peace or war—it is indifferent, my son, to yon English buccaneer, which is even now laden with the plunder of a Spanish galleon."

"But why should yon Spanish ship, if Spanish she be, twice in size, armament, and crew, fear to be known to the little Englishman?" asked Constantine.

"My son," replied the priest slowly, seriously, "you are young, but you have discretion beyond your years; you have been brought up in our holy faith and with a salutary abhorrence of all heretics, you have been my pupil; moreover it is too late for the disclosures I am about to make to be of harm, and so I will tell you."

"Then *you* know this Spaniard?" asked Constantine eagerly, and the father, believing the youth's mind to be bent upon an introduction to the commander, replied,

"I do, and since you have resolved upon seeking your fortune at sea, will beg of her captain, who is even now ashore in Argostoli, to receive thee on board."

"This is kind, father; but when?"

"Curb thy impatience, youth, but for three hours, and thou shalt have an opportunity of gloriously inaugurating thy career beneath the flag of the Catholic King, for long ere the morning sun the Spanish colours will float at the mast-head of yon English buccaneer," replied the priest with a malicious glance at the English ship.

"How, what mean you, father?" asked the astonished youth; adding, "Surely the brave English will never succumb without a good fight."

"Heaven forefend that the life of even one of his Catholic Majesty's subjects should be unnecessarily thrown away. No, my son, there will be no contest, the Holy Virgin hath delivered the pirates into our hands. It is by stratagem, by means of a part of her own crew, that she will be taken."

"Father," exclaimed the youth with more warmth than courtesy, "this cannot be, no English sailor could be found so base."

"That may, or may not be, my son; but give me your patient attention or I will hold my peace," returned the father angrily. "While in the Gulf of Siam," he continued, "the Englishman captured a piratical prahu. The chief and ten men, to escape being given over to the Siamese mandarin, who would have put them to a cruel lingering death, accepted the captain's invitation to join his crew. Now this chief and several of his Malays have been sent ashore these two or three days to fetch water. Even now"—as he spoke he pointed to a portion of the cliff which abutted into the sea—"the Malay is just behind yonder jutting rock awaiting the return of his men. The first day the Malay chief went into Argostoli he met with the Spanish captain, it appears they had met before at the different ports in India; the Malay told the story of his capture and his desire for revenge, moreover that the opportunity was fitting, for the English crew were nearly all sick in their hammocks. The Spanish

captain, having the service of his church and king at heart,
seized the fortunate chance by offering the Malay his liberty and
a portion of the booty, if he would aid in capturing the English
ship. The Malay readily agreed, but has since been awaiting his
opportunity. It has come; as I have said, the greater part of
the crew are sick in their hammocks, so this night he and his
men will seize the night-watch and fasten down the hatches, a
signal then being made, the Catholic King's captain will run his
ship alongside and complete the capture."

"It is at the best a treacherous scheme," replied the boy
quickly.

"*Treacherous?* boy! Surely even thou art old enough to know
that all strategy is fair in war; besides, have I not said that yon
pirate is laden with the plunder of one of the Catholic King's
galleons? Treacherous! I tell you it is a noble, a merciful
scheme."

A flush of indignation passed over the youth's face. An imprudent reply was at his tongue's end, but, dissembling, he said,
"Well, father, it is more merciful to make prisoners of war of
these Englishmen, than to leave them to be butchered by the
savage Malays. But thy friend, the Spanish captain, father, am
I to see him this night?"

"Nay, now I bethink me it will be inconvenient, for the Malays
are ashore fetching water, and he may be holding conference with
them."

"Surely that is a dangerous proceeding—one that must excite
suspicion?"

"It is, however, necessary, my son; besides, as the English
captain will not suffer these savages to bear arms, the Spaniard
intends to deliver to them one cask, which, in place of water,

will contain weapons for their use during the attack. But thy interview! thy interview!" added the priest, musingly. "Well, it shall take place to-morrow; in the meanwhile the Holy Virgin have thee in her keeping, and may God speed the good work in hand. My son, farewell;"—so saying, the father retraced his steps up the rugged pathway.

Now it must be remembered that Constantine was a Greek, and so owed no allegiance to the English. Nevertheless, as he gazed upon the retreating figure of the priest, he thus soliloquized :

"These treacherous Spaniards, I'll none of them. Ill would it become a descendant of the republicans of Greece and Rome to serve beneath the red flag of despotic Spain, the plunderer of the Indies, and the exterminator or enslaver of their ancient races. No! a born islander, I will seek to serve beneath the flag of the freest, greatest island in the world—brave, generous England, whose language I have learned, and whose people I have met and loved. Ah!" he ejaculated, "could I but warn this English captain of his impending danger, I should win his gratitude and good-will. But how? there is no time to go to Argostoli ; there is no boat near, while to swim so great a distance is beyond my strength. Yet, let me think," and Constantine, with folded arms, walked leisurely along the beach beneath the overhanging cliffs, in the direction of the jutting rock, behind which the priest had said the English boat was awaiting the return of the Malays from Argostoli with the water-casks. It was about half a mile along the beach, and stretched forth nearly to the water ; thus, like a partition, screening the boat, if boat there were, from his view, and, better for his purpose, his own person from the men who might be there awaiting their fellows. Having reached the rock, he stood leaning against it in deep thought, until the darkness of night set in. The moon, in her first quarter, was hazy and watery, but threw sufficient light upon the rippling waters and shingle to render the form of man or boat dimly visible.

While standing against the cliff, Constantine had resolved upon an enterprise, sufficiently desperate if there should be but one man in the boat, but impossible if more. To ascertain this, he crept round the point upon his hands and knees. There was little chance, however, of his footsteps being heard amid the splashing noise of the in-rolling waves; but with what anxiety and fear was he possessed as he passed around that point! for the safety of the English ship and her crew, perhaps his own fortunes, depended whether one or two men were in the boat. An instant, and he saw there was but one, a muscular, swarthy-skinned Malay, attired after the fashion of his race. A crimson handkerchief was around his head, a circular scarf or *sarong* of blue cotton hung over one shoulder and across to the opposite hip; another scarf of red and yellow bound around his waist, fell to the knees like a High-lander's kilt. His neck, legs, and feet were bare; and fortunately, as he stood in the boat, his face was turned towards Argostoli, and his back towards Constantine. The boat was about one half in the shingle, and swayed to and fro, so that the slightest movement from behind would have capsized its tenant. Observing this, the boy would at once have pounced upon him, but he also saw that the priest had deceived him in declaring the Malay unarmed, for from the waistband or sash of the man in the boat gleamed the polished barrels of pistols, and Constantine bit his nether lip with chagrin, feeling that to attack so formidable an opponent would be madness. Instinctively clutching the hilt of his dagger, he retreated behind the abutment, untied the sash from his waist, and, with the point of his dagger, slit one long strip of silk.

Having replaced the sash and dagger, he twisted the strip rope-like, and again stole around the point.

The Malay was now *sitting* upon the gunwale, but fortunately, as before, with his back turned towards the youth, musing, probably, upon his intended treachery, not more than ten yards from the rocky screen. "It is a desperate attempt," thought Constantine; "for should the fellow turn about before I reach him, all is lost—my own life, perhaps." These thoughts, however, only quickened his movements, so, trusting to the friendly plashing of the in-rolling waves to absorb the sound of his footsteps, he stole forwards, slowly, stealthily. Once, when within a couple of yards of the boat, the Malay moved as if to turn. The young Greek's heart beat quickly; it proved, however, to be a false alarm, for the man's attention was fixed towards the road from Argostoli, to the trampling footsteps of his returning comrades. The same sounds nerved Constantine to immediate action; there was no time to be lost. He sprang forward, and with unerring aim threw the rope of silk over the head of the unconscious Asiatic, who, in an instant more, was writhing, half-strangled, at the bottom of his own boat. Snatching the pistols from the Malay's waist, Constantine loosened the silk; the astounded man made a gurgling noise with his throat in an attempt to speak, but the boy, coolly sitting upon a cross seat, held both pistols close to his head, saying,

"Not a word, thou treacherous dog. Take up the oars and row me to yon English ship—quick," and he clicked the triggers.

With the pistols at his head the man stared in stupefied astonishment. The lad's face told him that an instant's delay would cost him his life, so, placing himself upon the seat, he sullenly took the oars in his hand. The sound of voices could now be heard distinctly, and, with eyes glaring with hate and disappointment,

the Malay would have turned to look, but again Constantine
said,

"Not a word. Pull off direct to the Englishman, and move
neither to the right nor the left, or I will send the contents of
these pistols through your head."

The tempest of hate and rage that filled the baffled rogue's
heart was plainly visible in his face ; but the tone in which the
young Greek spoke, the firmness of his attitude as he sat with his
feet upon the stretcher of the boat, the two pistols pointing within a couple of feet of his head, plainly told him that he had no
choice but instant death or compliance. True, once, when about
mid-distance between the shore and the ship, the motion of his
arms slackened, and his body bent forward as if to make a sudden
spring upon his youthful captor ; but, if such an idea passed
through his brain, it was but as the lightning's flash, for even
he, savage as he was, quailed beneath the gaze of the resolute
youth, whose eyes were fixed upon him, as, we are told, the unarmed Indian, when surprised, will fix *his* upon the beasts of the
forest.

Sitting with his back towards the English ship, and not daring
to move his eyes from the Malay, Constantine expected when they
were within a few yards of the vessel the watch would hail them.
He listened, but no, they had passed under the bowsprit without
hearing voice or footstep. In the deep gloom, alone relieved by
the pale light of the moon, the strange pair, boy and man, sat in
deadly fear of each other ; for, bold as he was, Constantine knew
that a false step at that moment of his enterprise would cause his
ruin.

"What will the master do now ?" asked the Malay, sullenly.

"What indeed !" thought Constantine. "To run up the side,

leaving this fellow to follow will never do, while to send him first will be, perhaps, to let him seize the first pistol at hand and send a bullet through me, after which, he can give his own account of what must appear to the captain this very strange affair."

All this flashed suddenly through his mind. Similar thoughts probably occupied the brain of the Malay, for again he said,

"My master is alongside the English ship; does he fear to ascend? He is right, the watch will shoot him down as a pirate."

This speech decided our hero upon the only course he could take. Still keeping the pistols pointed at his companion, he said,

"Up, fellow! but no tricks, or you are a dead man; for like a cat will I follow at your heels."

Without a word the Asiatic sprang up the sides with the rapidity of a wild beast. Constantine thrust the pistols beneath his sash, and followed; but, unused to the ship, he found some difficulty in the ascent. This delay was the advantage of the Malay, who no sooner gained the deck, than he gave the alarm cry, "Pirates!" and, snatching a pistol from one of the crew, he sent a ball with such effectual aim, that it tore away the lobe of the boy's right ear. One inch nearer, and, as Constantine had surmised, the Malay could have given his own account of this strange affair without fear of contradiction. As it was, as soon as the latter had placed his feet upon the deck, he found himself seized by two seamen, and saw others hastening up the hatchway.

"Unhand me!" he cried; "I am a friend who has saved you all, ship and cargo."

"May be, may be, lad, for sartinly one of your years ain't much of an enemy; howsomd'ever we'll have a talk with the skipper first. Hilloah!" he added, to the Malay, "Hilloah! mate, what's all this shindy about, and where did you catch this young fighting cock?" But the Malay paid no attention to the question, for he was backing slowly towards the side where they had left the boat. Perceiving this, and convinced that he was peering into the gloomy waters after the boat, Constantine made another struggle to escape, crying,

"Let go my arms, or take me to your captain at once; but seize that Malay dog. See! in another instant he will be over the side into the boat. Let him not escape, I say, for he would have fastened down the hatches to-night, and delivered you all, bound hand and foot, to yon Spaniard."

Struck by the boy's earnestness, one of the sailors who held him called out, "By Neptune! there is foul play somewhere. Seize Abdoul." But the order was unnecessary; for, as the Malay placed his hands upon the gunwale as if to clamber over, his arms were seized and pinioned behind by a stalwart youth, who said,

"How now, my friend? what treachery is this I hear? What, and who is this young Greek?"

The Malay kept a sullen silence, but Constantine again repeated his narration, and desired that they might both be taken before the captain.

"That shall you," replied the youth, adding, as he turned to a man near him, "But you, Jones, slip a length of tow-line round the arms of our friend here, for, by his silence, I fear me, yon Greek's charge hath some bottom in it."

"Aye, aye, sir," replied Jones, immediately obeying the order.

"Although but a youngster like myself," said Constantine, "you seem to have some command here; if it be so, just order these men to set me free, for to be held thus like a thief, is but a poor reward for having saved your ship and crew."

"Command! why, not much of that, bless you, except when my father the captain's sick, as he is just now; but look you, old fellow, whoever you may be, you seem to speak English pretty well; you are confoundedly plucky and straightforward, so, if you'll just give me your word of honour to play no tricks, you shall walk into the captain's cabin like a gentleman." Constantine having given his word to the frank-spoken youth, he was at once freed, and having had his wound dressed by one of the sailors was, with the Malay, led to the captain's cabin.

## CHAPTER II.

FATHER THOMAS had called the English ship a buccaneer; Constantine was therefore not surprised at observing guns upon the forecastle, the quarter-deck, and in the waist, nor, upon entering the captain's cabin, to see that its sides and ceiling were literally covered with arms, arranged in tasteful devices; muskets, arquebuses, flasks, bandoleers* and matches, swords, steel targets or bucklers, bills and spears. But notwithstanding these signs and symbols of war, and the priest's accusation, there was no good reason that she should be more than a simple trader; for in those days, when buccaneering was regarded by every nation but Spain, who desired to have no robbers upon the ocean but herself, in no very discreditable light, when there existed but a narrow partition between sea commerce and piracy, when nations, at peace by land, were continually fighting each other at sea, almost every vessel, whose owner could afford it, was similarly armed.

The captain, a middle-aged man, of stalwart build and noble form, but evidently just recovering from a wasting sickness, was reclining upon a couch, which was placed between the breeches of two small culverins. As the young sailor, Constantine, and the Malay entered, he raised himself upon one hand, and, observing the arms of the latter were fastened, said,

---

* Bandoleers were wooden cases covered with leather, containing a charge; each musqueteer carried twelve of these charges attached to a belt slung across the left shoulder, and resting on the right side.

"How? what's in the wind now, Blake, that Abdoul should be trussed like a fowl ready for the spit?"

"The spit—no; ready for the yardarm, sir, which will be a little too good for him, if what this youngster says be true; but listen to his story:" whereupon Constantine told how he had become acquainted with the plot to seize the ship, and the means he had taken to prevent such a calamity.

Now as the young Greek was not at that time by any means perfect in the English language, and he strove to make every item of his tale plainly understood, his narrative occupied some time, still the captain and young Blake listened with fixed attention. As for the Malay, he stood with head erect and a scowling brow, as if defiant of the probable fate that awaited him, nor did he move a muscle of his face till Constantine related how he had first surprised and then forced him to row his own boat to the ship, when the scowl deepened into a look, if not a glare, of malignant hatred and revenge.

The narrative being concluded, the invalid captain, by an effort almost beyond his strength, arose, and staggering forward caught hold of the young hero's hands, exclaiming,

"Whoever you may be, my gallant lad, if this tale be true—and I nothing doubt it—you have performed a service that a lifetime will be insufficient to .repay."

"I have done but little, sir. It is a duty to serve those we esteem; but I *love* the brave islanders of England," was the modest, or perhaps politic, answer. Not, however, noticing this, the captain, whose exhaustion caused him to stagger backwards to the couch, said,

"Now, treacherous, ungrateful Malay, have *you* naught to say —no denial to give?"

"Order the dog to be strung up to the yardarm, and mayhap he'll confess his accomplices," said the impetuous English boy.

"Dog in thy teeth, young scorpion," replied the Malay, scornfully; then to the captain he said,

"I confess naught, I deny naught; liberty was my birthright, you robbed me of that, and it has ever since been the object of my life to steal it back. Had *you* been the slave, and Abdoul the master, you would have done likewise. I have schemed and failed; am I a dog's son that I should fear to pay the penalty of failure, and beg my life of an accursed unbeliever?"

"That's plucky, too, for a midnight assassin, for the betrayer of those whose hands he has clasped, and whose salt he has eaten," interposed the English lad.

"The followers of Mahomet are less than dogs," replied the captain, "they betray those whose salt they have eaten; they are not men. Ungrateful wretch, when, after a fair fight, I captured thee and thy piratical crew, did I not save thee all from the horrible death reserved for pirates by the mandarins of Siam? did *I* not offer thee pay, and *you* promise with thy men to serve under my flag? In what, then, did I break my part of the compact, that thou shouldest eat thy words and betray us to the Spaniard?"

"The Spaniard, the Portugal, the Hollander, are, like thy own people, the sons of dogs; *they* have plundered and despoiled the East, *they* have slain the peoples, and dethroned the kings and emperors. The mushroom Hollanders have, in the guise of merchants, acted like thieves and assassins; they have overthrown ancient kingdoms, murdered or enslaved people who have ever been free, and I hate them: the descendants of my race will hate and pursue them till the end of the world. But *thou*, master of mine, laid hands on, dealt a vile blow with thy dog's hand to me—thy slave, it is true, by the capture of my prahu, but still the son of a race which never forgave the contamination of a blow; thus, partly for my liberty, but more for revenge, I betrayed thee to the Spaniard, who, in turn, I would have sold to his worst enemy;" then he added defiantly, "Now Abdoul has done, he would have no more speech with a dog of a Frank."

"Treacherous slave, for slave thou art, I have a mind to hang thee up to the yardarm within the hour," exclaimed the captain; but the very daring of the man subdued his anger; for the brave, to use an old platitude, admire bravery even in an enemy; and he added, "But no, it shall not be said that Edmund West sacrificed even a traitor and an assassin to his personal anger without a trial; besides, I do remember that I struck thee in my choler without sufficient cause—but lead him away, put him in irons, or I may change my mind;" and without a word, but with a glance of demoniac hatred towards the young Greek, Abdoul followed the sailor guard out of the cabin.

"Now, my brave lad," said the captain, "what can I do to show my gratitude for the service you have done me and the other owners of this vessel?"

"I would be a mariner, sir. Help me to be one, and you will more than repay me for any service I have done," was the straightforward reply.

"You can't refuse, sir; he is a plucky fellow: may I write his name, at least when we know what it is, in the ship's book?" interposed Blake.

"Patience, Blake," said the captain, with a smile. "Your name, good youth?" he asked.

"Constantine Phaulcon," was the reply.

"Constantine Phaulcon," continued the captain earnestly, "I know not how to refuse your desire, but have you seriously considered what it is you ask? You are young, have evidently been delicately nurtured, and can dream not what the change of life would be, of the perils, dangers, and withal, perhaps, but small profits to be gained by a life on the ocean."

"I know well what I ask, sir; I am well-born, but penniless; I am young, strong, and, God be thanked! blessed with health, and to remain poor would be disgraceful, sinful. In a word, sir, I have a great work before me, and, if I live, I have *willed* to carry it out."

"A great work," repeated the captain, with a smile at the warmth with which the boy had spoken.

"To become rich by my own exertions."

"Ah!" replied the captain, half in anger, half in disappointment, "so young, yet so avaricious, so sordid!"

Constantine's face became flushed with anger. "Sir," said he, "I am avaricious, but not sordid; for I desire wealth that I may replace those I love, my parents, in the position from which by misfortune they have fallen."

"Pardon me, my lad," replied the captain, "I misunderstood your motives, they are indeed commendable, noble; but your parents"—

"I will tell you about them, sir, and, having heard, you will not have the heart to refuse my prayer." He then related the tale of his parents' misfortunes, excepting only that it was upon a charge of *fraud* for which his father was then in the dungeons of St. Mark.

"It is a sad, very sad story, my lad," said the captain, when he had concluded; "but yet, bethink thee, that so gently nurtured as you have been, whether some less tempestuous life would not better befit thee."

"Sir, I *have* well pondered, and am fully resolved not to be a stay-at-home. Who indeed could, that knew by heart the stories of my mother's countryman, Marco Polo,—of Columbus, Sebastian Cabot, Vasco de Gama, Cortes, Pizarro, and your own great countryman, Blake? No, sir; for me, and such as me, there is but one road to fortune, distinction—the one traversed by the great men I have named."

"Well, well lad, I see it is of little use to attempt to turn aside your desire; it shall, therefore, as far as in me lies, be as you wish; your name shall be placed in the ship's book."

"And my pay?" interrupted the boy eagerly.

"Will be that of a master's mate, and paid regularly, doubt not that, lad," replied the captain sharply, angrily, for again he thought the boy's desire of gain uppermost in his mind.

"Pardon me, I do *not* doubt it, sir; but I was about to beg that three parts, be it what it may, might be at every convenient opportunity transmitted to my mother."

"Again I have misunderstood you, again I crave your pardon; you are a noble fellow, Constantine, and it shall be as you wish. But now, lad, as we cannot very well put you ashore to-night, get thee to Blake's cabin and turn in with him."

"By old father Neptune, youngster," said the English boy, as they entered his little cabin, "but you have done us a right good piece of service, and I am glad we are going to sail together. But," he added, as he glanced at the slender limbs and delicate features of the young Greek, and mentally compared them with his own robust, muscular form, "you won't be savage, old fellow, will you? but if I hadn't had good proof of your pluck, I should

have thought you more fitted for a priest or a bookworm than
a sailor."

"Yet," replied Constantine, with a smile, "I never heard that
size was a proof of courage, a cock pheasant has as much of that
quality as an eagle, and more than an ostrich; still, I am proud
to have won your good-will, and rejoice that we are to sail
together, Mr.——" and Constantine halting for a name, the other
said quickly,

"Taunton—Blake Taunton, but call me Blake."

"Indeed," replied Constantine, "I thought you were the good
captain's son, and I heard him name himself West."

"Ah!" said the other, with a half-sigh, "I call him so, and would
that he were; but it is wicked thus to repine, for captain West has
been a father—more than any father! Yet, yet old fellow,"—and
as he spoke a tear stood in his eye, "it's hard when one thinks of
it, to have no father, no mother, no blood relations, to be a kind of
stray link lost from the human chain, belonging to nobody, and
nobody belonging to you." Drawing his sleeve across his eyes, he
said, "But hang it, this will never do, there's a tear in my eye."

"There are occasions when we may be proud of our tears,"
replied Constantine; "but know you naught of your parentage?"

"Nothing. But you have heard of the great Admiral Blake?"

"I have; it was *his* deeds first taught me to love the English
name,—but more, I have seen him; for while a little child, and
living in Venice, the great admiral, who had a short time before
destroyed the piratical fleet of Tunis, and humbled the Dey, entered
the Adriatic, and was received by the Venetians with all the
honours due to his achievements."

"Ah! the chastising of those pirates was a great deed, and
gained for him and his countrymen the fear and respect of bar-

barous nations, who had hitherto held in contempt the sea power
of England.  But to my story.

"Well, you know, or perhaps you do not, that in the late war
between King Charles and his Parliament, the last strongholds
of the Royalists were the Channel Islands.*  To these Prince
Rupert had drawn those of his followers whose fortunes were
too desperate, or their loyalty too strong, to permit of their
remaining in England during the rule of the Lord Protector
Cromwell.  From these islands the Prince and his followers used
to issue forth like sea-robbers, as they were, attacking the towns on
the coast, or taking merchant ships wherever they fell in with
them, not too particular either as to what nation they belonged,
so that they were well laden.  To put an end to this organized
system of pirates, Cromwell sent a fleet under Blake, and very
speedily town after town, castle after castle, fell beneath his guns.
One of these islands was Jersey, under the command of Sir George
Carteret.  For two months did that gallant Cavalier hold the
castle of St. Heliers against the Parliamentary admiral and general :
indeed, it is doubtful if Blake would have succeeded in reducing it,
had he not received from Plymouth some mortars of extraordinary
size.  From these he was enabled to pour in such a succession of
missiles, that the defenders fell by hundreds, houses were toppled
down, and, lastly, the powder magazine being at length reached,
exploded and blew up nearly one hundred of the principal Cavalier
officers and men.

"Captain West was one of the first of Blake's officers to enter
the castle after the garrison had marched out, for that Blake
permitted them to do.  Great stores were found, such as beef,

* The story of the capture of these islands from the Royalists is well told
by Mr. Hepworth Dixon, in his Life of Robert Blake.

bread, beer, wine, powder, a park of artillery, and other matters.
But while the captain was congratulating himself and the admiral
upon the discovery of their unexpected acquisition, one of the
sailors, who had been probably looking through the castle in search
of booty, came forward, and told him that in one of the upper
rooms a lady was lying either dead or dying.

"He at once hastened to the lady's assistance, but, alas! she was
beyond human aid—a bullet had penetrated her brain from the back
of the head; but there was one to whom heaven must have especially
sent him, an infant, at least a little child, who was sitting, for he
was too young to walk or stand, smiling in his mother's face,
unconscious of the calamity that had overtaken him. That child
was myself, the lady, I *believe*, my mother. The kind-hearted
captain ordered all respect and honour to be paid to the dead,
and placed me under the temporary care of one of the women in
the town."

"But," asked Constantine, "was the lady not known to any of
the people in the town?"

"Wait, you shall hear. The captain, nay, the admiral, touched
by my forlorn condition, caused every inquiry to be made. Many
came to see the body, but no one could remember having seen her
with any of the Cavalier officers. That she was of gentle condition,
her attire and certain rich bracelets upon her wrists seemed to
prove. Several days passed in fruitless search and inquiry, when at
length a royalist soldier, who had been wounded nigh unto death,
told a comrade, from whom he heard the story of the dead lady and
her child, that on the night previous to the great bombardment
and surrender, a gentleman of noble bearing, a priest, and a female,
had, by means of the governor's own pass, entered the castle, nay,
had even been conducted to Sir George's own apartment; but *who*

they were neither he nor his comrades could tell, for the lady was conveyed in a close litter, and the gentleman's features were hidden by a large slouch hat, while his form was enveloped by a long horseman's cloak. The priest he should know if only by his accent, which was foreign.

"So far it was thought a clue was obtained, for although the priest had, for some purpose of his own, fled, it was certain that Sir George Carteret must well know the man he had admitted into the castle at such a momentous period. Unfortunately, the knight, according to the terms of the capitulation, had with the remnant of his force left the island for St. Malo on the coast of Normandy; still Blake sent an especial messenger to describe both child and mother, expecting that I should at once be claimed by my father if alive, or if dead by his relatives, but, in any case, that he should obtain my name; greatly, however, to his surprise, the knight denied all knowledge of me or my friends, and also that any such stranger or priest had had an interview with, or obtained a pass from him, upon the night in question.

"Strange," interposed Constantine, thoughtfully, "that strangers should be admitted at such a time, and more so, that the knight should know them not."

"More strange, my friend, that a noble gentleman should be guilty of a falsehood—and that it was such I have no misgiving—for the Royalist trooper solemnly swore that he saw, nay, read, Carteret's pass, and, moreover, himself led the party to the governor's quarters," replied Blake; adding bitterly, "Ah! I fear me, I had best not discover my father, lest it should prove that I am the son of a traitor from the Parliamentary army who was in secret coalition with the king's party."

"Nay, nay, it is sinful even thus to *suspect* thy parent."

"But it must be even so, as for no other reason, save to screen the dishonour of perhaps a noble name, could the soldier Carteret have told a lie."

"Had I such suspicion, I would even now seek Sir George, and upon my knees pray of him to disclose the secret of my birth," said Constantine.

"Impossible! he died in exile not long after his flight from Jersey. But to conclude my story, 'God tempered the wind to the shorn lamb'—Captain West, who had but one child, a daughter, adopted me, and, for want of a better, named me Blake Taunton; the first after his admiral, the second after the town which that great man held out and defended against the Royalists. But what scares you thus?" he exclaimed.

Constantine suddenly started backwards, as with fright; but turning his head, the cause was apparent enough; for by the light thrown upon the little window of the cabin, he saw the bust, and now really ferocious eyes of the Malay savagely glaring at them both.

"The fellow has slipped his irons—foul play somewhere—follow me!"

Before Constantine had time to comply, there was a flash, a report, and a bullet whizzed within an inch of his head. But seeing he had missed his aim, the intended assassin first muttering a malediction upon himself, screeched through the port, "Greek dog, we shall meet again! then beware of Abdoul, for he will be *thy* fate or *thou* his!"

In an instant Constantine ran up the companion-ladder upon deck. Blake and two of the men were loading their arquebuses.

"Thank Heaven," said Blake, "you are unhurt; the treacherous Malays it is who have helped their vagabond chief to slip his

irons. But," he added, pointing his piece in the direction of the
fleeing boat, "some of the rogues shall lose the number of their
mess."

"Nay," replied Constantine, quickly, "let them go, it is a
good riddance, a hundred of such scum would be no loss; but,
as you value our lives, the ship, the cargo, fire not a single piece;
the report will give notice to the Spaniard that his plot has failed,
and he knows that you have not twenty men able to fight him."

"Wise counsel, lad," said the captain, coming upon deck supported by two men. "Blake, you are too fast. Fire none of you.
See, Providence has sent us a wind in the nick of time. Douse the
lights, man the capstan, lower sail, 'bout ship, and we may run clear
of these waters before the Spaniard has time to shake himself out
of his first surprise." Thus, by such a fortuitous accident as the
treachery of a Malay, did Constantine realise the darling desire of
his soul, and find himself suddenly and literally afloat on the wide,
wide world. Truly it grieved him that he had been prevented
taking leave of his mother; but then the heart of youth is buoyant,
and if, in the bustle and novelty of his new career, he did not cease
to regret the accident which had torn him away so suddenly, he at
least consoled himself that it was no fault of his, and that he should
now be able to relieve her necessities.

Upon the arrival of Constantine in England, his career seemed
likely to be nipped in the bud, for the health of Captain West had
become so bad, that he was told by his physicians that if he would
save his life he must relinquish the sea. It was a painful decree,
for he had hoped to have made a few more voyages, not only that
he might realize a greater fortune, but that his adopted son might,
under his own eye, have obtained a knowledge of his profession
that would have justified him in taking the command out of his

hands, and even as it was, he clung so fondly to the hope that a
few months' rest would restore his health and enable him to carry
out his plans, that he persuaded Blake to seek service in no other
ship until he had fairly tried the experiment of retirement.

With Constantine he had greater difficulty; for although he
pointed out the difference between sailing under a commander
who had cause to like him, and another who, to say the least,
if not brutal, as were the majority of sea-captains in those days,
could only regard him as one of many, and offered to receive him
in his own home upon an equality with Blake, and to continue
his pay during his residence, the lad hated idleness, loved not
dependence, and burned to continue the career he had so
auspiciously begun.

Indeed, it was only when the kind-hearted captain promised
that, should the end of six months still find him unable for sea,
he would use his interest in obtaining him service in one of the
ships of the new East India Company, for which a number of
London merchants were then endeavouring to obtain a charter
from Charles the Second, that he agreed, and accompanied the
captain to his home in the north of England.

For nearly twelve months the two lads remained in the captain's
old country dwelling, not idle, for the greater portion of their
time was spent in rambling with their guns or fishing-rods across
the hills or moors, or by the sides of rivers, while their indoor
life was passed in listening to the captain's stories of his adventures in early life, the study of navigation, or in chatting
or reading to Zillah West, the captain's only child, a pretty
blonde, whose roguish blue eyes had even thus early made an
impression upon Master Blake Taunton's heart.

As for Constantine, if any such impression had been made

upon him, it was known to himself alone, for he was not one of those whose feelings can be read in their face. Quiet, earnest, impassible, Zillah would cry with vexation that she could not read his thoughts, while Blake, who carried his heart upon his sleeve, and was always talking, seemed to do so, only to fill the ears of the young Greek, who, always speaking to the purpose, seldom spoke unnecessarily—never—to divulge his feelings.

Still, notwithstanding the difference of their characters, nay, perhaps, in consequence thereof, day by day the lads seemed to grow more attached to each other; the strongest feeling might have been upon the side of Blake, but then although frank, bold, candid, he wanted the faculty of self-esteem, and possessed that of veneration; thus, he looked up to his junior, Constantine, as to an elder brother, and one, too, that was gifted with far higher powers of mind than himself. Poor Blake! his amiable nature had so practised him in saying *no to himself*, that his self-denial threatened soon to cause him many a pang.

As I have said, the lads passed nearly twelve months among the hills, and moors, and rivers. At the end of that time, news came from London that the *new* East India Company had received their charter, and were immediately about to send a fleet of ships to the East, one of which the captain was earnestly solicited to command.

Such an offer in those days was indeed a golden opportunity. The captain's health, however, was still so precarious that he was compelled to decline the appointment; but, unwilling to place himself any longer in the way of the professional advancement of the two youths, he asked, and obtained for them, the rank of master's mates, a position then about equivalent to a senior midshipman of the present time. Since, however, it was at the birth

D

of that wonderful Company which has performed such astounding acts in the East, and has so recently been dissolved, that Phaulcon entered upon his fortunes, it will not be out of place if I give a *résumé* of its origin and progress up to the time of Charles the Second.

In the year 1588, during the reign of Queen Elizabeth, a certain Captain Candish, or Cavendish, I believe an ancestor of the Dukes of Devonshire, returned from a long voyage in the East. He brought such wondrous accounts of the wealth of India, its desirability as a commercial mart, and the handsome conduct of the natives to him and his men, that a number of wealthy merchants raised among themselves 68,000*l.* (an immense sum in those days), formed themselves into an association, and petitioned the Queen to grant them a charter. By this they obtained a monopoly of the trade for fifteen years, and such wealth did they accumulate that at the end of their term they again petitioned the throne (James the First was then king) for a renewal. By the intercession of Lord Bacon, whom the merchants heavily bribed, they obtained it, as also a very *humble* letter from the King of England to the *Great Mogul* begging the latter to permit their subjects to trade with each other. The Asiatic Monarch complied with the request, and the merchants established several small stations along the coast; the chief, however, being Surat.

The profits of these men upon their capital was at least one hundred per cent.; but they hungered for more, they had studied the easy nature of the Asiatics, and had calculated the difference between their *physique* and that of Europeans, and doubtlessly having in mind the filibustering deeds of Cortes and Pizarro, swaggeringly craved the power to *make war* upon the people who had received them so hospitably. In the reign of that merry monarch, " who never *said* a stupid thing, or ever did a wise one," there were few things in the power of the Court to grant, that could not be obtained for money ; thus, by immense bribes to Charles the Second, his ministers and mistresses, they obtained powers similar to those granted by the Pope to the Portuguese and Spaniards over the New World ; namely, a new charter, which not only confirmed the Company's ancient privileges, but *first* vested in them authority to make peace and war with any prince or people *not being Christians,* and to seize within limits, and send home as prisoners, any Englishman found without a licence—in fact, a patent of sovereignty.

It was supposed, of course, by Englishmen at home, that interlopers being found they would be judged by the laws of England ; not so, thought one of the Company's chairmen, Sir John Child, the founder of the great banking house of that name ; for on one occasion, when one of the Company's Governors in India had been urged to enforce the penalties against certain private traders he replied, " That unhappily the laws of England would not let him proceed so far as might be wished." The banking knight perhaps remembering the immense bribes that had been paid to king and courtiers, replied, " *We* expect that *our orders* are to be your rule, and *not the laws of England,* which are a heap of nonsense, compiled by a few ignorant country gentlemen, who hardly know how to make laws for the good of their own families, much less for the regulating of companies and foreign commerce."

Let us thank our stars, or the bold brave men who have manfully spent their lives in battling against abuses, that in these days, bad as they still are for Eastern races with whom the

English desire to trade, the gentlemen who make our laws would
scarcely tolerate another Sir John Child.

\*      \*      \*      \*      \*

Of the lads' first five years or noviciate in the East there is
little to chronicle, except that by manfully doing their duty they
endeavoured to earn promotion, and a portion of the good things,
which in those days most Europeans found it easy to obtain in
the "Indies." To do the latter they wisely chose serving in a ship
that traded from port to port in the China and Indian seas to
making the "long voyage" to England, for by so doing, although
they had not the opportunities of shipowners or captains, they
were enabled to make small ventures upon their own accounts.
Again, they were fortunate in being employed a great portion
of the five years on shore at the Company's factory in the
chief seaport of Siam.   As we have seen, at the very commencement of his career, Constantine had *willed* to become rich ;
as he increased in years, the desire became the darling, all-
absorbing passion of his soul.   I am sorry to record this very
unheroic trait in the character of my hero, but then the great
Duke of Marlborough had the same passion, and in a more unworthy, sordid form : the Duke desired money as an end for itself
alone ; Constantine, but as a means to an end.   Moreover, with all
his passion, I do not think he would have done the dishonest
acts to obtain it that are on record of the illustrious John
Churchill.

By indefatigable toil, and using his fine abilities in the interests
of the Company, he gained the good-will and confidence of his
employers : thus promotion came, and with it additional opportunities of making money.   These opportunities he used to the
utmost, for not the most experienced European trader upon the

waters of the Meinam * knew better how to drive a bargain, and
but few so well how to secure the profits. Added to his desire and
faculty of making money, he practised self-denial to such an extent,
that but for his bold bearing and commanding intellect, which
enforced respect from all with whom he came in contact, he would
have been the most unpopular of the Company's servants. But
then it must be remembered, that although grasping and avaricious, the European traders were, for the greater part, careless,
dissolute spendthrifts. Indeed, but for the lawless, reckless character of the first Europeans in the Eastern seas, it is more than
probable that we should have heard of none of those terrible
massacres and wars between the Easterns and Westerns which
disgrace the pages of history, and that Christianity, at first so
warmly welcomed, would now have been the prevailing faith—
at least in *Eastern* India.

In favour of Constantine, I must say that, although he stood
aloof from new acquaintances and would not spend a superfluous
penny upon himself, he had become so dearly attached to Blake,
that had it been necessary he would have shared his all with him.

As it was, he more than once rescued his friend from pecuniary
difficulties into which he had fallen by the roguery of others ; nay,
by his interest obtained for him promotion and opportunities of
doing as well as himself. As for the generous, open-hearted young
Englishman, he was more rejoiced at his friend's success, than
regretful at his own want of it. But to the ambitious or avaricious,
success—never is, but always to be, *i. e.*, a little more than *is*
possessed, whatever that may be. Thus, one day, about the end
of the period above named, Constantine, when congratulated by
his friend upon the happy result of some commercial venture,

* The chief river of Siam.

replied, " Success, my dear Blake ! you are easily content ; do you
call a few thousand crowns—earned by years of toil upon these
tempestuous seas, or beneath this burning sickly sun, and saved
by a self-denial which, however I may think necessary, has gained
me the contempt of my fellow Europeans—success ?"

" Poh, poh, Constantine," said Blake ; " you are too—well, I
will not say avaricious, but in too great haste to gain wealth.
Be content, my dear fellow ; for who, tell me, among those who
came out here penniless, can, like you, lay his hands upon even
such a fund as you have stored ?   Why, in time you may be
able to buy a ship of your own."

" Like me, all *might* have made their own opportunities, or
at least have made the most of those they had ; all had the choice
between saving or squandering ; but," he added, " you are right,
Blake, I *shall* be able to become an owner, and *sooner* than you
anticipate—even now I am in treaty for the little Dutch Brigantine in the Meinam, for I am resolved no longer to remain a
subaltern, the little I have may prove the nucleus of a fortune
if properly laid out."

" You are mad to think of her," replied the astonished Blake,
" she is not seaworthy, or the Dutchman would not part with her."

" Nevertheless, when careened and overhauled by the carpenter,
she will carry Cæsar and his fortunes," he replied,'. laughing.
" But what say you, my friend, to joining me in a voyage to
England ? we can with our united means take a cargo worth its
weight in gold, and return with such another here, then with the
profits of the two voyages, charter a vessel so armed that, we
may coast the whole of China in defiance of all the Portuguese,
Spaniards, and Hollanders afloat."

" My dear friend," replied Blake seriously, " I see you are in earnest, and I know your talents and courage, but I fear me this will be a rash venture, for it is not well to carry all your eggs in one basket,.especially such an one as that you have chosen ; but despite my fears, I would still join you in all heart.  It cannot however be, for *I* have sought and obtained the command of a brig for a voyage between this and Macao." But, he added, " think well of this rash voyage ere you proceed farther."

" Poh, poh, Blake, nothing venture, nothing have ; all the thinking in the world will not alter my resolve," he replied ; adding earnestly, " My dear friend, every man has his opportunity if he knows when to seize it.  I believe mine has arrived, that my star is in the ascendant ; moreover, several times within the last month, in my dreams I have seen and conversed with my dear mother, who each time told me she was dying, and begged that I would not let her quit this world without seeing and bidding her a last farewell.  Oh ! Blake, *you* who have known no parents, cannot imagine my agony at the sight of that dear face beaming with maternal love, but so pale, so haggard, so wan."

" Enough, my friend," said Blake, excited almost to tears : " *now* I know full well that your resolve is unalterable."

" As the laws of the Medes and Persians."

" And all that remains for me," continued Blake, " is to pray that Heaven may take you in its safe keeping."  He said no more, for he well knew that Constantine had greater faith than even most sailors in dreams, omens, and his particular star, and feared to offend him.

Within a month after the foregoing conversation, Blake had received his maiden command, and with the first wind had sailed through the China seas for Macao.

Within a few days of the departure of his friend, Constantine found his little ship manned, victualled, and ready for sea. She was laden with such produce of the country as cardamums, gamboge, dragon's blood, gold, and valuable spices of the Celebes, which the owner had purchased of the Dutch merchants, and even after this outlay of ready money, he found he had a reserve.

It was with a proud heart that the prosperous young man set out for England, for not only was it his first command, but the vessel and the cargo were *all his own*, gained too by his talents and the sweat of his brow. Was it not the proudest, the most justifiable of prides, he had gained, and firmly planted his foot upon the first round of the ladder of fortune? Alas! who can foresee an hour beyond the present? But we will not anticipate.

# CHAPTER III.

FATHER AND DAUGHTER—AN UNEXPECTED .VISITOR.

THE abode of Captain West was situated in the valley of the
Alne, beneath the Cheviot hills and within a mile of Alnwick,
which for. five hundred years has been celebrated for the magnificent feudal palace of the Dukes of Northumberland. During
the middle ages, this place seems to have been the *bête noire*
of the kings of Scotland. In the reign of William Rufus, the
castle was besieged by King Malcolm, to whom it was on the
very point of surrendering, when the soldier who was appointed
to deliver up the keys, .pretending to present them upon the
point of his lance, stabbed the Scottish sovereign to the heart.
Malcolm's son again besieged the place to revenge his father's
death, but was himself slain in the attempt. Again in 1174,
William, King of Scots, made a similar effort, but being defeated
and made prisoner, he was carried with his feet bound under
his horse's belly to King Henry II., who detained him until the
Scottish people had agreed to pay £100,000 for his ransom. The
monarch, however, best remembered by the people of Alnwick is,
perhaps, King John, and if the following story be true, with
good reason.

"As his Highness (in those days the word Majesty was not
known) was one day journeying near the town, his horse stuck fast
in a great bog. Much enraged at finding himself in such an

undignified position through the neglect of the town's-people, who should have kept the roads in repair, the king, by way of punishing the inhabitants and their descendants for ever and ever, commanded a clause to be inserted in the charter, rendering it compulsory upon every man before taking up his freedom to jump into the bog, wherein," says the chronicler, "they some- times sink up to the chin." But to return to my story.

The captain's dwelling, or manor-house, as it was called, con- sisted of one tall square tower, which had, in all probability, been erected centuries before by some petty border chief; but the captain's father, from whom he inherited the estate, finding the little stronghold more imposing in appearance than convenient for residence, had, from the right and the left, thrown out in straight lines two wings of red brick, and of an elevation of two stories. The long and narrow windows were numerous and many-paned, being almost hidden by the ivy, which clustered and clambered over the whole front, and looked like little eyes peering through shaggy brows. Standing upon an almost conical hill, the grassy, gently descending slopes of which were dotted with tastefully planned flower-beds, overlooked from the back by the Cheviots, and overlooking from the front some two hundred acres of woodland, the view, the *entourage* was charm- ing in the summer months, but in the winter bleak and dreary.

It *was* winter, full two years after Constantine had sailed from Siam, at least dreary November, when the bleak winds from the hills seemed to pierce to the very marrow of the bones, the air was black, the leafless trees covered with hoar frost. It was night also; a pile of wood blazed upon the fire-dogs in the large parlour. The captain, now in better health, though still feeble, was seated in his great chair: before him, on the table, an ancient silver tankard, filled with good old "October" of his own brewing, and smoking a large bowled pipe of Asiatic manufacture; upon the opposite side of the table sat Zillah, also altered from when we last saw her, but then *she* had passed through that period when Old Time acts his kindliest, and had developed into—well, not a beautiful, nor a pretty, but a fine, handsome girl with liquid blue eyes, and, as became her as a maiden of the north, the fairest of skins, tinted with the red hue of health, and golden hair, which fell in luxuriant curls nearly to her waist.

The captain, although puffing the smoke as laboriously as if under a contract to consume a given quantity of tobacco within the hour, was intently listening to Zillah, who, with her head near the great lamp, *too* near for the sake of her lustrous eyes, was reading a letter aloud.  This epistle contained what we should now consider old news, for it was dated nearly two years before; but then it came from the far off Indies, from whence in those days it was not always easy to obtain a letter in England even in that time.  From the extreme care with which Zillah read that letter, and the attention with which the captain listened, a bystander would scarcely have thought it had been received twenty days before, and read almost as many times.  But then it was from one they both loved; and who is there that does not many a time and oft take up and reperuse an epistle from a far distant loved one, not so much with a hope of getting the contents by heart, as in a kind of semi-belief that some word or words, which would have thrown a further light upon the thoughts, feelings, or meaning of the writer, have escaped the eye.

That epistle, which was from Blake Taunton, contained much that the reader already knows, namely, the intelligence of his promotion, and Phaulcon's departure for England, but also that he himself hoped in another twelve months to obtain the command of some homeward bound ship. This was the *good* news of the letter, and caused father and daughter to rejoice. But there was that in it which was bad, and made them feel sick at heart. More than two years had elapsed since Constantine had quitted Siam, with the intention of making the voyage to England direct, and yet nought had been heard of him or his ship.

"Pray Heaven, he may not have been cast away in that small vessel," exclaimed Zillah, laying down the letter upon the table.

"It is not *that* I fear, Zil," replied her father, "for it is not the largest craft which can best weather a storm ; besides, the lad is a bold and skilful navigator ; but the Spaniards, the Portuguese, the Dutch, and, nearer home, the Algerine pirates. Foolish fellow," he added, "it was rash, headstrong, to venture upon 'the long voyage' without convoy, and in a mere tub, which although seaworthy, from Blake's account carried but a single gun."

"But, dear father," she said, eagerly clutching at a hope that passed through her mind, "*I* have heard you say that two years is no long time for a ship to be making the voyage from the Indies."

"Aye, aye, lass, true," he replied, shaking his head, "but then the time is occupied in trading from port to port ; but Constantine, Blake tells us"—as he spoke he placed his hand upon the letter— "had declared his intention of making a clean run for England ; that being the case, he should have been here full twelve months since. No, no," he added sorrowfully, "that boy's ambition has cost him life or liberty ; he would have all or none ; he was in too great haste to become rich, and I fear he has paid a heavy penalty for his impatience."

"Nay, nay, dear father," replied Zillah, her eyes suffused with tears, "perhaps this very haste to become rich, this ambition, may have inclined him after leaving Siam, to change his mind, and trade from port to port."

"It is a bare possibility, a last chance, the catching at a straw. But," he added, "now, child, get thee the chess-board, that by diverting our minds we may dream of that which we hope, and not that which we fear."

Zillah instantly complied; the chess-board was opened, the men were placed, the girl had made the first move, when they were both aroused by the loud barking of the watch-dog.

"Hiloah! what's in the wind now to make Pluto raise this disturbance?" said the captain.

"Oh, some person from the town to one of the servants," said Zillah; adding, impatiently, "it is your move, papa; be careful, never mind old Plu, or I shall conquer you again to-night."

"No, no," replied the captain, as the barking became louder; "Plu would not bark so savagely had he not a notion of a thief or a beggar."

"It is the latter, then, for Plu is a scornful dog, and always growls at tatters," said the laughing Zillah.

And at the same moment hearing the house-door open, and the voice of the servant severely rebuking some person for having presumed to come to the chief entrance, instead of round by the back to the servants' offices, they resumed their game. But before the captain had made his move the door of the room flew open, and the audacious beggar himself stood before them. Father and daughter started to their feet, and well they might, for never, perhaps, had so pitiable a sight been seen in that cosy parlour.

A man, young, tall, slender, his face nearly hidden by an old sou-wester, " bearded like the pard," and his limbs shivering in shreds of garments, which were held together by strings.  To add to the picture, his shoes were bound around with hay-bands. When the captain arose from his chair, he moved towards a sabre that was hanging by the side of the fire-place, exclaiming, "Who are you, my fine fellow?"

" Am I then so changed," replied the intruder, in tones that told of physical weakness and long suffering, " that my dearest friends do not know me?"

Altered as was that voice, wretched, miserable as the appearance of the speaker, Zillah ran up to him, exclaiming, hysterically, " Gracious Heavens!  Constantine!"

" God bless you!  God bless you, my brave boy!" said the captain, rather incoherently, but shaking him very heartily by both hands.

"It is Constantine, indeed—"  but ere he could finish the sentence, the old sailor led him to the chair in which he had himself been sitting, and, with tears rolling down his weather-beaten cheeks, exclaimed,

" Not another word, dear boy, not another word till you have rested and refreshed yourself."  Then, not waiting to summon the servants, Zillah and the captain both ran to the servants'-hall, the one to order a bedroom to be prepared and warmed, and the other to see what game there was in the larder that might speedily be dressed.  Then, when fresh wood had been placed upon the fire-dogs, and the host and his daughter returned to the parlour, so great was their joy, and so heartfelt the gratitude of Constantine at such a welcome after his long and many sufferings, that for some time the three in speechless pleasure sat gazing at each other, but through eyes which glistened with tears.—Well had Constantine once told Blake that *"there are occasions when we may be proud of our tears."*—This was one.

Little, however, could our hero tell that night of the terrible misfortune that had befallen him on his voyage from Siam, for his long tramp to the Manor House had exhausted his strength. Indeed, the following day he was seized with fever, which for a whole month kept him fluttering between life and death. But what disease, not mortal in itself, may not be cured by patience and loving tending? So, thanks to the careful nursing of Zillah—for the brave girl would trust him to no other nor meaner care—and to the affectionate kindness of the captain, at the beginning of the fifth week, although very weak, he was sufficiently convalescent to relate the story of his adventures. Thus, one evening, seated in the great arm-chair, by the side of a blazing fire, and with the captain and Zillah for listeners, he began.

## CHAPTER IV.

### WHAT BEFEL PHAULCON ON HIS VOYAGE TO ENGLAND.

"You, sir, once rebuked me for what you considered my too great impatience to become rich. Almost at my last parting with dear old Blake, he cautioned me to the same effect. From the adventures I am about to relate, it may seem that my experience has since proved you both correct, for had I remained in the Company's service, it is not probable that I should have encountered such terrible misfortunes ; but then, if the proverb which cautions us to 'make hay while the sun shines,' means anything, it means that youth is the season for work, and the most should, therefore, be made of its short duration. But apart from this great fault, if fault it be, it must be remembered that it was less a desire to realize a large sum of money by a voyage to England than to see my mother, that induced me to make so daring and perilous a venture."

"Let byegones be byegones, only profit by their teachings, my dear boy," interrupted the captain, apparently as much pained that his rebuke should be remembered as if he had been the cause of the young man's misfortunes.

Then, having told those particulars as to purchasing and freighting the Dutch brigantine, which are known to the reader, Constantine continued : "For the first month, with the exception of a typhoon in the China seas, all went merrily as marriage

bells, and we made a pretty quick run through the Straits of
Malacca, across the Indian Ocean, and through the Mozambique
Channel, without falling in with any worse mishap than a stiff
gale or two. Off the Cape we encountered a tempest that made
the little brigantine shake a bit; but about four days' run from
Ascension, at which island we had put in for water, we fell in
with a squall, and shipped such heavy seas that we were obliged
to cut away the masts. That loss, but little in itself in comparison with the saving of our lives and cargo, proved our ruin;
for, as we directed our course, slowly drifting, to the De Verdes
to refit, one morning we descried a ship looming in the distant
horizon. Instantly my fears were aroused; should she prove to
be a Spanish privateer or a Sallee rover, being powerless to escape
we were hopelessly lost.

"'What do *you* make of her, Jones?' I said, passing my
glass to the chief mate.

"Having carefully examined her about five minutes, he replied, 'A Spaniard, sir; a galleon, I think, and mayhap homeward bound from Peru with silver.'

"'Let us thank our stars for that,' I ejaculated, not a little
relieved to find that she was an honest craft; nay, hoping she
would help us to a few spars and some bread, of which we
were running short. Jones, however, not feeling equally satisfied,
replied,

"'Aye, aye, sir, when she has *shown* her honesty; but the truth
is, I don't hail well with these Spaniards,' and in the main my
man proved right, for about mid-day, when within gun-shot
of us, she rather uncivilly sent a twenty-four pounder athwart
our bows.

"'The cantankerous dog!' exclaimed the mate, 'that's a civil

E

way of telling us to stand to, any how.' However, there was no help for us, and so we obeyed. Shortly afterwards one of her officers asked through his trumpet ' Who we were and where we hailed from ?' I replied and asked the same questions, when I found that my mate's surmise was correct. She was a Spanish plate-ship bound for Cadiz. I then told him of our mishap, and begged him to let us have some spars, spare canvas, and a few bags of biscuit. For some time there was no answer, the officer had, I supposed, gone to consult his commander ; however, after a few minutes he returned, and not only very civilly complied with my request, but begged that I would go on board and dine with the captain. To this Jones objected, but refusal was useless, for if a friend it was policy, if an enemy we were powerless to prevent his seizing ship and cargo ; we could not run, we could not fight ; thus, accompanied by Jones, I went on board.

"The captain, who conducted us to his cabin, surprised me by his gentlemanly bearing, and at once, through one of his officers, the one I imagined who had hailed us in English, began to question me as to my cargo, how long we had been at sea ; and, my answers giving him satisfaction, he ordered the matters for which I had asked to be got ready while we were dining.

" During the dinner nothing could have been more satisfactory than the courtesy of the captain and his chief officer towards Jones and myself, and I believe he meant to be all square and above-board. During the meal the conversation had turned upon the respective disciplines on board English and Spanish ships, and so warmly did I argue the superiority of the former, that, piqued to prove me in the wrong, he invited me at once, before dessert, to accompany him through the vessel—hence my misfortunes— for upon reaching the top of the companion-ladder, a man stood

before me whom I had every reason to remember. In an instant
I felt that all was lost, and believe I trembled. That man was
the *Malay Abdoul*."

"*That* villain!" exclaimed the ·captain, dashing down his pipe
and starting from his chair. "Poor boy, poor boy, you were
indeed lost." Not, however, noticing the interruption, or even
the astonishment depicted upon the face of Zillah, Constantine
continued—

"Still, as I was but a boy at the time of the affair in the
roadstead of Cephalonia, was so differently attired, and even
altered in figure and face (Constantine now was bearded, and
browned by the exposure to the weather), I hoped he would not
recognize his old acquaintance. Well, when we had been through
the ship and had again reached the companion-ladder, one of the
officers spoke a few words in Spanish to the captain, whereupon
the latter, apologizing for leaving me, begged that I would re-enter
the cabin and await his return. I did so, but to my surprise he
remained absent nearly an hour. Candidly, sir, I then had my
suspicion that all was not right—in fact, that the cunning Malay
*had* recognised me, and was then communicating his discovery to
the Spaniard. The suspicion was well founded, for about ten
minutes after, our polite urbane host did return, accompanied
by the Malay and six sailors, armed to the teeth. These
fellows, having received their instructions beforehand, at once
pounced upon my mate and I, and lashed our arms to our
sides.

"'Allah be praised for giving thee into my hands, thou Greek
dog and son of a dog!' exclaimed the Malay with a demoniac glare,
and flourishing his crease before my eyes. Affecting, however, not
to recognize him, I exclaimed,

E 2

" ' What means this ? am I in the hands of pirates ?' adding, to the Spanish captain, ' Who is this Malay slave ?'

" ' One,' replied my old enemy, ' who, Allah be praised, so marked the *boy*, that he knows the *man*,' and he pointed to my ear."

" Apart from that, do you think he would have recognized you ?" asked the Captain.

" Perhaps not ; but with the long memory and sharp eyes of his race, his hazy remembrance of having seen my features somewhere before, became cleared at the sight of the ear the rogue himself had shorn of its fair proportions the night I made him row me to your ship. But, to resume my story, Jones and I were heavily ironed, thrown into the hold, and there left to contemplate or speculate upon the fate in reserve for us."

" But," asked the captain, " how came that Spanish captain to lend himself to the Malay's revenge ?"

" *That* we discovered the following day, when the fiend Abdoul came, and exultingly told me, that the captain was the same Spaniard who had plotted to seize your ship, sir, in the roadstead of Cephalonia. ' Greek dog !' he exclaimed, more with the hiss of a serpent than the voice of a man, ' did I not tell thee to beware of Abdoul—that he would be thy fate ?'

" ' Wretch, begone,' I cried, ' I fear thee not ; thou canst do no more than slay me.'

" ' Allah forbid,' he replied, fiercely, as he left the hold, ' that I should have so small a revenge. No, there is a punishment more feared by the Christian dog than death—slavery.'

" At this I despaired, for I could no longer doubt that, smarting under the remembrance of the trick I had played him off Cephalonia, the Spaniard intended to run into Tunis or

Algiers, where he could find a market for my ship and cargo, and sell us all into slavery; and such, indeed, I afterwards discovered, was the scheme he had laid down: but Providence, as if to punish him for his iniquitous designs upon fellow-Christians, interfered to prevent his having *quite* his own way.

"One night, after about ten days' run from the Canaries, I was awakened (for I slept soundly even in that dismal hold) by a fearful crashing against the ship's sides; you can imagine my sensations, I feared we had struck upon a rock—but no, for immediately afterwards I heard the screeching of human voices, the report of fire-arms, and the clash of steel.

"'Hurrah! the pirates are themselves boarded,' exclaimed Jones, in the full belief that our rescue was at hand by means of his fellow-countrymen.

"'Aye,' I replied, 'but not by Englishmen; those screeches come from the throats of savages or pirates.'

"Well, after about half-an-hour's struggle, if struggle it could be called, some half-dozen men were thrust into the hold with us. That they were manacled, we could hear by the sounds of the irons, and by their voices we knew that they were Spaniards. Thus, then, our captors *had* been in their turn captured, although by whom I could not tell. But to shorten a long story: as the Spaniard hugged the shore, he was hailed by one of two vessels which were sailing in consort. Being answered and hailed in return, one of the strangers replied that they were Algerines, in the service of Muly Ishmail, the Emperor of Morocco. The captain, thus thrown off his guard, permitted them to run alongside; when instantly the Algerines threw out their grapnels, hundreds of swarthy, half-naked men leaped on board, and the ship was irretrievably lost ere the Spaniards had recovered from their first surprise. Then, when too late, the Spanish captain found that during his absence a war had broken out between Spain and Morocco, and the Sallee ships had been for some time past cruising in these waters on the look-out for homeward-bound Spanish plate-ships."

"Aye, it was dog eat dog, and the Don deserved his fate," said the captain, chuckling at the Spaniard's capture ; "but after what sort did the fellow meet it ?"

"But sorrily," replied Constantine. "After the capture, all the prisoners were manacled, parties of ten or twelve being strung along a rope, and in this plight we remained until we reached Sallee, when we were taken ashore, and driven like a herd of cattle into a large barn, where we were kept for about a week, being tolerably well rationed during that time.

"About the eighth or ninth day, by which time our owner supposed we had become considerably improved in strength and appearance, we were driven into the public market-place to be sold by auction. As each human commodity was put up for sale, intending purchasers would come and examine the article; for instance, open the mouth, pinch the calves and arms, to try if they were firm and muscular, and look at the hands, to see whether they were hard and horny, or white and soft; if the latter, the article was estimated at a higher value, for there was a probability of its being a gentleman, and consequently possessed of friends at home who would offer a large ransom. They would also punch it in the chest, dig their fingers into its ribs, and run it up and down the market-place at a rapid pace to try its wind."

"The dogs, thus to treat Christians," exclaimed the captain, wincing, as if at that moment some intended purchaser had been about to experimentalise upon him.

"Gracious heavens ! is it possible you had to endure such things, my poor friend ?" interposed the plaintive voice of Zillah.

"Worse, far worse, dear Zillah ; for the master to whom Jones, the Malay Abdoul, and myself—it is curious that we three should have been bought by the same man—were sold, was a hard man, who hoped to be repaid his purchase-money by means of our physical strength ; thus, when we reached his house, which was at a town about seventy-eight miles from Sallee, we were made to carry burdens, only fit for horses, from town to town, dig in the fields or gardens, act as labourers to house builders, and toil on the roads, our food being for the greater part black barley bread and water. For six months I endured this existence without a murmur, ever trusting that Providence would afford me some opportunity of escape. The Malay bore his fate with equal fortitude, and with such cunning that he became a favourite with our master. Poor Jones, my mate, once endeavoured to reach the sea-shore, but being overtaken by the Malay, was re-captured, and having been severely beaten with rattan canes upon the soles of his feet, was afterwards, at least for three months, until it was thought his spirit was sufficiently broken, compelled to go through his daily work with irons upon his legs.

"Although our master was fast making money by trading, so loud and numerous were the reports of the wealth that had been found on board the Spanish ship and my brigantine, that his cupidity became excited ; consequently he bought a half-share in a rover, which he hoped might find another homeward-bound plate-ship, or two. Now, knowing that Jones and I were good navigators, he sent us on board with the civil intimation, that if we did not give our best services, or attempted to leave the ship

without permission, we should be bastinadoed to death ; but that if,
on the contrary, we were obedient, tractable to his commander, and
aided in the capture of another Spanish vessel, we should have our
liberty.  Thus, against my will, I became a pirate.  Thank Heaven,
however, that trade did not last long ; for when after a fruitless
cruise of ten weeks, we returned, my disappointed master, who was
anxiously awaiting us at the port of Sallee, finding himself half-
ruined by his venture, sold his share of the vessel, and took us
back with him to his residence.  To repair his loss, he now began
to reduce his expenses, and improve his property to the best of
his abilities.  To gain more profit out of us, he commanded that we
should pay him regularly every month twenty dollars each, or be
bastinadoed to death.  Now this, in effect, sounded like an order
for our execution ; for where the twenty dollars were to come from
was beyond all comprehension.  The cunning Moor, however, knew
very well what he was about.  He told us to take a shop, and
deal in lead, iron, shot, strong waters, and tobacco, for which
purpose he would advance the capital, the latter being to be
repaid by instalments monthly, with the twenty dollars.

"By this, however, you must not think he gave us an opportunity of saving a surplus that might ultimately enable us to
purchase our liberty.  No ; the wary old rogue knew full well that,
strive as we might, we should be for ever in his debt ; still, having
no alternative, we entered upon the business with a good will,
for it was at least a more agreeable occupation than field labour,
piracy, or household work, and by excessive toil each succeeded
in paying him ten dollars, and a small instalment of the capital ;
and even that must have been beyond his expectation, for he
never complained that it was only half the sum named.

"Now, although for the pursuing of our avocation for the

Moor's profit, we were *nominally* at liberty, escape seemed impossible, for we were seventy miles from the sea, and, under pain of the terrible bastinado, restricted to keep within a circuit of five miles, and, moreover, placed under the surveillance of Abdoul, the Malay, who, being a Mussulman, and full of hatred towards us, had obtained not only his liberty, but his master's confidence, and the latter, we knew full well, he never lost an opportunity of using to our disadvantage. The revengeful wretch was ever seeking to prove me guilty of some act, either of omission or commission, that would bring upon me the degrading punishment of the·bastinado, and at length he very nearly succeeded. How—I will relate.

"For six months we bought and sold with such success, that as regularly as the months came round, we punctually paid the ten dollars, and a small instalment of the capital; thus, to the chagrin of Abdoul, our money-loving master became so pleased, that he gave us leave, when he himself was not out upon a journey, to extend the limits of our peregrinations to within ten, instead of five miles, always providing we were accompanied by one of his servants, a Moor, in whom he placed the greatest confidence. Then again he endeavoured by many little acts of kindness to render our servitude more bearable, and so often and warmly did we express our gratitude, and so cheerful did we affect to appear in his presence, that I verily believe the foolish old fellow believed that we had accepted our fate, and resigned all hope of ever regaining our freedom; for having occasion to go upon a journey which would detain him some weeks from home, he took with him Abdoul, in full confidence that it was no longer necessary to employ that rogue to watch our every action. Whatever may have been the old Moor's confidence in his two slaves, I need scarcely tell you that from the first moment of our durance, no day nor night

passed without our brains being at work to concoct some scheme
by which we could regain dear liberty; but so closely had we been
watched, and so terrible was the punishment in the event of
failure, that we at length began to lose all hope. But now the
absence of the old trader, and more so, that of the ever-vigilant
Malay, presented at least a chance of flight, if only we could throw
dust in the eyes of the Moorish servant, who was forbidden to
let us leave the town during his master's absence.

"Luckily discovering that this man, who had been many years
in the old Moor's service, was writhing with jealousy of the Malay,
who he believed had supplanted him in his employer's confidence,
I so fanned the flame by abusing Abdoul, and talking of the
ingratitude of his master to so good, old, and faithful a servant,
that, like every man afflicted with one particular grievance, he
regarded with esteem the sympathizer into whose ears he could be
incessantly pouring his grief. Taking advantage of his new feeling
for me, one evening, after well plying him with strong waters, to
which, although a Mussulman, he had but little objection, providing he could drink on the sly, I told him that Jones and I
were becoming ill for want of exercise, and desired to take a
holiday, but that we were prevented for want of some person
whom we could trust to mind our shop. The cunning servant,
believing he should have an opportunity of robbing us, took the
bait; expressing his belief that we had no intention of attempting
to escape, nay, telling us that if we had, it would be impossible in
a country where no Christian slave could be a distance of two miles
from his owner's home, without being compelled, by the first Moor
he met, to show his master's written permission. He proposed
that we should go the next day, and offered to take charge of the
shop during our absence.

"It would be awkward, he said, to be without our owner's permission, but in the event of being arrested and brought back, we should be safe from punishment, as he would declare he had given us leave; but the dark-skinned knave, even while speaking, guessed our real intention, for within a week afterwards, old and faithful servant as he was, he took his revenge upon his employer by converting our, or rather the old trader's, stock into ready cash, and fleeing from the town.

"Early the following morning the Moor, to avoid our being questioned, or asked to show our pass, by the gate-keeper, led us out of the town, when, the first time since our slavery, we found ourselves under no surveillance. Then keeping in mind our want of a written permission, we determined to avoid, as much as possible, any native man, woman, or child. Hence we endeavoured to make for a lone, and, as we thought, deserted house, about three miles through the neighbouring forest, and there to remain until the darkness of night would cover our flight. Scarcely, however, had we proceeded a mile, through the pathway in the forest, when we heard the sound of horses' hoofs; turning round we saw six horsemen. Fearing they were in pursuit of us, we trembled in every limb, and sought shelter in a neighbouring thicket. It was, however, a false alarm, for they passed onwards without looking to the right or left. Our hopes of escape and fear of recapture had made us forget, that there was no person in the town who suspected our flight, and that even if these men had seen our backs, by our Moorish costume they must have believed us fellow-travellers; and within the hour we resumed our journey and soon came in sight of the house for which we were seeking, but to our dismay, we perceived in the distance that the Moorish horsemen were dismounted and standing by the door partaking of refreshments, by which we saw that the house we had hoped to find deserted was inhabited. It was fortunate, perhaps, that we discovered this mistake so soon, still our position was singularly unfortunate ; we *would* not retrace our steps, we *dared* not proceed by daylight. Luckily, to the right of the house I espied some limekilns. If we could reach them unobserved, they would afford us a hiding-place. Making a *détour* of a portion of the wood, we succeeded, and at once threw ourselves flat upon the ground beneath a low wall, but so near to the building that we could distinctly hear the horsemen conversing. After an hour's anxiety lest any one might chance to come to our retreat, we heard them mount and take their departure; but scarcely had we begun to breathe more freely, than we saw two Moorish women coming towards us, gathering wood as they approached. This was an awkward position, for to remain lying there would at once excite their suspicion that we were, what we really were, runaway Christian slaves; so, putting a bold face upon the matter, we arose, and in their own tongue, a sufficient knowledge of which we had learned, told them we were shopkeepers from the town out for a holiday, and offered to help them gather the wood. Pleased with our politeness, the women gladly accepted the offer, and having thus had their labours lightened, took their departure with much good humour depicted upon their faces, and we met with no further alarms that day. At night we recommenced our journey, and before daylight we had made a distance of twenty miles. During the journey we passed many Moorish tents, but the watchmen, if they noticed us at all, perceiving only our native costume, and hearing us speak in their own tongue, permitted us to proceed without a question. The next day we spent in a thick underwood refreshing ourselves with water and some bread that we had brought with us in bladders and two small bags."

"But to what point were you making; and by night, without chart or compass, how could you find your way?" asked the captain.

"To the sea-coast, south of Sallee, to which place Jones had more than once been with our master, and that, too, only with the desperate hope of finding a boat or materials wherewith to make a raft," replied Constantine; adding, "Well, for a week did we thus continue our journey, hiding by day, travelling by night, across plains, or rivers which we swam, through woods teeming with wild beasts, but none of which providentially assailed us, and living upon pumpkins, herbs, or wild fruits, when suddenly, as we were ascending a high, barren hill, a familiar sound greeted our ears, and we fell upon our knees, and thanked Heaven for having aided us so far. It was delicious music, the roaring of the sea, as its huge waves lashed the shore. How we panted for daybreak, and when it came, and from the summit of the hill we could once more see the ocean, our eyes were filled with tears of joy. The one drawback to our joy was that half a mile to the right, and at about the same distance to the left, were two villages, from which we could distinguish the people going out to pursue their daily avocations; we were, therefore, compelled to ascend an oak tree, and hide among its friendly foliage until night came again, and that, too, without water or other food but the acorns we could gather; still we bore both hunger and thirst joyfully, for liberty, dear liberty, was ahead; a degrading punishment, and, perhaps, perpetual slavery, in our wake.

"At night, much refreshed by our rest in the oak tree—for, that we might sleep without fear of falling, we lashed ourselves to the branches—we once more set out, and having descended the hill, proceeded about ten miles along the shore. On our way we fell in with a limpid stream, at which we replenished the bladders, and at daybreak we caught a land tortoise and about half a peck of snails, of which we made a plentiful meal. After this repast we rested but a couple of hours, for observing that the country was uninhabited thereabout, we ventured to continue our journey by broad daylight. That day we met no living soul; but towards evening we came in sight of the town of Sallee, whose houses and towers loomed through the distance; but more to our delight we could see a ship, we believed an Englishman, at anchor in the offing. You can imagine our joy, aye, and how quickly we determined to attempt to reach her, even at any risk of life or limb. But what a chilling sensation ran through our veins as we found how disproportioned were our means to the execution of our resolves; there was no boat at hand that we could take, no timber with which we could form a raft, while to swim would be impossible. No, there was but one plan; namely, to enter the town by night, and, at the risk of being discovered and re-captured, steal down to the harbour, where it was nearly certain we should find some boat.

"Well, having resolved to make this hazardous attempt, we hid in a large-foliaged fig-tree till night, and then set forth; un-luckily, when within half a mile of the town, we unexpectedly, and too suddenly to make a *détour*, fell in with the tents of some Moors; still more unfortunately, they were guarded by watch-dogs, who, scenting us, set up such a barking that the alarmed inmates came rushing out, and in an instant we should have been surrounded; but desperation lending us wings, we flew along the road, and, entering a thickly wooded valley, and forcing our way through a large bushy thicket, lay, or rather fell down exhausted, and, I may add, hopeless of escape, for we

had but little doubt the Moors had followed and observed our
hiding-place. Panting for breath, we lay with our ears to the
ground, listening, and expecting each moment to hear our
pursuers enter the thicket. But miraculously, as we then
thought, we could hear naught but the sound of our own hard
breathing. Thus, after the lapse of an hour, we became re-
assured of our safety. The Moors, after all, then, had not followed
us. Indeed, there was no reason that they should; for finding
they had not been robbed, and not having seen our faces or
heard our voices, they must have thought that their over-vigilant
dogs had only needlessly alarmed them, and equally so two harmless travellers.

"The thicket served for a retreat during the day, which
proved to be the most wretched of our journey. Perhaps,
it was that the nearer we seemed to be approaching liberty, the
greater became our fear of meeting with that proverbial 'slip
between the cup and the lip.' But be that as it may, we had
sufficient cause for our fears. About mid-day we were awakened
by the loud barking of a dog.

"'The Moors,' I whispered; 'let us run for it.'

"'Nay,' replied Jones, 'it is useless, for by so doing they
would see us, and there is a chance even now that they know
not our hiding-place; moreover, there can be but one, for I
hear no voices. Let us remain quiet.'

"Then the bushes near us were beaten by a stick, the dog
again barked, and we heard the whirr, whirr of rising partridges.
It was fortunate, however, for us that the birds did rise, for the
sportsman—as he proved to be—immediately made after them.
'A false alarm, captain,' cried Jones; 'nevertheless, you were
near betraying us both.'

" ' Aye, aye, it *was* a narrow escape,' I replied, as the sweat rolled off my forehead ; adding, as at that moment I heard footsteps, 'hush !'

"Again we lay down and listened, but this time we could see through a break in the thicket that the new comer was a countryman, who, having just washed his shirt in a neighbouring rivulet, had hung it upon the bush to dry, a process very quickly accomplished beneath an African sun. Short, however, as was the time that man sat there, it was terribly long for us, who feared lest he might hear even our breathing. My situation was painfully ludicrous. Not daring to move a limb for fear of rustling the underwood, holding my breath, I yet felt a painful desire to sneeze. Knowing that to do this would be, perhaps, to give myself again into slavery, I *willed* to resist, and succeeded ; but the agony—and it is no exaggeration—reminded me of some of the slow, but exquisite tortures of the Spanish Inquisition. Yet the delicious sensation of relief, when the man, having dried and aired his shirt, disappeared, almost repaid me for all I had endured."

"Then you had a comfortable sneeze," interposed the captain, provoked to laughter by this recital.

"No," returned Constantine, "I could not, mind had conquered matter, my *will* had conquered my infirmity, and, what is more remarkable, since that day I have never felt the least desire. But to continue my story, when night again came, we set forth to make our last great effort. Having refreshed ourselves at a stream, we proceeded towards the ancient Moorish town, intending to enter it by a gate not far from the sea-shore, and which Jones had observed was used chiefly by labourers and seafaring men, a class of people we thought less likely to take any particular notice of two strangers at night, even if they knew them to be Christian slaves, for numbers of those unfortunates were continually passing to and fro. Thinking that to avoid close observation it would be better not to enter the town by ourselves, we remained without the walls until we saw a company of Moorish sailors. As these fellows came along singing, laughing, and making merry about some European ship they had recently captured, and had that day brought into the harbour, we fell into the rear of their party without attracting any especial notice. As we entered the narrow gateway, our hearts thumped against our breasts—with fear that we might be voluntarily walking from the open country into a trap—with hope and joy that liberty was at hand. Imagine then our horror when, having passed through the entrance, we found ourselves encompassed by some fifty soldiers, one-half with their drawn swords, and the other holding torches above their heads, whose flaming light cast such a ghastly hue upon their savage, almost sable features and gleaming eyes, that we seemed to have suddenly fallen into Pandemonium.

" The chief coming forward selected Jones and me from the Moorish sailors, who, by the way, were little less astonished than ourselves; and muttering maledictions upon Christian slaves, sons of dogs who would run away from their Moslem masters, ordered us to be conveyed to the public prison, there to be ironed, hands and feet, and secured to the wall for the night, adding, with savage pleasure—

" ' There will be no fear of the dogs running away to-morrow *after* the bastinado.'

" Thus entrapped, but by whose means we could not divine, in an agony of hopelessness we passively submitted to be led to the dungeon, where, ironed, chained to the wall amidst the jeers and scoffing of the scum of the city, fetid stenches, squeaking of rats, and buzzing of mosquitoes, which stung us fearfully, we endured, in one night, sufferings which, in a Christian country, would have been deemed an ample punishment for almost any crime, much less for a mere attempt to obtain that liberty we had received, as our birthright, from the Creator. Nay, Zillah, if the relation thus pains you I will not proceed," he said, as he saw the tears trickling down her fair cheeks.

"Pardon me, dear Constantine, but the narration of such sufferings would almost bring tears into the eyes of a statue," she replied; adding, "but proceed, for I am impatient to discover by what stroke of good fortune we have you here."

"Whew," whistled the captain, who had been knitting his brows, puffing more vehemently at his pipe, stamping his foot to the ground, as if in fancy about to attempt Constantine's rescue; "it is a crying shame that England, nay, Christian nations don't unite to bring the strongholds of these infidel dogs about their ears, even as we, under Blake, burned to their very keel the whole fleet of the Dey of Tunis under the very walls of his fortresses, and thus made him give up the Christian slaves in his dominions. But proceed, my dear boy, for, like Zillah, I am impatient to hear how you managed to escape from these dogs."

Here I may step aside to remark that the captain had good reason for his anger at the supineness of the then Governments of Europe in suffering the practice of enslaving Christians, for he remembered the terrible lesson Blake had taught the Algerine pirates in the destruction of the Tunisian fleet. The following touching story of the generosity as well as bravery of Blake and his sailors is thus told by Mr. Hepworth Dixon in his Life of Robert Blake.

"There only remained Algiers. But force was no longer

necessary in dealing with the great pirate cities; the blow struck against the system at Tunis had cowed the corsairs from Tripoli to the shores of Fez and Morocco. When the English squadron stood into the Bay of Algiers, boldly, as if 'on a visit of courtesy to a friendly power, and Blake sent his officer, as usual, to demand restitution of property and the liberation of Christian slaves, the Dey received the messenger with great civility, paid a compliment to the English admiral, and to show his good will, sent a present of live cattle to the fleet—an extremely seasonable and politic gift—which at once made him popular with the ill-fed seamen. With regard to the specific demands of the admiral, he answered, with great adroitness, that the ships and men captured by his people in times past, whether from the English or from other nations, had become the property of private individuals, most of whom had bought them at full price in open market; that they had been seized during a period of recognised and inveterate war between Islam and Christendom, when no treaties existed, and when, therefore, none could be broken; that he could not restore the captives without using violence towards his subjects, and creating general discontent, if not rebellion in his dominions. He urged, moreover, that, considering the general prevalence of piracy in Europe as well as in Africa, the English required too much when they demanded the unconditional surrender of his prizes. Finally, if these objections should seem to the admiral as clear as they did to himself, he said he would procure the liberation of all English captives then in his country, at a moderate ransom per head, and enter for himself and his people into a solemn engagement not to molest English traders for all time to come. The humble tone of the pirate prince recommended his argument; a contract was, therefore, made for the ransom of all the captives at a fixed price, and the poor wretches were liberated and sent on board the ships of their deliverers. Before the fleet sailed from the harbour, a noble and touching incident occurred, adding one more to the long list of illustrations of the English seaman's character. The ships were lying in shore, not far from the mole-head, when a number of men were observed swimming towards them, pursued by several turbaned Moors in boats ; and on coming under the bows of our vessels, the fugitives cried to the sailors in Dutch to save them from their Moslem pursuers. Forgetting that only a few months before we had been at war with the Dutch, regardless of every consideration beyond the humane instincts of the moment, our sailors helped the poor wretches to clamber up, when they discovered that they were runaway slaves, and the men in chase of them their masters. Here, then, was a new difficulty! The Dey claimed the fugitives in virtue of the new treaty, and appealed to the accepted principle of compensation for all restored captives. But the idea of giving back Christian men, even enemies, from the freedom of an English man-of-war into the hands of pirates and infidels, was not to be entertained by Puritan sailors. Some one suggested to his fellows a subscription. How much the admiral himself paid into this fund he has carefully concealed, but every seaman in the fleet generously agreed to give up a dollar of his wages to buy the poor Hollanders their freedom. A bargain was soon made, the money was paid by the fleet-treasurer, and the liberated men went home to tell their countrymen this story of the magnanimous islanders."

Resuming his story, Constantine said—

"The means by which we were recaptured remained a mystery only till the next morning, when one of our jailers told us that the Moors, whose watch-dogs had alarmed them in the night, seeing us flying as if for our lives instead of remaining to demand their hospitality, as their own countrymen would have done, or at least to exchange the customary courtesies of travellers, at once suspected that we were fugitive slaves making our way from some town in the interior to the port of Sallee. They had therefore sent forward two of their party to put the authorities upon their guard, and, if their suspicions should prove true, to claim the reward always paid in that country for the recapture of Christian slaves; accordingly soldiers had been stationed at the different gates day and night, to examine every party or individual as they or he passed through the archway into the town. He further told us that intelligence of the seizure of two Christians had been sent to various towns and cities in the interior, that all those who had lost slaves might come and examine for themselves whether we were the runaways.

"Shortly after receiving this anything but consoling information, we were carried, ironed as we were, into a larger and better lighted room. Here we were visited by a great number of merchants and slave-owners, so many indeed that the greater part must have come out of mere curiosity. For two days we were not recognised, and thus began to have a dismal kind of hope that, by some remote possibility, we might be able to escape before our real owner discovered us; but, alas! upon the third day, among several who came to our prison, there was one who claimed us, not for himself, but for his master. It was *Abdoul the Malay!*

"'Ungrateful dogs!' he exclaimed maliciously, 'it is thus, then, you would have escaped from your master and benefactor. Allah be praised, He has not smiled upon the attempt.'

"'Do your will with us, we scorn your hate, wretch!' I exclaimed.

"'God is great,' he replied, 'but we will see;' and then he requested the jailers to take us to the tribunal of a certain judge or magistrate, before whom his master was required to swear upon the Koran, and prove his ownership, before we could be given over to him.

"Had they been about to lead us to instant execution, resigning my soul into the hands of the Creator, I could have died without a murmur, or certainly fearlessly. Knowing, however, the punishment awarded to runaway slaves, and also that it was inevitable, my brow became damp, and I trembled in every limb. But let me digress for a minute to describe the degrading punishment, and you shall judge whether I could be charged with cowardice for entertaining this horror.

"In the centre of a board about ten feet in length are two holes. The two ends of a cord being drawn through, a loop is formed, into which the two feet of the sufferer are secured by tightening the cord upon the other side about the ankles, and that, too, so tightly that the skin is cut through. The feet being thus placed, the ends of the board are supported upon the shoulders of a couple of stout men, and the sufferer, being thus with his head upon the ground, receives at the hands of another lusty fellow his allotted number of blows upon the soles.

"In the case of a recaptured fugitive Christian slave, the blows are dealt with might and main, and to the number of three or four hundred. Thus apart from its degradation, which to a European is by far the worst portion, the punishment frequently causes death, but in all instances many months of torture."

"Did the villains thus maltreat you, my poor boy?"

"Merciful Providence! is it possible that you can have thus suffered?" exclaimed both father and daughter, simultaneously.

"Thank Heaven, no; but patience, my dear friends." Then continuing his narrative, he said, "Upon being taken before the judge, we were at once confronted with our master, who, having satisfactorily proved his right of ownership, fell upon his knees and demanded that, as an example, we should then and there, in his lordship's presence, be bastinadoed according to law. The judge having consented, we were at once seized by his myrmidons, but, before they could fix our feet in the planks, a bald-headed old Moor, with a benevolent aspect, came forward from the crowd, and falling upon his knees, claimed Jones, me, and the Malay, as his property. The great man frowned savagely at the very notion of a Christian escaping punishment, but, as he was bound by law, gave the new claimant permission to speak.

"Our bald-headed friend—Heaven bless the old fellow, albeit he be an infidel—produced certain papers, by which our master, in consideration of a large loan to be expended in the purchase and fitting out of the piratical ship, in which we had been compelled to serve, had mortgaged to old bald-head all his slaves and other property, with permission to take or sell the whole, providing the money was not repaid within a month after the return of the vessel from her first cruise.

"To this claim our master had no reply in defence; the papers were proof sufficient of his forfeiture. The judge, therefore, although much against his will—for he was aware, from the known character of the claimant, that he would shield us from the punishment which could only be administered to a slave at the especial solicitation of his owner—at once adjudged that we should all three be given over to old bald-head. In an agony of disappointment and suppressed rage plainly visible upon his countenance, Abdoul claimed his freedom, upon the grounds that he had received his manumission ; but, as the latter had been granted *after* the mortgage, the tyrannical judge not only disallowed the plea, but, delighted that he could find an excuse to show his power of punishing some one, ordered him to receive fifty blows upon the soles of his feet for his impudence in having made it.

"Now, although we had not regained our liberty, we found our position greatly improved, for our new master treated us very kindly ; again, we were near the sea should an opportunity of escape offer ; moreover, we had for companions five fellow slaves, all Englishmen ; perhaps, however, the most important benefit we found in our change of masters, was that our new one taking a dislike to the Malay sold him to a ship captain, and so rid us of his hateful presence.

"I have said that bald-head was kind ; nevertheless, as his object was to make a good profit by his slaves, we were compelled to work at different trades, each slave choosing that for which he had the most aptitude. For instance, my mate Jones, who in early life had been a carpenter, chose that trade, and prospered so well that he soon became possessed of a good-sized house ; one, named Linder, was a bricklayer ; another, Thompson, was a cap-maker ; the other three, knowing no trade, were sent daily to wash clothes at the seashore, while I was permitted to help Jones as a kind of journeyman. Thus we all lived the lives of workmen, and were only compelled to pay our master a sum that enabled us to save something for ourselves ; we had, as Christian slaves, but little to complain of ; indeed, so accustomed had the five Englishmen become to their chains, for they had been captured more than ten years before, that, but for the efforts of the carpenters' firm of Jones and Phaulcon, I believe they would all have remained in slavery till now. As, however, I had no particular taste for my vocation, and had long been revolving in my mind a plan of escape that would be impossible without their assistance, I, little by little, endeavoured to shake them out of their apathy by frequent allusions to Old England, wives, sweethearts, children, and hints that, if they would act upon my advice, they might soon see those dear relations again; and at length I succeeded so far that, one evening after working hours, Linder the bricklayer and Thompson the cap-maker desired to know how I proposed to escape.

"'Let us take advantage of the first dark night, and put boldly out to sea,' said I.

"'Sheer madness, Phaulcon. How is it possible, for at night every ship's boat is hauled on board; and even could we find and seize some other, it would not carry us beyond the offing.'

"'My friends,' I replied, 'I propose that, night by night, in the cellar beneath this house we build a boat, not only sufficiently large for us all, but which, when finished, we can take to pieces. In that state, having between us carried it, bit by bit, to the sea-shore, there hide it until an opportunity occurring we can leave this city after dark and put it together again. Provisions and water can be conveyed in the same way. The boat my mate and I will undertake. To you we leave the finding of the provisions, and the carrying of them and the pieces of the boat to the shore. Do you agree?'

"For a time they hesitated, doubting whether the chances of escape were worth the certain punishment that would await us in the event of failure. When, however, I had more fully explained

our plan, they cordially agreed, and undertook to enlist the three
clothes-washers in our scheme. From that time Jones and I
commenced our labours, and continued them three hours each
night for nearly a month. The keel consisted of two planks
twelve feet long, each rib was made in three pieces, the ends of the
centre piece we did not join to the others by mortice or tenon,
but by simply laying them upon the flat surface. In each joint
there were two holes for nails, not parallel with the ends of the
wood, which would have formed one straight piece, but so bored
that when the nails were in each joint, would form an obtuse
angle, and the whole a semicircle, this being, as you will afterwards
see, desirable. For the clothing of the naked ribs we bought enough
strong canvas to twice cover the entire boat. To make the latter
waterproof, we painted it over with pitch and tallow, which we
melted in earthen pots. Having completed the boat, we took it
to pieces again, and then came the most difficult, most hazardous
portion of our task—the taking the various parts out of town
without being discovered. After a little consultation, it was thus
arranged.

"Linder the bricklayer, with his apron before him, and his
trowel in hand, carried one piece of the keel over his shoulder as
if going about his ordinary work; having hidden this in a small
copse about a quarter of a mile from the sea, he, the next day,
did the same with the other piece. The ribs, being made to fold,
were taken one by one by the washers in their clothes-bags. The
most difficult portion to carry was the tarred canvas, for its very
appearance would excite suspicion; at length, however, we resolved
to inclose it in a large bag, putting over it two pillows, in case any
passer-by might lay his hand upon it, and then entrusted it to one
of the washers, who, throwing it over his shoulder as if it were

an ordinary clothes-bag, but a little fuller than usual, safely placed it with the other parts. So far we had succeeded, when our scheme, by me concocted, was by me very nearly destroyed.

"We had ready stored in our cellar some bread in bags, and bladders for water, and had even named the night for our flight, when, suddenly remembering that we had provided no sail, I procured some canvas, and rolling it up in a bale, proceeded to carry it myself down to the sea with as much nonchalance as if on some message for my master, when suddenly I saw a Moor, whom I knew to be a friend of his, close at my heels. Believing he suspected something wrong, I trembled for our scheme, and scarce knew whether to go forward or return. Seeing our two washers busily engaged at the seaside, a happy thought struck me; going up to them, I threw the bale on the ground and bid them wash it while I waited; understanding my motive, my fellow-conspirators immediately seized upon the canvas, and began to wash as if it had been sent for that express purpose. This, and my returning to the town, disarmed my spy of his suspicions, and he went on his way. Still, thinking it possible he might casually mention to my master the next day (fortunately he had left the town and was not to return that night) that he had seen me take a bale of clothes down to the washers and so lead to a discovery, I mentioned the circumstance to my fellows, and urged them, since all was ready, to make their escape that very night, and, admitting the wisdom of the suggestion, they agreed.

"Accordingly, at night, we left the town by different gates; in this we had no difficulty, for no person suspected that kind old bald-head's slaves, most of whom had belonged to him so many years, would attempt, or even desire, to escape. We met again at the little copse, where, by the light of the moon, we put our boat

together.  This being done, four of the fellows, stripping themselves
naked and putting their clothes in the bottom, carried her into the
sea.  Thus launched, myself, Jones, and Thompson stepped in,
and in an instant every man felt sick at heart; the little craft was
too fragile to hold so many—she was sinking.  Alarmed for their
lives, two of the naked men leaped into the sea and swam ashore.
I called to them to return, but Jones and Linder, who had the oars
in their hands, asking me if I was mad, began to pull for their
lives, and thus did the cowardly fear of two of our party give life
and liberty to the rest.

"That night we rowed for our lives—more, dear liberty ; but so
contrary were the winds, that at daybreak we were still in sight of
the Moorish ships ; probably, however, our boat was too small to
call their attention, for they gave no signs that they saw us, or
at least knew who and what we were.

"Before night again came, we discovered that with all our foresight, we had been deficient in providing proper protection for
our bread and water.  The bags and bladders were defective : the
first let in the sea, so that the bread had become saturated with
brine ; the latter, excepting one or two, had burst and let out the
fresh water.  Thus, our plight soon became deplorable ; still, so
hungered we for our liberty, that by doling the water out almost
in drops at a time, and sparingly partaking of the bread, bad as
it was, we made it support life for three days ; but when on the
fourth we found the food nearly gone, and the wind still adverse,
two of our party, worn out with hunger and toil, even proposed
that we should return to Sallee.  Although I spoke vehemently
against such a proposition, and strenuously endeavoured to show
that death met in the effort to recover our liberty was far preferable
to slavery, I did not wonder at the suggestion, for our labour

against the wind was incessant, and the heat of the sun so bleached and blistered our skin, that while two rowed and the others attended to the rudder and sail, I continued, without intermission, to drench them with sea-water.

"On the fifth day, when our sufferings had become so fearful that two of the party lay helplessly in the bottom of the boat praying for death to relieve them, we fell in with a turtle lying asleep. This was indeed a godsend; we caught it, cut off her head and let her bleed into a pot. We drank the blood and sucked the flesh. Wonderfully refreshed by this, we toiled with renewed vigour, and were soon rewarded by the sight of land. The vision gave us additional vitality, and in less than two hours we had reached the land; still the rocks were so craggy, that we were two hours more before we could make a landing. Succeeding in that, however, at last we one and all lay down upon the beach, beneath the shelter of an overhanging rock, and slept; how long I know not, but probably five or six hours, for it was not sundown when we landed, and when we awakened it was night, with a full bright moon shining over us, and a stiff refreshing sea-breeze blowing in our faces.

"We were all famishing; but our two invalids, who had become somewhat better since we had squeezed the juice of the turtle flesh into their mouths, we were obliged to lift ashore, where they lay crying for water. To obtain this, Jones and I left them under the charge of Thompson and Linder, and proceeded along the coast till we came to a watch-tower, when, from the soldiers on guard, I found we had fallen upon the island of Majorca. Fortunately, having learned the Spanish tongue in my boyhood, I could tell them our wants, and beg of them to send some of their comrades with a litter for our invalids. This being com--

municated to the commander of the town, that officer at once
complied, and we returned at once to our companions, who, like
ourselves, had no little difficulty in passing even cakes softened
in water through their so long unused throats.

"Having remained three days at the tower, until the officer had
communicated with and heard from the governor of the island,
we were taken to the capital. Our story had travelled before us,
and such a spectacle did we present with our bare feet, shaggy
hair, and beards, and tattered Moorish gowns, that as we passed
through the suburbs, crowds of people followed, offering us meat,
drink, and clothing. When the governor had heard the story of
our adventures, he, like a noble gentleman, kept us at his own cost
until an opportunity afforded of giving us a passage in one of the
Spanish ships bound for Alicante. Upon our arrival at the latter
place, we shipped on board an English vessel. The captain, however, less humane than the Spaniards, compelled us to work our
passage, and because, when the ship put into the port of Newcastle,
I insisted upon leaving her, he sent me ashore without a day's
rations or a solitary coin, and only the clothes which I had
worn almost to tatters in the ship's work on the passage from
Alicante."

"The paltry rascal!" interposed the captain.

"From the moment of my landing at Newcastle, I lost no time
in steering for your house, cheerfully walking the whole distance
of forty miles, without other food than what I could beg by the
way, for I well knew the right good welcome I should meet."

"Welcome, indeed," exclaimed the captain, with tears in his
eyes; "a stray dog would have met with a kind reception in this
house, at the present inclement season; but to you welcome is not
the word. As a son I took to you years past by, as a son dear to

my love I now bid you regard my house as your own home, my purse yours to share, and there is my hand on it." Constantine took the hand and heartily returned the warm grasp, but his heart was too full to let words express his gratitude.

Why did Zillah shed so many tears during and at the close of this recital? Why did those sunshiny eyes beam with something like pride in the hero of the adventures to which she had been listening? Perhaps, like Desdemona, she loved the man for the dangers he had past. But I will not anticipate.

"Dear Constantine," she exclaimed, "Heaven be thanked for having brought you once more among us. Your sufferings have been terrible, your misfortunes great; it must have been a sad, sad blow, to have lost that for which you had toiled so hard and patiently; but that Providence which has brought you safely through so many dangers will, in the future, not forget the pious object for which you encountered them."

"Dear Zillah, if in too great haste to make money, it was chiefly that my parents might share it; thus, but for their sakes, I could forget that it had melted within my grasp, for what my hands and brain have once accomplished, at my age that can they do again. But my mother, my poor mother—" and he buried his face in his hands, as he added, "should she have *died* during my captivity, and there is something within me that declares she is no longer of this world, what new fortune, come it when or how it may, can console me for the loss of her for whose sake I was first spurred on to raise myself in the world?"

"Nay, nay, my lad," said the captain, affectionately placing his hand upon his shoulder, "I honour your feelings; but grieve not for that which may, perchance, be but imaginary. Your good mother may yet be living, aye, and mayhap grieving for her son's supposed loss.   Come, cheer up, and as soon as your strength will permit, I will procure you a passage in a Mediterranean trader."

"Dear sir," returned Constantine, brightening up, "it was my poverty, my inability to obtain such a passage that wrung my heart and aggravated my fears; but I thank you—I cannot thank you enough."

"Pooh, pooh," replied the captain, rather petulantly, "you knew it was to be had for the asking.   But now," he added, "bethink thee, my dear boy, of nought but furbishing up your strength."   And from that day so quickly did Constantine improve under the soothing care of the old sailor and his daughter, that within the month he had sailed for his native land.

# CHAPTER V.

### BLAKE'S "CONTINGENCY" PHAULCON'S OPPORTUNITY.

AFTER a short absence, yet long enough to confirm his worst
.fears, Constantine returned to the Manor House, sad at heart,
nearly broken-spirited. His mother had died about twelve months
before, and of his father, all that he could discover was, that he
had been released from the dungeon of St. Mark, but, unable
to hold up his head among his friends, had disappeared—
whither, no person could tell. The dear parent for whom, chiefly,
he had toiled so long and patiently, had passed away almost
simultaneously with the——well, comparative wealth he had acquired
for her; thus fortune herself seemed to be his enemy, and for
a time he despaired; but the *habit* of getting money had grown
into his nature; moreover, toil and adventure had become so
habitual to him that he loved them for themselves alone, and
not only as a means to an end.

Thus, although the captain, Zillah, and Blake were untiring in
their endeavours to make him forget his dependent position,
he soon became restless to re-visit the East, the scenes of his
early successes. Again, this desire was strengthened by a spirit
of emulation, for Blake Taunton, who had returned to England
during his visit to Cephalonia, had brought wondrous news of the
fortunes that Europeans were then making in the Indies, and,
moreover, by way of proof, a sum of money more than sufficient

to keep him, should he so choose, at ease for the remainder of his life. Without money to join in any venture, he would be compelled to begin *de novo*, or, at least, in a position very different to that at which he aspired ; still, he cared not, so long as he could only find himself once more traversing that ground which in those days was supposed to lead to fortune. Hence, without consulting his friends, he solicited the directors of the India Company to appoint him to a ship bound for Siam. Then, when in reply to his request, he was informed that the company, having taken into consideration his previous good service, would give him the first vacant second-officership, he gleefully told Blake of his application and its success.

"I am not surprised," said the latter, "at your resolution, and I congratulate you, my dear fellow, upon your success; still I do not take it kindly that you, who helped *me* so much, should not have asked something in return."

"My dear Blake," returned Constantine, "I feared you or the captain might have attempted to shake my resolution ; besides, I knew you could not aid me otherwise than by money, and to accept, either by way of gift or even loan, any portion of that for which you have toiled so long and hard, was out of the question."

"Hold, my friend, you are wrong; I can aid you by *other* means than gift or loan, nay, to that which even your proud spirit will deign to accept. Know that my gains, savings, are all invested in the new company ; hence I have it in my power to help you to a separate and independent command, even to that of the very ship I brought home from the East."

"Is this possible, Blake!" exclaimed the other, in gratified surprise.

" Aye, *very* possible, more, probable ; but listen," replied Blake, adding, "within a week or two my ship again sets sail for the factory at Siam ; it is also the earnest wish of the directors that I should again take the command. But, as yet, I have neither accepted nor refused ; what I *may* do depends upon a certain contingency over which I have but little control."

" *That* contingency ? " said Constantine interrogatively.

"I may not at present tell even you, yet, my dear fellow," he replied, "but my decision must be given within a week. Give me, therefore, your word that you will take no further steps in this matter till that time has expired, and I will pledge mine that should I refuse this command it shall be only in your favour ; should I accept, well—then, you, my friend, shall sail with me as you like, either as captain or chief officer."

"My dear Blake, if not in blood, in affection we are brothers," replied Constantine with more impulse than was his wont ; and shaking his friend by the hand warmly, he added, "but, astonished as I confess myself at your interest with the company, and still more so at this mysterious contingency, your generous offer is only what Constantine Phaulcon might have expected at the hands of Blake Taunton." .

But as the speaker continued to pour out his thanks, Blake, having returned his grasp, said, as he turned towards the house, "But even of thanks enough is as good as a feast, and now I go to seek Zillah."

"Zillah !" echoed Constantine, giving a keen look at his friend. "then you will find her in her own little charming boudoir, as usual, busily employed with her needle. I have just left her."

"Thanks, old fellow," replied Blake, but the keen, piercing eye brought a flush into his face, that must, either in fact or fancy, have revealed some secret to Constantine, for, as the former passed into the house, he muttered abstractedly,

"Well, well, it might have been, but *might have been* is a phrase significant of the past and regret. No, it is by other means that Constantine Phaulcon must attain his goal."

As for the mysterious contingency of which Blake had spoken, although it was deemed by the latter a matter to be kept secret from the ears of Constantine, it may at least be revealed to the reader by means of a conversation that had taken place during the morning, between him and the captain.

"Well, lad," said the old sailor, "dost think thou canst give over this adventuring in the Indies, take to thyself a wife, and sit thee down for the rest of thy days like a contented gentleman ?"

"I might, sir," replied Blake, adding thoughtfully, "yet although my means are more than ample for a bachelor, I fear they are scarcely equal to the wants of a wife."

"Poh, poh, lad, thou art over modest; dost think she upon whom I have my eye, and if I mistake not thou hast long had thy entire vision, will go to a husband empty-handed ?"

"What mean you, sir ?" exclaimed the young man, with sparkling eyes, but his whole frame tremulous with emotion. "Is it possible that *you* can have guessed my feelings towards——"

"Zillah," interposed the captain. "I will be more frank than you have been with me. Yes, he must have been a dullard indeed, who could have lived the last few months beneath the same roof with you both, not to have made the discovery. But hark you, master Blake, it was scarcely fair sailing of you or Zillah not to take me into your confidence."

"Zillah," repeated Blake ; adding, with the frankness of a

sailor, who speaks exactly that which he means, "Heaven bless you, dear sir! as far as I am concerned, the dear girl is as ignorant of my love for her as I believed you to be."

"Whew! but I have made a pretty mess of this voyage, then," exclaimed the captain, but with a look of doubt and astonishment that plainly exhibited the difficulty he found in giving credence to the young man's declaration. "What! a youngster woo a pretty girl without her knowing it? Master Blake, Master Blake. you must tell this to the sea-gulls."

"On my honour, sir, it is the truth," said Blake, warmly.

"Aye, aye, dear lad, to the best of your belief; but if this be so, tell me how is it that since your return you have almost entirely forsaken your so much loved field sports for Zillah's society, and about what—for if you have no love-secrets you may candidly tell me—have I so frequently found you in such earnest conversation?"

"Easily answered, sir. From the first year you adopted me I have loved Zillah—first, as a brother, then with a warmer affection, but, since my last voyage, as a woman I would woo for my wife; thus have I forsaken my gun, nay, all other pleasures, with a hope that a happy moment would come when I might find courage sufficient to tell her of my affection; that time or opportunity, however, as yet, has never arrived, for although pretty well accustomed to cruising in dangerous waters, when with her I have felt—well, the truth must be told—chicken-hearted, and as if I wanted a pilot to steer me free of the reef refusal; thus, instead of love as you supposed, our conversation has, most frequently I believe, been about my voyages and doings in the East, and Constantine Phanlcon's adventures and misfortunes— but chiefly about the latter."

"But," asked the still incredulous captain, "do you mean to say that you never have given the girl *any* reason to understand your passion for her?"

"By words never, save, indeed, those of the language of love, by which soul speaks to soul through the eyes."

"Bravo, my lad," returned the captain, with a laugh; "better and better. When a sailor talks like that it is a pretty sure sign that he has struck his colours to some pretty face. But tell me, Blake, has Zillah ever given you reason to believe that your addresses would prove *otherwise* than acceptable to her?"

"Nay, sir, had it been so, I could have answered your first question in the negative, for her refusal would at once turn my course to the East again.'

"My dear boy," said the captain, seriously, "frankly as you have spoken, as frankly will I tell you that for years it has been my hope that matters would take this turn. My son by adoption, I would have you my son by a nearer connexion. As I have said, I thought matters were somewhat better, or certainly more plainly understood between you than it appears they are, and that belief has given me infinite pleasure. All that I can now say is, that you have my hearty consent to address her openly, and may you prosper, for I would have you quit this voyaging about the East, and remain to cheer my old days with the presence of a son and daughter whose happiness and prosperity are my sole tie to this life."

"Dear sir, how can I express my gratitude?"

"By making my daughter a good husband," interposed the captain; adding, with a laugh, "but get thee gone at once, and make up for lost time."

"I pray Heaven that your wishes and my happiness may be

realized," returned Blake ; but quitting the room ere he heard the
captain's "Of course they will ; the young minx wouldn't dare
to love any one else without telling her father, and if she has
not, why who could she fall in love with but you?"

The reader has now learned what the contingency was to which
Blake had alluded, also for what purpose he was seeking Zillah.

Once having resolved to set about this terrible task—and to
Blake, who really had but a very small opinion of himself, it
seemed the most terrible that had ever been imposed upon him
—he determined to dash boldly, clumsily, perhaps, but straightforward and sailor-like.  Why, the silly fellow, who had all along
been hugging to his heart a hope, or a fancy, that Zillah was
as violently in love with him as he was with her, no sooner
found himself in the pretty, laughing girl's presence, for the express purpose of asking her the most interesting question of her
life, than instead of boldly asking himself what earthly reason
there could be for her refusing him, actually began to ask himself why so pretty, good, and amiable a creature should prefer
him to all other handsomer, richer, and better men.  The favourite
proverb or maxim "that none but the *brave* deserve the fair,"
women frequently negative by proving that few but the *im-
pudent* can win them.  Now, as, on entering the room, he was
mentally putting the above question to himself, Zillah, laughingly,
said,

"Why, Blake, dear, you look as serious as a Quaker.  What
ails thee?"

If he had replied that he felt sick at heart, it would have
been not only a gallant, but a perfectly true answer.  Then,
as we have seen, Blake was neither an adept in soft nothings
nor pretty sayings, but a frank sailor ; and so, in as lover-like a

roundabout way as his straightforward habits of thinking and speaking would permit, he began by speaking of their affection for each other since their childhood. Then, when he came to tell how that his love had developed into feelings far deeper than fraternal love, she put down the work, and placing her hand upon her fair throat, as if to suppress some rising emotion, seemed to be painfully distressed, at least so a bystander would have been impressed. Not so Blake. Having once broken the ice, he took courage, and became even eloquent. Guess, however, his astonishment, when, as he related his interview with the captain, Zillah, as if unable any longer to restrain some powerful emotion, arose, like another Niobe, all tears, and, placing her hand upon his shoulder, cried, in piteous accents,

"Blake, dear Blake, say no more, you will kill me, poor me; poor Blake, my poor dear father."

"Zillah," he exclaimed, shrinking backwards, "in Heaven's name what can thus have moved you? I am astounded. Is it possible that this subject is disagreeable—that I am hateful in your eyes?"

"Nay, Blake, dear Blake, my brother, my more than brother, be not offended, have pity on me; on my knees I ask you to forgive and forget me, save as a loving sister."

"Zillah," he replied, as he gently raised her from the ground, "you forget, you have explained nought. Why, tell me, I pray you, all this emotion, and in what can *you* have offended, that you should thus seek *my* pardon?"

"In much, Blake, for I shall cruelly, most cruelly disappoint you and my dear father, who, from that which now flashes through my brain like a long-forgotten dream, tells me that he has had our union near his heart for years. I might have fore-

seen, might have known· that this day would come, and have
been prepared for it."

"But, dear Zillah," said Blake, taking her by the hand and
looking into her streaming eyes, "what mystery is this that *you*
can have kept from your father? What, oh what! save your
hate, is there that can prevent our union?"

"Blake, be generous; trust, but ask me not, sufficient that it
is impossible; but why I may not, must not, nay," she added
firmly, "*will* not tell—at least now," she added soothingly.

"At least now," he echoed, as if there were balm in the sounds,
then walking towards the door, he said, firmly, kindly, but sadly,
as if his noble heart were breaking, "Zillah, I *have* your secret,
you love another. I could not have divined this, or would not
thus have pained you. In, perhaps, the last words I may ever
address you—May he deserve such love as yours; Heaven bless you."

While he had been thus slowly speaking, Zillah had listened
as if entranced, but as he passed from the room she rose, exclaiming, "Blake, dear Blake, come back, but for an instant; this must
not be, we must not part thus;" and she followed, but her voice,
her footsteps, were as nothing. He turned not his head, and
even in her agony, too proud to again solicit him who seemed to
shun her, she retired to her room, and covering her face with her
hands, gave free vent to her grief. She heard not even the footsteps of Blake, who, having returned, said, "Zillah, I have been
too hasty, too harsh, pardon me; thus we must not part, we who
have been friends from little children."

"This is, indeed, like my own dear kind Blake," she exclaimed,
seizing his hands; adding, "Oh! did you know that which is
now passing within my heart, you would indeed pity, forgive me."

"Zillah," he replied sadly, "no more of this, I pray. I have asked, and been refused; you say, you cannot, must not, dare not give the reason of this refusal. I, therefore, question you no more; but, Zillah, for your own sake, for your father's sake, think well ere you thus answer *him*."

"Ah, it is that which now fills me with misery. My dear, kind father! What, oh, what can I say to him?" then a sudden thought passing through her mind, she added, "Blake, dear, kind Blake, have faith in me; help me in this dire extremity; do not tell my father, for his own sake, do not tell him the match he has had near his heart so long is broken irrevocably. No," she added, with some hesitation, "for Heaven's sake, no; but by some means lead him to believe, at least for the present, that it is *my* wish, if you will, that it should be postponed until your return from another voyage, and in the meantime I will confess to *him* that which I may not disclose to you."

"Zillah," he replied sternly, "*how* long is it since you learned to practise subterfuge and deceit with your kind-hearted, loving father?"

"Blake, this is ungenerous, cruel, most cruel," and she sobbed as if her heart would break, and the simple-hearted fellow, notwithstanding her cruelty to him, said,

"Well, well, Zillah, it shall be as you wish, nay more, he shall not even know that the wish for the postponement originated with you;" and so saying he left the house, intending to meditate that most difficult of things to a brave, honest mind—*a white lie*, for he felt that without a short rehearsal he should not be able to face his kind-hearted, adopted father with an untruth upon his lips; before, however, he had proceeded a dozen yards he was met by the captain himself, who, observing his downcast looks, said,

"Why Blake, son, what can have happened to make thee look as glum as the captain of a Plate ship within the claws of a buccaneer? Has Phyllis proved unkind? well, then, never mind, women are all wilful in these matters; the wind, perhaps, will blow from a better quarter to-morrow."

"Nay, sir, you are in error, of Zillah I complain not; but—"

"But what?" exclaimed the captain, as Blake hesitated to proceed.

"But of my insufficient fortune to render her as happy as she deserves, of my want of a name, in fact, sir," he blurted out with more frankness than courtesy, considering what had passed between them earlier in the day. "After talking the matter over with Zillah, I have resolved to make another voyage to the East, and to make some other and greater effort to discover my parents, that I may have a legal right to the name I bestow upon my wife."

For a moment the captain stood speechless with astonishment, anger, and disappointment; but then placing his hand on the young man's shoulder, and looking him full in the face, he said,

"Blake, you are a bad hand at a falsehood,—never attempt it again. You, who but an hour since were mad with delight at this marriage, who told me that your making another voyage depended only upon one contingency, who quitted me with the light step and sunny countenance of a man whose years of hopes of anticipated happiness were about to be realized—you, who from boyhood have been careless of acquiring wealth, and who have ever found a difficulty in retaining it as it was obtained— you thus to become a miser in your desire for gain! You, whose countenance has in so short a time fallen from the height of delight to the depth of despair. No, no, Blake, I am not thus to be deceived, there is some mystery in this, at which that little minx is at the bottom, and I will fathom it out; but cheer up, my lad, all will yet be right. I will at once seek Zillah."

"Stay, sir, one moment, hear me," cried Blake, as the captain hastened towards the house; but the call being unheeded, he walked gloomily onwards through the grounds, revolving in his mind the names of the various young men of the neighbourhood with whom he knew, or had heard, that Zillah was acquainted, and wondering which could be his rival, for that he had a rival he did not now doubt.

It was strange that his suspicions had not fallen upon one nearer home, but they had not; they did not until, as he came near the gates of the grounds, he saw Constantine approaching; then the remembrance flashed through his mind, that Zillah had spent hours with himself conversing about the young Greek, his adventures, fortunes, and talents. Thus, then, his dearest friend was his rival. The thought was sickening to his heart, and, filled with jealousy, he turned upon his heel to avoid him.

"How now, Blake," cried Constantine, "what means this? Why this gloom? What can have chanced to have so suddenly brought down thy spirits from midsummer warmth to zero? But, above all, why seem to shun *me*?"

"Because," he replied, sharply, "of all men, you are the one I would have avoided at this moment."

"In Heaven's name, my dear Blake, what means this?" exclaimed his astonished friend.

"Constantine Phaulcon," replied Blake, coolly, "for better or for worse, we have been shipmates and friends for many years—too many to bring such an association to a sudden termination without a free and frank explanation on both sides."

"My dear friend," interposed the other, "you astound me, on

my honour. I know of no reason for such a calamity. You have
been imposed upon. But, proceed, let me know my sins, whether
of omission or commission, at once."

Blake, somewhat mollified by this, told in his own frank
manner, the history of his love, his hopes, the captain's wishes,
his own proposal to Zillah, and her refusal.

"It is a singular story—it is a great grief for you, my poor
friend," replied Constantine, when Blake had concluded. "Doubtlessly," he added, "you have a rival; do you not suspect who
he may be?"

"I do—a friend with whom I have offered to share my all—
yourself, Constantine Phaulcon. Now," he added, "be as frank
with me as I have been with you. Say, is it not so?"

"Blake, my friend, you are mad to have such thoughts; frankly
will I answer you, and on my honour, not one word of love has
ever passed between us, other than would have become a brother
and sister, for as the latter have I, and shall I, ever hold Zillah,
notwithstanding that she has jilted even you. Moreover, had I
loved her and she had deemed me worthy of her affection, I,
Constantine Phaulcon, a penniless adventurer, could not marry;
nor, to be frank with you, my friend, will I ever, save it
can at the same time help me to that fortune for which I
crave."

At this Blake's countenance brightened a little, and taking the
other's hand, he said,

"From my heart I believe you, Constantine, for assuredly no
man in love could speak thus heartlessly. But of Zillah you
speak wrongly, she has not jilted me, for although I have been
deceived by my own vanity into believing that she loved me as
one to whom she could unite herself, her affections have been

turned in some other direction, me she has regarded as a brother, a brother only."

"But," said Constantine, "you know not the reason of her refusal, you know not that there is even a rival in the way.  So cheer up, it may be only a woman's whim—that time may cure. Take my word for it, you and Zillah will yet live to sit in yon great parlour, a happy man and wife."

"Impossible," replied Blake, despondingly; adding, "but it is probable that time, absence, may do much, at least to relieve my mind; I have, therefore, resolved to take my ship back to Siam, and that, too, as soon as they have completed manning, provisioning, and lading her, and now I have only to renew my offer to you."

"Dear, generous friend, how can I—"

"See, here comes the captain.  Hush, not one word about Zillah before him," interrupted Blake.

"I will leave you, for, by his look, our friend has that to say which is not for my ears," said Constantine, retreating towards the gates.

"I fear you have but ill news, sir," said Blake, as the captain, with sad and dejected countenance, approached.

"Ill news!  Zounds, no.  It is no ill news to tell you of your escape from such an obstinate, ungrateful minx.  Why, lad, I could get nothing from her, but that she could not marry you, and prays that I would not ask her her reasons for such monstrous behaviour.  Oh, Blake, pray you may never have a daughter thus to vex and cross you."

"Nay, sir, Zillah is too good a daughter to vex you thus without some good reason.  But even now, time may bring about what we so earnestly desire.  By the time I return again from the East she may have reason to alter her present determination."

"Your *return !* then you have determined to accept the ship ?" replied the captain, with a downcast air. "But," he added, immediately afterwards, "I cannot blame you, at your age you could scarcely do otherwise."

Within three weeks after this conversation Blake and Constantine Phaulcon sailed again for Siam. The captain, by this time having become used to the notion of parting with Blake, had bid him a hearty farewell, with wishes for a successful voyage out and home. And, hearken, lad," he added, "if I don't see you back within three years, I shall be strongly tempted to take another voyage and fetch you."

It was the evening before the day of his departure from the manor house, that Blake had parted with Zillah. "Farewell, and Heaven bless you, Zillah ! we shall never meet again, but your image will ever remain engraven upon my heart."

"*Never* meet again !" repeated Zillah, almost mechanically. Then, with tears streaming down her cheeks, she said, "Dear Blake, recall that word, its remembrance in years to come will kill me. Oh ! that I should have been the cause of all this !"

"Zillah," he replied ; "you alone have sent forth the fiat— we never shall meet again, saving you see reason to change your present determination."

"Blake, Blake, refer no more to that."

"Zillah," he replied, solemnly, "these may be the last words I shall ever speak to you, I shall form them into a request. Should—and Heaven alone knows whether it be impossible—you, even years hence, find that your feelings are running back into that current—where I *know*, I say I *know* they were—leave no means untried to send that ring to me." So saying, he put a golden circle in her hand. But Zillah made no reply.

## CHAPTER VI

ADVENTURES IN COCHIN CHINA.

ONE of those terrible storms, so common and fatal to human beings in the Chinese seas, had just passed over. A noble ship, which had bravely lived out the hurricane, was feebly making her way into the bay of Turon in Cochin China. How bravely she had resisted, and gallantly fought against the elements, may be best told by describing her appearance. The bowsprit and foremast were gone; the decks were strewn with masts and yards, the ropes of which, still fastened to them, the sailors were cutting away with their axes; maimed and wounded men were lying screaming with pain, and praying for help, that could be afforded them but scantily and slowly. The entire forepart of the ship was stripped of its rigging and anchors. The crew, which was of many nations, were variously engaged. Siamese and Chinese were praying before little wooden gods, before which burned incense; or throwing into the sea little models of ships, of silver paper, as offerings to appease the sea goddess, Ma-tsoo-po. Some Portuguese were returning thanks to Heaven, and promising, if ever they got safe back to Siam, to offer up a votive mass in honour of Saint Francis Xavier, the apostle of the East. The most remarkable figure perhaps in the picture, was a very short, stout, yellow - faced man, with a small but perfectly globular head, lank black hair, neatly gathered into a top-knot; small dark laughing round eyes, a well-shaped, but nothing to speak of in size nose, and a very scanty, but dandily cultivated beard. From his eyes and rounded cheeks, it was easy to discern he was not a Chinese. His dress consisted of a handsome turban of thick black crape, a blue silk jacket, as loose as a shirt, which reached to the knees, and buttoned at the side, trousers of crimson silk, and a handsome pair of shoes or clogs; then there dangled from his girdle many little matters appertaining to people of his rank, such for instance as a pouch for tobacco, paper for cigars, an ornamental box for betel-mixture, to the frequent use of which his black teeth and encrimsoned lips testified, a pair of tweezers for the extraction of troublesome hairs, and lastly, a string of cash* slung across his shoulders.

This important personage, surrounded by his body-attendants, was standing upon the raised or quarter-deck, quietly and apparently contentedly watching the superstitious performances of his fellow-religionists, the Siamese and Chinese. The English, or greater portion of the crew, equally grateful in their hearts for the protection of Heaven during the recent storm, were better employed, namely clearing the ship, and attending to the wounded, under the direction of their two chief officers, Phaulcon and Blake.

"Thank God! we have weathered the typhoon," said Blake, as the two friends sat upon some spars to rest after their long mental anxiety and physical labour; "many a storm have I been in, yet grim death never before stared me so boldly in the face."

"Heaven be thanked, for saving so many human beings from a sudden and unprepared death," replied Phaulcon. "Yet," he

* The copper coin of the Chinese.

added musingly, " for myself alone, I would almost that we
*had* struck ; it would have been my *third* wreck, after which
I have a belief that my future will undergo a change for the
better."

" Poh, poh !" replied Blake, " why the classic figure three, why
not the mystic number seven ; but," he added, as he pointed to
another vessel, which, as it was struggling, unavailingly, to make the
mouth of the bay, seemed to have suffered more than their own
ship, " Yon Frenchman wants help ; she is water-logged, let us
send half a score of hands to work her pumps."

" Aye, true, we had forgotten all but ourselves," replied Phaulcon,
rising to give the requisite order to the sailors.   But while the
two friends are engaged in this Christian duty, I will digress
to tell you how it came about that they were then off the coast
of Cochin China.

As we have seen, the two young men, in again taking sea
service, were actuated by very different motives.   Blake had
sought active employment for the simple purpose of forgetting
his misplaced attachment ; thus, upon reaching Siam, he sought
and obtained those commands which would detain him longest
at sea, the only drawback to this being, that during a period of
three years he had met Phaulcon but twice.   As for the latter,
with whose affairs we are most concerned, he had returned to
the East to reinstate himself in his old position.   Still sanguine,
notwithstanding his misfortunes, Phaulcon hoped to find some
royal road to wealth and perhaps honour.   But rare indeed is it
that the honest man, however indefatigable his exertions, reaches
either fame or fortune by a leap ; and even where they *seem* thus
easily to have come to any individual, in most instances, it is
only because the lower rounds of the ladder, the smaller progressive

steps, are unseen or forgotten ; and that Phaulcon *was* an honest man, we have the testimony of the Père d'Orleans, who says : " His upright conduct retarded his advancement ; for although he had many opportunities of acquiring fortune which his natural love for honesty did not let him consider legitimate, he preferred the attainment of his object by slow and honourable, rather than quick, but unjust means."

Thus, although for three years after his return to Siam, Phaulcon toiled indefatigably, at the end of that time, he had but saved money sufficient for the purchase a very small ship, with which to trade to and from the Indian ports ; true, Blake, who was more prosperous, would have lent him money with which to traffic on his own account, but so much did our hero esteem his friend, so great were the risks to all but well-armed ships in those days in the Eastern seas, and so independent perhaps his character, that after his first loss, he had determined to endanger no property but his own, except indeed in the capacity of a carrier of goods entrusted to him by the merchants of the English Factory.

Once Phaulcon had raised himself to comparative affluence, which, as we have seen, suddenly melted away, leaving him a beggar and a slave ; undismayed by toil and suffering, he awaited his opportunity ; the wheel of fortune, aided by his own character, came to his help—he had once more a ship, therefore the means of regaining an equivalent for that which he had lost. He set out for Macao, but the fickle goddess, jealous of his ever buoyant and determined courage, scarcely permitted his ship to cross the bar of the Siam River, than she sent her to the bottom of the gulf ; and again, like Sisyphus, was he rolled to the very base of that hill he had fought so hard and apparently successfully to climb.

How few men would have held their heads up again after two such dreadful blows; for although, among the *inheritors* of wealth, many have been known to submit to its deprivation without a murmur, and even the fortune that has been gained by the sweat of the brow has been lost again without other pang than a feeling of submission to the dispensation of Heaven; he who can receive blow after blow undismayed, but to rise with renewed vigour after every such successive downfall, as if in defiance of fate (which in reality is self), is a hero. "To know thyself, all other knowledge vain," is a grand axiom; equally grand was the lesson taught by the great Napoleon to his army, that "every private soldier carried in his knapsack the baton of a French marshal," for it taught each man to rely upon himself. So Phaulcon, frowning back the scowls of fate, returned to the English Factory, determined to commence anew his toils and struggles for the Will-o-the-wisp, fortune, and more thankful to Heaven for having saved his life, than in grief at the blow which had ruined him. I said ruined—but youth, health, talent, and conduct can never be ruined.

A singular circumstance soon verified Phaulcon's favourite adage, that "the gods help those who help themselves." An ambassador who had been sent from the King of Cochin China to his Siamese majesty, was wrecked, with all his retinue, in the Gulf of Siam. The lives of his excellency and a portion of his attendants had been saved; but as all the valuable presents for the King of Siam had been lost, and he dared not appear before so great a potentate without gifts, he besought the India Company to send him back to Cochin China, in one of their ships, under the command of an able captain.

Thus did the ambassador's misfortune turn to Phaulcon's

advantage; for the chiefs of the English Factory, knowing that the great annual four months' fair of Hué, the capital of Cochin China, would take place at about the same time a vessel would reach there from Siam; and farther, having had experience of the Greek's talent for all commercial matters, appointed him to the command. And while the ship was being got ready for sea, Blake returned from a voyage to Surat, on the Malabar coast; the generous fellow, finding Phaulcon would receive no loan from him, by means of which he might trade on his own account, offered to accompany him as his chief officer, providing he would accept one-half the profits of any trading he might do with his own money, a proposition to which the other agreed, partly from fear of giving his friend real offence, partly that he should have his company. Thus we find them once more treading the same planks in the Bay of Turon. But to resume my narrative.

As Blake had surmised, when he had suggested that aid should be sent to the French ship, the latter *had* sprung a leak in several places; thus, and but for the timely aid sent, she never could have made the, at all times, difficult entrance to the harbour. Once, however, within the bay, which is land-locked, being nearly surrounded by mountains covered with wood to their very summits, and floating upon water as tranquil as an inland lake, the crews of both ships found an interval of repose, compared with their recent labours.

As soon as the anchors were down, the ambassador, sending for Phaulcon, told him that, as it was unsuitable to his rank and dignity to appear among his countrymen on foot, like a shipwrecked beggar, he desired to send one of his retinue to command the head-man of the town of Turon to prepare and send him a suitable state-barge, by which he could proceed to the capital, Hué. De-

lighted to show his attention to one who might prove of great
service to him and his crew, Phaulcon declared that he would himself take the attendant ashore. Accordingly, he at once ordered
a boat to be manned with Englishmen, and left the ship. At the
same time almost, a boat left the French vessel; but it was very
doubtful whether either would have been permitted to land but for
the presence of the Cochinese attendant in Phaulcon's boat, for
they were surrounded by swarms of fishing-craft, with three square
sails, and made of a kind of basket-work of very close texture, and
manned by more than half-naked natives. The Cochinese, however,
addressing the latter in their own language, informed them of the
important personage who was on board the English ship, and for
what purpose his excellency was going ashore, and instantaneously
a way was made through the fishers for the European boats.

Scarcely, however, had Phaulcon, the ambassador's attendant,
and half-a-dozen sailors placed their feet upon the shore, than they
found themselves confronted by fifty Cochinese soldiers, very short,
but exceedingly robust men, and admirably attired for Asiatic
troops, namely, with conical helmets of gilt basket-work, plumed
with crimson horsehair, loose red jackets faced with yellow, with
close collar, which reached to the knees and were fastened in front
with loops and buttons, a pair of wide trousers of white serge,
fastened at the knees; some few were armed with arquebuses, but
the majority carried javelins and swords. The appearance of these
fierce little fat warriors somewhat puzzled Phaulcon, for he knew
not whether they came with hostile intent, or as a force to protect
the new-comers from the swarm of half-naked natives who followed
in their rear, loudly clamouring at, or for something, but what he
he could not understand.

"Will the noble attendant of his excellency the ambassador ask

these warriors what they mean by thus opposing our progress, and
why the people behind them are so clamorous ?" asked Phaulcon, in
Siamese, of his Cochinese companion, who, having held a short
conversation with the chief of the soldiers, replied :—

"The people, some months ago, believing they suffered great
wrong at the hands of some Christian priests, drove them from
the land ; ever since they have kept jealous watch upon any newly-
arrived European ship, for fear it might bring others into the
country ; therefore, before they will allow you to land any more
men, or even proceed farther yourself, you must declare that you
have no priest in your ship."

"My friend has accompanied me the whole voyage, surely he
could answer the chief of the warriors to his satisfaction," said
Phaulcon.

"All that the noble commander could wish, his servant *has* said,"
replied the Cochinese, politely. "We may proceed." And thus,
thanks to having a native interpreter, the French boat-party might
have followed Phaulcon and his men to the town of Turon, for the
chief of the soldiers had applied the one answer to his question
both to English and French, but for an indiscretion on the part of
the latter, and thus it happened.

The French, eight in number, had landed almost simultaneously
with the English, when shortly afterwards two of the undisciplined
sailors, having a dispute as to which should remain in charge of
the boat during the absence of their shipmates, became enraged
even to the interchange of blows. Whereupon, another walking up
to the disputants, addressed a few serious words and instantly made
them friends. Astounded at this, the Cochinese chief exclaimed :
"Who, and what can be the rank of yon meanly attired man, that
he can so easily allay the angry passions of these barbarian Franks ?"

"A priest, no other than a Christian priest, who has dared to return here disguised," exclaimed one, whose garb proclaimed *him* an Omsaii, or priest of Buddha, and as when at the first sight of his game the hunter gives a cry of joy, his fellows take up the refrain, so the mob gave chorus—"Let us slay the dog who has *prevented the rain from falling*, and thereby *withered our crops and robbed us of our harvest*," and there and then the poor man would have been pressed to death, but that with the quickness of thought, Phaulcon, and his men, drawing their swords, ran to his aid. But the assistance of so small a party against so numerous a mob would not avail long, so calling to the Cochinese, Phaulcon said :—

"Haste thee, my friend, to his excellency; implore of him, as he is grateful for the perils I have brought him through, to forget his dignity, and come to the rescue of this poor man." The Cochinese complied with alacrity, but alas, a cordon of but little more than a dozen Europeans around the priest could not for many minutes stem the torrent of such a savage mob.

Probably the father saw this, for when one of his party called aloud to the savages to forbear, "that he was no priest, nothing but a slave, as his dress betokened," with every sign of joy and enthusiasm depicted upon his features, and regardless of the fact that the speaker, being a Frenchman, could not have been understood by the natives, he shouted above the noise of the multitude:

"It is the will of God that I should be blessed with martyrdom, on the verge of eternity, therefore, will I not shame my sacred calling by denial. Behold, O miserable men, I *am* a priest of Christ, and as he spoke, he took from beneath his ragged mantle his stole and surplice. At this the natives became more angry still; the enthusiastic priest began to exhort

them to throw aside their paganism and embrace Christianity as quietly and earnestly as if within the walls of his own church.*

Goaded by the clamours of the people, the soldiers brought their javelins to their sides, and were about to break through the thin line of Europeans. But the bloody struggle was prevented, for suddenly there fell some heavy drops of rain; instantaneously the warriors stood as if transfixed, the noise became hushed, the people stood aghast with their faces heavenwards, as will the beasts of the field at the first symptoms of relief from a long drought. Then the rain fell in torrents, and the natives, literally jumping with joy, begged of the soldiers to let them pass and kiss the hem of the good man's garment.

"Our priests are dogs;" they cried, "they have deceived us; it is they who have thus long withheld the blessed rain, and not this holy man."

"Thanks be to God and the Holy Virgin, who at the ninth hour have thus come to the succour of their servant, and have changed the hearts of these savages," exclaimed the priest; and then taking advantage of his position, as even in the midst of the drenching rain the people knelt around him, he exhorted them to recall the Christian priests he had heard they had expelled, and rebuild the churches they had destroyed; and as he spoke in their own tongue (there were few of the languages of the East that were not spoken by those early missionaries) they promised, with sobs of penitential grief, to obey.

* Among the earlier members of the Society of Jesus, this indifference to death and longing for the honours of martyrdom, was of frequent occurrence. One of these brave men, in a letter to the General of the Jesuits, relating an incident that had occurred to him similar to the above, says :—" Hereupon believing I was certainly a dead man, I resolved to die as what I was."

"Would my children prove their sincerity, let them declare the whereabouts of the holy fathers they have expelled, if indeed they have not impiously slain them."

"The holy men are safe in yonder island, awaiting the ship to bear them home," exclaimed some among the crowd.

"Then get thee thither on the instant and release them from their vile durance," replied the father, and scarcely had the command left his lips than several fishing-boats were put out to sea.

"A miracle," exclaimed one of the French sailors.

"A mystery, at least," said Phaulcon, who at that time knew not the causes that had led to that most extraordinary scene.

From the foregoing events, it will be easily understood that by the time the obese round-headed little ambassador, preceded by two men carrying bamboo canes with which they beat away from his magnificent presence all less important people, and followed by others of his retinue, came up, all necessity for his presence had passed away. Now the hasty summons of a mere barbarian captain like Phaulcon, the compulsory walking, and that too beneath a drenching rain, had changed his excellency's usual laughing countenance into another of a damp kind of dolefulness mixed with an unmistakable expression of offended dignity. But when, as he approached, the soldiers presented arms, the natives fell upon their faces, and the Europeans all respectfully saluted him, his little eyes twinkled with pleasure, for he felt that nothing but sheer necessity, and no want of respect, had been the cause of his being shaken out of his dignity. Thus when the Jesuit father had explained to him that some of his brother priests had been expelled the country, and he himself had nearly been slain, for having prevented the rain from falling from the skies, the little nobleman indulged in a laugh that extended his eyes, puffed out his cheeks, and shook the fat upon his ribs till he rolled from side to side like a tub at sea in a gale of wind.

Having revived from his cachinnatory fit, he pursed up his mouth, and having looked around upon the prostrate crowd with all the sternness or rather tragi-comic expression his merry countenance would enable him to muster, he cried out—

"The dolts, the dunderheads, the dogs, the rats, the sons of dogs, beat them to their homes!" and the soldiers, readily obeying, taking in hand the two bamboo sticks which they carry for the purpose of striking at intervals in order to show they are not asleep, fell to beating them off, as if they had been either of the animals whose names had been so politely applied to them. Those who were upon their feet lost no time in making the very best use of them, while the unfortunates who were prostrate, crawled and squeaked upon all fours under the rattans of the soldiers.

Having thus, like a thorough Asiatic, satisfied himself by means of the bamboo that his power was no myth, the ambassador returned to the ship to await the coming of his state-barge. Now for this act of what in England would be called tyranny, the reader must not think very badly of the little lord, for in the East, especially among the Indo-Chinese races, these beatings are regarded as parental corrections, for which the chastised are expected to return their thanks. No, the ambassador upon the whole was a good-hearted man, and moreover, intellectually and in liberality, far in advance of the majority of the Cochinese of his own rank. Thus he not only begged of Phaulcon, but of the Father Tachard, to accompany him to his palace at Hué. Greatly pleased at this invitation, for he believed it to be for the interests of religion, the father then returned to his ship to make preparations for the intended journey.

The following day at noon, as Phaulcon and Blake were conversing upon the means necessary to be taken for the repairs and provisioning of the vessel during the absence of the former at the capital, a boat from the French ship came alongside, bringing Father Tachard and another Jesuit. The thin emaciated features of the latter told a tale of long suffering and privation. He was in fact the only survivor of the seven priests who had been driven by the Cochinese to take refuge upon a desolate island a few miles from the Bay of Turon, and from which place he had been rescued the night before by the repentant natives.

The young men having respectfully welcomed the two ecclesiastics on board, Father Tachard, pointing to Phaulcon said, "This, reverend brother, is the gallant captain to whom, under Providence, I am indebted for my life; and you, for release from long suffering."

"Your name, my son, that I may enshrine it within my memory, and remember it in my orisons, as that of one who has served God and our holy Church by saving lives, worthless in themselves, but of inestimable value, inasmuch as they are devoted to the conversion of the heathen," said the wan priest.

"Phaulcon, captain in the service of the English Company of Merchant Adventurers trading to the Indies," was the reply, but as he mentioned his name, and saw that the priest, tremulous with emotion, was slowly and curiously scanning his features, he added, "Father, surely we have met before."

"Phaulcon?" said the father, "Constantine Phaulcon; the young Greek of Cephalonia? Impossible!"

The recognition now being mutual, they embraced, Phaulcon

exclaiming, " Father Thomas, my old tutor, early friend, I should not—did not, recognise thee."

" Truly the means by which Heaven works out its ends are as wonderful as they are inscrutable; this meeting is surely prophetic of good," said Father Tachard, adding however, as he pointed to the shore, " But look, brother Thomas, the state-barge is putting off from the land. Let us therefore lose no time in craving his excellency's permission that you may also accompany us to the capital."

" True," replied Father Thomas ; but as, turning to follow his colleague, his eye fell upon Blake, he started, and putting his hand to his forehead as if to throw a light backwards upon some distant memory, he said, " But this young man, this officer, who is he ?—surely his features are known to me ? "

" Blake Taunton, also an officer in the India Company," replied the young Englishman ; adding bluntly, " But father, to the best my memory we have never met before."

" Blake Taunton," said the priest, slowly repeating the names, as if making an effort to remember some long past event; " it is not possible," he murmured as if to himself; then, as if glad to crush the thoughts that were passing through his mind, he said, " But pardon me, my son. I am getting old, I have toiled and suffered much, strange fantasies sometimes pass through my brain, making me believe that I see the people of the past before me."

The good-natured little ambassador, put into the very best of humours by the approach of his state-barge, a magnificent craft with dragon-shaped prow covered with gold, and manned by forty rowers, very readily extended his invitation to Father Thomas, and moreover promised to become the friend of himself and his mission at court. Farther he gave Phaulcon a written authority for him or his crew to trade and barter with the people of

Turon, or the neighbouring towns. This Phaulcon placed in the
hands of Blake to use to the best advantage during his absence in
the capital, where he himself intended to barter in the interests of
the Company, and for which purpose he ordered the largest of the
ship's boats to be manned, and laden with British broad-cloth, to
follow in the wake of the barge.

The state-craft having arrived alongside the vessel, the attendants
of the ambassador went on board to see that the carpet was
properly adjusted under the silken-curtained canopy set apart for
his excellency. His betel box and pipe ready at hand, the great
man went on board and squatted down, his immediate attendants
lying upon their stomachs around him.

The two fathers and Phaulcon seated themselves in the stern,
where an awning or canopy had been erected for their accom-
modation. The ambassador then giving the word, the rowers struck
up a wild barbarian song, and keeping time with their oars, the
barge set out upon its voyage round the mountainous coast towards
the mouth of the great river of Hué. On the voyage, for the sea
was now as calm and smooth almost as an inland lake, Father
Thomas told the story of his adventures.

## CHAPTER VII.

THE STORY OF CHRISTIANITY IN COCHIN CHINA.

"I HAD long," said the Father Thomas, "felt within my
breast a burning desire to follow in the footsteps of the great
St. Francis Xavier: thus when our holy father the Pope commanded a new mission to China, I asked and obtained permission
to join it. Being arrived at Macao, I heard such glowing
accounts of the efforts of certain Portuguese fathers among the
pagans of Cochin China; for instance, that they had succeeded
in converting to our faith not only many hundreds of the poorer
people, but several great ladies, among whom was the *Infanta*
herself.

"Fired at this blessed news, I, with several other fathers,
demanded and obtained permission of our superior to follow
out this mission; guess then our surprise, on arriving in this
country, to find that the zeal of the Portuguese fathers had led
them to disseminate absolute falsehoods. In the first place no such
personage as the *Infanta* of Cochin China was known in the land.
Then, although numbers of the people were pointed out to us as
professing *Christians*, upon examination we found the poor heathens
ignorant of even the meaning of the word. They understood but
a certain form the Portuguese fathers were wont to ask—if they
would enter the bosom of the Church, and upon being answered in
the affirmative they would perform the rites of baptism, but alas,

the natives understood the word *Church* to mean Portuguese, and the holy rite of baptism to be the mere changing of their country.

"Is this possible, father?" asked Phaulcon in surprise.

"Aye, my son, and thus was it made manifest:

"Looking one day at a kind of play (the Cochinese are famous for their lively plays) that was being performed in the streets, we observed that the chief character was dressed to represent a Portuguese father, but in a gown that swelled him out to an enormous rotundity. The other character was a native boy, who being asked by the other the usual question, whether he would enter the bosom of the Church, assented, and at once entered into the other's immense body, to the great amusement of the spectators.*

"Dismayed at this mockery, we sought to learn the language, or at least, sufficient to make an appeal to the minds and hearts of the people, and at length, when we knew enough to explain to them the system of our religion, and by preaching and example exhorted them to conversion, a ray of hope dawned across our hearts. But the *Omsaii* or native priests grew jealous, and *their* power would have been sufficient to have crushed us, had it not been for that knowledge of the Mathematics, which has ever been the great support of our society in the kingdoms of the East. Thus, the royal astrologers having predicted an eclipse of the moon on a certain night, we declared that no such phenomenon would be visible. Astounded and enraged at this apparent contradiction of their predictions, the Omsaii repaired to the King and demanded our immediate expulsion from the

* This extraordinary incident is related by Father Borri in his "Relazione della nova Missione dei Padri della Compania de Jesus nel regno del Cocincina."

kingdom, and this his majesty promised, provided *he saw* the eclipse which we had declared would be invisible.

Now, you know, in these pagan lands it is universally believed that during an eclipse a huge dragon is endeavouring to devour the moon or the sun; accordingly it is the custom for the king to march out at the head of his troops, the artillery to be discharged, and every drum, gong, and trumpet throughout the kingdom sounded; nay, even for the kitchen maids to rattle their cans and pails, in order to frighten away the monster. Thus, upon the night named, the king and people came out; but, although they waited patiently until morning, nothing was to be seen of the dragon—as *we* had predicted, the eclipse was *invisible*. Whereupon the king was so disappointed with his astrologers, that he dismissed them from their posts, and appointed two of us in their places, with permission to preach to and, if we could, make converts of his subjects."

"A blessed result," exclaimed Father Tachard piously.

"True, my brother, and not an instant did we waste in endeavouring to make the most of our advantage; but, alas! at every step we were crossed and thwarted by the very shadow and likeness of the institutions of our own communion. Verily, the Evil One, to further his own ends, the encompassing of so many souls, must have given to the pagan priests, in all but the one thing needful, a counterpart to holy Church. If we have strings of beads, crosses, so have they; if we have processions, convents, monasteries, begging friars, so have they; as, indeed, like ceremonies, dresses, and offices of our Church. In nothing," continued the father indignantly, "are they wanting to complete the mockery, delusion, and snare, of a resemblance to the Church of Rome, but the knowledge of Christ and the

Virgin, and from that are they kept by these phantoms raised
by Lucifer. Nay, even when we exhorted the people to destroy
their idols, they mocked us by answering that they dared not,
for they were but the images of departed great men, whom
they worshipped exactly on the same principle and manner as
the farangs (Christians) did their images of the apostles and
martyrs." *

"Such difficulties and crosses did the holy St. Francis Xavier
have to encounter, yet *he* faltered not, neither did he despair,"
interposed Father Tachard with something like asperity.

"Humbly imitating the 'holy apostle of the East,'" resumed
Father Thomas, "we sought to counteract the influence of the Evil
One by self-abnegation, long vigils and fasting; and we were rewarded for our pains by the conversion of many people of the
lower classes. Our earnest desire then became to sow the divine
seed in the hearts of some of the great, knowing that their example
would be quickly followed by their vassals and servants, and at
length our desires became accomplished.

One day, while walking through the principal street of the city,
I met a long train of elephants, on which were seated a number of
richly dressed ladies. One of these, whom, from the splendour of
her dress, and the blaze of jewels with which she was covered,
I knew to be the chief, stopped, and earnestly exhorted me to
admit her into the bosom of the Church. "For," said she, "I
have heard of the doctrines taught by the Christian fathers, and by
the unblemished lives they lead, feel convinced that theirs is the
only true faith." Believing, however, that so sudden a desire might

* This marvellous resemblance between the forms and ceremonies of the
priests of Buddha and those of the Church of Rome, was a sore trouble to the
Jesuit missionaries.

carry with it but little earnestness, I desired her to take time, and
promised to visit her at her own house.  This I did, and day
by day she became more importunate ; nay, to show her humility,
even put aside her elephants, and repeatedly walked a distance of
two miles, barefooted through the mire, to my lodgings, to pray that
I would admit her into our communion ; then, when no longer able
to resist her importunities, I complied, she desired that her women
to the number of twenty, might receive baptism at the same time ;
but that, I told her, was impossible, while they all remained in
the capacity of secondary wives to her husband who was then
out of the country upon an embassy to a foreign king.  Hearing
my decision, one and all, to show their sincerity, declared they
would rather leave their lord and look out for a husband each,
than forego salvation.  Upon this condition they were baptized, and
immediately replaced their idols, which they broke in pieces, with
crosses, *Agnus Dei's*, medals and relics."

"But the pagan, her husband, how got ye on with him ?" asked
Father Tachard.

"Upon his return, which happened shortly after the conversion
of his family, he was aghast at the change.  Where he had left
pagan idols, he found crosses or images of the Virgin.  The women,
no longer bedecked with jewels in barbaric splendour, but in plain
attire, having about them the emblems of Christianity, instead of
receiving him with profane levity, now greeted him with sober
yet respectful joy.  At first he believed them mad, and wept ;
then thinking they had been set on, by his enemies at court, to
treat him with disrespect, he gave vent to his rage, even threatening
them with instant death ; but all the time the good in his heart was
working itself uppermost, for when his chief wife, of whom he was
passionately fond, earnestly and eloquently told him of her happi-

ness at the blessed change, he smiled approvingly ; nay, such was
her influence, that in a few days *he also* desired to be admitted into
the Church, and pressed that the ceremony should take place
immediately. This being a fitting opportunity, I told him that as
a preliminary he must dismiss all of his wives but one. Then
like fire by water his enthusiasm cooled, nay, became well-nigh
quenched, and he left me saying, he would take time to consider.

The next day he brought with him one of the most learned
Omsaii, who argued against the necessity of the wives being given
up, and finding I could concede nothing in that matter, he
begged that I would procure a dispensation from the Pope, but I
explained to both that such a course was impossible, and that
nothing but the absolute dismissal of all the ladies but one, would
enable me to receive him into our communion ; whereupon, to my
great joy, he, regarding the answer as final, promised there and
then to issue orders that the whole of them should be sent away
that very night.

After the stipulation made by the women themselves, I thought
they would have hailed this order with joy—But lo ! no sooner did
it reach their ears, than one and all with wild look, dishevelled
hair and tearful eyes, headed by the chief wife, came into their
lord's presence, and throwing themselves upon their knees, implored
of him not to send them away ; I exhorted them to *remember their
promise*, but it was in vain, for the principal spouse declared that,
as they had all been brought up together from their infancy, and
loved each other as sisters, they could not now be parted, and
as from this determination neither their lord nor myself could
make them swerve, it was at length agreed that they might
remain in the house, but only in the capacity of attendants upon
the mistress of the household.

"At this concession," continued Father Thomas, "the Cochinese noble was so well pleased, that after his own baptism he lent us his powerful aid in the conversion of his countrymen. We also speedily had permission to build a church, and the work of our mission prospered so well, that we had even hopes of bringing the king over to the faith; but in the mean time Lucifer was busy in the hearts and minds of the pagan priests. The latter, always powerful with the people, had been biding their opportunity for our destruction, and at length it came in the form of a long and terrible drought, a calamity the Omsaii openly ascribed to the Christian priests.

"It is no wonder," they preached, "that the gods deny us rain, when a body of strangers are permitted to preach a doctrine by which they are so deeply dishonoured."

Then the chief Omsaii, proceeding to the top of a mountain, invoked his devils, and thrice striking his feet upon the earth, there miraculously fell a slight shower, not indeed enough to be of use to the famishing land, but sufficient, in the minds of the ignorant multitude, to lend a semblance of truth to the charge their priests had brought against us.

"Even," said they, "if these foreign priests have not been the *cause* of the gods withholding the rain, it is certain they have not done so much for us as our Omsaii, therefore let them quit the land or die;" and the king's power being comparatively impotent against the *vox populi*, we were forthwith driven to seek refuge upon that desert island, upon which my brethren died a lingering death from exhaustion and starvation. As for myself, even now I wonder by what blessed accident I have survived and been rescued.

"Some Chinese traders," said Father Tachard, "being in the

country at the time of your expulsion, brought the news to Macao, and as soon as it reached the ears of our superior in that city, he despatched me hither to bring you relief, and to examine into, and take charge of the mission, while you and your fellow-sufferers returned to Macao to recruit your health. But, alas! their martyrdom, for martyrdom it was, has relieved me of one-half my charge. Still, my dear brother," he added, " but for this brave captain, even you would not have survived to relate the story of your sufferings in the blessed cause."

Profuse would have been Father Thomas's expressions of gratitude to Phaulcon, but they were curtailed by the coming of one of the ambassador's attendants, who said that his lord desired to hear, from the father's own lips, the history of his adventures and sufferings since he had been in that country. Delighted at such an opportunity, the father at once followed the servant into the presence of the Cochinese magnate, and re-told his tale, much to the edification of his listener, who, at its conclusion, with great warmth, renewed his promise of using his influence with the king in favour of the Jesuits and their mission.

Upon their arrival in the capital city, Hué, the little noble lost neither time nor opportunity in serving his European friends. He lodged them in one wing of his house, a large building with tiled roof and stone walls, situated upon the bank of a canal, having upon two sides a large garden, upon another the cook-house, and in front a large court-yard, the whole place being encircled by bamboo hedges. The two Jesuits he desired to keep within his house, or at least the grounds, until he had obtained the sanction of the king for them to appear in the public streets. As for Phaulcon, he introduced him to the sovereign within a very few days after their arrival, no very difficult matter, for as his majesty

like many other monarchs of the East, was the largest merchant and
trader in his kingdom, he was himself but too delighted to forestall
his subjects in bartering for the English broad-cloths, a commodity
which, at that time, was in great demand among the Cochinese.
And a very profitable bargain Phaulcon made for his employers, the
Company, taking in exchange for his broad-cloth (not alone the few
bales he had brought with him to the capital, but the whole cargo),
Tonquin crape, silks, satins, fans ; and, above all, a large quantity
of the edible birds-nests which then, as now, were purchased at
almost any price by the Chinese, who make of them one of their
most luxurious dishes.     Moreover, it was stipulated that the
Cochinese products were to be taken to the English ship, and the
broad-cloth brought back to Hué at the king's own cost.

As for the two fathers, the good little noble listened to their
exhortations until he himself became a convert.     Then, becoming a
vehement or enthusiastic propagandist, he repaired to his sovereign,
and having related the story of Father Thomas's sufferings, and the
miracle by which at Turon he had turned the feelings of the people
in his favour, further advised his majesty to permit the priests to
establish their mission upon a firm basis.

To this, the king, who was as liberal and far-seeing as his
noble, not only readily consented, but, at a special audience,
gave the brethren permission to invite to his kingdom others
of their order, to assist them in the work of conversion.     At
this unexpected success, the fathers offered up long and fervent
thanks to the throne of mercy, for having so directed the heart
of the heathen prince, and prayed for wisdom and judgment to
enable them to win over to Christ the many millions of souls
in that empire.

In the enthusiasm of the moment the Jesuits believed that they

were upon the eve of a mighty conquest; but, alas! how would their
ardour have been damped could they have foreseen the sufferings
in store for their successors.  Yet they must have had some mis-
givings, for they knew that but a few years before, Christianity,
which had once been planted (apparently) so firmly in the islands of
Japan, had been extirpated, root and branch.  Indeed, the horrors of
that most bloody persecution were so well known, that in those days
there was not an European in the East who did not tremble as he
heard mention of the boiling wells in which the Japanese Christians had been tortured.  But the story of Christianity in Cochin
China is doubly interesting at the present time, when the Emperor
Louis Napoleon has sent a large force to that country, with the
double object of avenging certain insults to French missionaries,
and of establishing for his countrymen a permanent footing, from
which to carry on operations in the East,* perhaps—who knows?—
to the ultimate disadvantage of England.  I will, therefore, turn
aside from my narrative to give a slight sketch of the doings of
European missionaries in the land.

Three of the greatest obstacles to the permanent establishment
of Christianity in Eastern India have been, first, the apathy of
all races professing the doctrines of Confucius or Buddha, the
only exception I believe being Japan, a people who are apathetic in
nothing, and whose passions are, extreme and violent, both for
good and bad.  Secondly, the utter impossibility of the Easterns
to comprehend why Catholics and Protestants, both worshipping
one God, should once have been so violently antagonistic to
each other.  Thirdly, the sovereigns being despots, the encourage-

---

* Since the above was written, the Emperor, in his speech at the opening
of the Chambers, congratulated the members upon the *consolidation* of the
French establishment in Cochin China by the valour of his soldiers.

ment or persecution of Christians depends upon the mere whim of any new monarch. Thus, in 1698, a young king, entirely devoted to the priests of Buddha, ascending the throne, commanded a raid upon the Christian churches which were then numerous in the land. In a letter dated December 9th, 1700, Father Pellison writes :—

"Several of our churches were pulled down, and the persecution would probably have raged still more, had not a furious storm arisen, obliging the idolaters to employ themselves wholly in repairing the damage caused by it ; not to mention that, I then foretold an eclipse in such a manner as seemed to please the court, upon which I was left in possession of my church, and the missionaries met with gentle treatment. The royal year (every twelfth) occurred soon after, and as the people at that time are allowed greater liberty, the Christians enjoyed it in common with them, so that we then performed the several exercises of our religion in as public a manner as we had before the persecution. In the beginning of 1700, some thieves, or rather some enemies to the Christians, hoping to bring them into trouble, pulled down and broke in pieces the idols dispersed about the country. The king accused the Christians of this action, not doubting but they were really the authors of it. He was told, at the same time, that our churches were very much crowded on Ash-Wednesday, whereupon he ordered the massacre of all the Christians the first time they assembled, but on the 6th of March, hearing of this, I prevented their meeting.

"There were then five European missionaries in that city. On the 12th of March the idolaters came armed into the churches, seized our servants, plundered our houses of everything they could lay hands on, and confined the several missionaries to their churches. Four of them, at that time in the city, were carried to the state prisons, and the cangu * was put about the necks of three.  I was also taken, but set at liberty the next day, being a mathematician.

"On the 17th the prince's edict was published, commanding all the Christian churches in the kingdom to be pulled down ; it likewise enacted, that the several books relating to our religion shou!.l be burnt, and all the missionaries seized ; that those who . had embraced the Christian faith should return to the established religion of the country ; and that, as a testimony of obedience, all persons in general, both Christians and idolaters, men and women, young and old, should trample under foot the image of our Saviour, the principal one we set up on the altar in our churches, in sight of the whole congregation.   This order was immediately executed in the palace, in the houses of the mandarins, and in the streets and places of public resort in this city.   We had the grief to see the blessed image trodden under foot by many un-worthy Christians, whilst others hid themselves to avoid doing so ; and some, generously refusing to comply with the king's orders, received the crown of martyrdom.   Most of the holy books were burnt that day, but all that belonged to me, with several others, were restored, the idolaters saying they might be of service in the mathematics.   By this means I saved a mass-book, and the life of Christ, represented in copper plates, which is of great use in order to give this ignorant people an idea of our Saviour's miracles.

"The king had commanded that whatever belonged to the Christians should be given as plunder to the soldiers, except such things as we looked upon as holy, which he ordered to be brought to him.   Many relics (some being entire bones) were carried to

* A wooden collar of great weight, commonly used in China.

him ; taking them in his hand and showing them to his courtiers : 'See,' exclaimed he, 'how impious the Christians are, they don't even scruple to take bones of the dead out of their graves, a circumstance which must surely strike every man with horror ; but this is not all, for having pounded them they put them into drinks, or make a kind of bread with them, which they give to the people, and thereby bewitch them to such a degree, that they run blindly after them and embrace their doctrine.' The king perceiving that this discourse animated the whole court with fury against us, ordered the bones in question to be brought into the place of public resort; and bid the people be told the uses which (he said) we put them to. Hence all the missionaries conclude, that it is not yet a fit time to expose such things in this country, nor to set them before the people in order to excite their veneration, lest, as the Gospel says, this should be casting pearls before swine.

"Three women of distinction being brought before the king, he ordered them to be bastinadoed, shaved, and the tips of their ears and fingers cut off ; all such of his male subjects as refused to recant, he sentenced to die, and most of them of starvation. The prisoners were confined in a hut, inclosed with thick stakes covered with branches of trees, eight feet long and six wide. After they were dead, their bodies were torn in pieces, and cast into the river, by the monarch's order, to prevent the remains of them from being preserved. On the 20th of May the Chinese vessels arrived, bringing the missionaries their small pensions from Canton. The Mandarins did all in their power to discover whether some supply was not brought to the fathers; but the Chinese captain played his part so well, that he eluded all their vigilance, and put into my hands whatever had been delivered to him for me, which has proved of no little service to all the imprisoned Christians.

" Four of our brethren are still confined, but I live in a little garden, which was given to me, standing near the palace, and as I bear the title of mathematician, I am allowed to go freely whither-soever I please, to visit the prisoners, and say mass every day. Several of the fathers have concealed themselves in the islands, or in the mountains."

Father Le Royer, another Jesuit missionary, but one who was *not* fortunate enough to hold the appointment of court mathematician ; gives, in a letter to his brother, an interesting illustration of the untiring perseverance of those heroic men under even the most fearful difficulties. " As to my way of life," says he, " and the methods I employ in order to win over souls, since you are desirous of being informed in that particular, I shall give you a plain undisguised relation of it ; such as becomes a brother. Were we to appear ever so little in public, we should easily be dis-covered by our complexion, and therefore, to prevent the persecu-tion from increasing, we are obliged to conceal ourselves as much as possible. For this reason, I pass whole days, either shut up in a boat, which I never leave, except in the night, in order to visit the villages lying near rivers, or retire in some lone house.

" Whenever I visit the Christians, of whom there are vast numbers upon the mountains and in the midst of the forests, I am com-monly accompanied by eight or ten catechists,* whom I am obliged

---

* Catechists were generally *native* converts, who, being perfectly instructed in the mysteries of the Christian religion, were sent by the Jesuits before them into the several villages to teach the inhabitants what they had themselves learned. One portion of their duty was to keep a register of all who desired to be baptized, or to receive the sacrament, as also of those who led bad lives.

to support entirely, they, like myself, having learnt to be contented with a little. We divide our time in the following manner: I labour the whole night, and that (as I can assure you), with very few intervals. The time not bestowed in hearing confessions, or in administering the communion to those confessed by me, is employed either in composing differences, in settling matters, or in resolving such difficulties as my catechists could not. After mass, which I celebrate a little before daybreak, I return to my boat, or to the house, which then serves as a retreat.

" The catechists, who sleep at night, labour in the day, during which I either pray, study, or repose myself. Their business is to preach to the infidels, to exhort the old Christians, and to prepare them for receiving the sacraments of penance, and the Eucharist; to dispose the catechumens for baptism, to visit the sick, in a word, to perform all those offices which do not absolutely require the sacred character of the priesthood. After having visited one village we go to another, or repeat the same exercises, so that we are never inactive."

For eighty years after these persecutions Christianity seems to have languished in Cochin China. In 1774, however, an internal revolution led to events which promised not only to plant the cross permanently in the land, but to give the French a mighty influence in India itself. The king, Caung-shung, was dethroned, and *supposed* to have been put to death, by four of his principal nobles, who not only divided Cochin China among themselves, but conquered the extensive neighbouring kingdom of Tonquin; the son of Caung-shung, on the assumption of his father's decease, was crowned by a few of the devoted followers of the royal house. The prince, however, finding it impossible to reconquer his inheritance, repaired to the court of Siam, where he passed through many remarkable adventures, and distinguished himself in a war against the Birmans. So remarkable, indeed, were his abilities, that he brought upon himself the jealousy of the Siamese king, who would have slain him, but for the interposition of Adran, a French priest, who took the royal youth with him to France.

The Cochinese prince was well received at the court of Versailles by the unfortunate Louis the Sixteenth, who promised to re-seat him upon his throne. Consequently a treaty was signed in the year 1788, by which, in return for being restored to his native dominions, the prince stipulated to furnish stores, &c. for fourteen ships of the line ; to permit French consuls to reside in all parts of his domains ; to cede the bay and peninsula of Turon in perpetuity ; to construct roads ; and, in case of *war in India*, to furnish fourteen thousand men for the aid of France, and sixty thousand to defend any portion of Cochin China.

This remarkable treaty, which might have changed the whole aspect of the Indian world by giving the French supremacy in the East, was to a great extent nullified by the outbreak of the French revolution, even as were the first treaties made between Japan and China with England, by the wars between Charles and his parliament. Undaunted by this disappointment, the Siamese prince returned to his native country, and having collected a few adherents, determined to try his fortune against the usurpers. Upon his arrival, he discovered that his father the old king was alive, and for two years had been living with a handful of his faithful subjects, upon a solitary island, their only means of subsistence being a few roots and herbs. The sight of the young prince brought thousands to his banner, and in a short time he had reconquered the crown for his father.

Restored to his birthright, the prince forgot not his good

friends the French. Their priests were admitted into the country under Adran, his old protector, who bore the title of Bishop of Cochin China, and ambassador and plenipotentiary extraordinary from the King of France. Wonderful stories are related of this prince when he became king. Like a second Peter the Great, he, in the course of ten years raised his navy from a single vessel to twelve hundred of various descriptions. He purchased a Portuguese ship for the purpose of taking it to pieces plank by plank with his own hands, and fitting in every one afresh till a new one was constructed on the same model. He increased his army, and disciplined it after the European system. He preferred the title of general to that of king. He knew the greater number of the soldiers by their names, and would inquire about their wives and children. He was the main-spring of every movement which took place in his kingdom; not a nail was driven in, nor a gun mounted, without consulting him. With regard to the arts of peace, he restored the culture of areca and betel, the plantations of which had been destroyed by the usurpers; he encouraged the growth of sugar, built bridges, and facilitated all kinds of commercial intercourse.

Under this great and liberal sovereign, Christianity began again to flourish; but, as I have said, one great obstacle to its permanent establishment in the East, is the despotism of its rulers. Thus, the successors to this wise prince being devoted to their ancient faith, French influence declined, and from that day a system of terrible persecutions has followed. The French missionaries have been imprisoned, tortured and crucified, driven to live in holes and crannies of the rocks, and perform the rites of their religion in secret, and in the daily expectation of martyrdom. It was to avenge these insults and cruelties, that the French in 1858 sent a force to Cochin China, which, after several severe battles, succeeded in taking possession of a portion of the country, and which they will doubtlessly continue to hold under the treaty of 1788. It is a curious title, for not having acquitted themselves of *their* share of the stipulations, and the French cannot with fairness, expect the Cochinese to perform their part of the treaty; but then, *when* did Europeans in the East forget that might makes right?

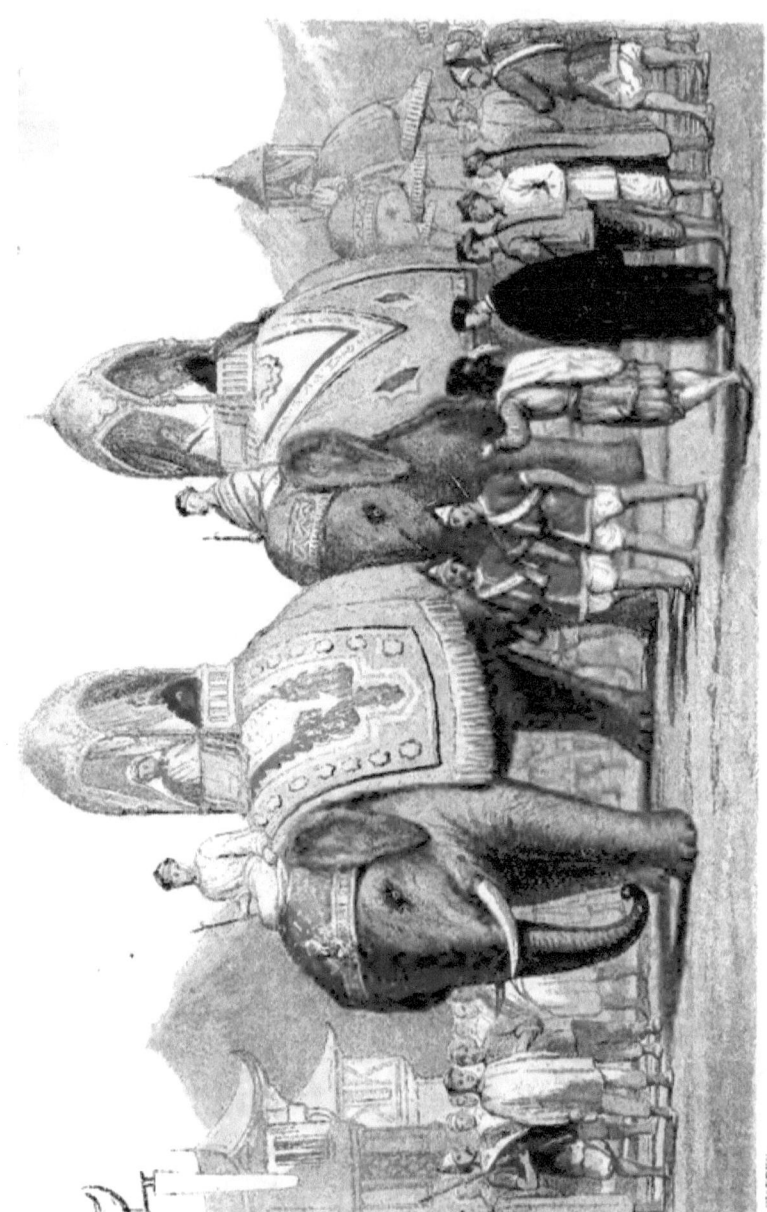

## CHAPTER VIII.

ADVENTURES OF THE LADY MONICA.

WHEN, after the lapse of about three weeks, the commercial transaction between the king and Phaulcon had been completed, by the due delivery of the merchandize upon both sides, the latter prepared to take his departure, no very easy matter with such a hospitable host as the fat little Cochinese noble. "Delays," saith the proverb, "are dangerous;" sometimes, however, they are attended by far different results—they have saved lives—they have brought fortunes—how, it will not be very difficult for the reader to imagine. To Constantine Phaulcon, the delaying his departure for a few days brought him the most remarkable introduction of his adventurous life. By what means we shall now discover.

The day prior to that on which he had appointed to quit Hué, Phaulcon and Father Thomas went to witness a great fight between a royal tiger and several elephants, which had been commanded by the king, for the amusement of himself and his court. As, towards evening, they were returning homewards, they were obliged to stand aside, or be trampled beneath the feet of three elephants which were bearing from the same sight to his palace some native lord, at least so they then believed him to be, and his suite. Each of these noble beasts was magnificently caparisoned, and carried upon his back a silken canopied howdah fringed with gold. In

the first of these were two men—the one a well-looking, olive-
coloured youth, scarcely twenty years of age ; the other, who sat
on the side nearest to Phaulcon, was in the meridian of life, of
much darker hue and a sinister expression of countenance, that
once seen could not easily be forgotten.  Both wore the costume
of Siamese mandarins of high rank, but the senior alone was
armed with scimitar and buckler.  The latter, as he passed, had
his head turned slightly towards his companion, still Phaulcon
saw enough of his features to cause him to start with surprise
—he could have sworn he had seen him before—but no, it was
impossible ; however, all thoughts of the dark-skinned Asiatic
left his mind as the second elephant passed, for in the howdah,
the curtains of which were drawn aside, sat a lady, so fair and
of such noble aspect, that Phaulcon exclaimed :

"Yon fair creature can scarcely be an Asiatic."

"Impossible, or if so, she is a Christian," replied Father Thomas,
and both were to a certain extent justified in their remarks ;
Phaulcon, for although her beautiful and abundant black hair was
dressed after the manner of the ladies of Japan—i.e. arranged into
the form of a small turban and stuck full of exquisitely wrought
and highly polished pins of tortoiseshell—and her form, after the
fashion of ladies of the same race, was enveloped in an ample robe
of purple silk, embroidered with gold, and clasped at the waist by a
rich scarf of the same glossy material,—she had neither the swarthy
skin, diminutive form, or black teeth of the women of the Indo-
Chinese races.  True, the eyes were slightly oblique,but then she
was tall of stature, elegantly shaped, with pearly teeth, and fair-
complexioned.  The priest must also have been correct in his
surmises, for around her neck she wore a string of beads, an *Agnus
Dei*, and a cross, the emblems of Christianity.  Who could she be ?

both were puzzled—the priest more especially, for as her eye rested upon him, she started as if she had either recognised in him some person she knew, or desired to speak with him. Taken by surprise, Father Thomas stared almost rudely at her, but, more to the priest's astonishment, the rudeness, if rudeness it was, was reciprocal, for the lady returned his gaze earnestly—almost, at least so he fancied, imploringly. He would have approached and spoken to her, but, as if suddenly reminded of the imprudence of permitting such an act, the lady turned to speak to a female attendant or companion, and the procession passed onwards, leaving both Phaulcon and the Jesuit in a state of bewilderment. The mind of the former seemed chiefly occupied with the two men upon the first elephant, for turning to a bystander he asked who and what they were, when greatly to his relief he was told, that the young man was Prince Soyaton, the son of a near relation of the King of Siam, from which potentate he was then on a mission to the monarch of Cochin China, and that his companion was a prince of Macassar, or rather one who had held that rank until the Dutch had taken possession of the Celebes, and driven him and his family from their native inheritance, since which he had been a fugitive and a wanderer about the East, sometimes living at one court, sometimes at another, where his services (for he was esteemed by all to be a great warrior) might be acceptable.

" But the lady, who is she ? " asked the priest.

" The chief wife of the Prince Soyaton, who has, within the last few days, been brought hither by the prince of Macassar," was the only reply, and with that he was compelled to rest content.

Immersed in thought, the two passed on to the house of the Cochinese, and without speaking to each other, neither did they have an opportunity of alluding to that chief event of the day till late in the evening, for the little lord, knowing it was to be the last day of Phaulcon's stay in Hué, had prepared an entertainment for his diversion.   When, however, that was concluded, and Phaulcon and the two Jesuits were again by themselves, the former said,

"Father Thomas, I would wager my life that I have seen that black fellow upon the first elephant before."

"It is not probable; but *who* didst take him for, my son?"

"Abdoul the Malay, the fellow whom *you* may remember would, but for me, have sold the English captain and his ship to the Spaniard off the coast of Cephalonia."

"Impossible! a mere fancy, my son," replied the father, changing colour; for either from gratitude to Phaulcon, his early pupil, or from policy, he had not once alluded to that famous night when the boy outwitted him and his colleague the Spanish captain. "Impossible, I say, for did we not hear that he was a prince of Macassar?—and we *saw*, by his being seated in the same palanquin, that he *is* a friend, an intimate, an equal, of the Prince Soyaton."

"Be he what he may *now*, prince or peasant, father, he is nevertheless Abdoul the Malay," replied Phaulcon firmly; adding, "and if he recognised me, and possesses any influence with this Cochinese king, the sooner my, perhaps *our*, feet again tread upon European planks, the better it will be."

"You fear this man, my son."

"Fear!" repeated Phaulcon, "I know no such feeling. Yet," he added, musingly, "what courage is proof against treachery?" Before, however, the priest could reply, one of the slaves appointed by the Cochinese lord to attend upon the Europeans announced that a lady of rank, then at the gates in her palanquin, desired immediate speech with the holy father. At this incident Phaulcon was not a little surprised; Father Thomas, however, having had experience that such visits from converts, or those seeking conversion, were of no unusual occurrence, told the slave to usher the visitor into the room, with all respect, adding to his companions, " Doubtless it is the wife of the ambassador of whom I told you ;" and he was correct in his surmise, for the next minute appeared a handsome, goodnatured-looking Cochinese woman, attired in a full, long, flowing silk gown, with loose sleeves, and buttoned close at the neck, wide pantaloons, a black mantle of flowered silk (an article of dress only worn by people of rank upon ceremonious occasions), and a crape turban, with the almost only distinguishing mark of dress between the sexes—a large basket-shaped hat.

A female slave awaited at the door of the apartment, while the lady, with all the humility of a recent convert, and great veneration for the father, fell upon her knees, and taking his hand in her own, congratulated him upon his having secured the favour of the king; adding, as he raised her from her kneeling position, that she had brought with her a beloved friend, who was in sore distress, and desired his aid. Without, however, awaiting a reply, she waved her hand to the slave, who at once quitted the room.

The father then expressed a wish that Phaulcon would leave the apartment, as the friend might not wish to be seen by other eyes than those of the priest, whom she was coming to consult; but the lady interposed, saying :

" *No ;* the noble captain is a farang (Christian) like ourselves, we are as if one family ; moreover, he is a man of war ; and my friend may want the protection of a weapon the holy fathers do not carry—a sword."

At this extraordinary reply, the Jesuit felt alarmed, for he feared that the lady in question might be, as was not unfrequently the case, the wife of some native noble seeking conversion, in defiance or without the knowledge of her husband; but ere he could question her, the lady herself was ushered by the slave into the room.

"The wife of Prince Soyaton!" exclaimed the astonished Phaulcon, in Siamese.

At the name, the lady, who had appeared either bewildered or as if ashamed of having forced herself into the presence of the Europeans, started as if suddenly stung by a serpent.

"The wife of Soyaton!" she exclaimed; "no! Monica is the wife of no man." Then throwing herself at the feet of the Jesuit, and convulsively clutching his robe, she said, "Man of prayer, a Christian maiden seeks the protection of Holy Church from a villain who has treacherously torn her from her home and friends."

"My daughter," said Father Thomas, "the cross has at present but little power in this pagan land to shield its votaries from the vengeance of the great," and he gently sought to raise her from her kneeling position; but resisting his endeavours, she said,

"I will not rise till you have promised. *He* of whom I speak is not a noble of this land, but a refugee from his own king and country. You have the favour and protection of the Cochinese monarch. Take me to his presence, and the great king will not deny my prayer."

"Lady," replied the cautious priest, "you exaggerate my power; the monarch has but recently, in a fit of penitence for the past, granted us licence to use our best efforts for the winning over of his people to the Church; my interference in matters of lesser import might cause him to revoke his favour. But," he added, "in your excitement, fear, you have not said what it is you desire."

"I have told you," she said, "that I am a Christian maiden, *that* surely should be sufficient to command your sympathies. Let me add that I have this night fled from the house of the miserable Soyaton, who caused one of his creatures treacherously to inveigle me from my home in Siam, aye, even in defiance of his king's command. From him"—and as she spoke, she turned nervously towards the door—"who may even now have missed and be seeking me, I claim protection, and desire the king's permission to return to Siam."

"And by my honour you shall have both, lady, or I much mistake the Cochinese king's desire to see justice done within his dominions," interposed Phaulcon, stepping forward. "But, lady," he added, as he gently assisted her to rise, and led her to an ottoman, "that I may seek the influence of our host with his majesty, I must be able to lay before him the story of your wrong."

"Noble, generous stranger," she replied joyfully, "Heaven will reward you; my story is soon told. I am the daughter of a noble and wealthy Christian family of Japan, one of those who during the terrible persecutions in 1630, chose rather to fly their native land and settle in Siam, than to abandon the faith for which so many of their name endured a joyful martyrdom; moreover I boast the blood of the English islanders, for my great-grandfather was that William Adams, the first of his race who ever set foot in Japan, and whose wisdom and bravery obtained for him the love and confidence of the Ziogoon, at whose court he lived in an exalted position for nearly twenty years. His son, my grandsire, fled the land, and as I have said, settled in the capital of

Siam, where my family have since lived. My father being the
commander of the king of Siam's Japanese guard,* his associates
were the princes and nobles of the land. During his life-time
(for, alas, he is dead) I had many offers of marriage, not one of
which could I have accepted had I even been so inclined, for
they came from idol-worshippers, who are permitted a plurality
of wives; still, notwithstanding my rejection of every proposal,
I remained free from persecution during my parents' lifetime, but
in less than six months after he had been slain in the war with the
savage Burmans, this Soyaton, the son of prince Petraxa, a near
relation of the king, began to importune me to be the chief of
his twenty wives. Often and openly this dissolute prince persecuted
me with his attentions and solicitations; neither my rank nor
wealth were sufficient to protect me from open violence, for one
night, he with his friend, a refugee prince of Macassar, broke into
my house and carried me to his palace. Fortunately, a devoted
servant, who had witnessed the outrage, had both wit and courage
to force his way into the very presence of the king, to whom he
recounted the story of my abduction. His majesty was so greatly
enraged at this insult to the daughter of a great officer, whom he
had regarded rather in the light of a friend than a servant, and
who had moreover fallen in his service, that, having set me free,
he ordered Prince Soyaton to be put to death.† But this sentence
coming to the ears of Petraxa, that prince threw himself at the foot

---

* At one period, when the Japanese were *not* " exclusive" people, and their
country was *not* the "sealed land," it has been the custom to represent it,
these warlike islanders used to take service in the armies of the other potentates of Asia, and as the kings of France once had a Scots regiment, so
the monarchs of Siam had a Japanese guard.

† In Siam and Asia, and some other countries in the East, princes are
executed by being put in a sack and then beaten to death with clubs, for
on no account must the sacred blood of royalty be shed.

of the throne, and begged his son's life ; and the good king, being
no longer under the influence of the demon passion, granted the
boon. Still, unable to bear the sight of Soyaton about the court, he
despatched him at once to this kingdom of Cochin China, nominally as a kind of envoy, but at the same time commanding
him, under penalty of death, to remain here until recalled to his
native land. Thus, I believed myself to be safe from all further
persecution. from that bad prince ; but, alas, I dreamt not the
cunning or extent to which the villain would carry his plot
against me.

"One evening, when returning from a pleasure excursion upon
the Meinam, a boat with one rower put off from a large trading
junk, and made towards my barge ; when within hearing, the
boatmen, calling to my attendants, desired them to tell their
lady that the junk had on board some rare and ancient china ; the
captain, they added, knew that the lady Monica was the pos-
sessor of great wealth, and loved to adorn her palace with the
rarities of foreign countries; he therefore craved the lady's permission to bring them to her house, for he felt assured that she
would purchase them.

"The cunning rogue was right, he knew my passion for rarities of
all kinds, but especially for *ancient* china, a passion which I have
in common with all wealthy women of China and Japan ; thus,
impatient to view these things, in an evil moment I went on board
the junk, with all my attendants, leaving only my rower in the
barge ; but no sooner did we enter the large cabin, than the door
was suddenly secured from without, and we were prisoners, but
worse, to the Prince of Macassar, who the instant after came from
behind a screen.

"'Pardon, O lady !' said he, 'this apparent violence, Heaven has willed it as necessary for the happiness of one who cannot, will not live without thee.'

"'Wretch!' I exclaimed, 'what means this violence? Art thou an agent of the hateful Soyaton? But I know thou art,' and as the suspicion of my real position passed through my mind, I fainted in the arms of my women."

"But the rowers, lady," asked Phaulcon, "missing their mistress, did they not attempt thy rescue?"

"Alas, no! the treacherous knaves had been bribed by my captor. But to conclude this story of my second abduction : I did not again see the prince until we arrived in this country, and then he confessed what I had long suspected, that he had brought me here to be the chief wife of Soyaton. At this disclosure, the rogue expected an outburst of rage ; but during the voyage I had had time to meditate upon my only chance of escape. Thus, although filled with indignation and terror, I merely bent my head as if in silent submission to à fate it was now impossible to withstand ; even when taken before Soyaton, I did but mildly reproach him for his treachery ; and, astonished at my apparent coolness, even that villain seemed to have some regret at the violent measures he had taken, as for two whole days he troubled me not with his hated presence.

"The next time he came, he importuned me to become his wife. Not as before, expressing my disgust at the proposal, I simply told him, that being a Christian it was impossible. To this he begged that I would listen to the arguments of the chief Omsaii of this country, who was his friend, and by whose learning he hoped to make me forswear the faith in which I had been born and bred. At this monstrous proposition, an indignant reply stood upon my lips ; but bethinking that delay might prove my greatest ally, I begged that he would leave me to myself for a time.

"The prince complied, but for his forbearance I had to thank his avarice, for if he could not obtain me as his *legal* wife, and by my own consent—for I have neither father, uncle, nor brother—he could not touch my wealth.

"Within a few days I heard, from one of the attendants my per-secutor had placed about me, of the persecution of the Christian fathers, then of their restoration to the king's favour, and also of the conversion of the wife and family of a Cochinese noble. The latter was joyful intelligence, for I entertained a hope that if I could but convey to the noblewoman the story of my misery, like a sister, she would fly to my aid. To do this, I charged one of my most devoted attendants (a Christian) to seek out this lady (as she spoke Monica pointed to the Cochinese lady). My servant having obtained an interview and recited my story, my new friend, by means of her husband, a man too powerful for Soyaton to disoblige, obtained permission to visit me.

"At our first interview she told me that two Christian fathers were then in the city, as also a European ship-captain, who was in great favour with the king. Further, she said, that in the evening of the day of the tiger and elephant fight, when Soyaton and the Macassar prince would be engaged in a distant part of the house, regaling themselves, she would visit me in her largest palanquin, and carry me to the lodgings of the fathers, under whose shelter I should be safe from my persecutors. Nay, the good lady further promised, that should the holy men be either unable or fear to protect me, that she would lodge me in her own house, until a fitting opportunity occurred of my returning to Siam."

"And the wife of the Cochinese lord will not eat her words. The Lady Monica will find the house open, even now, to her, should she desire so to honour it with her presence," interposed the lady in question.

"Daughter," replied Father Thomas deliberately, for he still kept before his eyes the possibility of the Cochinese sovereign revoking his recently granted concession to the Christians, "should the king not will it otherwise, and the good noble who is master of this house permit, you shall remain beneath this roof until we ourselves can offer thee a passage back to Siam."

"Lady," said Phaulcon determinedly, "confidently defy the power and enmity of these rascal princes of whom you speak. My brave ship is at your service, and with *your* permission I will not quit this city, nay, nor this land of Cochin China, except accompanied by you; and to-morrow I will seek an interview with the king himself."

"Noble sir," said the Lady Monica, her eyes suffused with tears of joy, "how can I express my gratitude?"—But suddenly she trembled from head to foot, and, falling at his feet, cried, "In the name of that God whom we both worship, protect me from these men."

This alarm, these words were called forth by the sudden appearance of Soyaton and the Prince of Macassar, accompanied by the little round-headed, good-natured Cochinese noble. A frown, however, now rested upon the brow of the latter, as he said, "Is it thus that the Christian priests show their gratitude to their protectors? Is it by inducing runaway wives to hide themselves from their husbands in my house that they repay me for my hospitality?"

Soyaton neither spoke nor moved while these words were uttered, but the Prince of Macassar, advancing to seize Monica, said, "Lady, this is no place for thee; return to the house of thy chosen husband before the scandal shall have reached over the whole city."

Before, however, his hand could profane even her robe, Phaulcon, enraged at the intended rudeness, struck him backwards with his clenched fist. The Macassar, raising himself, drew his dagger ; but presenting the point of his sword, Phaulcon exclaimed—

" It is, then, as I thought, Abdoul, the Malay impostor ! But one inch nearer, and that moment is your last." Then, seeing the angry frown upon his host's countenance, he said, " This fellow is a Malay pirate and a thief, who stole from her home in Siam this noble Christian lady."

" Ah, what words are these ? " exclaimed the old noble.

" They are true, oh excellent lord," replied the Cochinese lady, who then hastily repeated Monica's adventure.

"Then the princes Soyaton and Abdullah have made me eat dirt, I—a counsellor of the king," exclaimed the little noble sternly, angrily, and although the two worthies still insisted upon the truth of their own tale, and demanded that Monica should be given over to them, he would not listen to them in contradiction to his countrywoman, the wife, too, of a noble high in the land, and his own blood relation.

" No," he said ; " this noble lady's story is true, so get thee hence, and to-morrow the king himself shall decide this cause. In the meanwhile the Christian girl shall remain in my wife's apartments."

Whatever was passing in the mind of Soyaton, he left the room sullenly without a word, for he dreaded to embroil himself with the minister of a king who, did the whole truth reach him, might at pleasure send him back in chains to his own sovereign.

Not so Abdullah, who, grasping the hilt of his dagger significantly, hissed through his gnashing teeth—

" Again, O dog of a Greek, hast thou crossed my path ; beware the next time lest I crush thee. I am thy fate. I have said it, and a prince of Macassar eats not his own words."

"*Prince* forsooth—pirate, impostor, I defy thee," scornfully replied Phaulcon, who did not believe the story he had heard of Abdullah's being one of the sons of the last king of the Celebes.

Becoming soothed at the discomfiture of her two enemies, Monica, with a countenance beaming with hope and gratitude, took leave of Phaulcon, and with the lady who had so greatly befriended her, followed the old Cochinese noble to the apartments devoted to his wife and the women of her household.

The next day our hero, accompanied by the old noble, sought an audience of the king, and his majesty, having heard Monica's story, at once gave her permission to quit his dominions, when and how she pleased. She chose to place herself under the paternal care of Father Thomas, who intended to accompany Phaulcon back to Siam, *en route* for Macao, at that period the head-quarters of the Jesuit fathers in Eastern India. As for Father Tachard, he went with them only as far as the Bay of Turon, from which place he took his departure in the French ship for France, his great object being to report to his superior, and through that personage to Louis the Fourteenth, the chances of a grand scheme for the conversion of the people of Cochin China and Siam proving a success; nay, the possibility of making those countries an appanage of the crown of France—plans very dear to the heart of le grande monarque.

## CHAPTER IX.

"'Tis an ill wind that blows no one good"—so the squall which wrecked the vessel and sent to the bottom the sumptuous presents the Cochinese ambassador was carrying to the King of Siam, thereby rendering it necessary for his excellency to seek a passage back to his native country at the hands of the India Company, blew fortune into the lap of Phaulcon, for upon calculating the results of his voyage, he found that, what with presents from the little Cochinese noble, his share of the gains upon his transactions with the King of Annam,* the profits made by Blake in his dealings with the Turonese, which the generous fellow insisted, according to agreement, to hand over to his friend, and though last, not least, a handsome sum of money forced upon him by the grateful and wealthy Monica, he had realised sufficient money once more to set him afloat in the world upon an independent footing.

"I have never despaired," he said to his friend, after recounting the above result of his voyage, "and at last, or rather *again*, am I rewarded."

"Fortune has indeed smiled upon you during the last voyage ; nevertheless, my friend, as of yore, I repeat, do not tempt thy evil fate by carrying the whole of your eggs in one basket, for should you again——"

* Cochin China is known to the natives only as Annam.

"Be ruined," interrupted Phaulcon, impatiently. "Well, even so, I shall have to do as I have done before, begin afresh, for while I live, I'll strive. Look you, Blake, many, yourself included, accredit me with mere sordid avarice, or ambition; but it is not so; I tell you I feel that within me which impels to difficulties for the mere pleasure, excitement, of overcoming them. Besides, the fair lady the proverb tells us that was never won by faint heart is assuredly Dame Fortune, and she I am determined, under Providence, to wed."

"Still," said Blake doggedly, "don't again carry all your eggs in one basket, for even Dame Fortune will reject you if wanting in prudence."

"Well, old friend, you shall have your way this time," replied Phaulcon, laughing; and, luckily for himself, as the sequel will prove, he kept his word.

The next passage of importance in our hero's life was a "venture" to Surat, the then chief station of the English Company in India. Within six months after his return from Cochin China, he had purchased and equipped a ship, and had laden her with the most valuable products of Siam, at an outlay of all he possessed, excepting only two thousand crowns, which he took with him in the shape of bills upon the English Company at Surat. And again the heart of Phaulcon beat with pride at the prospect before him—a pride, however, slightly chilled by disappointment, for he was not to be accompanied by his friend. Blake would not accept of a partnership in the venture; he could not go as second officer, because he had, he said, some intention of again seeking the command of a ship bound for England.

"So much for your determination never to return till a certain

ring had summoned you," said Phaulcon, whereby the reader will
see that Blake had made his friend a confidant in the matter of
his parting gift to Zillah; but perhaps Blake's weakness in this
was more commendable than Phaulcon's sneer.

Now, notwithstanding the coolness that had suddenly sprung
up between the two young men, Blake, hearing that our hero's
vessel was ready for sea, went on board to bid him farewell and
*bon voyage.*

Phaulcon was standing upon his little quarter-deck giving
instructions to a European, who appeared to be his first officer.
Seeing Blake, he turned, saying, rather coolly, "Welcome, my
friend." The former, however, did not notice the coolness; his
attention was fixed upon the more than half-naked bodies of the
sailors: Chinese, Malays, Siamese, Moors, indeed, any and every
race but Europeans, who were engaged upon the decks, or clamber-
ing the rigging—in vain his eye sought a white man.

"You have but a small show of Europeans, Phaulcon; how
many can you muster?"

"Captain Taunton wishes to inspect our European force; call
them all aft, Johnson," said Phaulcon to his companion.

"Bob!"

"Aye, aye, sir," and forthwith a small boy some twelve years
of age tumbled from behind a bale of goods in the waist, and,
coming aft, stood bolt upright before his captain, who turning to
Blake, said—

"Here we are all. Three—no, two and a half. What do you
think of us?"

"Phaulcon, you must be mad to dream of trusting yourself and
valuable cargo to such a nest of rascals, one-half of whom are
old pirates, and the other willing to become ready pupils."

L

"Tut, tut, my cautious friend, the fellows cannot help being scarecrows; besides, they are honest enough, and we have all the arms to ourselves. Look," and as he spoke he led him to a cabin built upon deck, and well furnished with sabres and pistols. In the centre was placed a small brass swivel gun, so mounted that, if necessary, it would sweep the whole length and breadth of the vessel.

"This but proves to me the desperate nature of your venture, Phaulcon; but I see how it is—I might have known it—European sailors are not to be had just now for love or money."

"You have hit the mark, Blake; nevertheless, I am not to lose my profits."

Placing his hand to his brow for a minute, Blake remained in deep thought, then, offering it to Phaulcon, he said, "I retract my refusal; you *must* not sail alone; now I *entreat* permission to join you."

"Thank God for this," exclaimed Phaulcon, warmly grasping his friend's hand, "less for your proferred assistance than the proof that your love for me is as of old."

"Stay," replied Blake, "open that, and you will learn whether I had not good reason for desiring a voyage to England," and he placed a letter in his hand.

Phaulcon opened the epistle. It was from Captain West, earnestly entreating Blake's return. Not a word did it contain from Zillah; but there was inclosed the little gold circlet, which endorsed the father's invitation more warmly than written words could have done.

"I see, I see;" said Phaulcon, "to obey such a summons one would joyfully traverse the whole world;" then, as he gave him back the letter, he added, "I comprehend the generous sacrifice you

would make for my unworthy sake; but this must not be, my
friend, so get you the command of this homeward-bound ship
with all speed, and return to comfort the dear souls. Would that
my own future was as clearly defined."

"Nay, Phaulcon, not so; it were foul shame did I not stand
by thee at this juncture; besides, this run to Surat and back,
will delay me but a few months, and should you have the luck to
ship a half-score of Europeans at 'any of the Malabar ports, why
then I may chance to find a passage to England in some homeward-
bound trader."

Blake then went ashore to prepare for sea. The next
day they sailed, and from that time till near the end of their
voyage the friends saw but little of each other, or at least were
never together long enough to hold much conversation, for tempestuous weather and the want of European hands, rendered it
necessary that one of them should be upon deck both by night
and day.

Having traversed the long line of the Malabar coast, from Cape
Comorin until through the glass they could trace the shadowy
forms of the spires and towers of old Goa, they became becalmed.
So near the end of the voyage, this was vexatious. However, to
keep the crew in good humour, Phaulcon had them "piped to
mischief," and served with a double allowance of grog. To the
latter they had no objection, for although Asiatics, frequent
service with Europeans had destroyed the temperate habits of
their race.

While these half-savage mariners were engaged, some with cards
or dice, some at shuttlecock, and others preparing little ships and
crews of tinsel-paper, in readiness for the Goddess Ma-tsoo-po,
who, they hoped, during the next storm, would find too much

mean, and far baser birth than mine, have successfully lifted their hopes as high."

" True," replied Blake, " there have been adventurers, who have dragged themselves into high places, by clinging to a woman's robe, and to become either slaves or tyrants, but such an achievement is scarcely worthy of the high-spirited Phaulcon.

" Blake," he replied, " these words are as unjust as they are severe. But then," he continued abstractedly, " how is it possible that *you* who love the gentle Zillah, and seek your highest happiness in a moderate competency, and a contented domesticity, can comprehend the love of a restless being like me, or the workings of the mind of the noble Monica, to whom misfortune is as an heirloom, and in whose heart love can only be developed through her sympathies with high resolves, great actions, and even physical peril. But *you* are right, Blake, she *is* far above such as me : exalted beyond mere self, there is room in her breast but for one passion—the dissemination of the faith of Christ throughout this land of Siam."

" My friend," replied Blake, " now more than ever I think thee bewitched, for canst not see that her woman's mind has been worked upon by the cunning Jesuit, Father Thomas, for the furtherance of his own ends ; but, even shouldst thou make thyself a hero worthy of this lady's love, there still remains an insurmountable obstacle—she is of the Church of Rome, an enthusiastic disciple of the Jesuit fathers.

" The Church in which *my* childhood was cradled, the Church of my ancestors," replied Phaulcon, thoughtfully.

" True," answered Blake bitterly ; for in those days the *odium theologicum* ran very high between Catholics and Protestants, and Blake knew that although Phaulcon during his long association with

the English had attended the services of the reformed religion,
the bent of his inclination had ever remained towards the faith in
which he had been educated, and remembering this he wisely
discontinued the subject.

As it was Blake's turn to keep watch on deck that night,
Phaulcon turned into his cabin, and throwing himself upon his
couch soon became lost in thought, or rather ambitious dreams.
Once more upon the high road to wealth, he like many a wiser and
greater man, began to calculate his profits by anticipation, a process
which, when the result chances to be successful, gains men reputation for great foresight; but when the reverse, that of " Builders of
castles in the air "—dreamers, who, to use a homely proverb, foolishly
" count their chickens before they are hatched."

Now, one of these *chateaux en Espagne*, or unhatched chickens—
which you will—was the realizing of a large profit by the sale of bar
gold for dollars, then the bartering of Siamese commodities for the
products of the Malabar country; but his hopes of gain chiefly
rested upon the sale of several large casks of petroleum, or earth oil,
from the kingdom of Ava, a natural production at that time so difficult to obtain, that it readily found liberal purchasers among the
English merchants, and who could deny that so far these were fair
and admissible calculations, for had he not brought his ship and
cargo safely through the dangerous seas of China, to within a few
miles of the English station, but then his thoughts took higher flight.

" Fortune is indeed propitious," he murmured, " patience, perseverance have overcome all difficulties, and at length I see a hope
of quitting this wandering life ; my homeward voyage equally
prosperous, my hopes and aims may take a less sordid shape.
The Jesuit's scheme of converting the Siamese is grand, glorious,
holy.   The king is, in intelligence, far beyond his age and

race. I will seek a post at his court; the aid and advice of a wealthy European he will, doubtlessly, accept. Yes," he continued, " the country, the people *are* capable of being raised to greatness, they are ripe for Christianity, the revenues want but careful handling, the commerce may be extended, nay relations opened up with the great French king, who they tell me is burning with desire to plant the Church and his people in the lands of the East. Then—the beautiful Monica"—and with that name upon his lips, he glided into the arms of Somnus, the pleasant chain of thoughts being kept alive in his brain by the God of dreams. Who shall blame him? Who that could as reasonably claim such dreams would not command them to his couch? Who in fact that dwells upon the glorious, because unknown future *does not* " count his chickens before they are hatched ?"—Nonè, save the fool, " who, caring for to-day, leaves the morrow to care for itself."

From these pleasant dreams Phaulcon was awakened by a noise, as if of a scuffle, apparently just without his cabin. To leap to his feet, and place his hands upon his ready loaded pistols, was the work of an instant. The next, he had jumped upon a side table, and was looking through a small aperture which had been left by the builder for the cooling of the cabin. A bolder heart than even our hero's would have been dismayed at the sight before him. The grey streak of dawn exhibited the ghastly features of his only English seaman lying slain upon the deck. Blake was unwounded, but bound hands and feet, while the little boy Bob, was struggling in the hands of some of the Asiatics who were endeavouring also to secure him. What had happened was obvious at a glance.

The crew had mutinied, and were about to seize the ship which, with the cargo, at that time they would find but little difficulty in

carrying to a good market, and that too without fear of being asked
any troublesome particulars.   Oh ! what a spasm shot through
Phaulcon's heart !   Again at the eleventh hour was he to be ruined
—worse, murdered !   Of what use all his care and precautions
during that voyage, when he had lost all by reposing in a false
security at the last moment.   However, not an instant was to be
lost.   He knew the craven nature of the men.   One bold stroke
might *regain* him the mastery.   I have said, that in the centre of
his cabin was affixed a small brass swivel gun.   This, nominally
for signals, but really in readiness for such a moment as the present,
he had always kept loaded.   Well, it was pretty certain that when
they had secured the boy, the mutineers would rush into his cabin.
Thus, he prepared a match and stood at the breech of the gun
ready to fire it on the instant.

Many terrible minutes, however, passed, and he could hear
the fellows debating, as to whether they should make some
alarm that would awaken the captain and so bring him forth
into their hands, or burst open the doors and seize him at once.
Then one, more cowardly than the rest, suggested that they
should fall upon him while asleep, as, if awake, he would sell
his life dearly.   This suggestion seemed to have some weight,
for it was followed by a lull.   Suddenly, however, there was a
scuffling of feet ; they were preparing for action.   Phaulcon
lighted the match ; the door was burst open with a hatchet ;
the fire was near the touch-hole, and the next instant the majority
of the mutineers would have been blown to eternity ; but, prepared
for the discharge of the death-dealing instrument, the savages
held Blake before them, in front of the muzzle.   Aghast at
the sight, Phaulcon retreated some steps, match in hand.

"Nay, care not for me, one must be sacrificed.   Fire, Phaulcon,

THE MUTINY.

fire, and you will clear the ship of enough of these dogs to render the others harmless." And the leader of the rogues, a Chinese, must have read compliance in the stern countenance of our hero, for he called out:

"Let the noble captain submit, and by the bones of my ancestors, he shall come to no other harm than confinement until we can put him, his lieutenant, and the boy ashore."

It was a terrible, but the last and only alternative; besides he knew that a Chinese would never break that oath, so dashing the still burning match upon the floor, Phaulcon came forward, and without a word submitted to be bound with cords. The two friends, with the boy Bob, were then left upon the quarter-deck to console each other as best they might, while the piratical crew, now their own masters, proceeded to inaugurate their victory by a terrific saturnalia.

"From my soul I grieve for you, my friend," said Blake, as they lay huddled together upon the deck.

"Nay, grief is useless; my turn will come again, the next time to be lasting. Have I not said that *three* times I should be ruined before my tide of permanent fortune would come; true, I expected another shipwreck, but it matters little in what form misfortune comes; but hearken, Blake," he whispered, "if we could only manage to slip these ropes I have hopes that all would not be lost yet, for long before midnight these wretches will be helplessly drunk."

"There is that faint possibility," replied Blake dismally; "it is also probable that these savages once rendered insane by drink may murder us. Ah, my friend, I deserve my fate, for had I kept the watch, as has always been my wont, this would not have happened, but being becalmed almost in sight of the port,

I was thrown off my guard and seized by the villains before I dreamt of danger." And in such self-accusation and sorrow did Blake pass the rest of the day.

Having captured their officers at so early a period in the morning, the mutineers had sufficient time to get drunk, sober, and drunk again before evening. At night, however, they commenced a great saturnalia ; the ship became a very pandemonium, and the men, from their insane tricks, more like maddened monkeys than human beings ; but, extraordinary to relate, they offered neither insult nor injury to the prisoners, but supplied them with both meat and drink.

As night approached, the rogues, one by one, disappeared from the deck, some to sleep off the fumes of the liquor, others to commence new orgies below ; but two remained on deck as a nightwatch, and these observing that the prisoners were slumbering, soon succumbed to the effects of their potations, by stretching themselves at full length upon the boards.

"Should a stiff night-breeze spring up and blow in shore, nothing can save us from destruction," whispered Blake.

"Aye, and with these cords around our arms and legs we shall go to the bottom like bales of merchandize," replied Phaulcon.

When all seemed quiet, and every hope of escape passed, Phaulcon felt upon his shoulder the hand of Bob, who at the same time whispered, "Captain, I have managed to get one fist free."

"Cleverly done, boy, then thrust it into my pocket and you will find a knife," was the reply.

Slowly, noiselessly, without moving another limb the lad complied, and in a minute the bright sharp blade had severed the cords which bound the captives.

For nearly an hour they remained as quietly as possible, stretching their limbs and listening for the voice or footstep of some more sober reveller. At length, feeling assured that all the mutineers were in deep slumber, Phaulcon whispered :

" Let us creep into my cabin."

Once within the little deck-room they breathed more freely, for the means of defence or attack were in their hands.

" The rogues still sleep, unconscious that we are at liberty," said Phaulcon. "Now, if we can only toss the two rascals who are snoring at their posts into the sea, or even silently gag them, we can fasten down the hatches and so trap the whole gang ; the signal gun will then bring us aid from the shore.

The advantage of gagging, if possible, the sleeping sentries being obvious, Phaulcon and Blake, each with a handful of tow and their neckerchiefs in their hands, followed by the boy, who carried two lengths of cord, crept stealthily forward. A death-like silence prevailed, which was broken alone by the rippling of the water against the ship's sides.

Wrapped in drunken slumber, the two sentries were stretched upon the deck, about a yard beyond the principal hatchway. The friends had passed the latter, in another instant the men would be in their power ; but their movements are suddenly arrested, Phaulcon aghast places his hand upon Blake's shoulder ; a thin column of dark smoke rises through the hatchway, as if direct from the hold. Their plans are now defeated by a more terrible enemy than the mutineers.

"We are lost, hopelessly lost, the drunken brutes have fired the ship."

Then kicking the nearest sentry, he cried, " What ho, there, arise, the ship's on fire ;" and the two men awakening, although

wise Phaulcon must inevitably have perished. As it was, it was only by the aid of the breeze which was blowing in shore, and the almost superhuman exertions of Blake and the boy Bob, that his head was kept above water until they reached the land.

159

## CHAPTER X.

AT THE DEPTH OF MISFORTUNE BEGINS PROSPERITY.

For nearly an hour did Phaulcon lie stretched senseless upon the sand. Consciousness returning, he sat up, and placing his hand upon his brow, gazed wildly around as if to recall past events. Then, as his eye caught the low hull of the barque, and the black smoke ascending from the still-burning oil, he said mournfully,

"Again hath ruin fallen on me;" then, as if cheered by some sudden thought, he added, "But cheer thee up, Blake, 'tis the *third* and last shipwreck, my fortunes will now be built upon a firmer basis, for had not good been in store, those dark-skinned rogues would have been permitted to end our lives at the first onset."

"'Tis at least a cheerful view to take, at such a terrible crisis," said Blake.

"Aye, my friend, and it is to you I am indebted for smoothing my road to the next success, for this voyage I did *not place all my eggs in one basket*—Look;" and as he spoke, he thrust his hand beneath his vest, but fearful was the consternation, the utter misery depicted upon his face, and he withdrew his hand, as if it had been stung by a scorpion.

"It is gone; now am I indeed hopelessly ruined, Blake;" he added, perceiving the latter's astonishment, "I have lost my pocket case, and with it bills upon the merchants of Surat for two thousand crowns—two thousand crowns;" he repeated, "the nucleus of a fortune in any part of the world;" and for the first time in his life Phaulcon wept in an agony of despair.

" 'Tis a cruel disheartening loss, but remember," said Blake, soothingly, "thy former misfortunes, how bravely you battled against them; and that you still have youth, health, and strength— a trio, formidable enough to battle a prosperous route through a mountain of difficulties."

"True, Blake, this despair is unworthy of my manhood;" replied Phaulcon, with a return of his old confidence in himself and his fortunes, " 'Tis the third shipwreck of my hopes, the change for the good is now assuredly approaching, for *at the depth of misfortune, begins prosperity.*"

"Constantine Phaulcon is once more himself," said Blake, "but see, fortune has already commenced to befriend us;" he added, pointing to a small hut at a short distance from the sea, "a few hours' rest, sheltered from the storm which is now brewing, will prepare us for to-morrow's toil."

Upon entering the tenement which Blake had taken for a hut, they found it to be a stone grotto, which, at some former time, had been built as a hermitage for a Brahmin recluse, and as it would serve them admirably as a place of refuge during the coming storm, they all three stretched themselves upon the floor, Blake and the boy to slumber soundly; as for Phaulcon, who to the last day of his life had good cause to remember that night, he afterwards declared that he knew not whether he had slept or fallen into a half-dreamy state, between sleeping and awaking. He could not, however, have remained in the grotto more than two hours, for Blake awaking very early the next morning found his friend missing ; going in search of him, he found him rapidly pacing the sand to and fro, buried in such deep thought, that he did not perceive the approach of Blake, until the latter, touching his arm, said,

"Constantine, is it possible that *you* can permit a temporary misfortune to weigh thus heavily upon your mind."

" Blake," replied our hero hastily, as if impatient at the interruption to the current of his thoughts, "you are wrong, I have already cast the past from my thoughts."

" Good," replied Blake, "you were brewing resolutions for the future, meditating a means of release from our present difficulties. *I* have been doing likewise. Remember, my fortune is unimpaired, therefore if we can but reach Surat, where I am sure to be recognised by some of my countrymen, a voyage to England is easily procurable."

" A voyage to *England*," repeated Phaulcon abstractedly.

" Aye, this time to the old country, for surely, even thou must at length have become tired of tempting the fickle goddess upon the treacherous ocean."

His black eyes lighting up as if with inspiration, and with an earnestness of manner that startled his friend, Phaulcon replied :—

"Blake, return *you* to your native country, where love, perhaps, and a peaceful prosperity await you ; *my* future is cast in the East, where alone the web of my destiny can be unravelled."

" Destiny ! poh, poh, my friend, what superstitious fancy hath taken possession of thee now ?  Destiny forsooth, what is *that* but the future carved out of the present by man's own strong will ? "

"Stay, listen," he said, with a solemnity of manner that at once arrested Blake's attention, "Last night, as stretched upon the floor of yonder grotto, I lay, neither asleep nor awake,

M

pondering upon the past and future in a kind of waking dream, there seemed suddenly to spring from the earth, silvery jets of light, which, becoming more voluminous as they rose, resolved themselves into a fountain, that appeared not only to fill the grotto, but to be throwing its sprays for miles around. Then, when my attention had become most fixed, there came a few steps forth from this luminous fountain, a man attired in all the magnificence of an eastern monarch, but whose benign countenance and form of majestic symmetry, reminded me of the sculptured gods of my own ancient race. Startled, nay with a thrill of pleasure running through every nerve, at this glorious apparition, I threw myself upon my knees, crying.

" ' For what great purpose, oh ! god-like shadow, hast thou thus appeared to the thrice ruined Phaulcon ?' The words having left my lips, I trembled at my temerity in having dared first to address him. But with a gaze, which has no comparison but that of the pure heavenly smile of a young mother, as she thus speaks love to the heart of her firstborn, he replied :

" ' To direct thee to *return from whence thou camest. Hesitate not an instant, my son, for 'tis in Siam that thy fortunes will be built, thy future developed.' '*

" Poh, poh ! a dream ; the result of physical exhaustion and an over-excited brain," said Blake, adding laughingly, " But did'st tell the old gentleman of your bad luck in the country, or what is more to the purpose, did he tell thee how to get a passage back again ? "

" As these words," continued Phaulcon, regardless of the badinage, " fell upon my ears, I awakened ; but the majestic figure, the voice, the tone in which it had spoken, were so impressed upon my brain, that I could sleep no more, so rising I came here to meditate, to ponder upon the means of obeying that which I cannot but regard to be a command from my good genius."

"Poh, poh !" exclaimed the matter-of-fact Blake.

"Nay, nay, speak not deridingly. See, fate is even now working in my favour," he said, laying one hand upon his friend's shoulder, and with the other pointing to a small black object which seemed attached to the very spar upon which they had floated ashore from the ship, and turning his eyes in the direction indicated, Blake for the instant almost became a convert to Phaulcon's superstitious fancies ; for it was no other than the pocket-book, the loss of which had caused our hero to despair.

"This is indeed extraordinary—at least, very fortunate," said Blake.

"It is more, it is the work of Providence," exclaimed our hero, as opening the little book, he saw that his two thousand crowns' worth of bills had been preserved from injury by the tightly folded seal-skin covering ; "surely," he added in the ecstasy of the moment, "it would be pleasing to heaven and propitiating fortune, to devote a moiety of this money to some charitable object."

" 'Tis a pious purpose, my friend, and hereafter, if you remain in the same mind, you will have time and opportunity of carrying it out," replied Blake ; "but for the present, if we would not die from exhaustion, we had better seek for sustenance ; let us therefore at once make for Goa, and on the road refresh ourselves with what fruits we may find."

"Aye, aye, it is a good and practical suggestion," said Phaulcon, aroused out of dreamland by certain twinges of the stomach. "Look!" he added, pointing to some distance along the coast, "yonder must be the mouth of the little river which divides the island from the mainland."

Accordingly the boy Bob was aroused, and the three set off along the coast in the direction of Goa. Scarcely, however, had they proceeded a mile than they descried a man approaching.

"Heaven is indeed bountiful;" exclaimed Phaulcon, "if we can only make this fellow understand our language, he will lead us to some inhabited house, or at least a stream or well at which we may refresh ourselves."

"Truly we *are* fortunate," answered Blake, but then, as they approached nearer to the stranger, he added, in a tone of disappointment, "Faith, my friend, here is one whom *even we* may pity, for he is worse off than ourselves;" and the remark was justified by the appearance of the new comer, for although stout, and rather tall for an Asiatic, his faltering steps, scanty dress, dripping with wet, and scared features betokened him to be one who had recently suffered some misfortune.

"You are right, Blake," replied Phaulcon, "he is some poor shipwrecked wretch; but look you, he is from Siam," he added, pointing to the distinguishing tuft upon the stranger's head, "we shall at least have a companion to whom we may talk of our troubles;" and as they were now within a yard of each other Phaulcon would have addressed him; but the Siamese, as if in doubt as to whether the three Europeans might be friends or enemies, anticipated him by falling upon his knees after the abject manner of his race when in the presence of those whom they know to be, or their fears compel them to recognise as superior, and in tones which bespoke his utter hopelessness of their being able to understand him said,

"Let the noble strangers vouchsafe to take pity upon a wretch whose misfortune it is to have fallen under the displeasure of the sea-goddess."

"My elder brother," replied Phaulcon, adopting the colloquial style of the Siamese, "must not demean himself by falling at the feet of his servants; let him arise, for like himself we have also fallen beneath the displeasure of the sea-goddess, and thus are friends and companions in misfortune."

The effect upon the Siamese of these words, in his own language, it is scarcely possible to describe. A shipwrecked stranger upon a foreign shore, suddenly meeting with white men, and mistaking them for Portuguese, the terror of all orientals, he, even hopeless that they would understand his language, had fallen at their feet abjectly to beg his life, or that he might not be carried into slavery. But when Phaulcon replied in his mother-tongue, offering both friendship, and sympathy, for a few seconds he gazed in wild astonishment and delight, clasped his knees, and wept.

Then, when raising him from his kneeling position, Phaulcon asked the cause of his being in such a sad plight, he replied, that his name was Prenawi Consitt, a Mandarin of Siam, and that many months before he had been sent by his sovereign as ambassador to Solomon, the then reigning shah of Persia; having successfully performed his mission, and being on his return homewards, his ship had struck upon a rock during the night, and all hands, as far as he knew, but himself, had perished.

"Truly," he concluded, "heaven hath visited the unhappy Prenawi with a misfortune, great as doubtlessly it was deserved, yet 'out of evil cometh good'; for, although cast away and dashed senseless upon these shores, thy servant hath awakened to find himself at the feet of generous strangers, who have suffered like himself, and speak his language."

"The words of my elder brother," replied Phaulcon, "are good, he *has* fallen in with friends, who can sympathize with his misfortunes. We," he added, "are now on our way to the Portuguese city of Goa, which cannot be many miles distant."

"Alas, that I dare not accompany you, for who without power, wealth, and not a worshipper of the God of the Christians, would venture within the city of the terrible Portuguese," replied Prenawi, who had heard of the dreadful Inquisition, and the cruelties of the Portuguese towards all natives of the East, not professing Christianity.

"Fear not, noble Prenawi," replied Phaulcon, smiling at the terror of the Siamese at the very name of Goa, "you *shall* accompany us; for if thou art a heathen and in poverty, we are Christians, and have wealth, at least sufficient for our purpose, that of purchasing a ship which may carry us all back to Siam."

This seeming to sooth Prenawi, he replied :—

"It shall be as my elder brother desires, and may heaven vouchsafe us a safe voyage to Siam, that thy servant, who possesses both wealth and power in his native land, may show his gratitude."

"The exercise of his gratitude is a pleasure in store for the Lord Prenawi," replied Phaulcon; "In the mean time, it will be my luxury that, in the midst of misfortunes, it is yet in my power to assist one more distressed than myself."

It then being agreed, that for Prenawi's greater safety he should, if questioned, announce himself as the slave of the Christians, they all proceeded on their way to the Portuguese city. After two days and two nights, during which they slept in caverns or woods, and lived upon fruits, they reached Salsette, a town directly opposite the island of Goa. At this place, by representing themselves to be shipwrecked mariners who were desirous to reach the opposite city, wherein they expected to meet with friends, they were charitably entertained for one night.

The next morning they set forth in a barge, accompanied by one of the officers of the town of Salsette, a person however who was well nigh the cause of their career being brought to a premature termination ; for, upon their arrival in the city, he led them at once before one of the viceroy's deputies, charging them with the terrible crimes of being unknown wanderers and heretics ; whereupon, they would have been there and then cast into a dungeon, from thence, in all probability to be taken to the Inquisition, but that Phaulcon mentioned the names of several great Portuguese merchants who had traded with him in Siam. These gentlemen being sent for, and recognising both Blake and his friend, they were released. More—one of the merchants learning from Phaulcon that he had bills for two thousand crowns upon a merchant at the chief Indo-English station, offered to negotiate them, and, while they should be tarrying until they had purchased and equipped a ship, to lodge them at his own house.

Although Phaulcon had been fortunate in changing his bills into money on the first or second day of his arrival, and still more so in purchasing a small barque, they were detained for a month while she was being prepared for sea. During their stay took place some of the most important and solemn festivals and pro-cessions of the Romish Church, and these religious displays well nigh caused an estrangement between the two friends ; for in the hearts of both were aroused long dormant feelings, equally wrong, perhaps. They regarded these pageants from totally opposite points of view. The Puritan Englishman with the contempt, almost hatred, taught in *his* childhood for the ancient Church, with sneering look and cynical words. Upon the other hand, the

Greek, having from boyhood been associated with wild, reckless seamen, who, if of any religion, belonged to the reformed Church, saw in these solemnities, and outward grandeur, that which reminded him that for so many years his soul had been bent upon the things of this world alone, and reproached him with forgetting the teaching of his childhood. Perhaps he thought of the hopes and wishes, and plans meditated and talked of by the Father Thomas, and of the holy desire of Monica that the cross of Christ should be raised in every city, the banner of the Church be hoisted upon every tower, and the faith planted in every heart of the far East.

The two friends were standing in the verandah of their house as a great procession of the priesthood was passing. Blake had watched Phaulcon remove the covering from his head, and how reverentially he bent his body. Moreover, he more than suspected that ancient memories had been recalled; nay, that every superstitious feeling in his friend's nature had become excited. Taking him by the arm, he exclaimed, petulantly—

"Bah! let's away from this mummery; these jewels of paste, and spurious imitations of the precious metal. It is sickening—it palls upon one's senses."

"Blake," exclaimed Phaulcon, starting from his reverie, "you speak irreverently of holy matters." Then, as if fearful that his friend's speech might be heard by the passers-by, he added, "For heaven's sake let not these monks catch thy words. In Goa, less have cost people their lives."

"Yet," persisted Blake, "it is of these cruel, blood-stained priests you would have *me* speak *reverently*."

"Hush! ministers of God, whatever garb they wear, or creed they profess," whispered Phaulcon, "should be treated reverently. And if," he added, "the Fathers of Goa, like wise parents who chastise their children for their own good, have been severe, it has been as a means to an end. Aye," he continued enthusiastically, "an end that would be purchased cheaply at the cost of a million of heathen lives—the upraising of the cross in every city of the East."

"Phaulcon," exclaimed Blake, startled at the warmth and fervour of his friend, "beware; there is a change coming over you that bodes no good; the scarlet woman of Rome is engaging thy senses by her glitter, show, and mummery."

"By glitter, show—tinsel and gaud, if you will—ceremony, and mysterious symbols, the hearts and brains of men have been ruled from all time. By such means, and the example of their own ascetic lives, shall these holy men gather beneath the banner of Christ the vast millions of the East."

"And," said Blake, bitterly, "the sceptres of Indian kings like those *gathered* in Mexico and Peru. Phaulcon, it is the *lands*, with their teeming wealth, and the *store chambers* of the sovereigns that are coveted, rather than the conversion of the people. When did a European leader let human lives obstruct his path to plunder. No, like the followers of Mahomet, but with less honesty, because with less regard for conversion than wealth, these Portuguese have marched through strange lands, sword in one hand, Bible in the other, sacrificing their thousands beneath the shadow of the holy book, nominally in its name and by its sanction; but with their greedy eyes ever fixed upon the lands and treasures of their victims. No, my friend, the great and holy work will never be performed by these men of Portugal; for every land trodden by them did they sow with blood and water, with the tears of its people, and now are they reaping bitter hatred. Already is

their power passing into other hands. These people, who
boasted an empire extending along twelve thousand miles
of coast, from the Cape of Good Hope to the frontier of
China, who conquered and possessed kingdoms in Africa, Arabia,
Persia, and even the Spice Islands ;—where, for the greater part,
are their possessions now? And in this mournful city of Goa, where
have the seeds of Christianity, sown as they were in bloodshed,
sprouted in aught but hatred and contempt? From Japan, where
the soil was most promising, they have been uprooted. In China,
as they gave forth promise, they were extirpated."

"True," replied Phaulcon, thoughtfully ; "as the jackal for the
lion, so have they seized commerce and dominion in the East, to be
snatched from them by the Dutch—those vile Hollanders, who
purchased their slavish position in Japan, by aiding the heathen
to massacre their fellow Europeans, and retain it by the cowardly
and blasphemous tenure of annually trampling beneath their feet
the image of the Redeemer."

"Aye," said Blake, "these Dutch I love not, they are either
tyrants over the weak or sycophants to the strong, and ever bringing the very name of European into contempt among the Asiatics ;
but their punishment is at hand ; they in turn will prove but
jackals for the lion of England, who, even now, is scenting the
prey and biding his opportunity to take it from them. But these
Portuguese"—

"Enough of them," interposed Phaulcon, almost angrily ; "give
honour where honour is due; the Portuguese have been the pioneers
of European civilization and Christianity in the East ; and, which-
ever of the Western nations may snatch the ripening fruit, theirs
were the toil, dangers, sufferings, and therefore glory, of clearing
the orchard."

Astonished at his own enthusiasm, perhaps, one-sidedness, and still fearing to cause ill-blood between them, Blake adroitly changed the subject of the conversation to the manning and provisioning of the barque, and the two friends there and then proceeded together down to the harbour, where she was laying at anchor. As, however, the doings of the Portuguese in Goa teem with interest, I may be pardoned if I step aside from my narrative to repeat a few anecdotes illustrative of the means by which this nation sought to convert the natives.

"The main and most glorious object of conquest in the East," cried the monarchs of Spain and Portugal, "is not commerce, the gain of wealth, but the conversion of the heathen."

Hence, as soon as it became known at home that any country had been conquered, large bodies of priest-missionaries were at once despatched, to cure souls, by fair means, if possible, if not, by removing them from their bodies. So, when the news came to Portugal that Albuquerque had taken Goa from one of the Mahomedan sovereigns of Malabar, a host of missionaries departed for the henceforth capital of the Portuguese possessions in India.

The enthusiastic priests had scarcely calculated upon the difficulties in their way, for upon their arrival they found that the people were about equally in the hands of two different classes of Brahmins. One of these lived in the cities, mixed with the inhabitants, and possessed so much influence over their minds, that no undertaking of any importance was commenced, by prince or subject, until the Brahmins had first consulted their demons. The other class were hermits, who existed by begging, and lived in deserts and caves, or in the tops of trees. Then the pride and insolence of the Nairs, or soldier class, who would not look at, or speak to any of the inferior rank, was utterly incompatible with Christian humility. Finally came that *bête noire* of the Jesuits, the great similarity between the forms of the heathen worship and those of their own. Nay, so terribly like were these forms, that young missionaries, or those new to the office, declared themselves unable to perceive any difference.

To obtain something like a counter-influence, the priests had recourse to cunning. First, as quack-doctors, they issued through the people little cheques, pieces of paper upon which were written certain sentences that they assured their patients were cures for all diseases. In this practice, however unworthy of Christian ministers, it must be admitted they exhibited a shrewd knowledge of human nature, for the Orient is not by any means the only part of the world where Catholicons are snapped at with greediness. Then again they set up as magicians, or at least conjurors, pretending that they could discover any article that was lost. They even claimed the *merit* of recovering two holy cows lost by a Gentoo king, and Christian priests as they were, of restoring them for the purpose of idolatrous worship. Bad indeed must have been their visible chances of success ; still, any means were admissible if they could but attain their end.

Knowing the love of all Orientals for glitter and imposing effect, they next erected an image of the Virgin, set with gold and jewels, and this promised a great result ; for one day, a hermit, at least eighty years old, but so black and sunburnt that he appeared scarcely human, came in from the woods, and being shown the image, was so stricken with delight, that he fell at its feet soliciting instant admission within the pale of the Church.

The example of so holy and venerated a man was followed by numbers ; and now, in order to allure as many as possible into baptism, that they might send home glowing accounts of the

number of their converts, they prepared to perform the ceremony
with all possible pomp. The church was adorned with rich cloth,
flowers and branches of trees ; every priest and candidate bringing
from his house or garden whatever could serve to adorn it, while to
heighten the solemnity, it was performed upon a great number
at once.

By these means *some* way was made, but the result was very
discouraging. For so deep-rooted in the minds of the majority of the
people, was the influence and teaching of the Brahmins, that the
moment a man became a Christian he was excluded from all civil
privileges, and from all the charities and relations of social life.
His parents and nearest connexions would neither see nor speak
to him, nor give a cup of cold water to save him from perishing.
A boy of twelve years having been converted, his mother took him
out into the fields, where she contrived to *bury him alive*, covering
him up in such a manner as to make it impossible to rise.
Fortunately, some Portuguese happening to pass immediately after,
heard his cries, dug him out, and carried him back to Goa.

After the hermit, their next great sensation was the conversion
of a young princess, only daughter to the King of Goa. This
success was triumphantly announced to the Portuguese Governor,
who, however, instead of receiving it with the expected joy, like
a wise man, was a great deal perplexed by the intelligence, being
much afraid that it would involve him in an open rupture with
the royal family. He judged it prudent, therefore, to communicate
to her parents the tidings of her conversion. Never was there
such a scene of horror and dismay as followed this communication. The queen instantly raised a shriek, which echoed to
the remotest extremities of the palace ; and all her women
crowding to inquire the cause, the royal mansion became one

scene of tears and lamentations. The subject of this woe being sent for was implored in the most pathetic terms to renounce her fatal design, her parents declaring, that though she was their only hope and delight, they would a thousand times rather see her lying dead at their feet. The young lady, however, remained immovable in her purpose, and apprehensive of force, took to flight, and ran full speed to the Portuguese church, where she was received, and lodged in the house of a lady of distinction.

Doubtful as had been their success in Goa, the missionaries cast longing eyes upon Salsette, a large and populous island in the vicinity, which was considered by them to be the main stronghold of idolatry. Being governed by Brahmins it presented a still more unbroken front of resistance than any other. Here, too, their only gleam of success was among the young ladies. The daughter of one of the ruling Brahmins ran off from her parents and joined their communion. The distracted father raised an action against the missionaries in the civil courts, insisting that she had been impelled to this step only by the most nefarious means of deceit and intimidation, but the cause being tried before Portuguese judges, judgment was, of course, given against the parents.

This decision, however, so increased the odium against the fathers, that even all respect for their cloth was set aside; so that a certain priest refusing to pay the customary dues at passing a ferry, the people fell upon him, and gave him a beating. This personal chastisement of one of their order so raised the indignation of the whole body, that they represented to the government the absolute necessity of some strong measures, which might either incline the Salsettines to receive the faith, or at least, might punish them well for rejecting it. At their urgent request an armament was suddenly equipped and landed at Salsette with such expedition, that it carried the city, destroying 1,200 temples with all their images.

The Christians, it is said, now lifted up their heads and counted a greater number of converts. They were soon astonished, however, to find themselves regarded with the most rooted and deadly hatred, and the Salsettines become the warm allies of every power that raised its standard against the Portuguese. In the course of some wars in which that nation was involved with the neighbouring states, they took repeated occasions to rebuild their own temples and raze to the ground those of the Catholics. The missionaries, finding that the mild measures hitherto pursued had failed of success, now called loudly for something on a greater scale, and to be conducted in a more sweeping manner.

Their entreaties at length prevailed ; a new expedition was fitted out which landed as before, and not only destroyed the temples, but by setting fire to the cities and villages, in a few hours reduced the whole island to ashes. The affrighted inhabitants fled almost naked from their houses, and sought shelter on the shore of the neighbouring continent ; and this fair scene of culture and crowded population was converted at once into a smoking desert.

The dismayed and humbled people sent to implore peace and permission to rebuild their ruined habitations, which was granted, on condition that they should not erect along with them any edifice destined to an idolatrous purpose. They returned ; and Salsette began gradually to resume its former aspect. To their surprise, however, the missionaries found themselves regarded with increasing execration by the natives, and scarcely less so by their lay fellow-countrymen, who imputed to them the recent disaster. They complained bitterly, that all the blame should be imputed

to them; yet admitted that the governors would infallibly have
adopted lenient measures, but for their earnest and constant
exhortations. At last, however, news arrived from Spain, that
their deeds, misrepresented they said, had 'struck with horror
even Philip II. and the Spanish Inquisition ; and that an order
was coming out to allow the Indians the free exercise of their
religion. But *happily*, to use the word of one of their priests, a
Father Pacheco, happening to be on a mission to Europe, persuaded
the king to modify this order, and to leave it to the discretion of
the governor to follow the course which circumstances might dictate.

The fathers then persuaded the Portuguese ruler that there was
no occasion to make any change in the present system ; under
which Salsette was maintained in a state of perfect tranquillity.
In fact, the Salsettines no longer exhibited the same daring and
rebellious front; their manners were become mild and submissive,
and they showed to the missionaries all that respectful courtesy
of which they were ambitious. The priests were therefore convinced, that their *gentle* behaviour had at length produced fully
its natural effect, and they determined to *reward the docility* of
the people by founding at their capital a splendid church, which
might at once dazzle their eyes, and remove all remaining obstacles
to conversion.

Five heads of the mission therefore set out for the town, and
having repaired to the appointed spot, began making preparations
for the ceremony. While they were thus busied, a Brahmin sprung
out into the street, and called aloud to the people, that the
time was come to avenge their gods. Small and great flew to
arms. They began with blocking up all passes by which the
missionaries had come, or could return. While the fathers then
were wondering at the delay of the inhabitants in coming to pay

them the usual compliments, they heard, echoing on all sides the cries of "Kill! kill!" They saw at once that resistance was vain, and laid open their breasts for the blow. Instantly a thousand darts were in the hearts of the unfortunate victims; the earth streamed with their blood, and the infuriate Indians heaped on the lifeless bodies all the indignities which they had so often seen inflicted by the Jesuits on the prostrate native deities. Pacheco alone was reserved for some extraordinary punishment, and being set up as a mark, was covered with arrows, till he no longer retained any trace of the human form.

Vengeance being at length satiated, the Indians seem to have stood aghast at their own audacity, and allowed, without resistance, the mangled remains of their victims to be carried away and interred. When the news of the dreadful tragedy arrived at Goa, the assembled friars were affected first with grief, and then professedly with joy, on account of the glorious martyrdom of their brethren. This did not prevent them from joining in a loud cry for vengeance; but the viceroy was a prudent man, and seeing from this fearful example, the state of desperation to which the minds of the natives were worked up, positively refused to commit his conduct any longer to such guidance. He merely abridged the guilty town of some trifling privileges, and withdrew all further restraint on the religion of the people. It is said, that after this time more conversions were effected than before. These were probably owing to this very toleration, though the fathers attribute them to the soil being watered by the blood of their martyred brethren.

To resume my story.

The barque being ready for sea, Phaulcon, Blake, Bob, and the Siamese noble embarked; and as Père d'Orleans, who seems to have regarded the money's worth for the two thousand crowns as nothing, quaintly remarks, "Now that they had no longer anything to lose they reached Ayuthia without any unlucky contretemps."

Ayuthia, called by the Siamese, "Terrestrial Paradise," and, for its numerous canals and the grandeur of its public buildings, by Europeans the Oriental Venice, is now in ruins, having been destroyed by the Burmans in 1751. The present capital is Bangkok, a great city, constructed after a similar model, about thirty miles up the river Meinam. Describing the old metropolis, Mandelsloe, the traveller, writes :—

"It is built upon an island in the river Meinam, and is the ordinary residence of the King of Siam ; having several very fair streets with spacious channels regularly cut. The suburbs, which are on both sides the river, like the town itself, are adorned with many temples and palaces. Of the first of these there are about three hundred within the city, distinguished by their gilt steeples or pyramids, and afford a glorious prospect at a distance."

Two hundred years ago, Ayuthia presented a busy bustling scene, and was a mart of great importance for ships of all nations. Chinese, Malabars, Malays, Persians, Parsees, English, Dutch, Portuguese, and French, were to be found upon its waters, while in the city most of these people had their factories, wherein they resided and carried on their traffic.

As, however, in manners, customs, and all that concerns my narrative, the Siamese, as elsewhere in the unchangeable far East of that age, were the same as those of their descendants of the present day, Sir John Bowring's graphic description of life upon the Meinam, will afford an admirable illustration of the people among whom Phaulcon earned a page in history.

"The Meinam is skirted on the two sides with forest trees, many of which are of a green so bright as to defy the powers of art to copy. Some are hung with magnificent and fragrant flowers; upon others are suspended a variety of tropical fruits. Gay birds, in multitudes, are seen on the branches, in repose, or winging their active way from one place to another. The very sandbanks are full of life, and a sort of amphibious fish are flitting from the water to be lost among the roots of the jungle-wood. On the stream all varieties of vessels are moving up and down, some charged with leaves of the *atap palm*, which at-once adorn and cause them to be wafted by the wind along the water. A few huts of bamboo, with leaved roofs, are seen; and in the neighbouring creeks, the small boats of the inhabitants are moored. Here and there is a floating house, with Chinese inscriptions on scarlet, or other gay-coloured paper; and, at greater distances from one another, are temples, adjacent to the river, whose priestly occupants, always clad in yellow garments, their heads shaven bare, and holding a palm-leaf fan between their faces and the sun, sit in listless and unconcerned vacancy, or affected meditation, upon the rafts or railings which skirt the shore.

"But the houses thicken as you proceed, the boats increase in number, the noise of human voices becomes louder, and, one after another, pyramidical temples, domes, and palaces, are seen towering above the gardens and forests. Over the perpetual verdure, so emerald-bright, roofs of many-coloured adornings sparkle in the sun. Sometimes white walls are visible, through whose embrasures artillery is peeping; multitudes of junks grotesquely and gaily painted, whose gaudy flags are floating in the breezes; each junk with the two great eyes, which are never wanting, in the prow; ('No have eyes, how can see?' say the Chinese;) square-rigged

N 2

vessels, most of which carry the scarlet flag with the white elephant in the centre; while, on both sides of the river, a line of floating bazaars, crowded with men, women, and children, and houses built on piles along the banks, present all the objects of consumption and commerce. Meanwhile, multitudes of ambulatory boats are engaged in traffic with the various groups around. If it be morning, vast numbers of priests will be seen in their skiffs on the Meinam, with their iron pot and scrip, levying their contributions of food from the well-known devotees, who never fail to provide a supply for the multitudinous mendicants (if mendicants they can be called), whose code alike prohibits them from supplicating for alms, and from returning thanks when those alms are given.

"Seldom is music wanting to add to the interest of the scene. The opulent Siamese have invariably bands of musicians in their service; the gongs of the Chinese, the sweet pipes of the Laos, the stringed and wind instruments of the native population, seem never still.

"The city of Bangkok extends along the banks of the Meinam a distance of several miles. The greater proportion of the population is on the left side of the river. The limits of the city are marked by a semicircle of the Meinam on the western side, and by a canal on the eastern, whose two extremities joining the river make the city almost circular. There is an inner island, formed by another canal, also joining the Meinam. There are two other canals, viz., one from north to south, and another from east to west, crossing the city at right lines, besides auxiliary canals on both sides the river. The highways of Bangkok are not streets, or roads, but the river and the canals. Boats are the universal means of conveyance and communication. Except about the palaces of the kings, horses or carriages are rarely seen, and the sedan of the Chinese appears unknown in Siam; but a boat is a necessary part of every person's household; to its dexterous management every child is trained—women and men are equally accustomed to the use of the oar, the paddle, and the rudder. From the most miserable skiff which seems scarcely large enough to hold a dog, up to the magnificently adorned barges which are honoured with the presence of royalty—from the shabbiest canoe hewn out of the small trunk of a tree from the jungle, up to the roofed and curtained, the carved and gilded, barques of the nobles— every rank and condition has its boats plying in endless activity, night and day, on the surface of the Meinam waters.

"A great proportion of the houses float on large rafters, and are sometimes seen moving up and down the river conveying all the belongings of a family to some newly selected locality. It is a curious sight to witness these locomotive abodes, sometimes consisting of many apartments, loosened from the cables which have attached them to a particular spot, and going forth on their travels to fresh destinations. On the borders of the river there are scarcely any but floating houses, which can at any time be detached and removed bodily, and without any inconvenience, at the will of the owner.

"There are a few houses built of stone and brick; but those of the middle classes are of wood, while the dwellings of the poor are constructed of light bamboos, and roofed with leaves of the atap palm.

"Fires are frequent; and from the combustible character of the erections, hundreds of habitations are often destroyed, but in a few days the mischief is generally repaired, for on such occasions friends and neighbours lend a willing hand.

"A house generally consists of two divisions ; one occupied by the males, the other by the females. The piles on which they are built are sunk three or four feet into the ground, and the floor is raised six or eight feet from its surface, and is reached by a rude ladder, which, if the front of the house be towards the river, is made accessible at low tide. Of the floating houses, some are of boards, others of bamboo, or either wicker-work or palm-leaves. These houses have generally a verandah in front, and a small wing at each end. When used for shops or ware-houses the whole frontage is removed, and the contents exposed for inspection to the boats which pass by on the river.

"The existence of the people may be called amphibious ; the children pass much of their time in the water, paddling, diving, and swimming, as if it were their native element. Boats often run against one another, and those within them are submerged in the water ; but it seldom happens that any life is lost, or mischief done to the persons whose boats are run down. I have again and again seen boats bottom upward, whose owners have floated them to the shore, or otherwise repaired the damage done, as speedily as possible. The constant occurrence of petty disasters seems to reconcile everybody to their consequences.

"The gilded barges are among the gayest objects which float upon the Meinam waters. They are some of them one hundred and twenty feet long, scooped out of the trunk of a single tree. The prow, rising high aloft, represents the head of a serpent, a dragon, a fish, a deity, a monster, or any fantastic object. The poop, which is also elevated high above the water, is like the tail of a bird or fish, but generally ends in a wavy point.

"The concussions of boats, and the knocking of their rowers and crews into the water, are of constant occurrence, and seldom produce any expressions of irritation. I have seen cargoes swamped and destroyed, and the calamity has been submitted to without any vituperation of its cause. Generally speaking, the boats are paddled about with consummate dexterity, the practice being acquired from the earliest trainings of childhood.

"The tides rise from six to seven feet at Bangkok, in October, November, and December; they overflow almost all the ground on which the city is built. In April, May, and June, many of the canals are dry during several hours of the day, when communication is interrupted. These canals, which are multitudinous, are the principal means of intercourse. Much inconvenience is experienced by the inhabitants, from the want of highways or paths, for with the exception of some principal streets within the walls, and a smaller number without, the land passages are scarcely passable, and frequently will not allow two persons to walk abreast.

"The streets are crowded with persons in chains, men and women, in larger or smaller groups, attended by an officer of police bearing a large staff or stick, as the emblem of authority. The weight of the chains is apportioned to the magnitude of the offence for which the bearer is suffering. I understood a large portion of these prisoners to be debtors. If a person cannot pay what he owes his body is delivered over to his creditors, at whose absolute disposal his services are placed. There is no redemption but by the act of the creditor, or the payment of the debt; friends and relatives often interfere for its discharge. The legal rate of interest being thirty per cent. it may well be conceived how rapidly ruin will overtake an unfortunate debtor. An individual, or family, may be released from servitude by any party who is willing to discharge the original debt and accept the services of the debtor.

The value of a slave is about 100 ticals (£12 10s. sterling). If the slave can find security, his personal liberty is less restrained.

"Pallegoix gives the following contract for the sale of a slave :— 'Wednesday, the sixth month, the twenty-sixth day of the moon of the era 1,211, the first year of the cock, I, *Mi*, the husband, and I, *Kot*, the wife, bring our daughter *Ma*, to be sold to *Lúang Si* for eighty ticals, or to be taken into his service in lieu of interest. If our daughter *Ma* should take flight, let me be seized, and be required to restore her. I, *Mi*, have placed my signature in witness.'

"To complete this picture let me add, that the public prisons are suspended over the water like bird-cages, and the inmates, who exist only by the charity of passers by, are compelled to hop from side to side, as the shade shifts—that it is by no means uncommon to find the bodies of human beings, floating upon the surface of the river, regardless of respect for the dead or the health of the living—that among vendible articles men do not hesitate to expose their own daughters for sale, stipulating only, that should the purchaser quit the city, he must restore the girl, together with another sum equivalent to the original purchase-money, to her affectionate father. No man, except he be in a state of absolute poverty, is to be met without his betel box, and the black teeth and blood-red saliva issuing from his mouth, the consequence of the continual use of that mixture; nor the smallest boy without a cigar between his lips, or in the hole perforated in the lobe of his ear, for its reception. Lastly, gambling and cock-fighting are passions; and the debasing enervating vice of opium smoking is common among all classes, high and low."

185

## CHAPTER XI.

A GOOD ACTION BRINGS ITS OWN REWARD.

"RETURN from whence thou camest; hesitate not an instant, my son, for 'tis in Siam that thy fortunes will be built, thy future developed."

Acting upon these words which had sunk deeply into his mind, Phaulcon found himself once more lodged at the English Factory upon the banks of the Meinam. His notions, however, as to the means by which he was to arrive at the promised future, were vague in the extreme. True, the European residents, sympathising with his last great loss, had given him a very warm welcome, and sought to repair it by raising among themselves a subscription; but this the proud Greek had politely declined, declaring to Blake, that he would owe everything to his own hands and brain—nothing to charity.

"All I possess," said he one day to his friend, "is my little barque, but then it will sell for at least one thousand crowns."

"By which you will lose one-half its value," replied Blake. "No, no!" he added, "this must not be; swallow your pride and desire of independent action. Let us become partners; you can find the ship, I will find cargo, and so together let us make a venture to the Dutch ports in the Java sea. What say you?"

"That I have two objections, Blake. One, that it will delay your return to England ; the other, that as I believe the fates have appointed Siam for the working out of my destiny, it would be madness to again trust to the sea."

"Poh, poh!" exclaimed Blake, "Let not your superstitious credence in that dream-gentleman's prophecy stand in your way ; as for the first objection, that concerneth me alone ;" and after much persuasion of this kind, Phaulcon consented to grasp the substantial present, leaving the shadowy future to care for itself.

This resolution being agreed to, the friends set to work with such good will, that in a few days the little barque was again nearly ready for sea. The evening, however, before the day of their intended departure, as the two young men were standing upon the river's bank, watching the shipment of the last bale of merchandize, a slave, whose portly appearance and gay colours bespoke him to belong to the household of some mandarin, came up to Phaulcon, and falling before him, said—

"Thy mean servant is the slave of the great Lord Prenawi, who trembling to think that the preservers of his life may be even now charging him with base ingratitude, hath sent him to beg of the noble Farangs to visit his lordship's poor house to-morrow." "Should," he added, "the noble Farangs be pleased to comply, the Lord Prenawi will send a state barge to convey them to his presence."

"We have arranged to sail to-morrow ; delays are dangerous," said Blake, vexed at the chance of a postponement of their departure.

"Sometimes, they may be propitious," replied Phaulcon, adding, "at all events we cannot refuse, it would be churlish."

"Well, well, as you will," replied Blake. "Phaulcon, my friend, like a drowning man catching at a straw, you seize upon this invitation; but then," he added, with an ironical smile, "who knows, perhaps your shadowy friend the dream-gentleman is at the bottom of this delay.'

"Who knows, indeed?" replied Phaulcon, quite seriously; then turning to the slave, he dismissed him with a reply to the noble Prenawi's invitation; so long, so tedious, and so formal, that I can only chronicle its pith—"Yes."

The next day the state barge, with its gilded dragon-shaped prow and twenty boatmen, made its appearance, and the two friends were rowed to Prenawi's residence, a large hand-some building on the banks of the river, at a distance of about three miles from the European factories.

Being ushered into a spacious and lofty hall they found Prenawi sitting in a very ugly statuesque position; that is, upon a kind of wooden pillar about twenty-four inches square, and three feet in height, with his legs bent under him, and supporting his body with his left arm, the elbow of which was bent inward. This unnatural protrusion of the left arm is considered by the Siamese to be a mark of the highest gentility; to perfect themselves in which, the children of the nobility are practised from their earliest childhood; even as the gentry of Japan are trained to the skilful performance of the Hara-kiri, or ripping up of their own bowels; so that should misfortune ever bring them within the ban of the law, they may honourably evade its punishment, and thereby secure to their families their fortunes, which would otherwise be forfeited to the state. But the Siamese have for their ugly and painful fashion neither the excuse of, the people of Japan, nor one even so good as that of the Chinese for the crushing of their women's feet, viz. to keep them at home. Worse, however, by far than this bending the elbow inward, is the slavish humility of any Siamese in the presence of a superior.

At the time of Phaulcon and Blake's visit, several persons of but a shade lower rank than Prenawi, honoured with an audience for the transaction of some business, were prostrate on the floor before him. When addressed by the magnate, they did not dare to cast their eyes towards him; but raising the head a little, and touching the forehead with both hands united, their eyes still fixed upon the ground, they whispered their answers in the most humiliating tones. But sad, degrading to humanity as is such grovelling in the dust before one's fellow man, the Siamese find some consolation in the universality of the custom— the next hour Prenawi's visitors would probably be receiving similar adulation from a grade lower than themselves; while the present exalted mandarin might be crawling at the feet of some personage a grade higher. Of this slavish custom, as it exists at the present, a late governor of Hong-kong* says :— "The humiliation of one order or rank of men to another, from step to step, is the object which first excited the marvel of the traveller. To me who have been accustomed to witness the subjection of the multitude before high office and dignity in China, the scenes in Bangkok were almost incredible. Every grade is in a state of humble submission to that above it, till, culminated in the person and presence of the sovereign, all the concentrated reverence takes the character of uni-versal adoration, and announces less a mortal raised above his fellow mortals, than a god in the presence of trembling, abject men."

Is it to be wondered that of such a slavish people, one of their kings, who is accounted among the wisest of Siamese

* Sir John Bowring.

sovereigns, said to the French ambassador, that his subjects had
the temper of asses, who trembled so long as one holds the end
of their chain, and who disown their master when the hand is
loosed. But to return to the two friends.

The audience being concluded, their arrival was formally
announced to Prenawi, who at the intelligence forgetting his
dignity, jumped off his pedestal, and with many words of welcome
shook them, English fashion, by the hands.   He then led them
to another apartment, upon the floor of which were placed three
small carpets, all upon the same level, a complimentary signification
that he acknowledged his visitors as of equal rank with himself.
Not content with this, the grateful mandarin also offered Phaulcon
the piece upon the left-hand side, which, opposed to the custom
of China, is considered by the Siamese to be the place of honour.

The trio being seated, the host gave a sign to one of the slaves,
and a few minutes afterwards several servants entered with
refreshments ; that is, they crawled forward upon all fours,
supported on the elbow and toes, the body being dragged upon
the ground.   In this manner they pushed the dishes before
them, from time to time, in the best manner their very awkward
and painful position would permit, until they had succeeded
in placing them near their master ; after which, without turning,
they crawled backwards again.

The meal, for meal it really was, consisting of fish, rice, and
nam-phrik, a sauce made of bruised pepper, garlic, onions, brine,
citron juice, ginger, tamarind, and ground seeds, having been
taken in solemn silence, the dishes and the mother-o'-pearl
spoons * were removed, and tea and tobacco brought upon the
table, i. e. the floor.   It was now that the Mandarin expressed

* Among the Siamese these spoons serve for knives and forks. ]

his gratitude to the young men in the most extravagant language, concluding his speech by saying :—

"But surely thy servant would be the meanest of small beasts could he not show his gratitude otherwise than by words ; yes, the man who has been saved to return to his king, and his family, hath prepared for his noble preservers presents that monarchs might envy, and which will lengthen their lives by causing them to pass in comfort and happiness."

As Prenawi concluded, there fell upon the ears of Blake and Phaulcon sounds of tittering and whispering in low tones at one end of the room. These arresting the attention of the guests, they observed that that which they had believed to be the end wall of the apartment, was simply a perforated screened partition, curtained upon the other side.

"The noble Farangs," said Prenawi, "are vexed that the eyes f the women of the house have been resting upon them. But my brothers may pardon them, for truly these wives, daughters, and slaves of thy servant would have been less than the least of little beasts, had they not longed to gaze admiringly upon the preservers of their lord."

"A confounded nuisance to have been stared at like a couple of strange beasts by a parcel of women," *thought* Blake.

"We should be less than dogs not to feel flattered at such a mark of attention from the beauties of the Lord Prenawi's household," *said* Phaulcon.

"Of their beauty and accomplishments my brothers shall judge for themselves," replied the host, at the same time he made a sign to a slave who lay near the door.

"Hang me if he isn't about to let these she-creatures loose upon us," exclaimed Blake, in English, with quite a scared look.

"Never mind; take courage my friend," replied Phaulcon, laughing, "our suffering will not last long; but look," and as he spoke, the before-mentioned perforated partition opened in the centre, disclosing to the view several groups of diminutive, but dark-skinned and prostrate beauties of Laos.*

At a signal from Prenawi, they one and all arose, as gracefully as water nymphs from out their native element amidst the swelling sounds of the Laos organ, an instrument of peculiarly sweet tones, and arranged themselves for the dance. Their black hair contrasting with ornaments of white fragrant flowers, gave a zest to the meek and modest eyes, while at every movement their flowing scarfs and petticoats of silken tissue added additional grace to their symmetrical forms. But one action destroyed the *tout ensemble*, and that was the very perfection with which they would every now and then practice that most difficult and ugly act of protruding the elbow forward.

"Very graceful and charming," said Blake, as the sylph-like forms of the girls passed through a kind of minuet; "but," he added, "these wonderful presents, when will they be forthcoming, for, I confess, my curiosity is aroused."

"At the end of this entertainment, doubtless," returned Phaulcon. "But, Blake," he added, "thou art a Goth to think of aught but the grace and beauty before us."

"May be, may be," replied Blake; "but then I prefer the country dances of Old England."

"Aye," replied his friend with a smile, "and one fair, blue-eyed, golden-haired maid, to a dozen of these meek-eyed daughters of Laos."

---

* From Laos, a kingdom tributary to Siam, the nobles of the latter country chiefly choose their wives.

"Bah ! my countrywomen would not feel flattered even at the suggestion of such a choice. But the presents, these presents, my friend, canst guess what they will be like."

"Tut, tut, this impatience is childish, still it will soon be satisfied, for now comes the close of the entertainment," replied Phaulcon, as at another signal from the host the girls discontinued their dancing.

Then four of the maidens, of greater beauty, and more richly robed than the others, with their eyes, nay their bodies, nearly bent to the ground, came forward and knelt by the side of the mandarin.

"What 'on earth' is coming now?" muttered Blake.

"From these four maids, the jewels of my heart and household, let each of the noble Farangs choose a wife. Thy servant hath no more valuable gift to offer in return for the preservation of his life ; and as Prenawi, not dreaming of the possibility of a refusal, uttered these words, his eyes were filled with tears at the thought of parting with two of his daughters.

The astonishment, the surprise of Blake, were both grotesque and painful ; he stared aghast, yet he knew that the Siamese noble believed he was conferring a great honour, as well as the most valuable presents upon strangers. The girls too, what would be their feelings at rejection, for, like many other young men, he had vanity enough to believe they would feel a refusal keenly ; but recovering a little his presence of mind, he stammered forth something about thanks, the honour done to him by the offer ; but also his surprise, and the impossibility of his acceptation of the valuable gift.

Phaulcon, equally surprised, but less disconcerted, came to his rescue by declaring that his friend was already engaged to be married, and that his religion forbade more than one wife.

At the latter declaration the girls looked incredulously, and as if some such thoughts were passing through their minds as—"Only to think how like a prison must be the home of a poor woman whose husband has no other wives for her companions!" They then lifted up their eyes to Phaulcon as their only remaining chance, wondering which among them *he* would choose; but, alas, for their hopes of obtaining a European husband, the pitiful fellow, regardless of their rank, beauty, and accomplishments, replied, that although dazzled by the proffered honour, and its rejection might cut him to the heart, he had always had a prophetic feeling, a presentiment, that it would be unlucky for him, aye, and his wife also, to marry until he had reached a certain age and station in the world.

For a minute the mandarin looked as much chagrined as his daughters, but then bowing submissively to fate, he replied:—

"Truly these words are unpleasant, but doubtlessly they are good, for they come from the mouth of the noble Farang." And as, after what had happened, all · present felt and looked ʻanything but comfortable, our two friends arose and took their departure. By his cunningly-shaped answer Phaulcon removed the sting from his refusal, for to the superstitious nature of a Siamese an appeal meets with as quick a response as to the honour of a high-souled gentleman of Europe. Writing of this, the weakest point in the character of the people, Loubere says :—

"The Siamese are of opinion, that there is an art of prophecy, and are so superstitious, that neither prince nor people will undertake any affair or expedition, till the diviners, who are Brahmins or Peguans, have fixed an hour prosperously to set upon it; and they have an almanack made annually by a Brahmin astrologer, which tells them the lucky or unlucky days for the things they wish to do, and they never stir from home, or return, so long as this prohibits. They take the howlings of wild beasts, and the cries of stags and apes, for ill omens. A serpent that crosses the way, a thunder-bolt that falls on a house, anything that falls as it were of itself and without any apparent cause, are subjects of dread to the Siamese, and the reasons of laying aside the most important matters. Many other superstitions they have, but so foolish that this taste may satisfy the intelligent reader."

"Confoundedly unfortunate our friend Prenawi took it into his head to bestow upon us these live presents," said Blake, as they were returning to their lodgings. "Never was so uncomfortable in my life, for I feel as if we had done the whole family an injury."

"It is indeed to be regretted," replied Phaulcon, "for Prenawi will feel himself and family disgraced until he has hit upon some means of proving his gratitude."

"Out of sight out of mind, my friend ; the gratitude of Asiatics goes not far below the surface ; his mandarinship will not fret long after we have sailed."

"As a rule, you are right, but Prenawi is an exception, or I am much deceived," was the reply ; and Phaulcon's estimate was the correct one, for the very next morning the mandarin waited upon the two young men with presents of silks and gold ornaments.

To Phaulcon he also brought a message from the Barcalon, or Prime Minister of Siam. The latter having heard from the grateful Prenawi of the great service he had received from Phaulcon, desired to see our hero, that in return for his service to so exalted a personage as a king's ambassador, he might eward him, either with money, or, should he prefer it, an office of emolument.

"Now, indeed," exclaimed Phaulcon, grasping the hand of Prenawi, "do I know that my brother is grateful, and desirous to serve me, for he has remembered a conversation that passed between us long since."

"My brother's words were, 'That as he had thrice lost a fortune upon the ocean, he earnestly desired the opportunity of pushing his fortunes ashore.' "

"They were, they were, and well hast thou remembered them, my good friend." Then the words, "*Hesitate not for one instant, for 'tis in Siam that thy fortune will be built, thy future developed,*" rang in his ear, and he added impatiently—

"If the noble Prenawi is willing, and the time fitting, we will at once go to the Barcalon's palace."

"It is well that my brother is impatient to pay his respects to the minister; but it cannot be until the first night of the moon, the fifth from this, for to-day is the beginning of a Tham Khuan.* The great lord's eldest son is to have his head-tuft shaven, to cast aside the white and girdle on the red *langouti*;† to take upon himself the business of a man."

"Impossible, Phaulcon, we dare not delay our voyage another five days, we shall lose the wind. This audience, therefore, desirable as I admit it to be, must be postponed till we return," interposed Blake.

"My dear friend," replied Phaulcon firmly, "in *this* instance delay

* The Tham Khuan are certain festivals or ceremonies which mark the principal epochs in the lives of the Siamese; for instance, shaving the head-tuft, becoming a Bonze, marriage, or the accession of a new sovereign.
† The garment which girdles the waist.

*would* be dangerous, both to your sailing and my prospects with this Barcalon. Go thou, therefore, alone; to me it would be to fly in the very face of fate;" and, as no persuasion was likely to make him break a once formed resolution, Blake submitted.

But as this ceremony, which placed a hiatus of several days between Phaulcon and his fortunes, is one of the most important among the Siamese, and bears a family likeness to the adoption of the *toga virilis* among the Romans—the one, indeed, by means of which a boy is legally and formally raised into manhood, its description must be interesting.

This head-tuft, which is as sacred to a Siamese as the tail is to a Chinese, is of the shape of the lotus flower, and formed by removing the hair, both back and front, leaving but the tuft upon the crown. In any rank of life the occasion of the shaving of the head-tuft is one of singular importance, but in the case of a prince of the blood royal, it is one of rejoicing for the whole kingdom.

This formal entrance into manhood of a prince takes place between the thirteenth and fourteenth years of his age. On the first day of the ceremony a vast procession of nobles, soldiers, and children, of all the nations tributary to Siam, each splendidly attired, and carrying a lotus flower, is formed in double file. The prince, who is almost covered with golden ornaments, is seated in a chair of state, upon the shoulders of nobles. Thus the procession moves towards the palace of the king, amid the sound of flutes, tambarines, trumpets, and tom-toms, a rattle being at intervals shaken before him, to signify that he is as yet in his infancy. The princess who is to be his future wife, goes before with her hands joined, bearing a plume of peacock's feathers.

Having arrived at the palace, his highness descends from his chair and prostrates himself before the king, who taking him by the hands leads him into the temple where the ashes of his ancestors are deposited.

This ceremony is repeated three consecutive days ; on the fourth the talapoin cuts his hair in the ancestral temple, and removing the white dress, which he wears until this moment, replaces it with a red one. Later on the same day, the prince is conducted to an artificial mountain ; the latter is constructed for the occasion, with a pathway to the top, upon which is erected a tent or pavilion, and a little lower down two fountains, in the form of elephants, from which water flows into a large basin at the foot of the hill. First washing his hands in the basin, his highness, accompanied by four of the greatest of the nobles, ascends to the pavilion, where it is superstitiously believed he receives some mysterious communication from the Gods. In this pavilion closes the ceremony of shaving the head-tuft, and henceforth his highness is esteemed a *man* by the people of Siam.

\*       \*       \*       \*       \*       \*

A little after sunset, on the first night \* of the new moon, Prenawi conducted Phaulcon to the Barcalon's house. It was a low, but spacious, stone-building ; but large as it was seemed insufficient to accommodate the vast number of attendants and slaves which native custom rendered necessary appendages to the high rank of its owner. Upon the appearance of Prenawi, the chief of the

---

\* The Siamese reckon not by days but by nights ; repose, instead of activity, is the instrument by which time is measured. They generally inquire, " Where did you rest ?" instead of " What did you do ?" They say, " This is the first night of the moon ; how many nights did you take for your journey ?"

household, walking backwards, and with his head so near his toes
that one might almost have trundled him like a hoop, led them
through an avenue of dusky prostrate human beings to the hall of
audience, a large square apartment, decorated, after the Chinese
fashion, with long narrow slips of paper, upon which were written
moral sentences and axioms, and lighted by lanterns fancifully
wrought into the forms of divers animals.

The Barcalon, who, like most of the native nobles, was very
corpulent, or as the Chinese say, " a man of full measure," was
evidently enjoying his *otium cum dignitate*, after the labour of the
day, for instead of being perched with his legs doubled, and his arm
painfully twisted, upon the customary pedestal, he was reclining
upon a slightly raised platform or dais, his back being supported
by a velvet cushion, smoking, while some six or seven slaves lay
ready to replenish his betel box, or to hand him a cheroot.

With stately steps and erect form had Prenawi walked through
the avenue of slaves, prostrated in deference to *his* rank; no
sooner, however, did the good man reach the entrance to the hall
of audience, than *he* fell upon all fours, and in that beast-like position remained till the Barcalon motioned to him and our hero to
approach, and, oh ! wonderful condescension, not prostrate, but
seat themselves upon two pieces of carpet which had been placed
at a little distance from the dais in readiness for them.

For about ten minutes the minister maintained—well, scarcely
a *dignified* silence, for during the whole time he puffed the smoke
in columns from his mouth, as if to hide from Phaulcon that
he was gazing at him as curiously as if he had been examining
the joints and calculating the value of a horse offered for sale.
Then taking the cheroot from between his lips, and placing it in
the hole in the lobe of his right ear, began to question his visitor,

as to his history, age, the countries he had visited, how they were governed, and whether they were at war or peace.

These queries being answered to the magnate's satisfaction, he desired to know whether Phaulcon understood accounts, and if so, whether he was desirous of accepting employment in his service. The reply being in the affirmative, the minister expressed much pleasure, and invited his two visitors to partake of sweetmeats, betel mixture, and tobacco. Now among all people good eating brings good humour, and a nearer approach to equality between opposite ranks, so, after the refreshment, the Barcalon unlaced his dignity, and frankly told our hero that Prenawi had given such an account of his talents that he had desired to see and converse with him, and that, having done so, he was so pleased with the result, that he would then and there make him his own private secretary, and apportion certain apartments in his house for his convenience.

Both surprised and gratified that his good points were so vivid upon the surface, that they could be seen at a glance, Phaulcon accepted the offer; and, moreover, promised to enter upon the duties of his new vocation the following day, much to the satisfaction of the Siamese chief, who then courteously dismissed them.

That night Phaulcon went to his bed a happy man, and dreamt again of the majestic personage whom he now believed to be a kind of patron saint, the source of his good fortune; for such he esteemed his new appointment. Père d'Orleans, however, more reasonably ascribes the cause of his luck to have been the generosity of disposition that led him to find a pleasure, even in the midst of his own misfortunes, in assisting the shipwrecked ambassador. "For," says the father, "the Siamese

(Prenawi), filled with gratitude, had no sooner rendered to the
Barcalon an account of his negotiations with the Persians,
than he related to that minister, in detail, the benefits he had
received from Phaulcon; and so warmly did he praise him that
the all-powerful chief, who was himself an intelligent man and
admired what was good in others, earnestly desired to make his
acquaintance; an interview took place, during which the Barcalon
became so charmed with the young Greek's talents and manners,
that he there and then secured his service."

# CHAPTER XII.

LIKE many another great statesman, the minister's mind and time had been so deeply absorbed in the affairs of the nation that his own had become terribly entangled. His revenues were large, even sufficiently so to have supported the lazy multitude attached to his household, had they been faithfully administered ; but although honesty is a jewel rarely found, or even expected, in Asiatic servants, whether those of king or tradesman, it is rare, even in the East, to find so great an amount of pilfering and wanton wastefulness as our hero discovered had been going on, for some years, among the servants of his patron. The latter, however, who had hitherto only known of the disease, having its cause pointed out at once gave his secretary a *carte blanche* to clean out the Augean stable, and remodel his establishment upon a more prudent footing.

It was a hard task, and could not be achieved without making many enemies ; yet, so determinedly did Phaulcon set to work, that within a very short period he had not only removed or punished the pilferers, but had succeeded in gratifying the two great passions of an Asiatic noble—pride and avarice, by doubling his state and magnificence at nearly one half the former outlay.

Then, in commercial matters—for, like the king his master, the

Barcalon was a great trader—Phaulcon made such good use of his past experience that the minister speedily saw in perspective, riches beyond his wildest dreams. In a few words, so indefatigable was the industry, and so great the skill of the new secretary, in the business affairs of his employer, that the latter admitted him to an equality and friendship that would have been impossible had he been a native; for so slavish are the Siamese in their humility to those but a single grade above them, and haughty to those but a shade beneath, even as between an elder and younger brother, that the minister would have been degraded in the eyes of the whole nation, from the king to the boatman.

How often do we find that the most successful men, in any given profession, have stumbled upon their particular careers without any previous training. The cause is obvious : free from the trammels which compel others to pursue the beaten track, as they fall into a new sphere by the weight alone of the true metal within them, they shape and press out a place for themselves. So Phaulcon, commencing his new vocation as an useful servant, soon rendered himself indispensable, and thence a *friend* of the Barcalon, who now, having faith in his probity and fitness for the office, sought his advice and assistance in a matter pertaining to the state itself. To fully comprehend, however, the causes which led to the great man's asking the advice of his humble secretary, we must take a slight view of the then Court of Siam and its surroundings.

Phra Narai, the reigning king, like many another Asiatic monarch, had obtained the throne by the assassination of his predecessor ; "still," say the Jesuit fathers, "his majesty was, by the admission of all who travelled in the Indies, one of the most enlightened princes of the East, who quickly penetrated into character, and had the greatest regard for intelligence. This we may well believe from what is known of his choice of ministers, encouragement of commerce, desire to enter into treaties with European powers, liberality in matters concerning religion, and the ability and humanity by which, with but little bloodshed, he so speedily suppressed the revolts which at the beginning of his reign broke out in all parts of the kingdom.

The native priests (of Buddha) being opposed to the liberality with which the king permitted the exercise of all religions, conspired to assassinate him, while he was attending some religious rite in one of the temples, but they missed their mark; the plot was discovered and the conspirators executed. This destruction of the Bonzes, albeit they were regicides in their hearts, was never forgotten, or forgiven, by the people, among whom their order became but the more popular; his majesty, therefore, as a matter of policy, endeavoured to conciliate the ecclesiastics by treating their chief, a personage by the way almost as high and mighty in Siam as the pope in Rome, with all kindness and honour. But the arrogant priest, assuming that his sovereign was repentant, grew so intolerably insolent that his majesty resolved upon punishing, or at least rebuking him, in a manner that might check the priestly order, without giving cause of serious offence to his lay subjects.

Thus one day, after the chief priest had been more than usually presuming, the king, who had listened with dignified silence, no sooner saw his departure from the audience chamber, than he ordered that a great baboon, which was known to be full of mischief, should be taken to him as a present from the throne, with a command that the holy father should treat the animal well, and permit it full liberty of action. Now, insolent as had been the priest hitherto, a command direct from the

king was too serious a matter to disobey. The beast was
therefore installed with all due dignity, and freedom of action,
in the episcopal residence. In a few days, however, it had become more intolerable to the priest than the latter to the king,
for the animal had spoiled, broken, or damaged every article of
value in the house. In this strait he furbished up his courage,
and presenting himself before the sovereign humbly, and in tones
of misery and suffering, implored his majesty to take back his
valuable present.

"How!" replied the king, affecting surprise, "I am astounded
at this request; you, a priest, so greatly wanting in patience
that you cannot bear the gambols of a poor animal for a few
days, while I, the king, have to endure the bad conduct and
insolent treatment of thousands of my subjects every day of
my life."

The dignitary submitted to this rebuke in silence, but henceforth
he was to be numbered among the secret enemies of the king.

Now, during the reign of this monarch, there were two factions
in the state, which in these days would, in all probability, be
named, at least by Europeans, Old Siam, and Young Siam.
The first, at the head of which was the chief priest, and Petraxa,
a prince of the blood, were desirous of keeping Siam to the
Siamese; or in other words, of excluding all religions but that of
Buddha from the land, and not permitting reaties to be entered
into with foreign powers. On the other hand, the Young Siam
party desired to enlarge the minds of the people, and develop
the resources of the nation, by giving freedom of opinion in
matters of faith; and entering into treaties of commerce with
European governments. The *nominal* head of the latter was
the Barcalon, but it was shrewdly suspected by the opposite party

that the king himself was their real chief and leader, for, although
his majesty punctiliously attended to the forms and ceremonies
of the worship of Buddha, he had permitted certain Jesuits to
erect a church in the capital, and invite any of his subjects to
become converts to Christianity. Then, again, he had not only
granted a like permission to certain Mahomedans, but had
appointed several of the latter to offices in the state, nay, even
one of the most important departments, namely, the ordering
and regulating, with proper magnificence and dignity, the sending
out of embassies to foreign sovereigns, and the reception of others
in the capital; indeed, such confidence did the king seem to
place in the Mahomedans, that the native nobles feared the
aliens would in time usurp all the offices of the state, and the
priests, that they would induce the sovereign to adopt the Koran,
and make its faith the established religion of the land.

On their part the Mahomedans saw with jealousy that the king
gave an undue share of favour to a certain French Jesuit, with
whom it was known his majesty was frequently closeted; and thus,
in a greater degree than the Buddhist priests feared the introduction of the Koran, did the astute Moors fear that the Jesuits
might ultimately gain precedence for the Bible, and so, to their
discomfiture, Christianize the people. Thus, for a time, forbearing
to make proselytes to Mahomedanism, and even affecting to look
upon Buddhism with as much veneration as they regarded Christianity with dislike, they succeeded in forming a coalition with
the Old Siam party against their common enemies, the Jesuits.

Notwithstanding this alliance, disputes would occasionally happen
between them that called for the interference of the only two honest
men in the empire, the king and his Barcalon, who had more
than sufficient occupation in watching their intrigues, and playing

one against the other, so that neither could injure the state; was it, therefore, surprising that frequently, after an interview with his majesty, the minister would return to his house soured and angry?

It was upon one of these occasions that he ordered the attendance of his secretary, who, finding his patron impatiently pacing the apartment, said—

"Some misfortune has happened, for my lord is displeased?"

"These rats of Moors* are gnawing at the very foundation of the throne."

"It is a great evil, which the king should remove; but anger, oh! my lord, will kill neither rats nor Moor," he added, boldly, for he had more than once tried out-speaking, and had discovered that the minister, Asiatic though he was, liked it—perhaps, for its very novelty to him."

"Thy rebuke is just, he replied, mildly; "it is not fitting that the minister of a great king should, like a child, weep at the sting of an insect."

"May thy servant ask in what these dogs have offended my lord?"

"Listen," he replied; adding, "and if by advice or action thou canst aid me in recovering the king's favour, by opening his eyes, thy fortune is made."

"Has so heavy a blow as the anger of the great king fallen upon my lord?"

"Truly it has, and by means of these rats," he replied; adding, "the king having determined to send an embassy to the mightiest ruler of the West, charged the Moors with its preparation, and

---

* Moors or Moormen, was the name by which, at that period, all Mahomedans were known to the Siamese.

upon a fully magnificent scale; but the rats, misliking the purport of the embassy, after long delay reported that, 'It was impossible, for not only was there insufficient wealth in the royal treasury, but that, in addition, his majesty was already indebted to them sixty thousand crowns.'

"Astounded at such an unexpected report, the king sent for me; but instead of receiving his servant graciously, as usual, he exclaimed—

"'How is this, O dog of a minister, that there is not wealth enough in my treasury, for the sending of an embassy, with the magnificence worthy of my greatness! In what have the precious metals, jewels, silks, and gums, sent by tributary princes, been squandered, that thou, in whom I have placed my confidence, shouldst have feared to open thy lips?'

"Now," continued the Barcalon, "although long surmising the cause of the king's poverty, I had not dared to accuse the Moors, but now a fitting opportunity had come, and I replied—

"'Mighty and august lord! divine mercy, master of life, sovereign of the earth, I, a dust-grain of your sacred feet,* can only answer, that thy coffers were filled with a goodly amount of treasure till the Moors were entrusted with the management of the embassies; since then the wealth of the king has dwindled; yet, if thy servant may speak the words and live, there yet remains sufficient in the royal treasury for the furnishing forth of this embassy.'

"'How! what dog's words are these!' he replied; 'who shall gainsay the men in whom the king places his confidence? Has not the chief of the Moors declared, that not only are we

---

* In this fulsome language are the kings of Siam addressed by their nobles.

indébted to him sixty thousand crowns, but that the wealth in
our treasury is not enough, by one half, for the purpose of the
embassy ?'

" 'Should it cost him his life it is the duty of thy slave to
offer counsel in all matters.  Let the chief of these Moors be
commanded to deliver into the hands of one skilled in accounts
the papers and books wherein are written the expenditure for
the last three embassies, then, O king! it may be found that
there is yet sufficient wealth remaining for thy wise purpose.'

" But the king, who, prudent in all other matters, yet loves
magnificence in the appointment of his embassies, replied, with
still more anger—

" 'Dog of a Barcalon, get thee hence, for thou wouldst degrade
thy master in the eyes of a mighty prince, by reducing the state
of his envoys to the level of those of a petty chief or tributary.'  Thus," concluded the Barcalon, " with dust in his eyes,
that prevents his seeing the roguery of the Moors, I left the
royal presence."

"Thy pardon, O my lord!" replied Phaulcon; "but is there
any proof that these Moors are rogues?"

" Is there any water in the ocean?" answered the minister,
adding, as he placed a packet of papers in the hands of Phaulcon,
"see, there are the details of those things necessary for the
embassy, and also of the sums demanded by the Moors for the
proper furnishing thereof; get thee to thy chamber and examine
if they are not exorbitant."

"My  lord!"*  replied Phaulcon,  and  immediately he  left
the room.

Having occupied the greater part of that night and the whole

* " My lord !" is equivalent to, " Thy will shall be obeyed."

of the next morning, in examining the papers and making fresh
calculations, in the evening Phaulcon presented himself before
his patron.

"Hast discovered these rats to be thieves?" exclaimed the
latter, eagerly.

"My lord, they are robbers."

"Buddha be praised!" and the minister chuckled.

"The Moors," continued Phaulcon, "demand one half more
than is required."

"Can this be proved beyond questioning?"

"Truly it can," replied Phaulcon. "Moreover, there is one man
in Siam who, at the risk of his head, would not only undertake
to send forth this embassy, with a magnificence and state worthy
of the king, at less than one half the sum now demanded, but, if
the necessary papers were placed before him, would prove, perhaps,
that the roguish Moors are themselves indebted to his majesty."

At this reply, the Barcalon, who, as we have seen, had had
good cause to place faith in Phaulcon's arithmetical talents,
became in ecstasies.  All thoughts of their difference in rank
seemed to have passed from his mind, for, motioning to him to
sit upon his own raised platform, he exclaimed—

"My friend, my brother, *that* man is my secretary; for him
is it reserved to save the minister, and, perhaps, the king.  But,"
he added, "how may this thing be done?  The office cannot be
transferred from the Moors to thee without the permission of
his majesty, whose faith in the honesty of these rogues is, at
present, unlimited."

"Truly, my lord, this matter is beset by difficulties," replied
Phaulcon; "yet might this affair be accomplished, could the dust
be removed from the eyes of the sovereign."

P

"Who is there mighty enough to cure the vision of the wilfully blind?" muttered the Barcalon, thoughtfully. "Yet," he added quickly, as if a sudden thought had flashed through his mind, "it is *possible;* but to attain it my friend will risk his head."

"Let my lord speak, and the possible shall be accomplished at any risk to his servant," said Phaulcon.

"Thou hast, oh Phaulcon! the cunning of the fox with the courage of the tiger, yet may this enterprise be beyond even thee ; but listen—

"There is one whose influence over the king is sufficient to cause him to deprive the Moors of their office—the pearl of the kingdom, the princess, his majesty's only child. The royal lady loves not the Moors, for they are now in junction with the Lord Petraxa, who is ever importuning the king to compel her to marry his second son ; so, if we can but place in her hands proofs that the Moors are rogues, and that her father will be benefited by their removal, our end will be attained."

"But this is not possible, for it is instant death to be found within the precincts of the women's division of the palace," said Phaulcon gloomily.

At this the minister looked grave, but, after a minute's reflection, replied—

"That is true, yet a packet might reach the princess by the hands of her chief friend and companion. This lady, being a Christian, has obtained the royal permission for her confessor to visit her house ; but fortunately the holy man is now absent from Ayuthia, so that didst thou dare to assume habiliments like unto his it would be possible to introduce thyself into the very

house of the Christian lady; but 'tis a dangerous task, think
well whether thou wilt undertake it."

"I dare not refuse, for my lord could trust none other."

"Good, then to-morrow shall you attempt to penetrate the
sacred quarter of the palace; the day, however, will be in your
favour, for it is the first of the Rëkna, when King Hop reigns,
and the people will be too much engaged with their follies to
give special attention to thee. In the meanwhile I will prepare
a letter to the Lady Diamond, and inclose for the princess's eye
thy calculation, which will be all-sufficient to prove the Moors'
extortion, and thy fitness for the office they so roguishly perform;"
so saying, the minister signified by a motion of his hand that the
audience was at an end, and Phaulcon withdrew to dream of the
morrow's enterprise, and perhaps King Hop.

By the way, the Rëkna, of which the Barcalon had spoken,
is a kind of Tom Fool's festival, which lasts three days, during
which time the king keeps his palace, and upon the first of which
a mock king is invested by the people with temporary sovereignty.
This sham monarch is named King Hop; he sends out his
ministers to take what they can from the bazaars and open shops,
and even confiscates junks that arrive during the exercise of his
short rule. On the first day of the festival the mock sovereign
proceeds in state to a field in town, and makes some furrows
with a golden plough; leaning against the trunk of a tree he
places his right foot on his left knee, and is bound to stand on
one leg in evidence of his legitimacy; hence his title. A variety
of vegetables are scattered in his presence, and a cow being
brought in, whatever she first eats is pronounced likely to be
scarce, and the people are advised accordingly.

For the origin of this mummery, it seems to me to have

no deeper meaning than had similar exhibitions in Europe, during the middle ages, and under the most despotic governments, when the people were permitted at a certain season of the year to burlesque their betters with impunity. For instance, when the Lords of Misrule held temporary sway. Bowring, however, thus philosophizes: "The whole farce is probably intended to throw scorn upon popular influences, and reconcile the subjects to the authority of a *real* king; for the reality of the royal authority of a Monarch of Siam is a fact not to be mistaken, and may well be contrasted with the doings of a temporary impostor."

## CHAPTER XIII

### KING HOP.

Towards evening the next day the Barcalon went to Phaulcon's apartments, taking with him the habiliments of a Christian priest; but upon examining them and finding that the gown was hooded, he said—

"What are these things? my lord hath been deceived, for the brethren of the Society of Jesus wear not hoods, but caps."

"Then," replied the Barcalon, "the Father Antoine hath a purpose of his own in attiring himself differently from his brethren; for not only have I seen him wear the hood, but these very garments have been *borrowed* from his own house by one of the most cunning of my slaves."

Hearing this, our hero did not trouble himself as to the father's whim, but rejoicing at the better chance of disguise the hood offered, he attired himself, and set out by water for the royal residence. As the minister had foretold, the people were so much engaged with the boisterous merriment and mischievous pranks of King Hop and his subjects, that he passed to the very walls without, as far as he knew, attracting any especial attention.

The royal palace of Ayuthia was in size a town of itself, consisting of three inclosures, one within the other, the space between each forming large court-yards, and the women's apartments or rather houses being the innermost of all.

So well, however, was Phaulcon disguised, and so admirably did he imitate the slow thoughtful steps of the Jesuit, that he passed the first and second gates without exciting the smallest suspicion that he was other than the Father Antoine. But as he feared that the keepers of the entrance to the most sacred division of the palace would more closely examine, nay question him, he loitered about the second court-yard, among the soldiers, slaves, and attendants, until dusk.

This precaution, however, was unnecessary ; for the porters and sentries were so accustomed to the in-comings and out-goings of the Christian priest, that they allowed our hero to pass, as indeed they were commanded by the king to permit the real Simon Pure, without even taking him before the officer whose duty it was to examine the robes, and smell the breath of every person entering the sacred precincts, to see that none should pass therein either armed or drunk.

Having passed the door-keepers and sentries, it suddenly occurred to him that his greatest difficulty was to come. He knew not which of the many residences before him was that of the Lady Diamond, while to ask the question would be to betray himself, for so constant a visitor as the Father Antoine would certainly not have required any such information.

In this dilemma, luck came to his aid in the form of a female slave, who, bending her body before him, yet in evident surprise, exclaimed—

" It is the Farang man of prayer ; how pleased will be my mistress, for it is certain she thinks thee far from Ayuthia ;" so saying, she skipped nimbly along the paved court towards one of the buildings.

" That then is the house. I am fortunate," muttered Phaulcon ;

he felt, however, far from comfortable, for speak he dared not, neither did he know whether the real Father Antoine would have followed the slave into the house, or have waited in the vestibule until his visit had been announced to her mistress. In this dilemma, he chose the intermediate course of proceeding at a slow pace with his head bent towards the ground, as if in deep contemplation. It was a wise resolve, for before he had reached the house, the nimble-footed slave came running back and begged that he would follow her at once to her mistress's apartment.

The Diamond of the Palace indeed, thought Phaulcon, as upon entering the room he saw—rare sight in Siam—a studious lady, whose mind seemed absorbed in the pages of a book—probably some work on religion; for as our hero walked towards her, she, with one finger upon the page as if to mark a particular passage requiring his explanation, said—

"Holy Father, this visit is as opportune as it is unexpected;" but, as with her eyes still fixed upon the book, she approached him, the mock priest, startled out of all prudence, exclaimed—

"Is it possible! Monica! The Lady Monica!"

In her astonishment, she dropped the book, then hastily glancing towards the door, as if fearful that other ears might be opened, she said, as her eyes sparkled with pleasure—

"My preserver! The Farang, Captain Phaulcon!"

"True, O lady, and the misfortunes of a life are redeemed by a meeting, which, although so sudden, so unexpected, thy servant has longed for through many, many months," replied Phaulcon, with more warmth than prudence.

"Hush!" she whispered, "for great is your danger." Then summoning her attendant, and telling the girl to permit no other

slave to enter while the priest remained with her, she turned
to Phaulcon, and in a tone of anger, said—

"How is it that the Farang Captain has dared to penetrate
the sacred precincts of the palace? for what purpose is he
here in the garb of the Father Antoine? It is not well, for
it is the dishonest of purpose alone who adopt deceit and
disguise."

"Lady," he replied, "I crave thy pardon for my boldness; yet
must my excuse be, astonishment at finding the Lady Monica
in the Diamond of the Palace, to whom I am charged with a
mission from the Barcalon."

"Comest thou to me from the Barcalon? then thou must be
the Farang Secretary, of whom the good minister hath said so
much."

"If the great lord hath poured such words of praise into
the ears of the Lady Monica, then indeed is his servant amply
rewarded."

"But," interposed the lady, impatiently, "Wherefore this
disguise? for what purpose hath the Barcalon sent thee?"

"Is the Lady Monica still desirous that the faith for which
her fathers fought and suffered shall take root in the land?"

"With my whole heart, and at the cost of life if need be,
do I desire this thing," replied the beautiful enthusiast, her whole
frame tremulous with pleasure, and her dark eyes flashing forth
the hope with which she was filled. "But," she added gloomily,
"such a glorious consummation can never be attained; for
although the king listens to the teaching of Father Antoine,
upon his right hand sit the priests of Buddha, and upon his
left the Moors, who are even now praying his Majesty to
embrace the tenets of the Koran. Alas," she continued, "the

only hope for the true faith was the embassy to the mighty sovereign of France, who might have sent to this benighted land a mission; but all chance of such an embassy is at an end, for the Moors, I doubt me not for the gaining of their own ends, have declared the royal treasury exhausted."

"Lady," replied Phaulcon, placing in her hands the Barcalon's packet, "the object of this my visit to thee, is to check the power of these Mahomedans; their influence over the king is already waning, and to be utterly uprooted requires but the aid of the Lady Monica, as this document will advise her."

Having perused, and well pondered over the contents of the Barcalon's letter and inclosures, she placed them within the folds of her robe, saying—

"Noble Farang, let the good minister know that his will shall be obeyed; these papers *shall* be laid before the king, by means of his daughter, who is the light of his eyes, the very pearl of his existence; and the office of these Moors being once transferred to thy hands, as I doubt not it will be, the embassy may be accomplished, and the faith, the true faith, yet shine resplendently, throughout the kingdom. Oh, noble Phaulcon!" she added, "to this end, to this glorious result, let thy toil be directed, and thy reward—"

"Lady," interposed our hero, as he profanely gazed into the eyes of the beautiful being before him, whose majesty of form, rich-toned voice, and dark glistening eyes, gave the notion of an inspired prophetess, "for that which I may and will accomplish, I shall claim but the happiness of having served thee. The reward of which I dream, only dream, would be the asking for the highest star from the heavens."

"Monica," replied she, as at these bold words of Phaulcon her face, hands, even to the tips of her fingers became encrimsoned "can never forget that it was thou, oh brave Phaulcon! that preserved her from a terrible fate; still, all selfish thoughts must be banished from our minds, until the conclusion of that good work, which but commences the instant the king places in thy hands the office of the Moors."

The allusion to the past and incidentally to a future, the soft tone of her voice, all tended to make our hero forget himself, he seized her hand, would have pressed it to his lips, but now really angered, though assuming to misinterpret the action, she withdrew it quickly, saying as she quitted the room, "The thanks should not be tended till the benefit be received," and Phaulcon, the politician, who was seeking to over- turn almost an institution of the Empire, as he made his way through the palace knew not whether he was upon his head or his heels, nor did he even notice that, as he quitted the lady's residence, a little slave darted from behind a pillar and followed him through the palace, unto the very water's edge.

It was only upon getting into his boat that he became awakened to more mundane things; then indeed it was very necessary, for the river was now literally crowded with the noisy revellers of "King Hop," most of them, too, in a state that made it desirable to avoid coming in contact with them, for whatever pranks the subjects of the burlesque sovereign played that night would be winked at by the authorities.

Forcing his way as best he could through the crowds of boats and barges, laughing (for it was policy to assume good temper) at the sallies, and even mischievous practical jokes the most boisterous would at every opportunity play upon some more quiet and temperate passer-by, he had rowed to within a mile of the Barcalon's residence, when he suddenly found himself

between two small barges, whose crews (noisiest of revellers)
were evidently endeavouring to foul each other's boats. Phaulcon,
knowing that any call would be unheeded at such a time,
endeavoured, by a dexterous manœuvre, to shoot his little craft
between them. It was then he saw that their show of fouling
each other had been but a feint, and that he was the real
object of attack, for quick as lightning, and with a dexterity
only known to the amphibious Siamese, one of the boats
darted forward with such velocity, that striking Phaulcon's
boat about midships, placed its keel uppermost, and its owner
in the river.

Conscious of the scurvy joke that had been played him, our
hero made for the shore; but the jokers were not to be so easily
deprived of their fun, for the instant the boat was capsized,
the little slave, who had followed him from the palace, and who
was now in one of the boats, cried aloud, "caught, caught,"
and before our sham priest had made a couple of yards, he was
dragged into one of the barges a prisoner.

Greatly enraged that *fun* should be carried so far, Phaulcon
threatened the boatmen; but, in reply, they proceeded to greater
lengths, for they bound his arms behind him, placed a gag in
his mouth, and tied a bandage round his eyes; still, notwithstanding this anything but comical treatment, he believed himself
to be only in the hands of the subjects of King Hop, until in
about half an hour his tormentors landed and led him through
what, from the smooth pavements upon which he trod, he
guessed to be the different courts of a palace. It was then he
began to suspect that he had fallen in with a much more serious
affair than a reveller's prank, and this suspicion became confirmed,
when upon their removing the gag, cord, and bandage, he saw

he saw that he was in a small square apartment lighted by a single horn lantern.

"For what purpose, and by whose orders, oh my friends, have you brought me here?" he asked. But the men, although they bowed as reverentially to his garb as if it had been the attire of one of their own priests, quitted the room without making a reply, leaving him to ponder upon the meaning of so strange an adventure.

What had he done to bring upon himself the vengeance of the government? Nothing; but even so, his patron the Barcalon would not have permitted such violence. Then, with the exception of the minister's pilfering servants whom he had dismissed, he could remember no enemy in Siam; the enigma, however, was soon solved, for as he sat shivering in his wet garments, and pondering, Prince Soyaton entered his prison-chamber.

Surprised, for he knew not that this personage had been recalled from his exile in Cochin China, Phaulcon exclaimed, "It is to thee then, oh dog of a prince, that I owe this violence and kidnapping;" but the astonishment depicted upon the prince's countenance, at hearing such words from the lips of a Jesuit, whose brethren were renowned throughout the East for their meekness, reminding him of his assumed character, he added quickly, and in a humble tone—

"In what can the poor priest have injured the great prince Soyaton to merit such violence?"

"If violence hath been done, it was without the knowledge of the prince, the near relation of the king, who, forgetting his exaltation, is even now here to seek the holy man's friendship," replied Soyaton with an hauteur that clearly belied his words.

" If it is *thus*," replied Phaulcon, exhibiting the red marks upon his wrists caused by the cords, and pointing to his dripping garments, " Prince Soyaton creates friends, cruel, indeed, must be his manner of making enemies."

" Man is the slave of the hour, the creature of circumstances, and it is not always given to him to choose his own means of gaining his end ; thus, thy servant desired and resolved to obtain thy friendship and aid in a matter of importance to himself, and knew no other means than that of bringing thee to his palace."

" Honest men speak not in riddles ; how is it that a prince of the blood seeks the friendship of a poor priest ? What aid can he desire, or obtain, from one so lowly ?" replied Phaulcon.

" The holy man is the priest of the Christian Monica, named the Diamond of the Palace."

" I am," replied our hero, with knitted brows, and hand placed, where in another costume would have been his dagger. " What would the prince with the Lady Monica."

" The Diamond of the Palace is beautiful, a jewel rare enough to be set in a crown."

" This is true," replied Phaulcon. But he added quickly, " She is more, she is the adopted daughter of the king, the friend, almost sister of the princess, and thus should be high above the profane wishes of Prince Soyaton."

" For all those reasons, and others, would I make her my chief wife, *I*, the near relation of the king."

" *You*," repeated our hero, with a look of withering scorn, and again he had almost forgotten his assumed character. " But," he said, " does not the prince know that the lady being a Christian, such a marriage is impossible."

"Therein," said Soyaton, "hath hitherto been my misery, but for that she would long since have been my willing bride."

What were our hero's feelings at this audacious falsehood, may be imagined; the blood rushed to his temples, his hand sought his dagger, the harshest of contradictions was at his tongue's end, but prudence curtailed the word ere it left his lips.

"Li—'est thou not in error, oh prince! for albeit all that passes in the royal family is held sacred from the ears of the people, it *is* whispered that it was to the Japanese lady thou wert indebted for thy banishment to Cochin China."

"Ah!" exclaimed the prince, "what dog's tongue hath wagged of affairs in his sovereign's family? How knowest thou this?"

"The confessor hears many things kept sacred from the ears of others, oh prince!"

"Then she hath made thee her confidant in other than the matters of her religion," replied the prince; adding, "Well, it is good that it is so, for the better canst thou aid me."

"May thy servant ask thee, oh prince! in what manner it is in his power to help thee?" replied Phaulcon, who was burning with curiosity to know the rogue's scheme.

"Thou, oh holy man! hast this lady's ear; pour into it words in praise of Soyaton; tell her that the prince is dying for Monica's love, that for her he will resign his wives, making her sole mistress of his heart and household, and, perhaps, in time, share with her a throne. Do this, and thy reward shall be the success of that which is dearest to thine heart, thy religion; for my father, who is the prince nearest the throne, myself, and all the lords of the party now in such deadly opposition to the Christians, will uphold them and their creed."

"Prince," replied our hero, "you demand that which is impossible, for the maiden is a Christian, and thou art a Pagan, a worshipper of false deities; as for thy promised reward, it is needless, since the one true and only God will promote His own good work in *His* own time."

"Priest, you dream not of the consequences of a refusal," said the Prince fiercely; as if, however, some other thought had flashed through his mind, he added in milder tones—"But stay, tell her that if otherwise a marriage is impossible between us, that for her sake, Soyaton will forsake the ancient gods of his ancestors, and worship the God of the Christians."

"If thou art sincere in this, oh prince! no aid of mine is required; for having once been received into the bosom of the Church, thou hast but to throw thyself at the feet of the king, and demand his permission to openly address the lady."

"Dog of a priest," exclaimed the prince, now losing all command over his temper, "art laughing in thy sleeve? for well thou knowest that the king's enmity to me is such, that if not by secret means, this marriage can never happen. Lend me thine aid," he continued fiercely, "or I will have thy garb torn from thy shoulders, and pass as thyself into the lady's presence."

"How easily could I crush this miserable worm," thought Phaulcon; conscious, however, that the least attempt at violence would bring about his own immediate destruction, he merely ventured upon a covert threat.

"Be it as the prince wills," he replied, "better to die than betray my trust. But," he added, "my death will be followed by thine own, for the Christian priest being missed by the king, and the Barcalon, such a search will be made, and rewards offered, that even thou wilt not be able to escape detection."

"Dares the dog of a Farang threaten?" replied Soyaton, now

well-nigh choking with rage, "then let him listen to the words
of the prince; till two hours after to-morrow's sunrise thou shalt
be left to reflect, but if then contumacious, I will have thee
beaten to death in a sack, and thy body thrown into the
Meinam."

"Wretch, I defy thee," replied our hero, as the prince quitted
the chamber.  But left to himself, he began to regret the course
he had adopted during the interview.  He had no doubt that
Soyaton would keep his word; should he choose death, he would
not have the miserable satisfaction of believing that his murder
would be avenged, for although as a *ruse*, he had threatened the
prince with the certainty of discovery, Phaulcon felt that, as a
stranger in the land, even the Barcalon would speedily forget him;
that missed, like a stone thrown into the water, there would be a
plash, a ripple—no more.

To die, so young, just as he had placed his foot upon the first
round of fortune, was a cruel thought.    But a far worse one—that
Monica would be left to the evil machinations of the prince, from
which he had the vanity to believe he could protect her.  Thus
pondering, he resolved at length to fight Soyaton with his own
weapon, deceit.  To do this he must feign compliance with his
will.  But afterwards—well he would take time to consider;
and so he stretched himself upon the floor and slept till some
time after sunrise.

Awakening, his first thoughts were so to frame his words that
the cunning Soyaton might have no doubt of his sincerity in
offering to assist his designs upon Monica; but while meditating,
his ears caught the sound of voices in the corridor or passage
leading to his prison-room.

"It is the rascal Soyaton," he muttered ; but, "No !" he added, as his ears caught the sound of what appeared to him to be a familiar voice, "or if it is, he is bringing some other prisoner;" but the next instant the door stood open, and two slaves, followed by a guard of several of their fellows, ushered into the room a man, attired like himself in the garb of a Jesuit.

"Father Thomas!" exclaimed our hero, breathless with surprise.

"Phaulcon! and in priest's attire," cried the no less astonished ecclesiastic.

Now, as the slaves entered the room, they did not see our hero; for he was lying stretched upon the floor, in an obscure corner. As, however, he arose, to shake the father by the hand, the eyes of the natives opened unnaturally wide, their legs trembled beneath them, and with something very like shrieks, they receded to the doorway; one, no less terrified than his fellows, but who preserved the use of his tongue, exclaimed—

"A devil, a magician; for he can be everywhere, within and without, at the same time."

"What mean these idiots?" asked Phaulcon.

"I understand it now," replied the father; "they believe that you and I are one person, a magician or a demon, who has the power of being two separate men at one and the same moment. As I was passing this house, on my way to visit the king, one of these fellows stopped and stared me full in the face, then, suddenly darting within the house, he fetched others, who declared that I was their prisoner, their master's prisoner, and must have escaped from the room in which they had confined me. As my men fled on the instant, I had no alternative but to come with them, believing that I had fallen into the hands of madmen. But now the cause is plainly apparent; they mistook me for you, and

well they might," concluded the father, with a look of curiosity
at our hero's attire.

"You are surprised to see me in this garb; I will explain,"
said Phaulcon. But at that moment Soyaton made his appearance,
exclaiming aloud—

"Magician! Demon! It is a trick to rob me of the dog of
a priest;" but, upon entering the room and seeing that, as his
slave had told him, there were *two*, he added savagely, "Which
of the dogs is the Farang Priest Antoine?"

"*I* am he called Father Antoine," replied the Jesuit, to the
great astonishment of Phaulcon, who said—

"Thou the father Antoine, impossible!"

"It is possible; it is true, my son," replied the priest, with a
smile; adding, by way of explanation, "From my noviciate in the
Society of Jesus, I have been known as Thomas; but upon being
sent to this Mission, I added Antoine, the name I received at the
first to distinguish me from another brother now in Siam, who
bears the same surname."

"*Thou* the Father Antoine, *thou* the confessor of the Lady
Monica!" exclaimed Soyaton. "Then," he added, as, half-suffocated
with rage, he seized Phaulcon by the throat, "who is this vile
dog, that feigning to be thee, has learned the bosom secret of a
prince?"

Our hero replied for himself, but I am afraid very rudely, for,
unable to endure the indignity or pain of Soyaton's clutch, with
one blow he laid H. R. H. low, and then removing the hood
from his face, said—

"Phaulcon, the Farang captain, who rescued the Lady Monica
from thy villainous clutches at Hué."

"At this insult to the prince, the slaves present raised such a noise, that, in a very few minutes, the room became thronged with members of the household, and ill would it have fared with both our hero, and the Jesuit, but for the presence of mind of the latter, who, familiarly tapping the infuriated scion of royalty upon the arm, said—

"Be warned, oh prince, in time, or the club and the sack will be thy fate. Having already lost the king's favour, thou hast in my person outraged his authority; for when molested by thy slaves, I was, by the royal command, on the way to the palace; even now, if I make not all haste, my cowardly attendants will carry the news of this outrage to the king's ears."

Terrified at this threat, Soyaton, in softened tones, replied— "*Thou*, oh holy man! art free to go; but this dog, who by the laws of the land hath earned death by entering the women's division of the palace, shall—

"Accompany me, oh prince," interrupted the father; "for he is the secretary of the great and good Barcalon. Let him depart at once, and I promise that not a whisper of thine own doings shall reach the ears of the king; touch but his smallest finger, and thou wilt seal thine own death-warrant."

The effect of this speech upon the foiled prince was instantaneous; for already in disgrace with the king, and not loved by the all-powerful minister, he knew that to add another to his list of offences would be but to give an excuse for his immediate execution. His consanguinity to royalty would not avail to save him; for in Siam, as in all the despotisms of the East, the nearer to the throne the nearer to the grave. Thus check-mated—more, compelled to feign humility, Soyaton sullenly quitted the room, and taking refuge in his own inner apartment, there gave vent to his rage in impotent howlings against his enemies.

"This rogue of a prince shall be made to feel the vengeance of the king, if I have any influence with the Barcalon," said Phaulcon, as he and the Jesuit left the house.

"Not so," replied the father, quickly, "it would be imprudent, even if I had not passed my word. For, although if this man's delinquencies were made known, he would assuredly be punished with death; yet he would not suffer alone; thou wouldst also be put to death; for not even the king could save a man who has outraged the dignity and pride of the whole people, by forcing his way into the women's apartment of the royal palace."

"Thou art right, father, I will abide my time," replied our hero, adding fiercely, "This fellow's chastisement must be deferred; nevertheless it shall come."

"It will be wise," replied the Jesuit. "But," he added, "was it not imprudent, nay worse, infinitely worse—criminal, to endanger thyself, and peril the reputation, and perhaps the life, of the Lady Monica."

"Father," replied Phaulcon, "thou hast done me a great service, and may deem me ungrateful to keep silence in this matter; still, speak out I cannot, lest I disclose secrets not mine own. But," he added, as they approached the Barcalon's palace, "here we part, and, until we meet again, harbour no harsh thoughts of me."

"Enough," replied the priest, with offended dignity; adding, as Phaulcon turned to leave him, "One word, my son; be warned in time, lest thy fall be the greater; look not so high as this Lady Monica; for if she would even unite herself with an adventurer, she dare not with a heretic."

The Jesuit then went on his way; and Phaulcon entered the house, muttering to himself, "This officious meddling priest—an adventurer—poh ! *who* in this world is *not* an adventurer ; but she dare not marry with a heretic ; there may be truth in that ; indeed, she *would* not ;" and in this frame of mind he entered the apartment of the Barcalon, who, seeing his secretary again, joyfully exclaimed—

"Buddha be praised, thou art still in the flesh, for truly I had begun to lament thee as one with the ghosts."

"My lord honours his servant," he answered ; and then related the story of his adventures, since they had parted the day previously, to which the minister, having listened very patiently, replied—

"Thy mission was well and carefully performed. As for this dog of a Prince Soyaton (alas ! the unhappy hour that the king was prevailed upon to recall him from exile), the Farang priest Antoine advised well. Vengeance must sleep, at least till a fitting time, for did he disclose the secret of thy entering the palace, both thou who went, and I, who sent thee, would speedily be made to keep company with ghosts. But from this moment be on thy guard, for sleepless is Soyaton's hatred, and not a stone will he leave unturned in search of a means for thy destruction."

"But little care I for this man's hatred," replied Phaulcon ; "yet much that he may have the means of communicating my lord's scheme against the Moors, for assuredly will he set spies to watch whether I again enter the palace."

"In this," replied the Barcalon, "thou hast no cause to fear, for thou wilt not need again to visit the palace in disguise."

"But my lord knows not that my visit must be repeated this very day, for the purpose of receiving the required document from the Lady Monica."

"Not so," replied the minister, "this hath been a lucky

day, the papers are here," and, as he spoke, he lifted the lid
of a casket in which lay a packet. " Quickly, indeed," he added,
" must the Lady Monica have interested her royal mistress in this
affair of the Moors, and even with greater speed must the
princess have prevailed upon her royal parent, for, shortly after
sunrise this morning, the king, summoning me to his presence,
desired to know who and what was this most skilful man, who
dared to declare that he could prove the Moors dishonest, and
rescue his treasury from embarrassment.

" When I told him it was my secretary, thyself, and of the
things thou hadst done for me, he replied ; ' Lo, oh my
minister ! I am inclined to believe that this secretary of thine
may be able to do the thing he proposes ; take thou the papers
which the Moors have laid before me, and let him peruse
them, and draw up others that will prove them false. This
being done, see thou that they are placed before the board
who examine into the accounts of my kingdom, and if this
board declare the secretary to be neither a braggart nor a teller
of lies, but a good and true man, he shall find the king not
unmindful of his merits.' Thus," said the Barcalon, in conclusion, " came into my possession these documents. Take them
oh my Phaulcon ! into thy keeping, discover and make it plain
upon paper wherein lies the roguery of the dogs of Moors ; and
draw up another, showing what the cost will be of the embassy,
the sending of which is so near the king's heart. But," he
added, " it will be well that these things should be declared to
the board of examiners before the first night of the moon, as
upon the third, the chief of the Moors has demanded, and his
majesty hath consented to an audience, at which they will lay
their grievances at the foot of the throne."

"My lord has named the time in which this task is to be accomplished, and, God willing, the end shall be as successful as the beginning," replied Phaulcon, who then, receiving the casket from the hands of the minister, took his leave, at once to enter upon his task.

## CHAPTER XIV.

### PHAULCON OUTWITS THE MOORS.

In despotic countries, but small opportunities, if seized upon the instant, and used to the best advantage, are frequently sufficient to lay the foundation of a man's fortune. The foot once upon the lower round of the ladder, the uppermost is attainable by judicious climbing. Knowing this full well, Phaulcon toiled so hard at the wilfully entangled accounts of the Moors, that punctually, to the time appointed, he laid before his patron so lucid an unravelment, and so plain a statement of his own, that even, in spite of any bribes from the Mahomedans, the board of examiners would be compelled to admit the dishonesty of the Moors to be a proven fact. But, as the decision of this board would be given only in the presence of the king, it was with no little anxiety that Phaulcon awaited the audience.

Upon the day appointed, the Barcalon, to do his secretary the greater honour, invited him to a seat by his side in his own state barge. Thus, attended by a vast retinue, in barges gilded and decorated according to the respective ranks of their occupants, they proceeded to the royal palace. Passing through crowds of mandarins of different grades, officers, soldiers, slaves and attendants, all of whom fell upon their hands and knees in deference to the exalted rank of the minister, they at length reached the ante-room of the hall of audience. In this apartment, the Barcalon desired Phaulcon to await, until summoned, and proceeded to take the place appointed for the chief minister.

Being left to himself, our hero had leisure to contemplate the novel scene, in which he was himself soon to form an element. A Chinese screen, covered with landscapes without perspective, pieces of looking-glass, and scraps of paper, with moral sentences from the works of Confucius, formed the partition or doorway into the great hall. The screen, however, was moved sufficiently aside for him to obtain a good view of the interior.

This audience chamber was of great length and breadth, and lofty, the roof being upheld by circular pillars of red and green; the ceiling was painted gaily with wreaths of flowers, and · the floor covered with carpets of different colours. At the furthermost end of the hall were suspended by silken cords, from wall to wall, two magnificent curtains of gold and silver tissue; these, meeting in the middle, entirely screened the throne. The hall was crowded with people of every station, from the first prince of the blood, to the peasant, each in the place which marked his rank.

For a few minutes great was the confusion of voices; but suddenly, as the soft strains of musical instruments fell upon the ears, the whole assembly lay prostrate on the earth, their mouths almost touching the ground; not a body or limb moved; not a sound could be heard; not an eye was directed towards the curtains, as, to the sound of the music, they were slowly drawn aside, and disclosed the throne itself, which was raised to a height of twelve feet from the floor, and enshrined in a kind of glass-case, through the front open window of which, like an image of one of his own gods, was to be seen the object of all this adulation. Before the window was a magnificent chutt, *i. e.* an object like three umbrellas surmounting each other, reaching from the floor to the ceiling, made of cloth of gold, the stalks being of the same precious metal. Within the curtains, between them and the throne, sat Soyaton, his father Petraxa, and some other princes of the blood. Nearest to the curtains, lay the great officers of state, each having in front of him a golden cup, and a betel box, insignia of their rank, presented by the sovereign on their taking office.

The king, a well-looking Asiatic, at that time about fifty years of age, was magnificently attired, wearing a crown enriched with diamonds, set upon a cap of rich material, a vest wrought with flowers of gold, and diamonds about his neck, arms, wrists and fingers. Of this monarch the French Ambassador wrote:—

"The king is of regal disposition, brave, a great politician, governing himself, magnificent, liberal, loving the fine arts ; in a word, a prince who, by the power of his genius, has thrown off many foolish customs anciently kept up in his kingdom, and has borrowed from foreign nations, and especially from those of Europe, all that he considers most worthy to contribute to his own glory and to the happiness of his people."

The dead silence was broken, and the business of the audience commenced by the king, who commanded the prince and chief of the Moors to state the grievance for the redress of which he had petitioned the crown to grant that audience.

"This, then, is the rogue whose malpractice it has been my duty to discover," thought Phaulcon ; but, as at the king's command the Moor arose, and he caught a full view of the man's features, he started, as if bitten by a snake, and with good cause, for he was *Abdoul the Malay*, otherwise Abdullah, Prince of Macassar.

"Justice, oh dread king! justice. It is now three moons since at the royal feet thy slaves and servants laid a memorial, in which they claimed the sum of fifty thousand crowns, expended by them in the royal service, and over and above the monies in the treasury—yet have they been denied repayment."

"We remember," replied the king, "the memorial was presented to us at the same time that thou and thy brethren, who have been charged with the care of the royal treasuries, declared us too poor to furnish forth an embassy to the greatest king of the West. Your cry," added the king, frowningly, "is for justice, and justice you shall have. Let the chief of the board of accounts," he added, "give his report upon this weighty affair."

At this command, an old mandarin arose. "Thy slaves, oh great king! *have* patiently examined into the claims of these Moors, and that too with the assistance of a light more brilliant than any they have hitherto possessed."

"The result," exclaimed the monarch, impatiently.

"Is, that by a long system of fraud, cunningly managed, these Moors have contrived to make it appear that our lord, the king, owes them fifty thousand crowns, and such the board of examiners of accounts believed to be true, until, by the aid of a new light, they are able to prove that, instead of being creditors, these rats of Moors are themselves indebted to the king sixty thousand crowns."

"Is this thing possible? live there the rogues who dare to rob the sovereign under his own eyes?" replied the monarch, affecting surprise. I say affecting, for of course he and his ministers had thoroughly sifted the accounts in readiness for this *coup-de-théâtre*.

"The lives of thy slaves, oh dread king! will answer for the truth of these words," replied the old mandarin.

"Can the king believe this thing of the slaves who have

been honoured with the royal confidence ?" replied the prince, adding, with cool effrontery, "this old man is in league with our enemies."

"Place before the eyes of this dog of a prince, and chief of robbers, the papers of the Farang secretary, and let him, if he can, prove them false," said the king.

At this command, great was the astonishment of the prince, who dreamed not that his accounts had passed through other hands than those of the official examiners; but, when the papers prepared by Phaulcon were placed before him, and he saw how clearly his fraud was proven, both in the past and also in the matter of the embassy so much desired by the king, he trembled from head to foot. It was however with rage, not fear, for impudently addressing the throne, he said—

"The game has been played, the loser must pay the penalty, let it be as the king wills;" whereupon the soldiers stationed in the hall, turned their eyes towards their sovereign, as if expecting to receive the royal command to lead him forth to instant execution; but his majesty, addressing the Moor, said—

"Prince, thou camest here a wanderer and a beggar, we found you shelter, and even offices by which you have become rich and powerful. In return you have betrayed us. You demand justice, you shall have it. It is this. If before the next moon thou and thy brethren have not only repaid the sixty thousand crowns, but treble that sum, into our treasury, thy lives will be forfeit and thy bodies cast to the dogs."

"Now, oh worthy minister, whose wisdom hath chosen the instrument for the discovery of this great fraud," he added, turning to the Barcalon, "we will perform another act of justice; fetch thou this marvellous Farang, thy secretary, of whom we have heard so much, but seen naught."

The Barcalon, arising, then went for Phaulcon, who, as he approached the throne, not like a Siamese, crawling, but with bended body, became the cynosure of all beholders, but one ; that one was the prince, who, iu the cause of his ruin, saw once more the man, who as a boy had foiled his plans ; and fearful was the expression upon his countenance, for he dared not for his life, in that presence, show his emnity by any other sign.

" Great are the things we have heard of thee, oh stranger ; but still greater are those thou hast performed for us," said the king, as Phaulcon knelt before the throne.

"Thy servant, oh great king !" replied our hero, " hath but performed honestly, as was his duty, that which he undertook ; and if so little merits reward, he has it now in the king's praise."

"The king would be less than the least of dogs did he not offer thee a more profitable reward," replied the monarch ; adding, " since, however, thou hast served us so well, thou shalt have the opportunity of serving us even better. From this moment the office of Treasurer, so badly filled by this rogue of a prince, is in thy hands ; and, that our people may treat with proper submission and respect one whom it is the king's pleasure to honour, we create thee Luang,* with the ten thousand marks of dignity, in right of thy office. The king hath said it."

The last words uttered by the monarch being a signal to certain dignitaries, they came forward and presented to him the emblems of his majesty's favour, and his office ; the first being a rich garment, the latter, a golden cup and a betel box of the same metal.

---

* Luang, the lowest title of nobility. The grades of rank are regulated by marks of dignity, the highest number being ten thousand.

Overwhelmed with surprise and gratitude at his unexpected promotion, Phaulcon knelt at the foot of the throne, but his majesty, motioning to him to be silent, said—

"Now to prove to our subjects that we have not again misplaced our confidence, do thou, with all convenient speed, prepare and furnish all things necessary for the embassy to the French king, and with a magnificence befitting the state and dignity of the throne."

His majesty then reclining backwards, the strains of music again filled the air, and the golden curtains, moved by some invisible agency, glided towards each other, shutting the monarch from the view of his people. The prostrate crowd then sat upright, and began to chat, smoke their cigars, or take their departure; in fact, became as boisterous and joyful as a school of boys just dismissed from their studies and sent into the playground. As, however, Phaulcon arose to depart with his patron, the highest in rank flocked around to congratulate him, less upon his promotion than the great future they, as Asiatics, could foresee was in store for him; and with slavish humility, the great nobles bent their bodies before the man "whom the king had delighted to honour."

Two alone stood aloof—Soyaton, in sulky jealousy, and the Macassar prince who, silent from compulsion in that place, regarded him with a look of fiendish malignity, which, to one less fearless than our hero, would have made his new seat of dignity a bed of thorns.

"Didst regard the deep hatred of thee expressed in the eyes of the Macassar prince, as we quitted the hall of audience?" asked the Barcalon, as they again entered the minister's own apartment.

"My lord, that man's evil heart will some day work his own destruction," replied Phaulcon calmly.

"Nevertheless, be ever on thy guard, for those eyes spoke plainly as words, that he and thou cannot long exist together in this kingdom." As, however, our hero did not deem it policy to notice the dark hint which his words conveyed, the Barcalon, changing the subject of conversation, congratulated his protégé upon his success, and offered him the loan of a large house until the new Treasurer and Luang could provide a fitting establishment of his own.

## CHAPTER XV.

" THERE is a tide in the affairs of men, which taken at the flood leads on to fortune." Phaulcon's flood-tide was the defeat of the Moors ; for so popular did that make him with the people, and so well and speedily did he order all things necessary for the much talked-of Embassy to France, that within six months of his victory he had become "a man famous in the land." Nor was his sudden rise so much owing to the satisfaction he had given the king in the matter of the embassy, as to the good and wise counsel he had offered his majesty in such affairs as the defences of the kingdom against its ancient enemies the Burmans, the making of roads, the improvement of commerce, and the general welfare of the people, by which the shrewd monarch discerned the importance of attaching so good a servant to him by every mark of favour and encouragement.

Thus one would have thought so ambitious a person as our hero could have desired nothing more for the completeness of his own notion of happiness. But no ; although ennobled, high in office, upon the sure road to greater dignities, and, as " he whom the king had delighted to honour," surrounded by flatterers, who were never tired of sounding his praises, there was yet a void in his heart ; for since the night of his interview with the Lady Monica, he had neither seen nor heard of her. To have mentioned in the hearing of others even the name of a female of such high rank, and in connexion with the palace, would have been esteemed an unpardonable breach of good manners, at least in Siamese estimation. Thus had he but one source through which to obtain intelligence of her; namely, her confessor; but then the father, his old tutor, had, as if studiously, kept aloof from the house of the rising favourite; doubtlessly offended at Phaulcon's silence as to his purpose in visiting the palace in disguise. Nay, the priest ultimately admitted that, since the motive had not been openly confessed, he had regarded it as a lover's *ruse*, an attempt, in fact, to steal the best sheep from his flock.

Many an hour, in the midst of his employments, had our hero brooded over the cause of the father's absence from his house, pining perhaps more for the praises and congratulations of one he had known so many years, than gratified at the laudation of the native nobles. Thus, when one evening he received a message from the Jesuit desiring that, on the following morning, he would visit him at his house near the Christian church, he was both delighted and vexed; delighted that he should now become reconciled to the old man, and, perhaps, hear of Monica; vexed, because he could not comply till evening, for the next day was the annual festival of the inundation of the Meinam, and he would have to attend the king.

But a word or two about this festival.

Like the valley of the Nile, Siam is irrigated by the yearly inundation of its own mighty river. In June the waters begin to rise, and in August they sometimes reach to a height of six feet above the ordinary level, overflowing the whole country, to the destruction of the rice harvest and sugar plantations. "The day

R

upon which the turn of the inundation happens, the king," says
the traveller, Diego de Couti,* "comes out of the city, accompanied
by the whole of the nobility, in barges richly gilded and covered
with ornaments, with great display and noise of musical instruments. They proclaim that the king is about to order the waters
to disperse ; and this is the greatest festival in the year. A mast
is raised in the middle of the stream, adorned with silken flags,
and a prize suspended for the best rower. All the contending
boats put themselves in trim, and, at a given signal, start, with such
cries, shoutings, and tumults, as if the world were being destroyed;
the first who arrives carrying off the prize. But in the contest
there is terrible confusion—boats running against and swamping
each other ; oars tangled and disentangled, in a disorder admirable
to look at from around. So that the people are not so barbarous,
but they imitate the ancient Trojans (as in the manner Æneas,
when he arrived in Sicily, had the festival of his galleys, giving
precious prizes to the most alert) ; and when these Siamese
have won the prize, they return to the city with such rejoicings,
shoutings, and tumultuous music, that the noise shakes both the
water and the land. Then the king, having returned to the city,
the people say he has driven back the waters, because these
heathens attribute to their kings all the attributes of God, and
believe they are the source of all good."

Such was the ceremony at which the impatient Phaulcon was
compelled to attend till near sun-down, when, being dismissed by
the king, he at once went in his magnificent barge to keep his
appointment. The church stood about a quarter of a mile from
the banks of the river, being adjoined by the priest's little house.
To the latter our hero proceeded, unattended by any of the

* Bowring's Siam.

thirty men who had rowed him. As the father met him at the threshold, and led him within, he said—

"Thou art welcome, my son, for I have weighty matters to talk over with thee."

"But first, father, say in what have I offended, that you should thus long have kept aloof from your old pupil."

"Till yesterday, I believed that your object in visiting the palace in disguise was to steal the affections of the Japanese girl ; to bring her mind from spiritual to mundane things ; in other words, to rob me of the most worthy sheep of my flock."

"And if so, my father ?" said Phaulcon.

"As I *then* thought," replied the priest, almost savagely, "I would myself have betrayed thee to the king."

"Nay, nay, good father, I will not believe thee."

"Well, well, it matters not ; sufficient that now I see this affair in another light ; it may be even good for the Church that thou and Monica should ultimately become man and wife."

"Say you so, father ; how is this ? to what am I indebted for this change in my favour ?" replied Phaulcon.

"My son, I will be candid ; it is because I see that thou must become powerful in the land, will recant thy heresy, and help in the good work so near my heart. But hadst thou remained but the poor, aye, or even wealthy shipman, never shouldst thou have had opportunity of whispering words of love in the ear of the Japanese Monica."

"It is a daring assertion," replied Phaulcon, who, with the vanity of most brave amd handsome fellows, believe that they can at will establish a kind of magnetic telegraph between their own hearts, and those of any particular woman upon whom they condescend to fix their affections.

"Nay, my son, it is true; the descendant of martyrs would never have become the wife of a heretic."

"But," replied our hero, "suppose *that* difficulty had been removed?"

"Then I," replied the father, determinedly, "would have saved her from falling into the possession of a *mere* adventurer, powerless to aid our cause; for is she not the very key-stone of the arch, across which the faith is to be carried into this realm? But *tut*, it is useless to talk of a difficulty when it is no longer before us; I sent for thee to converse upon matters of moment."

"*Sent* for *me*," interposed Phaulcon, hastily and haughtily.

"Pardon, my son, if I have offended the minister, but it is to Phaulcon I am speaking, and as he, keeping in mind the rich reward, will aid me, we will not quarrel about words."

"From my soul I declare that no reward, nay, not even the hand of Monica, shall tempt me to do aught against my conscience," replied Phaulcon hotly.

"But that in which I seek thine aid, my son, will fit thy conscience. Nay, it is a portion of thy destiny; but listen."

"Proceed, my father."

"Know then," continued the priest, "that the time has now arrived when the faith of Christ may be firmly planted in the land; true, several attempts have been made, but the periods having been unfitly chosen, they have all failed. When the holy St. Francis Xavier was throwing broadcast the seeds of Christianity in Malacca and Singapore, then tributaries of Siam, some were wafted to the land where Christianity took such root, that, in the year 1616, the reigning King of Siam sent an embassy to Goa, requesting the Portuguese governor to send some missionaries to expound and preach the Gospel to his subjects.

The request being complied with, the king received the fathers with all kindness, offered every opportunity for the dissemination of their religion, and even built them a church at his own expense. But, alas! the monarch being dethroned by one of his chief noblemen, the usurper drove the brethren from the land, and commanded those of his people who had become converts to recant under penalty of death. Other similar attempts have been made, but without success. The time, however, has arrived when the holy banner may be unfurled, and upheld triumphantly; for the king is willing to become a convert, and thou art his chief favourite, and at his elbow; while his daughter, upon whom his whole earthly affections are fixed, is under the control and guidance of the Lady Monica."

"Alas, father! I fear that his majesty is but lukewarm in this matter."

"Not so; for but yesterday he told me that there were three thousand slaves, prisoners of war, adding: 'You, holy man, may make Christians of these people, if you can, and if, when you have succeeded, you will let me know, I will place a governor over them.'"

"True father," replied Phaulcon, "the king is liberal, far-seeing, and desirous that his people should choose for themselves; but a convert will he himself never become, for, but a few days ago, he said to me—

"'As different countries, oh Phaulcon! produce various fruits and flowers, so do they different religions. Your faith is excellent for you, mine for me; and although it is good that the subjects should be permitted the exercise of their own judgments, the king would be degraded in their eyes did he easily set the example of forsaking the religion of his fathers.'"

"Truly, it is less difficult to bring over to the faith its fiercest antagonist, than to sow the divine seed in the hearts of the apathetic; nevertheless, I do not despair of the conversion of this king; already is he about to send forth an embassy to Louis of France, to solicit the establishing of commercial relations, aye, and at my desire, even to beg that several fathers of the Society of Jesus, learned in the mathematics, may be sent to him."

"Then what more can you desire?" interposed Phaulcon.

"That," and the Jesuit whispered, as if he feared other ears than our hero's might catch his words, "the King of Siam should beg of the great Louis to send him a regiment of French troops."

"Father," replied Phaulcon starting, as if bitten by a serpent, "what mean you? would you have the conquests of Mexico and Peru played over again in this country by the Frenchmen, and suggest that *I* too, should be the means of betraying this good king, my friend—fie!"

"Be not too hasty, my son, you mistake my meaning. The presence of European troops will be for the benefit of all—the king, the people, thyself, and Christianity. You," he added, "are destined to rise to great power in this land; how think you can that power be consolidated, upheld, in the midst of such enemies as Soyaton, the Mahomedans, and the Buddhist priests and nobles, who even now are regarding thee with jealous eyes, aye, and perhaps intriguing to prevent your upward rise, if not displace thee; how, I again ask, with such treachery around, can you hope to remain in safety without European troops?"

"Father," replied Phaulcon thoughtfully, "this is a wily scheme, yet fraught with both good and evil; good, inasmuch as a few European troops might be made the nucleus of a well-drilled army for the king's service and protection, good again, as they would serve to keep intriguing traitors at bay—yet evil, should they prove but the vanguard of an army of conquest to be sent hereafter, for assuredly the ambitious Louis would claim some reward for so costly a loan."

"Princes of the earth," replied the father, "can desire no greater reward than the acclamations of grateful millions, the knowledge that they have conferred benefits upon humanity; and Louis seeks no greater than the establishment of a treaty of commerce between the two nations of France and Siam, and the dissemination of our holy faith. But," he added, "weigh this matter well in thy mind, and, having approved it, seek the king, and place before him the advantage of having at his command an army, so disciplined by European soldiers that he may set his hereditary foes, the Burmans, at defiance, and he will hug thee to his heart for thy counsel."

"Father," replied our hero, thoughtfully, "I will think this thing over."

"Do, my son, for it is near the heart of her you love, and she may—"

"Nay, father," interposed Phaulcon, "say no more, at least now, for I am but mortal, and selfish motives might make me blind, either to the good or evil of this my adopted country and its king. But," he added earnestly, "hast seen the Lady Monica of late?"

"Yesterday, my son, at the palace; but now it occurs to me that, ere we part, you may get sight of, nay, have speech with her."

"How! what mean you, father?" exclaimed Phaulcon, trembling with delight.

"Accompanied by the Princess, but unknown to all but her most favoured servants, she comes to attend the service for

which I am even now about to prepare," said the Jesuit, with
a searching glance into our hero's countenance, that probably
meant, "Surely, such a foretaste of the promised reward must
secure thee to my purpose."

"Is this possible?" replied Phaulcon. "Then she even now
approaches," he added, as, looking through the window, he saw
a gilded barge of great length, and with dragon prow, moored to
the bank of the river.

"It is, my son."

Then, with bated breath, Phaulcon watched the two ladies
disembark, and enter their palanquins or sedan chairs, which,
each borne by six men, stood in readiness for them. Scarcely,
however, had the bearers moved forward towards the church,
than, from another great barge, there leaped ashore some twenty
armed men, who surrounded the vehicles.

"Holy mother of Heaven, they are attacked by revellers,"
exclaimed the priest.

"Nay, it is the rascal Soyaton," cried Phaulcon; and with a few
springs, like those of a tiger-cat, he had thrown himself into the
midst of the party which had surrounded Monica and the Princess,
and with one blow of his sword lain the prince low; but dearly
did he pay for his temerity, for the next instant he was stretched
upon the earth by the dagger of the Prince of Macassar, who,
placing his foot upon our hero's breast, exclaimed—

"Accursed Greek, at length I have thee, did I not say
I would be thy fate;" and again would he have plunged his
weapon into the breast of his prostrate foe, but his upraised arm
was arrested by the heroic Monica, who, seeing Phaulcon's danger,
darted forth from her palanquin, exclaiming, as she prevented the
blow—

THE LADY MONICA SEIZED BY THE PRINCE.

"Is the Macassar Prince tired of his life, that he would slay the king's friend, in the presence of the king's daughter?"

. The words were all-powerful, the assassin's hand was stayed, he trembled as he repeated—

. "The Pearl of the Palace! The Princess!"

"Is here," said a soft, but a firm-toned voice, as the curtains of the other palanquin were drawn aside, and disclosed to view a young lady in the very pride of youth and beauty. "How is this, oh dog of a Moor! that even the daughter of the king cannot pass on her father's highway without molestation at thy hands?"

"Pardon, oh illustrious lady! for this thing could not have chanced, had it been possible for thy slave to have imagined thy sacred presence," replied the Macassar Prince, throwing himself at her feet. But, knowing his vantage ground, he added, "Who, oh royal lady! not being a magician, could have divined that the Princess of Siam would, in defiance of her great father's will, have been found paying a secret visit to the Farang priest?"

"Dog of a Moor, well knowest thou that the lives of thee and thy friend depend but upon a small word from my lips, still thou believest that for fear of vexing the king that word may not be uttered. But it shall not save thee, since thou hast given the noble Farang his death wound."

At these words Monica, who was endeavouring to staunch the blood from Phaulcon's wound with a silken sash, cried passionately—

"Royal lady! Mistress! command thy slaves to seize that bad man, for the noble Phaulcon is slain."

"Nay, nay," said Father Thomas, who had just joined the group, "it were better for all that he should depart. But take comfort, lady," he added, as he saw the grief upon Monica's countenance, "Phaulcon has but fainted from loss of blood, and, by God's help, he will speedily recover."

"Thank thee, father—Thank heaven for those words," replied the lady.

"Noble, beloved Monica," murmured our hero, suddenly recovering, as if through the tones of her voice.

"He revives," said Monica, joyfully ; and then she ordered a party of her attendants to carry our hero to the house of the Jesuit, who promised to tend him until he should be able to be removed to his own palace.

The Princess and the Lady Monica then returned to their barge. As for their late assailants, humbled, if not terrified at the mistake they had made in attacking the princess' party, they made the best of their way to their barge, taking with them the wounded Soyaton.

351

## CHAPTER XVI.

BLAKE'S RETURN AND DEPARTURE FROM SIAM.

WHEN, about three months after the incident related at the end of the last chapter, Blake returned to Ayuthia he was astounded at hearing, from the European merchants, of his friend's speedy rise to power and fortune. From a similar source he also learned that the Siamese people were, at the same time, rejoicing and weeping over two recent events. Rejoicing, because the renowned and popular Farang favourite, Phaulcon, had just been rescued from the very jaws of death, some said, by the king's physician, who had but that day declared his recovery from a violent fever certain. Weeping, and their grief was as genuine as their joy, at the death of the great and good Barcalon. Now, as Blake knew nothing of the latter minister, he could have little sympathy with the natives in their grief. But with the rejoicers he rejoiced, and, as we generally estimate the more highly that which we have been upon the point of losing, he lost no time in repairing at once to Phaulcon's *palace*. As he proceeded to the quarter where he was informed the latter was situated, his countenance alternated with smiles and sorrow. Phaulcon to have a palace! The good Lord Phaulcon! as he heard the natives call him. Phaulcon, always the unfortunate, but ever persevering; once a ship-boy, not long since a penniless adventurer, now the favourite of a king, a popular minister, and the owner of a palace! Well, after all there *was*

something in having "a star," in being visited by a majestic gentleman
in a dream, and in prophecies and presentiments generally.  Such
thoughts brought smiles upon his countenance.  But then, his
friend was climbing a dizzy height, and the greater would be his
fall ; and who that pondered for a minute over the histories of
king's favourites and popular ministers, could doubt that such a
fall was probable—and at these thoughts the smiles were lost in
an expression of sorrow.

It was, however, only upon reaching the palace that he could
realize to himself a notion of his friend's state.  Entering
the first court-yard, he found it crowded with guards, slaves, and
attendants, who, from their prostrate positions, were evidently
momentarily expecting the out-coming of some great man ; and, as
by the magnificent trappings of an elephant which stood, or rather
was kneeling before the chief entrance, and carried upon its back
a gorgeous howdah, bearing the insignia of royalty, he knew that
dignitary must be the king himself, he felt but the more
astonished, as for a King of Siam to visit a minister seemed a
monstrous piece of condescension.  Nevertheless, so it was, for
almost the next minute the king entered his howdah, and the
elephant arising, commenced his stately march back to the royal
residence.

"Now, for my Lord Mushroom himself," muttered Blake,
walking towards the entrance through which the king had just
passed; but the attendants, feeling the honour paid to their master
by the royal visit, reflected upon themselves, rudely forced him
back, declaring that majesty having once passed that portal,
henceforth it must be sealed up ; then, with insolent laughing,
they cried—

"Pray who is this mean fellow that hath the presumption to

endeavour to force his way so unceremoniously, into the presence of the great Lord Phaulcon?"

"I wonder if it be like master, like man," muttered Blake; and then he begged one of the men to tell Phaulcon, that his friend, Blake Taunton, was awaiting to see him. But this request only made my Lord Mushroom's slaves laugh the more, for what man, beneath the rank of a prince of the blood-royal, could presume to call his lordship friend; and it became very questionable whether Blake would have had his message conveyed at all, had it not been that the mandarin Prenawi, who had just quitted Phaulcon, passed through the court-yard at the time. Recognizing Blake, he shook him by the hand, after the English fashion he had been taught during the voyage with the two friends, then to the slaves he cried—

"Room there, ye dogs, for the great Lord Phaulcon's brother;" and in an instant every man prostrated himself, and the mandarin led Blake to my lord's chamber, at the door of which he left him.

It was a noble apartment, gorgeously furnished, but after a mixed Oriental and European fashion. Phaulcon, who was reclining languidly upon a pile of velvet cushions, no sooner saw his friend than, starting to his feet, he embraced him.

"Welcome, thrice welcome, Blake; long has my heart yearned for you." But so feeble were his steps; so wan, emaciated his appearance, and weak his voice, that Blake could not forbear exclaiming—

"Great Heaven! my friend, is it thus I find you; the fever has left you low indeed."

"Aye," replied Phaulcon, when they were seated; "but it was a fever caught at the point of the villain Abdoul's dagger—the

weapon was poisoned ; " and then he related the story of his visit
to the Father Thomas, the blow he had received from the Macassar
Prince ; adding, that to prevent its coming to the ears of the king
that the princess had been about visiting the Christian church,
he had caused it to be given out that he had been attacked
by fever.

"Dagger, blow, or fever, it has left you "—

"A remnant of my former self, Phaulcon's remains," said our
hero, impatiently ; adding, " But enough of this, I like not dwelling
upon that which I can neither prevent nor avenge. Tell me,
Blake, how has it fared with *you* since our parting."

"Well, passably well ; that is, I have neither won nor lost a
fortune. But my best news is from home, at least *my* home,
England."

"From the Captain ! Zillah ! God bless them both. What
say they ? "

" That all is well with them, except that the Captain has the
gout, and Zillah's getting aged ; at least so saith the old
gentleman himself, who, but for the state of his leg, declares he
would make the "long voyage for the purpose of carrying us both
back to England."

"I wonder whether it will ever be *my* lot to see those kindly
shores once more," said Phaulcon thoughtfully.

"Aye, to be sure, old fellow, when you are tired of playing
the hidalgo among these slippery, saffron-faced Siamese," replied
Blake ; adding, with a laugh, "*I* wonder what your old friend
the dream gentleman would prophecy thereat. "

"Tut, tut, my friend, no banter upon that incident in my
life."

" But what saith the Captain about me ? " replied Phaulcon.

"*Lege, lege*, Constantine," said Blake, placing a letter in his friend's hand.

Phaulcon perused the epistle, and tears started to his eyes, as they fell upon the many kind things written there about himself, and as he saw an offer of a home among the Cheviots should he not have been successful in his voyaging. Returning the letter to Blake, he said—

"God bless him, God bless him."

"But I have another letter," said Blake, "written a month after, yet which reached me at the same time. In this the Captain gives me the welcome intelligence that he has at last discovered a clew to my birth, and desires that I will return to England with all speed, to help him follow it out."

"Ah, that is indeed joyful news; from my soul I congratulate you, Blake," replied Phaulcon, "yet now more than 'ever shall I miss you, my friend. When do you sail?"

"By the first homeward-bound ship,—in a week I hope," said Blake. "But enough of my affairs; how about thine own? tell me by what strange chance *you* have risen so high that even the king condescends to visit you at your own house."

Very attentively and admiringly did Blake listen to the story of his friend's adventures, since their parting; but when, in conclusion, Phaulcon told him he had that day obtained his majesty's permission to solicit from the King of France the loan of two regiments, Blake, laying his hand upon Phaulcon's shoulder, said—

"Phaulcon, do you mean honestly to this king and people of Siam? Is it not rather the scheme of thy ambitious brain, perhaps even with a notion of grasping at the highest dignity in the realm, to place beneath the yoke of the priests and soldiers of France the souls and bodies of these Siamese? Such daring ideas have been attempted, aye, and successfully in the East ere now." *

"By my soul, no," replied Phaulcon. "But," he added, almost haughtily, "it is not of such things that *you* and I must speak, my friend."

"Stay," said Blake, " this may be the last time I shall have the opportunity of speaking upon this matter. Be warned in time, Phaulcon, the higher you climb, the better target you will be, and the more numerous the shafts that will be sent against you; forget not the proverbial treachery of Asiatics ; nor, that this Soyaton and his father, being near the throne, head a powerful party."

" For these reasons do I seek to place around the king a bulwark of European troops," replied Phaulcon. " Do you still doubt my moderation ?  Know then, my cautious friend, that this morning his majesty begged of me, as a further reward for my past services, and as a testimony of his regard, to accept the office of *Barcalon*, so recently rendered vacant by the death of my good patron.† Well, fearing to give umbrage to the native nobles, I refused to accept it."

"It was a prudent course, indeed ; but how took the king your refusal ? "

" At first angrily, but then, admitting the justice of my reasons, he commanded me to ask a favour of him, and such an one, that

---

* Kempfer avers that Phaulcon's intention in introducing French troops into Siam was, that he might seize upon the supreme power.

† "Phaulcon," says the Père d'Orleans, "prudently excused himself accepting the Barcalonship, fearing in the dawn of his prosperity to excite the jealousy of the nobles; but, although refusing the position, he fulfilled nearly all the duties connected with it; for any affair of importance was referred to him and the king had such entire confidence in him that he was the channel of all the requests of the people and of all the favours of the sovereign."

in its bestowal, he would feel that he was granting an equivalent to. the rank and office I had rejected."

"Didst ask him for the hand of his only daughter?" said Blake, laughing.

"Not so, yet a boon almost as great, which he could and did promise to grant in due time. What that is, however, must be known to none until it is completed," replied Phaulcon. "But now," he added, "*I* have a favour to ask of thee, my friend. Wilt take charge of the ship that is to convey the Siamese embassy to France?.by so doing you will serve me, and, at the same time, obtain a handsome sum for the passage. I ask thee not to bring her back, it will be unnecessary, for a Frenchman will then take the command."

"On the latter condition, I accept your offer," replied Blake, who was pleased at the opportunity of sailing much earlier than he expected.

The rest of the day was spent by the friends in talking over old times and future prospects. The favour that Phaulcon had asked of the king, yet could not tell Blake, was the hand of Monica; but, even had he not been barred by etiquette, our hero *would* have been equally silent to his friend upon this matter, for the secret involved another, which he knew would deeply pain Blake, and perhaps the Captain and Zillah, namely, that during his illness he had returned to the faith in which he had been born and bred. How that conversion came about we will hear from Père d'Orleans, who says :—

"Phaulcon was born of Catholic parents; but the education he had received among the English, during ten years of his life, had insensibly caused him to embrace the Anglican faith, in which he had continued up to this time. The captain of the

s

English factory, having perceived in him a leaning towards the faith of his fathers, omitted nothing to retain him in error. Happily, Father Antoine Thomas held several conversations with him, in which, the discourse being adroitly led to controversial points, Phaulcon took so much pleasure, that he himself invited the father to see him often, that they might have farther conference together. The earliest discussions were on the real presence of Jesus Christ in the Eucharist, of which, two or three conversations easily convinced a man who was in good faith striving to discover the truth.

"However much Phaulcon was occupied with the king and the prime ministers, he did not fail to find time to converse with his doctor upon religious subjects. They spoke of the pope, of the head of the Anglican Church, and of the origin of the last-mentioned power; the abuses of which were so clearly demonstrated to him by the father, that he was shortly persuaded of them.

"It was just at this time he fell sick; and he had not so entirely determined what part to take, but that he might have hesitated for some time to declare himself, had not his determination been hastened by the fear of dying out of the pale of the Church. Being at length resolved, he desired the father to come during the night; and, after having narrated to him the cause of his fall into heresy, he discovered to him the present condition of his heart and mind.

"As it was not very pressing, though the illness appeared dangerous, nothing was concluded upon that day; but on the morrow, when there was a sensible improvement, the sick man said to the father that he desired to return to the Church, entreating him to be his guide and director in this important matter, and assuring him that he should find the most perfect submission to all that he should direct.

"As the peril diminished, the father would not press his penitent to abjure his errors, but took care to converse with him frequently during his illness, encouraging his good intentions, and waiting his entire restoration to perform what was needful.

"Father Thomas, wishing to proceed cautiously in an affair of so much importance, and render his work secure, persuaded Phaulcon to seek a retreat, in which he read and meditated at leisure on the exercises of St. Ignatius. He instructed him also, during that time, to make a general confession, and made him promise to take a *Catholic* wife, as soon as he had abjured his errors, believing it to be a principal means for the solid conversion of a man who had lived in the disorders common to those of his age.

"Things being thus disposed, Phaulcon made his abjuration in the church of the Portuguese Jesuits. He experienced unspeakable consolation during the ceremony, thinking he had now returned to the bosom of the Church after so long straying from her fold. His gratitude was indeed so lively, that he told those who assisted at the rite, as he embraced them, that since God had shown him this favour, which he had so little deserved, he would thenceforth endeavour to serve the cause of religion in the kingdom of Siam, and so procure for others the happiness he now enjoyed. Some days after he received the communion; and his fervour still increasing, he addressed the father in these words :—

"'I promise, before our Lord Jesus Christ, whose presence I here acknowledge, that from henceforth I will devote all my endeavours to the reparation of having passed my life in error,

s 2

and to the extension of the Catholic Church.  I pray Him who
has inspired the intention to give me grace to perform it.'

"A few days after, he married a young Japanese lady of good
family, distinguished not only by rank, but also by the blood of
the martyrs, from whom she was descended, and whose virtues
she imitated.  He ever lived with his noble partner in such
peace and harmony, as might be a model to all who are united
by the sacrament of marriage.  The king and his nobles offered
him congratulations and handsome presents, and the Catholics
testified great pleasure on the occasion."

Shortly after his marriage, Phaulcon was prevailed upon by
the king to accept the title and state of barcalon, or prime
minister.  Thus, next the sovereign, the most powerful personage
in the empire, husband of the woman he loved, and in the
possession of wealth sufficient to keep up an almost kingly state,
it may be thought that our hero had reached the uppermost
round of fortune's ladder, and was therefore content.  But not
so; for knowing the treacherous nature of Asiatics, and the
slippery grasp by which the favourites of Eastern monarchs
have ever held power, our hero felt that he had built his house
but upon sand; that surrounded as he was by the party headed
by Petraxa, and the Mahomedans ever upon the look-out for a
means to work his ruin, he should know no real peace of mind
until he had obtained the loan of the regiments he had demanded
from the King of France.  The French alliance would moreover
enable him to effect that which had now become the darling
object of his soul; nay, since his abjuration and his marriage,
a burning passion, in comparison with which all other feelings
seemed of ice—the conversion of the Siamese nation to Christianity.
Great was the joy therefore of Phaulcon, when, after an absence

of two years, the envoys sent to France returned with the welcome intelligence, that the great Louis had not only readily complied with all their demands, but that, within the next two years, a French ambassador would be sent to the court of Siam, for the purpose of arranging the terms of a treaty, and also, that a regiment or regiments would accompany the ambassador. Now, upon hearing this, Phaulcon, who feared the kind of reception foreign troops might meet with, took every means to have it disseminated among the people that the soldiers and priests of the great western king were coming for their especial benefit. Thus, having as it were smoothed the way, and prepared for his expected allies a popular welcome, it was with no little anxiety he awaited their coming.

In the interim, Phaulcon lost no opportunity of adding to his own popularity with king and people. He devoted himself heart and soul to the duties of his high office, and with such signal success, that in less than three years from the time of his marriage, the monarch of Siam had become one of the richest and most prosperous sovereigns in Asia. For the people who could work he found employment, and (what had never before been heard of in Siam) regular payment. As for the halt and lame, who could not labour, there were few who did not receive charity at his hands; four hundred he fed and lodged within the walls of his palace. Nor did he forget his promise to the father, made in the Portuguese chapel; for he built churches, and sent envoys to the different governors of European settlements in the East, desiring that they would send missionaries to Siam.

# CHAPTER XVII.

## THE FRENCH ALLIANCE.

Now the Mahomedans and those of the native nobles who acted with them had, as we have seen, striven and intrigued to prevent the sending of the embassy to France; but, being defeated, they next sought to nullify its probable consequences, by procuring an embassy to be sent from the court of Persia to the sovereign of Siam—the main object of the latter being to induce the king to accept the Koran. But again were the Moors defeated; for although the Persian ambassadors reached Siam some six months before the French envoy, Phaulcon had, by means of some excuse or another, prevented their obtaining an audience of the sovereign. Then so glowingly and so often did our hero paint to the king the great benefits to be derived from the Gallic alliance, and so well did his emissaries work to the same effect among the people, that the day of the arrival of the French ambassador at the mouth of the Meinam was regarded as an occasion of national rejoicing.

On the 30th day of September, 1685, as Phaulcon and Monica were about commencing matutinal prayers, the Father Antoine Thomas entered their presence, in breathless haste, and, with signs of joy upon his countenance, announced that the Chevalier de Chaumont, the French ambassador, and his suite, with two ships, had crossed the bar of the Meinam.

"Is it indeed so, father? then God be thanked, for it is most opportune," said Phaulcon.

"God be thanked," repeated Monica; and not another word was spoken, until, in their orisons, they had offered up their gratitude to heaven.

"Now," said Phaulcon, when prayers were concluded, "the Persian may have his audience."

"Aye," muttered the father, who cared not that other ears than those of our hero and his wife should catch his words, "for the completion of our holy work is at hand. The king will doubtlessly now embrace the faith."

"Be not too sanguine upon that point, father, for I fear me, that although his majesty will give liberty of conscience to all— nay, even aid in the conversion of the people—he is himself yet far from the kingdom of God."

"My son," replied the father, triumphantly, "it is almost alone upon that condition, that Louis of France will consent to lend his regiments. It is the chief purpose of the Chevalier de Chaumont's coming.

"Is it possible, oh my husband! that thou didst stipulate, without the king's knowledge, that in return for these French troops his majesty would openly embrace the faith of Christ?" asked Monica, in alarm.

"If there be any blame in this matter, my daughter," replied the father, "it is mine."

"Thine, father?" said Monica, in surprise.

"Aye, daughter, for by one of my holy brethren who returned to France with the Siamese ambassadors, I sent information to Louis, through his minister, of the certainty of the King of Siam's embracing the faith."

" And this without my knowledge, father ? " said Phaulcon.

"Truly so, for I feared that you would not speak with certainty as to the king's intentions, and a doubt would have kept from us the regiments ; for think you the great Louis would have believed the King of Siam sincere in his desire to aid in the conversion of his subjects while his majesty himself wavered ?"

"Father," replied our hero bitterly, sternly, "you have thrust upon me the part of a double dealer ; nay, you have plunged me into a difficulty that may bring about my ruin, and that of the Christian cause !"   So saying he left the apartment to prepare for a visit to the king.

As soon as his majesty was informed of the arrival of the French ambassador at the mouth of the Meinam, at the suggestion of Phaulcon, he summoned a council of the chief officers of state, and ordered them, under heavy pains and penalties, to prepare to give his excellency a reception worthy of the great sovereign he represented ; indeed, such a one that had never before been given to an ambassador in Siam.

This order, for the greater part, was obeyed with alacrity and joy.   Two lords upon the part of the king, and two secretaries upon the part of the minister, Phaulcon, were sent to the mouth of the river to congratulate the Chevalier de Chaumont, ambassador of France, upon his arrival, and to present him with a supply of fruit, oxen, pigs, poultry, ducks, and other provisions, for the use of his ships' companies.

The Chevalier was greatly pleased at the cordial manner in which the two lords welcomed him, and not a little surprised at their recognising him as an old acquaintance of the Siamese ; —very old—for conformably with the Buddhist doctrine of the transmigration of souls, they declared that they knew very well

that his excellency had some thousand years before been employed
in great affairs, having, indeed, at that distant period, come as
ambassador from the King of France to the King of Siam, and
brought about a friendship between the two monarchs, and which
he was then in Siam to renew.  The French of that period
were no less polite than their descendants of the present day,
nevertheless De Chaumont could not resist a laugh at the mandarins' assertion, making reply, "that he could not remember
so distant a period, and moreover, to the best of his belief, that
the present voyage was the only one *he* had ever made to Siam."
The mandarins, then telling his excellency that the king, who
was overjoyed at his coming, was impatient to receive him, and
had commanded his astrologers to select a fortunate day for the
audience, and his nobles to have a palace prepared in the capital,
and to see that every honour was paid to his excellency and party
during their progress to Ayuthia, took their departure.

The voyage of the Chevalier from the mouth of the river
resembled a royal progress; the bosom and banks of the Meinam
were crowded with sight-seers.  At every town the governor and
his chief officers came to give him welcome, and the batteries
fired salutes.  In the capital he was received by the prime minister,
Phaulcon, in person, who conducted him to a magnificent palace,
which had been formerly tenanted by the Persian ambassador.
With this interview came a great difficulty to Phaulcon, for no
sooner had the arrangements been made for De Chaumont's
audience with the king, in order to present his majesty with the
autograph letter from Louis of France, than the ambassador
desired to know whether the conversion to Christianity of the
King of Siam would take place during his stay in the capital.

"My lord," replied Phaulcon, "I cannot but confess my surprise at your excellency's question, for surely the King of Siam's envoys could have promised no such thing to the great Louis."

"My lord Barcalon, they did not," replied De Chaumont, "they touched upon nought but a treaty of commerce and friendship between the two nations; nevertheless the Father Antoine Thomas, in a secret despatch, in which he craved of his majesty, King Louis, to send to *thy* aid French soldiers, promised that in return for such aid, the King of Siam, already convinced by you and him of the truths of Christianity, would, upon the coming of a French embassy, set the example of conversion himself, by publicly abjuring the worship of his false gods."

"My lord, the conversion of the King of Siam is the one object nearest to my heart, and I doubt not that ultimately it may be attained; but the father, enthusiastic in the good cause, was too precipitate. It is not by a leap, but by little and little that great ends are achieved. At present I have not pressed his majesty to this, and conjure your excellency most earnestly not to forward this matter at your audience, for by grasping at the whole we may lose all. No, for the present let us be content that the king is willing to permit churches to be built throughout his dominions—the coming and preaching of Catholic missionaries."

"My lord Phaulcon," replied the Frenchman, "I have heard much of your wisdom, and it must be true, for you have raised yourself from small beginnings to great power; but the same wisdom teaches you upon what a treacherous base that power if not supported by European troops."

"By heaven!" returned our hero, passionately, "your excellency wrongs me by imputing mere selfish motives. Like other men, I love power, and would keep that which I have gained; but

the honest, the heartiest, and most earnest desire of my soul is
to use it for the good of the people of this land and holy
Church."

"Your pardon, Monseigneur, I intended not to offend, but to
praise your great talent. I believe all you have said, and know
what you have done, and *will* do for the benefit of the souls of the
people of Siam ; still, as the chief object of my mission, and the
great desire of my royal master, is the *king's* conversion, as the
best, the only guarantee of his majesty's sincerity in promoting the
faith, I must declare either by word of mouth or letter King
Louis' message, and receive his majesty's reply, from his own
lips, or if it please you better, in writing, under the royal sign
manual."

This answer being decisive, the representatives of the kings
of France and Siam took leave of each other. The next day,
however, Phaulcon again sought the Frenchman ; it was arranged
between them that De Chaumont should at the audience touch
but slightly upon the subject of the king's conversion, and that
afterwards he should prepare a memorial in writing, which
Phaulcon not only undertook to present to the king at a private
audience, but to support with all the eloquence at his command.

Accordingly, after the grand reception of the French ambassador,
at which his excellency delivered King Louis' letter and presents
to the sovereign of Siam, Phaulcon performed his part of the
agreement. How honestly, we shall see from the Father Tachard's
account of the conversation between him and the king.*

"'Sire,' said Phaulcon, throwing himself at the monarch's
feet, and holding the paper in his hand, ' the ambassador
of France has placed in my hands a memorial which contains

* Sir John Bowring's translation.

certain propositions, of which he is to render an account to the
king, his master ; but, before giving it to your majesty, permit
me to represent to you the motive which has engaged the most
Christian king to send this embassy. That wise prince, your
sincere friend, sire, well knowing the greatness of soul, and
generosity of your royal heart through the ambassadors and the
magnificent presents which you sent to him, without other
interest than that of securing the friendship of a prince so
glorious and renowned throughout the universe ; seeing also that
your majesty's ministers had sent to the ministers of his kingdom
two mandarins with considerable presents, to congratulate them
on the birth of a grandson to their great king, worthy of a
perpetual posterity, which may ever represent his admirable virtues, and secure the happiness of his people : this great monarch,
sire, surprised at so disinterested a proceeding, resolved to respond
to those obliging compliments, and to do so he conceived a method
worthy of him, and suitable to your majesty.  Should he send you
wealth ?  No, for it is in your kingdom, sire, that strangers come
to seek it.  As to forces, it is well known that your majesty
is feared by all your neighbours, and well able to chastise them,
should they violate the peace which they have won by their
entreaties.  Should he think of ceding lands and provinces to
the sovereign of so many kings and the ruler of kingdoms
which make up nearly a fourth of Asia itself ; neither did he
send his subjects hither solely for the purposes of commerce,
which is an interest common alike to his own people and to
the subjects of your majesty.  He considered, however, that it
was in his power to offer to your majesty something of infinitely
more importance, and well befitting the dignity of two such
great sovereigns.  .

"'Remembering what had been the cause of his own glory, giving him power to take so many towns, subjugate so many provinces, and gain so many victories—which had made his people happy, and attracted to him, from the extremities of the globe, so many royal ambassadors and princes desiring his friendship—which had caused your majesty to seek the favour of such an incomparable prince, by sending so magnificent an embassy;—having, I repeat, attentively considered all these things, this wise and enlightened king saw that the God whom he worships was their author, His divine Providence having thus ordered them, and that he owed them all to the intercession of the Holy Mother of the Saviour, under whose protection he has consecrated his person and his kingdom to the true God. This conviction, and his great desire to secure to your majesty these great privileges, made him resolve to put before you, sire, the means which obtained for him so much glory and happiness, and which are indeed the knowledge and worship of the true God, as taught by the Christian religion, and by that alone. He therefore sends his ambassador, trusting that your majesty will, together with your whole kingdom, accept and follow the true faith.

"'This prince, sire, is still more to be admired for his penetration, enlightenment, and wisdom, than for his numerous conquests and victories. Your majesty is acquainted with his generosity and royal friendship, and cannot do better than follow the wise counsels of so great a king, and so good a friend. For myself, sire, I have never ceased to implore the God whom I worship for this grace for your majesty, and would willingly give a thousand lives to obtain it from the Divine goodness. May your majesty consider that by this you will exceed all that you have already done during your illustrious reign, that your memory will be immortalized, and that you will obtain for yourself everlasting glory and happiness in a future life !

" 'I beseech you, sire, reject not the proposal made to you by the ambassador of so great a sovereign, who desires thus to establish and render inviolable your royal alliance and friendship together.  Should your majesty have the intention of doing so, and feel even the slightest inclination towards it, allow it to be known. No more welcome news could be carried to the king, his master.

" 'Should your majesty have determined not to concede this point, or give a favourable reply to the ambassador, I would beg to be excused from conveying the royal answer, which would indeed be displeasing to the God I worship.  Let it not be deemed strange that I speak thus ; one who is not faithful to his God cannot be so to his sovereign ; and could I act differently I should no longer deserve to be honoured by continuing in your service.'

" The king listened to this discourse of Phaulcon without interruption ; then, seeming to collect himself, as one occupied with a great thought, he replied in the following terms :—

" 'Fear not that I should desire to constrain your conscience. What, however, has induced my esteemed friend, the King of France, to suppose that such were my sentiments ? '

" 'Who could imagine otherwise, sire,' replied Phaulcon, 'seeing the protection your majesty affords to the missionaries, the churches you are building, the alms you bestow upon the reverend fathers in China ?  This, sire, has persuaded the King of France that your majesty was favourable to Christianity.'

" 'But when you informed the ambassador,' added the king, 'of the reasons which kept me in the religion of my ancestors, what answer did he give ?'

"'The French ambassador,' rejoined Phaulcon, 'considered them weighty; but as the proposal of the king, his master, was entirely disinterested, and this great monarch had in view only the good of your majesty, he thought that these reasons should not prevent him from executing the orders of the king, his master, especially as he has learned that the Persian ambassador has arrived in Siam, bringing with him the Koran, that your majesty may adopt it. The ambassador of France felt himself obliged to offer to your majesty the Christian religion, beseeching your majesty to embrace it.'

"'Is it true,' replied the king, 'that the Persian ambassador is bringing me the Koran?'

"'So it is said, sire,' answered Phaulcon: to which the king immediately rejoined—

"'I wish with all my heart that the French ambassador was here to see how I receive the Persian. Were I to choose a religion, it would certainly not be Mahomedanism.

"'But, in answer to the French ambassador,' pursued the king, 'you will assure him from me, that I am greatly obliged to the King of France for the marks of friendship bestowed by his most Christian majesty; the honour done me by this great prince is already publicly known in the East, and I cannot sufficiently express my sense of his courtesy; I regret, however, that my excellent friend the King of France has proposed to me a thing so difficult. I refer myself to the wisdom of the most Christian king, who can judge of the importance and of the difficulties of a matter so delicate as the change of a religion acknowledged and followed uninterruptedly throughout the kingdom for the space of 2,229 years.

"For the rest, it is surprising to me that my esteemed friend,

the King of France, should take so strong an interest in an affair
which seems to belong to God, and which the Divine Being
appears to have left entirely to our own discretion.  For, would
not the true God who made heaven and earth, and all that are
therein—who has given to His creatures natures and inclinations
differing from one another—would He not, in giving souls and
bodies to men, have inclined them to follow one religion, the
form of worship most acceptable to Himself, giving one law to
all the nations of the world?  This order among men, and this
unity of faith, depending absolutely upon Divine Providence, who
might so easily have introduced this, as the diversity of sects
which have subsisted through all time ; must we not believe that
the true God is as well pleased to be honoured by different worship and ceremonies, as to be glorified by other beings, each after
his own manner?

"' Are the variety and beauty we admire in nature less admirable
in supernatural things, less worthy of Divine wisdom?  However,
this may be,' concluded his majesty, 'since we know that God
is the absolute Master of the world, and are persuaded that
nothing is done contrary to His will, I resign myself and my
states into the merciful hands of the Divine Providence, and
beseech of His eternal wisdom that He will dispose of them
according to His good pleasure.  I explicitly desire you to inform
the ambassador that I will omit nothing in my power to preserve
the royal friendship of the most Christian king ; and that I will
so act during the time it shall please God to preserve my life,
that my successors and my subjects shall on every occasion show
their gratitude and esteem for the royal person of his most Christian majesty, and for all his successors.'

"After the king had thus spoken, he kept silence for some time, and afterwards, looking at Phaulcon, pursued. 'What do you think the ambassador will reply to the reasons I have desired you to give him in writing?'.

"'I will not fail, sire,' said Phaulcon, 'to execute the orders of your majesty; but I know not what the French ambassador will answer to what you have just said, which appears to me exceedingly forcible. I am sure that he cannot fail to be surprised at your great wisdom and wonderful penetration. Nevertheless, it appears to me that he may reply, that although it be true that all the beings whom God has created glorify Him each in his own manner, there is this difference between men and beasts, that God in creating the latter has given them different properties, and peculiar instincts, to know what is good for them, and to seek it without reflection, to discern what is bad for them, and avoid it without reasoning. Thus the deer flies from the lion and the tiger, at first sight; chickens newly hatched, fear the kite and hide themselves under their mother's wings, without other teaching than that of nature. But God, in creating man, formed him with understanding and reason, to discern good from evil; and His Divine providence has willed that, in seeking and loving the good, which is proper for him, and flying the 'evil, which is contrary to the great end of knowing and loving God, man should obtain from the Divine goodness an everlasting reward.

"'It is, indeed, as easy for man to use his eyes, hands, and feet, to do evil as to do good, if his prudence, enlightened by Divine wisdom, lead him not to seek the path of true greatness, which is to be found only in the Christian faith, which teaches man to serve God according to the Divine pleasure. But all men do not follow the holy light. In like manner, your majesty's officers are

T

not all equally attached to the interests of your majesty, though
all call themselves your subjects, and account it an honour to be
in your service. So all men, indeed, serve God, though not all
in like manner. Some, like the beasts, live according to their
unruly passions, professing religion without following its precepts,
or examining its tenets; while others, seeing themselves raised
so far beyond the beasts that perish, rise above the dominion of
the senses; and their reason being enlightened by the Divine
Being, they seek to know Him, and to worship Him according
to His will, without other interests than those of obeying and
pleasing Him; and to this sincere following after truth God has
attached the salvation of man. It follows, then, that negligence
in learning, and weakness in our following what we believe to be
best, make us guilty in the eyes of Him who is justice itself.'"

Thus did Phaulcon essay the difficult task of serving two
masters at one and the same time, and for this course he has
been accused by his enemies of being a double-dealer, and actuated purely by selfish motives.    "But," says the Père d'Orléans,
"the words he addressed to the king are a proof of his zeal for
his religion, for the infidel monarch never having shown any
decided evidence of an inclination to embrace the Christian faith,
it was a delicate step for his minister thus to join a foreign
sovereign in opening the subject. The reply of this monarch,"
adds the father, "shows that his majesty had no idea of becoming
a convert; *but it was sufficiently moderate not to take away all hope
of his conversion,* as, however little inclination he had to embrace
the faith, he showed no small desire for its establishment in his
kingdom, thinking it might be advantageous to his people."

The whole of the conversation between king and minister was
reduced by the latter to writing and presented to De Chaumont.

Its perusal gave the ambassador great dissatisfaction, and very nearly brought the negotiations to a conclusion. The very moderation, however, of the king's reply, which left room for a hope of his ultimate conversion, and the splendid privileges Phaulcon granted to the French, one of which was a *monopoly* of all the pepper produced in Siam, to the great injury of the other Europeans, but especially the Dutch, induced his excellency to conceal his chagrin, and conclude a treaty by which the sovereign of France, upon his part, agreed to send a body of troops, not only to instruct the Siamese army in discipline, but to be at the disposal of the monarch of Siam or his minister, either as body-guards or to garrison fortresses.

# CHAPTER XVIII.

As we have seen, the question of the Siamese king's conversion well-nigh proved the ruin of Phaulcon's great designs. Having, however, dexterously extricated himself from that difficulty, by appealing to the Frenchman's cupidity, and holding out a hope of its ultimate probability, nay, by that very dexterity having given signal proof of his ability to aid the Gallic king's schemes for the conversion and conquest of the people, our hero's fortunes took an upward bound. True, surrounded as he was by enemies of the old Siam party, and the Moors, he had to struggle manfully, if warily, and make skilful use of his experience of the people and his great natural powers, in order to maintain his position during an interval of three years which transpired between the departure of the ambassador De Chaumont and the arrival of the promised succour from France; but, nevertheless, his success was complete.

Faithful to his part of the stipulations, the King of France sent five hundred veteran troops under Des Farges, the Count de Fourbin, and other experienced commanders. These being placed in garrison at Bangkok and Merguy, the two most considerable fortresses in Siam, served *nominally* to protect the kingdom from the invading Burmans, but really to overawe the discontented nobles, and to discipline the native troops so that, like the sepoys of the English possessions in India, they might ultimately serve to keep their fellow-countrymen in subjection.

Then, with a view to the spiritual conquest of the people, and the court in particular, Louis sent several learned Jesuits, who, after the example of the celebrated fathers Verbiest, Le Comte, and their colleagues in China, might introduce the Gospel at court indirectly, by teaching the mathematical sciences, in which royalty was known to take an all-absorbing interest; and of this scheme it was intended that Phaulcon should be made the scapegoat. The latter, however, not ignorant of the ultimate intention of his allies, yet conscious of the rectitude of his own conduct, at the same time that he knew he could do but little without their aid, resolved *seemingly* to be advancing the French policy, but, in fact, had determined to do so only while it was not incompatible with the interests of his adopted king and country.

Now, tortuous as undoubtedly was our hero's policy, laying him open to the intrigues of his enemies, the animadversions of his friends, and paving the way to his own ultimate ruin, at the period I shall again bring him before the reader, he had every reason to be satisfied with its result, for his power seemed consolidated and established upon a firm basis, and his happiness complete. He had European troops in possession of the chief fortresses, a well-disciplined regiment of Portuguese, English, and Dutch, to serve as a body-guard to the king and to himself; and of the latter corps he reserved the chief command, taking great delight in drilling and reviewing them; he had Jesuits in constant communication with the king, and other priests continually preaching to the people, among whom he was popular in the extreme; .Christian churches were being raised, under his auspices; and he was happy in the conviction that ere long Christianity would become the established religion of the land. It must not, however, be supposed that his path was free from thorns, for from time to time he would discover some intrigue, either of the Moors, the native Priests, or even the Dutch, to destroy his power; but then so badly were his enemies organized, so incapable were they of acting with secrecy and in concert, that it was but to strangle them at their birth. Thus Phaulcon had his hands full; but while his talents for government are to be admired, we can scarcely wonder at the hatred of the old Siam nobles and priests, for in their Greek minister they saw the man who had introduced into the kingdom the French people, who day by day were taking upon themselves the insolent airs of conquerors; and who, having already gained the king's confidence, and being in possession of some of the highest offices of state, they feared would soon become masters of the kingdom; nor was their hatred of the foreigners the less, that they were compelled to acknowledge their superiority in the art of war. Thus the old Siam party, having no alternative, sulkily resolved to bide their time.

Not so resolved, however, were the Dutch. These people had from the very first jealously watched the progress of Phaulcon and his French allies. The treaty had materially injured their own commerce; so, having colonies near the territory of the King of Johore, at that time a tributary of Siam, the Hollanders induced the king to send envoys to the Siamese sovereign, begging of him to expel the French from the land, and offering to send troops for the purpose. In counselling this course, the Hollanders affected a belief that the King of Siam had been coerced by his all-powerful minister to accept the treaty with France, and that he would therefore rejoice at an opportunity of clearing these foreigners from his kingdom ; at least, thus they told the Prince of Johore, further advising that sovereign to send as envoy a prince of his own blood, whose rank might entitle him to demand a private audience with the King of Siam. The king complied to the letter, but the Dutchmen soon discovered they had calculated without their host, for although the Johore prince obtained the private audience, he had no sooner delivered his message than his majesty, enraged at the insult offered to his dear friends the French, summoned Phaulcon to his presence, and, having explained the object of the envoy's mission, he added—

"See you not, Lord Barcalon, that it is at thine own destruction this King of Johore aims ? but for *what* reason ? what knoweth he of thee, or thou of him, that he should endeavour to encompass this thing ? "

" The King of Johore, thy tributary, oh my sovereign, is innocent ; he is but the tool of the Hollanders, who, envious of your majesty's good friends the French, and hating me, whom they regard as the cause of the French alliance, have induced him to send this message."

"Knew you of this man's coming ? " asked the king, with astonishment.

" A good minister should know all things concerning the interests of his sovereign," replied Phaulcon ; adding, " For three moons have I known that this envoy would come, as also the purport of his coming."

"Hadst told us of this, the dog's feet should never have soiled our land," said the king.

"Thy servant, oh my lord king, would debar his *friends* from entering thy presence, for he cares not that his praises should be ever pouring in the royal ears, but his enemies he would conduct to thy presence, fearless of their power to harm him."

"This may be well, my Lord Barcalon; nevertheless, to show our unwavering faith in a good minister, and our sensitiveness at the insult proposed to our friends the French, we will have the head of this dog hewn from his body—see that it be done."

"My lord the king," cried Phaulcon, falling upon his knees, "saving thy sacred presence and command, this thing may not be done. This prince of Johore is innocent of crime; moreover he is an ambassador, a character held sacred by all those nations of Europe, to the rank and civilization of which you would raise thy beloved Siam; nay, it would be, perhaps, to forfeit the friendship of your majesty's ally, the great French king, who would feel it foul shame to be in amity with a monarch who could be guilty of so barbarous an act as the destruction of an envoy."

For an instant this contradiction to his imperious will sent the hot blood to the temples of the monarch; a moment's reflection, however, showing the wisdom of his minister's advice, he replied—

"Then be it as thou wilt, yet take care that this fellow's feet tread not the earth of Siam after to-morrow's sundown."

"My lord the king hath said it," replied Phaulcon, and the audience was at an end.

"Thus, again," pondered our hero, as he entered the innermost apartment of his palace, "even as the poisoned dagger-blow of the rascal Abdoul did but strengthen the king's love for me, widen my popularity with the masses, and speed my union with Monica, so this cowardly attempt of the Höllanders, becoming known—and it shall soon float upon every breeze—

will but further exalt me in the eyes of all. Aye," he added aloud, "and but the firmer cement the foundation upon which my power is built."

"Hath my lord discovered another intrigue, that his eyes glisten with pleasure, although his brows are knit with thought?" said Monica, who was reclining upon a pile of cushions, holding in her hand a book, from which she had been reading to a raven-haired, dark-eyed little boy, about four years of age, who was kneeling by his mother's side.

"A wasp's nest, darling, nothing more; but the insects have been deprived of all power to harm me;" and he told her for what reason the king had so suddenly summoned him to his presence. Then, to check her reply, he playfully placed his finger upon her lips, and sitting by her side, and drawing the boy upon his knee, he said—

"But how now, master Mouse,* art tired of thy lesson, and longing for a game?"

"Blake glad pap-pa has come back; Blake don't like lesson; Blake likes mokish, and games with pap-pa," replied the child.

"Mokish? ay, then mokish we will have," replied Phaulcon, taking up a European flute and playing it. When the child became tired of the music, or mokish, as he called it, our hero said—

"Now, master Mouse, for a game!" and the next instant he and the boy were romping together upon the floor; and so they continued to amuse themselves, to the great delight of the mother, who seemed no less vexed than the child himself, when a lady of the household came to take him to his midday meal.

* Master Mouse, a term of endearment used by the Siamese to their children.

"Pap-pa not go away. Mokish soon come and play again," said the child, as the attendant led him from the room.

Then Phaulcon, forgetting affairs of state, as was his wont at every opportunity, began to talk to his wife of his early days, his adventures, of Blake, Zillah, England, and his beloved Cephalonia, subjects of which Monica never tired of hearing.

"Dear Phaulcon," said the lady, "how I long to visit that Cephalonia, of which you speak so warmly; yet more so England, the birthplace of my ancestor, William Adams."

"Dear Monica," said our hero, placing his arm around her waist, "wouldst be content to sink from the rank of wife of the first minister of this, our adopted land, to the station of a simple dame of Cephalonia or England ? "

"Indeed," she replied earnestly, " I would, were the great and good work accomplished ; for proud as is my woman's heart of so noble a husband, and his career of glory, I am *but* a woman, and so never cease to fear for thee."

" *Fear ?* " replied her husband ; " nay, Monica, the wife of Phaulcon must know no such feeling."

"For myself," she added. "No, I have no fear but for thee and for the boy. How can I but dread what might be his fate, should thine enemies ever succeed in encompassing thy ruin ? for in this land, as in other countries of the East, the ruin of the family is seldom slow to follow the destruction of its chief."

"Tut, tut!" replied Phaulcon, with brow somewhat clouded ; "these fears are unreasonable. Dost think thine husband but some effete Asiatic, who may be borne down by the first adverse breeze ? Nay, wife, nay. Besides, the king is my friend ; more, I am indispensable to his own safety."

"Even so, my dear husband; thy power, nay, safety, fortune, depend but upon the life of one man, for the king dead, thy greatest enemy, Petraxa, the father of Soyaton, would ascend the throne."

"Monica," replied Phaulcon, "almost bred in the palace, its secrets are known to you, yet is the succession of Petraxa improbable, while the princess, and her uncles, the king's two brothers, survive."

"But tottering are your plans for the future, my dear lord, if built upon such a foundation. The people, the nobles, of Siam, would never submit to be ruled by the princess, while the king himself, with his dying breath, would forbid the accession of either of his two brothers, he hates them both; but even if one of the princes were chosen, thou wouldst have—"

"Command of the position," interposed Phaulcon impatiently; adding proudly, "for know, wife of mine, that the monarchs who henceforth are placed in the royal seat of this land, will alone be enabled to retain their position by aid of their European allies, and are not these at my beck and call?"

"Alas, my lord," she replied sadly, but firmly, "by those words I fear for thee now more than ever: they were the promptings of an ambitious soul."

Angry words, the first angry words he had ever uttered to her, were upon his lips; but, luckily for his future peace of mind, before they were spoken, the Jesuit father, Antoine Thomas, stood in the room.

"Peace be with you, my children!"

"Welcome, father; yet by coming to Louvo to-day have you but anticipated our meeting by a few short hours, for to-morrow the king goes in state to Ayuthia, and I accompany his majesty," said Phaulcon.

"Whither he goes to be in readiness for the pagan ceremonies attending the inundations," replied the father. "Oh, my son," he added, "when will the blessed day come that shall bring the last of these pagan doings? When will the king, by embracing the true faith, set an example to the whole people?"

This was a sore subject to our hero, who replied—

"Remember, father, that once, by imprudent haste, you well-nigh brought about the very adverse of our hopes and desires. It would be still premature to again moot the question. The path already hewn out for thee and thy brethren is a vast one; toil in it unceasingly, and await patiently the crowning of our hopes by his majesty's conversion."

"My son, if by a mistaken judgment I brought about that evil, I did much to ward off its consequences; for my influence with De Chaumont was great, or the French alliance would not have been completed. But listen, my son," added the father, impressively, "this alliance cannot be lasting if the king continues to refuse conversion; for knowing that that was its basis, the French leaders are becoming impatient; nay, they begin to doubt thine own sincerity."

"Which among them dares to question my honesty?" asked Phaulcon, with warmth.

"All, my son, and with some reason. The reception given to the Mahommedan ambassadors of the Kings of Achen and Golconda but the other day, has filled them with disgust. They fear that these men were sent to induce the king to become a convert to Islamism."

"Their fears, father, are without cause; for although state reasons rendered it necessary that these ambassadors should be received with all due magnificence—and it is true that one object of their mission was to offer his majesty the Koran—the king

declined its acceptance, and I, father, to counteract the preachings
of the missionaries of a religion which flatters the desires and the
passions, have obtained the royal permission, that, at the expense
of the state, you and your brethren may print and disseminate
throughout the kingdom Christian catechisms, and other books,
explaining the mysteries of our holy faith."

"My son," replied the father, evidently both surprised and
pleased at this information, "this is, indeed, adding to what you
have already done for the great cause, and may do much to remove
from the minds of the French captains any idea that you have
been carrying on a double-dealing policy."

"Then, my father, as you love your old pupil, nay, even the
cause upon which the heart of every Christian in Siam is set,
get thee at once to these troublesome Frenchmen, and show them
that what I have done is but an earnest of my future actions."

"I am happy, my son, that you have given me an opportunity
of convincing these French captains of your sincerity, for many
are my fears that you will require their aid, nay, even now; and
to tell thee this, is one of the reasons of my being here to-day;
troops should be drafted from Merguy and Bangkok into
Ayuthia."

"Aye!" exclaimed our hero, with surprise, "what reasons have
you for this?"

"My son, within the last few days the city has been filling
with the followers of Abdullah and Soyaton; Mahommedans and
Buddhists seem united in bonds of brotherhood; that indicates
some great purpose in view. Beware, Phaulcon, while yet there
is time; order a body of European troops to the capital, for there is
mischief brewing, or I am no reader of men's countenances."

"Phaulcon, my lord, husband," interposed Monica, "the advice of the father is wise; such signs indicate danger to the king or thee; order the French troops to the capital!"

For a few minutes Phaulcon sat in deep thought, then he said—

"Tut, tut! am I to be taught my duty by a priest and a woman? No, father," he added, "these fears are groundless; and of this I will convince you both." Then, summoning a slave, he ordered him to fetch the captain of the Portuguese guards.

"Pedro d'Aguilar," he said, as the officer entered the apartment, "when where the princes Soyaton or Abdullah the Macassar *last* in Ayuthia?"

"About six months since, my lord."

"Have they entered the city within the past week?"

"Impossible, my lord, Prince Soyaton is—"

"Enough, captain, that will do," interposed Phaulcon; and, bowing, the officer left the room.

"D'Aguilar," said our hero, "has but this day arrived here from Ayuthia. It is his duty, as captain of the guards, to chronicle the entry and exit of every man of rank, for my information. Father," he added, "let me tell you *why* I have little to fear. It is that, by my advice, the king has sent Soyaton as governor to the province of Chantaburi, and Abdullah as commander of the forces against the Prince of Laos. With the distance of an empire between them, these princes can do but little harm; as for the stray Moors to be found in the streets, a handful of my European guard will suffice."

The father was about to reply, but at that moment an attendant brought little Blake into the room, and Phaulcon, impatient of further conversation, cried—

"Master Mouse back again?"

"Pap-pa *not* gone; *good* pap-pa!" cried the little fellow; and the next minute a change had come over the scene; the Jesuit had left the room; the father and son were at their romps, and so heartily enjoying them that Monica had almost forgotten her fears for our hero's safety. Such moments were the only ones of real relaxation that Phaulcon's career permitted. In boyhood he had possessed some of the feelings and aspirations of a man. In these moments of his manhood he had all the feelings of a boy. Alas! that such snatches of real happiness should have been disturbed; but so it was; a slave announced the coming of the mandarin Prenawi, who desired to see the minister on important affairs.

Phaulcon, who was lying upon the floor, holding the child in his hands, indignant at being so rudely aroused out of his temporary boyhood, fiercely ordered the slave to quit the room, telling him he would see no person; and again he began romping; but again the slave came, this time followed by Prenawi himself.

The great minister, rolling over and over with the child upon the floor, was a sight so incomprehensible to the mandarin, that doubtlessly he believed him demented; recovering, however, the first shock, and Phaulcon having risen from the floor, Prenawi, bowing low and presenting him with a letter, said—

"Pardon, my lord Barcalon, but my business is of the last importance, and admits of no delay; thus, at the risk of life itself, perhaps, have I forced myself into thy presence."

"Nay, nay, friend Prenawi," said Phaulcon; but looking at the superscription upon the letter, he said, with a smile, "How is this?—this letter is addressed to thyself, the mandarin Prenawi."

"Let my lord open and read it; his servant dared not, for,

from the messenger, he believes it bodes evil," replied Prenawi; and he trembled as he spoke.

Having opened the letter almost mechanically, and perused its contents, our hero's face darkened; placing his hand upon the mandarin's shoulder, he said, "Prenawi, my friend, knowest thou aught of the contents of this letter?"

"As my life is at stake, oh, my lord, no. The writer is my brother; but from an expression used by the slave who brought it, I feared to break the seal."

"That word, or words!"

Prenawi whispered in the ear of the minister.

"Thou hast done well, my friend; but wilt serve me by setting out even on the instant to Bangkok?"

"Let my life answer for my fidelity."

"Then follow me."

"My dear lord, there is danger at hand!" exclaimed Monica; but, kissing both wife and boy, our hero replied—

"Fear nought, Monica, all will soon be well." So saying, he left the room, leaving her in an agony of doubt and fear.

"Pap-pa soon come back to Blake," said the boy.

"Pray Heaven he may;" and the good wife retired to her oratory to pray for her husband's safety.

# CHAPTER XIX.

### THE PLOT.

THE wats or temples are, without doubt, the most artistic structures in Siam. "They are of a magnificence," says the French Bishop Pallegoix, "of which, in Europe, we have no idea. There are among them some which have cost more than 4,000,000 francs. There are eleven within the walls of the city, and about twenty extra-mural. In the pagoda of Xetuphon is a gilded statue of a sleeping Buddha, one hundred and sixty-six feet in length. In that of Bovoranivet, no less than four hundred and fifty ounces of gold-leaf were employed in the gilding only. From four to five hundred priests, with a thousand boys to attend them, are provided for in a single temple. The pagoda is, in fact, only the prominent ornament of a vast expanse, filled with beautiful edifices, among which will be found a score of Chinese belvideres; a succession of halls, accessible from the water-side; a vast building for preaching; two magnificent temples—one to hold the image of Buddha, another devoted to the worship of the priests, who occupy from two to three hundred prettily built houses, some in brick, others in wood. They have ponds with decorated rock-work, in some of which are crocodiles, in others gold and silver fish. They have extensive gardens, filled with flowers and fruits; many pyramids of elegant forms, gilded or covered with vitrifications or porcelain, raise their ornamental spires to the height of two or three hundred feet. Tall masts, with golden swans at their tops, from which are hung gay flags in the shape of crocodiles or other fantastic forms, are seen amidst the erections. At the entrances are enormous statues of giants, warriors, sages; lions and monsters brought from China; whilst the pagodas are made accessible for boats by canals and water-courses. They have piles for burning the dead, bridges for the convenience of passengers, libraries for the sacred books. The walls of the temples are gaudily painted, representing the facts of history, the traditions of fable, the costumes of foreign countries, and not unfrequently gross and licentious stories. A detailed description of any one of the larger pagodas would occupy a large volume, and leave much to be said. Generally, a colossal figure of Buddha is the prominent object, looking like an inert mass, and surrounded by a multitude of costly ornaments.

About midnight of the day when Prenawi visited Phaulcon, seven persons assembled in the preaching-room of one of the largest wats, or priest-villages, in the suburbs. It was a vast apartment, and, but for the colossal figure of an enthroned Buddha which stood at one end, might have been mistaken for the interior of a Christian church, for its doors were many, arched and carved, its pillars richly ornamented, and its windows were fitted with glass panes, stained in various colours, and decorated with the figures of saints and holy men.

That these men had met for no honest purpose was evidenced by the hour, the securely closed shutters and doors, and the small glimmering light, which was but barely sufficient to enable them to scan each other's features. But who were they? Well first, upon a slightly raised platform at the base of the image, sat the high-priest of Siam, he whom the king had tormented or rebuked by the present of a baboon; upon the ecclesiastic's right hand sat Soyaton, and upon his left Abdullah, Prince of Macassar, while upon the floor beneath, as became their inferior rank, sat four *Chaou Wats, i.e.* lords of temples, or abbots, who, like their chief, had shaven heads and eyebrows, and were attired in garments of yellow, that colour, resembling gold, the most precious of metals, being adopted to show reverence to Buddha. Each priest held in his hand a fan, which, at a signal from the chief, he placed before his eyes, then bending his head towards the floor, remained in prayerful contemplation, invoking a blessing upon the object of the meeting.

The profound silence, which lasted about ten minutes, was broken by a subdued cough, seemingly from the bowels of the image. At the sound, each man looked towards his neighbour in superstitious terror, except Abdullah, who, placing his hand upon his dagger, exclaimed—

"We are betrayed!"

"Not so, prince," said the high-priest; but, looking at Soyaton, whose mind he desired to impress with the miraculous powers of his order, he added, "it is a token that God has heard our prayers, and that our enterprise will succeed."

Of course, the Moorish prince had no faith in such a superstition; but, perceiving that it helped to sustain the courage of his colleague Soyaton, he replied—

"It is well, then; and we have chosen a fortunate day. But, oh holy man! wherefore comes not this Farang? Hath the dog betrayed us?"

"Prince," replied the high-priest, "thou art impatient; but," he added, as at that moment a door opened, "lo! true to his appointment, the noble Farang is here." And before another word

could be spoken, a tall man, of military gait, but enveloped in a
cloak, and with a slouched hat so drawn over his features that they
could not be recognised, stood with folded arms confronting the
high-priest and the image which towered above him.

"Thou art welcome, friend," said Abdullah. "But first say,
has this accursed Greek, Phaulcon, any suspicion that either myself
or the Prince Soyaton is at present in Ayuthia?"

"None! as I can answer by mine honour." As he spoke, a
groan fell upon his ear, and he exclaimed, "An unearthly
sound; what was it?"

"Bah!" said Abdullah, whose mind was too much absorbed
in the object for which he was there to have noticed the noise,
"is the Farang soldier a mouse to be frightened at the rustling
of the wind?"

"By my faith, no; yet, I could swear that I saw one of the
eyes of yon cursed pagan idol glisten," replied the soldier, as he
pointed to the image.

"Dog of a Farang!" exclaimed the high-priest, angrily;
"thou art blasphemous!" then, perhaps, remembering that he
could but ill afford to quarrel, at that moment, with the new
comer, he added, "Buddha (his name be praised) is giving visible
signs of his approval of our enterprise for the regeneration of
the kingdom;" and so impressively was this uttered, that the
soldier, but little less superstitious than the pagan whose religion
he scorned, felt awed.

"Hast told this Farang what it is we desire of him?" asked
Soyaton.

"Prince, he hath been told all, and with willing ears he
listened, for he hates the Greek," replied the high-priest;
"moreover, he will aid the good cause with heart and hand

at the fitting time. Say," he added to the European, "have I
spoken aright?"

"By mine honour, yes," was the reply; "I will aid thee to the
best of my power; that is," he added, "if, according to our
agreement, one-half the gold be lodged at my house in the city
by sunrise, and a guarantee be given me that I may, should I
so wish, quit this land the day after the success of our enterprise."

"It is well; here, then, is the [guarantee for the future," said
the priest, giving him a slip of paper ; adding, "the first half of
the gold is even now on its way to thine house. Is the Farang
content?"

"I am," replied the soldier, as he glanced at the paper.

"But what security have we that you will not betray us even
before sunrise?" asked Abdullah.

"My honour, the word of—"

"One who has promised to betray the man whose salt he
hath eaten;" interposed Abdullah. "Are we dogs, that we
should be so easily satisfied?"

"Does the Greek know your written characters?" interposed
the high-priest.

"He does ; but why this question?" replied the soldier.

"Then write thy name herein," said the priest, as he placed
upon the carpet, before him, a book in which were already painted
the names of the other conspirators.*

For an instant the traitor hesitated to commit himself so far,

---

* The books of the Siamese open in one continuous sheet, folded fan-like ;
the usual length of the page is from eight to twelve inches, the breadth three
or four ; the paper is black, and the characters are written generally with
gamboge, though sometimes with white paint.

but observing the savage glances of the Macassar, and the determination expressed upon the features of all the others present, he snatched the pencil and gamboge from the hands of one of the priests, and complied. But as he threw down the implement by which he had recorded his treason and treachery, and looked upwards, he trembled, although with a swaggering air he said—

"What mummery is this? I swear that the eye of yon image again glistened in my own."

For an instant something like an expression of contempt played about the features of the high-priest; then, suddenly, as if the man's superstitious terror might be turned to useful account, he said—

"Beware, oh Farang! how thou keepest thine oath of loyalty; for the eye of Buddha is upon thee."

"Pagan priest," replied the soldier, "the best surety thou hast that I will not break faith with thee, is my hatred for this upstart Greek, and my longing to clutch the other half of the promised reward; but for thy mummery, this image, I care not." But as he quitted the apartment, and his eye again caught that of the figure, a shudder ran through his frame that belied his words.

"Princes," softly said the high-priest, as the door closed after the Christian, "hast laid thy plans so secretly, securely, that they cannot fail?"

"Fear not, oh holy father!" replied Abdullah. "Thanks to the cunning of thee, and thy brethren here, our secresy is complete; as that book will witness, the mandarins of highest rank and nearest the king's heart await but the signal to strike with us, while the Greek knows not but that his deadliest enemies are still where they were placed by his cunning."

"But should this Farang show the heart of a mouse at the eleventh hour?" asked the high-priest.

"It will be too late to serve him or injure our enterprise; for five hundred of my own people, and a goodly number of the slaves of the noble Soyaton, armed, will surround the king, so that he cannot escape," replied Abdullah. "But," he added, fiercely, "let no man stand between me and the Greek. He must die by my sword alone."

"Buddha be praised!" ejaculated the priest, piously, "for to-morrow shall the usurper expiate the crime of making the high-priest of Buddha the jest of the whole people. Oh, my children," he added to the princes, "be wary, but strike well, and great shall be your reward. The princely Soyaton, in seeing his father, the great Petraxa, placed in the royal seat. Thou, oh noble Macassar! by the gratification of thy righteous vengeance, and the restoration of the offices formerly held by thee and thy people. I, who seek nothing for myself, by seeing the accursed Christian dogs swept from the land, and the priests of Buddha once more in the full exercise of their ancient privileges. As for thou, oh Soyaton! as the heir of thy great parent, the princess, the daughter of the Usurper, will be for thy espousal, and so give additional security to thine inheritance."

"While his greater reward will be the adding to the number of his secondary wives, the Japanese Monica," replied Soyaton, with a sardonic smile.

"Be it so," answered the priest, and rising to his feet, the council of worthies broke up and retired to make their respective preparations for the next day's raid upon their sovereign and his minister. One remained behind, the high-priest; for a few minutes he listened to the retreating footsteps of his brethren and colleagues, then securing the door through which they had passed, so that he could not be interrupted, he sat upon the floor, and opening the book which contained the signatures of the conspirators, became lost in contemplation for about half an hour.   Then rising, he proceeded to cross the apartment towards a large pedestal, upon which stood the images of the three Buddhas—the past, present, and future; but, as he moved, his eye fell upon the eye of the great statue, and he started.

"Truly," he muttered, "the eye of the god glistened as I have never seen it glisten before;" then he stared at it for a full minute.  "Bah!" he added, "I have been fooling the Farang till I have fooled myself."  Then he went up to the pedestal, and having first looked cautiously around, pressed his foot against a plinth at the bottom, and a portion of the front fell away, exhibiting a recess.  In this he placed the book, and having again closed the aperture, left the apartment.

# CHAPTER XX.

## THE COUNTER-PLOT.

RARELY, indeed, do the potentates of Siam condescend to show themselves to their adoring subjects. The return to Ayuthia was to be one of these occasions, at least so it had been rumoured. Thus, shortly after sunrise, the streets became crowded with people, on their way to the gate through which his Majesty was to enter, and several hours did they patiently await to obtain what, even at the best, could be but a sidelong glance at royalty, for as his majesty's elephant passed they would be compelled to fall upon their faces. Now the Portuguese, or rather mixed European regiments, were drawn up on either side of the road near the gates, so that at the coming of the elephants and howdahs carrying the king and his court they might fall into the procession, and act as the royal body-guard to Ayuthia.

A little before midday the acclamations of the multitude rent the air, for an *avant courier* arrived, announcing the coming of the royal procession. Shortly afterwards came the first elephants of the train, about fifty in number, whose curtained howdahs betokened that they bore the women of the household. These were attended by a native guard of about two hundred men, and a band of musicians, playing upon trumpets and other instruments. Then, after an interval of ten minutes, came a procession of fifty more elephants, all with howdahs on their backs. The king's, known by its greater magnificence, and the bearers of golden umbrellas, who attended upon either side, was about the middle of the line, and as soon as this came in sight, the people, as well as they could in such a crowd, prostrated themselves; but, as they did so, a murmuring, as of the sea in the distance, ran through the mass, and with reason, for they found themselves deprived of what should have been the best part of the show, for the king and his court were hidden from view. Some freak had led his majesty to command that the curtains of all the howdahs should be closely drawn. The murmuring, however, was speedily suppressed when they saw the manly form of their favourite Phaulcon, who, attired in the uniform of the Portuguese regiment, rode at the head of the native guard of the Louvo Palace; nay, would have broken forth into loud acclamations but for the presence of the king; as it was, the people, by signs and but half-suppressed cheers, gave every indication of their love for the handsome Greek.

Not so well, however, was he received by the Portuguese and their commandant, D'Aguilar.

"*Peste*," muttered the latter to a lieutenant by his side, "the Greek wears our uniform to-day; some devil's freak has put it into his head to take the command of the regiment to-day."

"Faith, it *is mal apropos*," replied the subaltern, and such must have been the thoughts of many others in the corps, for something more than a murmur ran through the ranks as Phaulcon rode up to the Portuguese regiment. When, however, addressing the officer, he said—

"Captain D'Aguilar, the Louvo Guard will form the escort to the palace. Get you in advance and form the men round the inner court, for his Majesty, as he alights, is desirous of inspecting his faithful European guard"—a murmur of satisfaction arose.

"So far it is well for our purpose," said the lieutenant to D'Aguilar, as, in obedience to Phaulcon's command, they were marching to the palace.

"Aye; the upstart's love of pomp and glitter may aid our plans. But look you, Pedro, it *is* possible, nay, do not look so frightened my friend, for it is not probable, the Greek *may* suspect us. Thus, at the slightest sign that he *has* discovered our plans, I will pistol him on the instant. Then, even if we fail in cutting a path through these miserable Asiatics, he will have paid a fair price for our heads."

Thus conversing, the worthy pair marched their men to the palace; but, upon entering the inner and greatest court-yard, the lieutenant started at seeing that on either side leading to the entrance to the king's apartments were drawn up a double column of native troops. The captain, however, soon placed him at his ease, by telling him that they were all followers of Soyaton, and officered by mandarins of that prince's party. "Moreover," he added, "at the first pistol-shot the gates will be forced by a body of Moors, and we shall have the king, the Greek, and their followers at our mercy! Nay," he continued, "that Phaulcon knows not that these troops are here is evident by his having ordered us to form the men in line around the court."

D'Aguilar then, dividing his regiment into two equal portions, one under himself, the other under his lieutenant, formed them into an avenue through which the royal procession must pass.

Among the last of the great dignitaries who entered the court, to be in readiness to welcome the sovereign to his capital, was the high-priest. As, however, at the head of a procession of ecclesiastics, he passed up the avenue of Europeans, and cast his eyes nervously around, he trembled in every limb. D'Aguilar, who as chief of the guard came forward to receive him with a low bow, said, in tones so soft that he could not be over-heard—

"What hath troubled the holy father; surely he suspects naught?"

The priest, advancing a couple of yards, and motioning to his attendants to remain where they were, replied—

"The officers of the native guard yonder are *not* those chosen by the princes, *they have been changed.* My friend, the Greek scents something wrong; the day is unfortunate for our purpose, let it therefore be postponed."

"Then it will be a struggle for our heads, father; and a bloody one too, for I can trust *my* men."

"Nay," replied the priest, "our enterprise *must* be postponed, to make the attempt now would be unwise—fatal. Remain quiet this day, and no harm can accrue to thee, thy men, or us; for albeit the Greek *may* expect a blow of some kind, he cannot be *sure* from which quarter it is to come; he can *know* nothing if we keep our own counsel, for the list of names is in my possession."

"Aye, priest, and accursed be the hour in which I added my name to that roll."

"Hush!" replied the ecclesiastic, "they come;" and, as he moved forward towards the door at which it was expected the king would alight, the royal procession began to enter the court-yard.

"*Peste!*" exclaimed D'Aguilar, twisting his moustachios; "what meaneth this manœuvre?"

This exclamation of surprise and anger was called forth by his observing that the elephants, having passed into the court-yard, instead of advancing up the avenue formed by his men, so that, as he intended, their riders would, if necessary, be under a cross-fire, filed alternately to the right and left behind the troops, thus exactly reversing the position. Far greater, however, was D'Aguilar's astonishment and fear when he saw that, although the double column had halted, the curtains of the howdahs still remained drawn; indeed, so great was his terror, that, although the elephant which bore the monarch was within a few yards of him when the animal halted, he omitted to give the word to his men to perform the customary salute of the European troops.

"How is this, captain," cried Phaulcon, riding up to him; "the king present, and no salute from his faithful Europeans?"

"My lord!" stammered forth the captain.

"Tut! Give the word instantly," interposed Phaulcon; adding scornfully, *"Beware, oh Farang! how thou keepest thine oath of loyalty, for the eye of Buddha is upon thee."*

"Ah! then we *are* betrayed!" exclaimed D'Aguilar. "But, Greek, I am prepared for thee, and die not alone;" and at the same time he discharged his pistol in Phaulcon's face.

Anticipating such an attempt, our hero had seized the assassin's arm, and the ball winged its way harmlessly. At the same moment, the heavy gates of the court-yard closed, and the curtains of the howdahs opened, disclosing to the astonished eyes of the Portuguese, neither king nor court, but in every one some *four or five well-armed French soldiers,* whose pieces were pointed in their faces.

"Ground arms—pile arms! and every private man's life is safe," cried Phaulcon. For an instant, a few of the troops, in very desperation, seemed inclined to receive and return the fire of the French; but as the native soldiers now found their way between the elephants, and thereby formed such a barrier that the mutineers could neither recede nor advance, in fear that to disobey was to invite instant death, the order was obeyed.

"Now," said Phaulcon to the captain of the native troops, "as you value your life, see that none of these fellows escape. As for you," he added to D'Aguilar and his lieutenant, "treble traitors as you are to your king, your religion, and your fellow-Europeans, lose not a moment in making peace with heaven, for by to-morrow's sun-down neither shall be alive on earth."

"My lord," said the dastard Portuguese, probably with a hope that by betraying the chiefs of the conspiracy his own life might be saved, "I am but a link of the conspiracy, the tool of others more potent and powerful—" But, ere he could utter another word, two soldiers seized, gagged, and led him away.

Then when the mutinous troops, deprived of their arms, had been marched each between two natives to the palace prison, Phaulcon, approaching the high-priest, said—

"Holy priest, a great crime has been prevented, for it was the intention of these men, and those who employed them, to have encompassed the deaths of our good king, and I, his unworthy minister."

From the commencement of this scene, the priest had been trembling with fear, and in expectancy of being denounced and seized. Taking hope, however, from our hero's apparently kind manner, that his share in the conspiracy might be unknown, and knowing that without the *book* no certain evidence could be brought, at least, that would suffice with safety to convict and punish one holding an office so exalted and holy in the eyes of people, he replied—

" Great, oh my lord ! is the goodness of heaven, for having saved the nation from so deadly a calamity."

"And *thou*, oh priest !" said Phaulcon sternly, but in whispered tones, "*from so deadly a sin.*"

" Who, oh my lord ! would dare—"

" Hush," interposed Phaulcon, "*I* dare." Then showing the book in which the names of the conspirators were written, he added, "And herein is the proof. Truly, the *eyes of Buddha are all-searching.*"

" At the sight of this book, which he believed to be so securely hidden from the eyes of men, the cunning traitor trembled from head to foot. Taking courage, however, from our hero's low tones and manner, both of which evinced that he himself had no desire that what was passing between them should be overheard, he said—

" Mercy, my lord; for surely Buddha himself must have turned against his priest and servant. Yes," he added, in a piteous whine, "the great and wise Farang minister of the king is too generous to crush a miserable wretch."

" Priest," replied Phaulcon sternly, "did I mete out to thee thy deserts, the next hour would see thee hanging in a cage over the river. But, in the name of the great king whom thou wouldst have murdered, I pardon thee, providing that you repeat to no living soul a word of what has passed between us; and farther, that you take the first opportunity of resigning the sacred office which, in thy person, hath been contaminated and disgraced."

" My lord shall be obeyed."

" Enough !" replied our hero, who, seeing the French soldiers had alighted from the elephants, and now stood in line on either side, then went up to their commander, the Count de Fourbin.

"Count," said he, "never did sovereign receive from an ally more timely aid than has my master, the King of Siam, this day from the French, and in his Majesty's name, I thank you and your men."

"My Lord Barcalon," replied the Frenchman, "is pleased to award praise where but little praise is merited, for it is to his wisdom and foresight alone that this most foul conspiracy has been suppressed so quietly and with so little bloodshed."

"Nevertheless, count, the king, as an acknowledgment of your individual services, desires that you will accept the governorship of this city of Ayuthia ; while to your brave comrades he has commanded to be paid a month's pay each."

The count bowed his thanks, the men cheered, and as the cheers were taken up by all the natives present, the din was deafening as our hero, attended by a small guard, passed out of the court-yard.

# CHAPTER XXI.

OF the many thousands of people who saw the royal procession, the two most deeply interested in its arrival at the pa'ace were Soyaton and Abdullah. Those princes, disguised in the habits of Buddhist priests, were hiding in a peasant's house upon the banks of the Meinam, about a hundred yards without the walls of the city.

At this place they had arranged with the high-priest and the Portuguese captain to await the report of a small piece of ordnance, and the coming of one of Petraxa's barges. At the discharge of the cannon, which was to be the signal of the death, or seizure of King and Barcalon, they were to enter the barge and make their way into the city, there to mix among the people, and exhort them to fall upon and massacre every foreigner and Christian in Ayuthia. In this treacherous work they were to be aided by the talapoins (priests) of the different wats. The necessary excitement having been created, Soyaton and Abdullah, at the head of their respective followers, were to enter the palace; and thus complete the work commenced by D'Aguilar.

Well, the procession *had* passed, and for two full hours the princes sat silently and anxiously awaiting the agreed signal. But it came not. Another hour passed, and Soyaton exclaimed—

"Abdullah, my friend, this suspense is unbearable." But the

x

Prince of Macassar only clutched the handle of the dagger, or *kris*, beneath his robe, the more firmly.

"I will send a slave into the city to gather intelligence," said Soyaton. .

Abdullah continued to play with the hilt of his weapon; but this time, with a glance of contempt at his more timid companion, he replied—

"Have patience, prince; the longer we are kept from the feast, the keener will be our appetite."

"Is it possible that the dog of a Portuguese can have failed us at the eleventh hour?" asked Soyaton.

"*Failed* us," was the scornful reply; "when did a dog of a Christian fail when gold was at stake? The *honour* of which these Farangs boast so much is naught, but their greed, everything; the bait by which you may catch them, one and all."

"Hark! is that the signal?" exclaimed his companion, as the sound of a fire-arm reverberated through the air.

"Prince," replied the other, "art bewitched, to mistake the report of a pistol for that of a cannon?"

"They come; my father's barge," joyfully cried Soyaton, who was looking out upon the river.

"What words are these? it is not possible, the gun has not been fired," replied Abdullah; but at the same moment he arose, and seeing the well-known water conveyance of the Prince Petraxa, he added, "yet it must be; the barge is ashore, and see, a slave is leaving her."

Almost as he spoke, the loud report of a cannon boomed through the air. At the sound both princes clutched their daggers, and gathering up their robes, prepared to descend the ladder of the house. But they were met by a slave, who, running up the rounds with the rapidity of a cat, fell at the feet of Soyaton.

"Prince, thy noble father, the great Petraxa—"

"My father!" exclaimed Soyaton with surprise. "Is it possible that the enterprise hath failed?"

"Alas! my lord, that I am alive to speak the word—yes; but the prince is here to convey thee and thy friend to a place of safety, for the Greek has discovered that you are near the city."

"The dog, the dog, the accursed dog," exclaimed Abdullah; but then, with his wonted coolness and presence of mind, he said—

"Come prince, let us to the noble Petraxa; fortune has but deferred our vengeance that it may be the surer."

"To the barge, my lords, to the barge; for so cunning is this Greek, that even now he knows that you are hidden here."

"By the head of the Prophet, then, it is our only means of safety," replied Abdullah, and the next minute they had descended the ladder, and were on board.

The state-room, if it may be so termed, upon the platform was closely curtained, an unusual occurrence, but then, the occasion obviously required it, and so without doubt or hesitation they passed in—but who shall picture the wretched fears of the miserable Soyaton, or the hatred depicted upon the countenance of the Macassar, when they found themselves with their arms pinioned, and in the safe keeping of a dozen French soldiers.

Nevertheless, not a word was spoken as the barge proceeded along the smooth waters of the Meinam, until Abdullah, observing that she had stopped at Phaulcon's palace, exclaimed, "God is great, and has doomed his servant to be ever at the feet of this dog of a Greek."

From that moment Abdullah, who had no doubt that the

successful minister would sentence him to a lingering death, resigned himself to his fate; not so Soyaton. The cruel doom of the traitor in Siam was ever present to his mind's eye, and he gave way to the most piteous lamentations.

Upon returning to his palace, Phaulcon's first care was to visit the princes; but how different the reception he met with from the two men. Abdullah, greeting him with a defiant look, exclaimed, " Dog of a Greek, the advantage is thine, use it as thou wilt."

" The Lord Phaulcon, the king's favourite, is great and generous," cried Soyaton, "he will not use his power to crush his miserable slave."

" Traitors," replied Phaulcon, "what canst thou offer to avert the terrible fate of those who attempt the life of a king of Siam ? "

"Naught, oh my Lord Barcalon ! naught; for it is deserved. Unfortunate was the hour of the miserable Soyaton's birth," cried the prince, with tears in his eyes. " But," he added, "the Lord Barcalon is great, he is merciful, let him save the life of his servant, and he will remain his slave the remainder of his days."

"Bah ! " exclaimed our hero in disgust, "this from a prince of the blood, and one so near the throne."

" A throne, Greek," interposed Abdullah, "which, backed by the Frenchmen and their priests, thou art plotting to usurp." Not noticing this, Phaulcon said—

"And thou, Malay ; what hast to offer to avoid the fate of a foul traitor ? "

" My father's son will ask naught of thee," replied Abdullah. " Yet," he added, "declare who was the base dog that betrayed us into thy hands, and the Prince of Macassar will go as joyously to his doom as a bridegroom to his wedding."

Assuming a most serious air and tone, Phaulcon replied,

"The eye of Buddha penetrates into the hearts and most secret doings of the wicked ; it glistened upon the traitor captain when he added his name to the book ; it glistened when the high-priest hid the list of conspirators beneath the image ; it glistens now upon the names as they stand here upon its black page." As he concluded, he exhibited the book itself to the two prisoners.

Then, a light shining over his brain, Abdullah exclaimed bitterly—

"Mouse that I was thus to eat dirt, to let dust be thrown into my eyes by a Christian ; would that I had thrust the point of my kris into that eye. But," he added, "enough ; God is great, and I submit to his will. Now, Greek, glut thy vengeance in thine own time and manner, for Abdullah, Prince of Macassar, will waste no more words."

"Abdoul, for by that and no other name will I call thee," said Phaulcon, sternly, "after the fashion of your own barbarian race, I ask, if our position had been reversed, what would have been my fate ?"

"Death—instant death ! No power on earth should have saved the dog whose very life hath been spent in foiling me at every step."

"Good !" said Phaulcon. "Now listen to the king's sentence, as administered through me and by my counsel, and thou wilt find how a Christian gluts his revenge."

The Macassar Prince listened eagerly, but resignedly.

"Abdoul, thou art a refugee in this kingdom of Siam. Your misfortunes have been great, and it is not the king's wish to put thee to death. *Thou art free*, conditionally that you quit Siam, and never again set foot on its soil."

It would be difficult to depict the astonishment of Abdullah at these words; for an instant a savage joy gleamed in his eyes, but then, in a subdued voice, he replied—

"Greek, more than ever do I hate thee, for doubly, trebly, hast thou conquered me. A Prince of Macassar dares not, will not, accept his life from his dire enemy."

"Man," exclaimed Phaulcon, "this is to be a demon; what is self, hast no children, no wife to whom even thou art dear?" and so saying, he cut the cords which pinioned his arms.

The mentioning of wife and children caused a tremor to run through the frame of even that barbarian. Nay, it was perhaps a feeling of self-reproach that another, and he his greatest foe, should have been the first to think of them. A tear stood in his eye as he replied—

"Greek, you have brought my head to the dust; but you have set me free. Know you not that a Macassar's vengeance can never die, dost not fear for the future?"

"No! For, albeit a rogue, thou art still a prince, a warrior, and a man," replied Phaulcon; adding, "now, at nightfall (for only in the dark canst thou escape the vengeance of the people) get thee hence." Then, as he left the room, he said to Soyaton—

"Prince, the rebellion is crushed in the bud. The king would not scandalize his family by punishing thee according to thy deserts, for, at present, it is known but to his majesty and myself who were the leaders in this conspiracy. The people know only that the Portuguese regiment has mutinied, the punishment of its officers alone will suffice for justice; but," he added, "you will return no more to your government, henceforth your post will be about the royal person."

Profuse would have been the expressions of gratitude by Soyaton but Phaulcon, exhausted by his many hours' exertions, went to h apartments, and, in the company of his wife and child endeavoured: to forget the troubles of the day. Monica, however, was curious as to the details of the conspiracy, its discovery and suppression.

He told her that Prenawi's brother, a priest of rank, being but a lukewarm traitor, had sent the letter to the mandarin by a slave, who was charged to tell him that he must open it on the instant, for it contained great information concerning his own safety. Prenawi, having long known his brother's connexion: with the party antagonistic to the king and his minister, was afraid to break the seal, thus he had brought it to Phaulcon. The latter, having perused the epistle, at once sent Prenawi to Bangkok to summon the Count de Fourbin to his aid. Then going to the penitent priest-conspirator, he terrified that worthy into a confession of the whole plot, and, moreover, discovered that the image of Buddha being hollow, he could there hear and see all that was going on. Thus, as the reader will have surmised, it was Phaulcon who made the eye of the image glisten, and who frightened the priest as he was hiding the list of traitors.

After the departure of the conspirators, our hero hastened to the royal palace at Louvo, and suggested to the king his plans for the immediate suppression of the rebellion. They being accepted, he at once proceeded to carry them out, with what success we have seen.

The able manner in which Phaulcon had detected and destroyed the incipient rebellion becoming known, as it speedily did, notwithstanding all our hero's efforts to prevent publicity, his praises were sounded throughout the land. Thus, when fortunately about the same time a second embassy arrived from France, his popularity had become so great, that he was permitted to send back with the Frenchmen three Siamese nobles, with power to beg of Louis the Great the loan of two hundred additional troops.

The late services of the French had proved the wisdom of bringing an additional force into the country, and such a high opinion had the French sovereign of the ability of Phaulcon, that, occupied as he then was waging war with the greater part of Europe, leagued against him by the Protestant powers, he at once sent to Siam the required soldiers.

Upon the arrival of these French troops in Siam, Phaulcon strengthened the garrisons and encompassed the king, so that he had but little fear of native conspirators. His mind now set at rest, he was enabled to further the cause of Christianity. "Thus," says the Père d'Orleans, "he founded a college for the French Missionary Propagandists, he sent Jesuits to China, and while awaiting the arrival of more for some other kingdoms to which he intended sending them, he built houses for those who were to reside in Ayuthia and Louvo. The king often visited the church and observatory preparing for them, hastening the workmen, as if impatient to see the work finished. In the meantime, the fathers endeavoured to convert the talapoins (native priests), and for this purpose learned the language of the country.

In order to avoid bringing upon himself the vengeance or hatred of the great party at the head of which stood Petraxa, Phaulcon had pardoned Soyaton, and even endeavoured to ignore the past altogether, though the former prince had been in reality the main-spring of the conspiracy. Petraxa, however, either unwilling to meet the eye of the king he had intended to put to death, or perhaps in hourly dread that the monarch, or his minister, would find some excuse to destroy him, sought refuge in a monastery of tala-poins, where he simulated the greatest devotion to his religion ; and so great a reputation did he obtain for holiness and austerity, that at the end of three years the good-natured king, having full belief that the black spots had been expunged from his relative's heart, desired his recall to court. To this Phaulcon was at first opposed, but, confident in the stability of his power, and the inability of Petraxa to harm him, he at length consented—to, as we shall see, his own ultimate ruin.

# CHAPTER XXII.

## CLOUDS GATHERING.

ONE evening, about six months after Prince Petraxa's recall to court, Monica sat awaiting the return of her husband from an audience with the king. At length he came, but with frowning brow, and looking pale and dejected.

"What can have chanced, dearest," she said, placing her arm around his neck, "to have worked this change in thee since the morning? You are ill, your brain is overwrought. Oh!" she added, "that we were away, far away from this land."

"Nay, Monica," he said, "this is to be ungrateful to fortune, who hath helped me to wealth and power, and thee to the accomplishing of thy heart's desire—the disseminating of our holy faith."

"Phaulcon, dear Phaulcon, this is evading my question; no uncommon event must have happened to pale thy cheek, and bring thee to me with knitted brows; say, what is this misfortune, for if it be misfortune I have a right to know, to share it."

"Dearest, it may be naught; it may be much. A cloud is passing over our fortunes. The king is sick nigh unto death. The mandarins of Petraxa's party are already speculating upon their chief's exaltation to the throne. To-day they slurred over their usual homage, and eyed me with looks which betoken hate and threats of vengeance for having so long kept them in awe and obedience."

"But what matters this? What chance hath Petraxa of the succession while the princes, the brothers of the king, and the princess live?"

"Monica," he replied, sadly, "should the calamity I dread take place, there are but two persons in this land who have a chance of holding supreme power. The one, Petraxa; the other, myself, in the name of the Prince Monfit; and by the bones of my ancestors," he added vehemently, "it shall not be the dog, Petraxa. But, but," he mused, "this is folly, foolish in the extreme, for what have I to dread; the outpost fortresses in my possession, a guard near the palace, the chief offices of the kingdom in the hands of my friends. No, no, Monica; there is naught to fear. Come, come, fetch the boy; and in his romping and merry laughter I will seek to forget the cares of state." But before Monica could leave the apartment, the chamberlain entered, announcing that the General des Farges and the Count de Fourbin desired immediate speech with the Lord Barcalon.

"A murrain on the Frenchmen," he murmured, adding, "admit them." Then turning to Monica, he said, "Dearest, get thee to the boy, and having dismissed these officers, I will join thee;" and as the lady quitted the room by one door, the two soldiers entered by another.

"By our lady," said the general, after the mutual greeting, —"my Lord Barcalon, but your amiability in letting loose that fellow Petraxa, is likely to bring a nest of hornets about our ears."

"Ah!" exclaimed Phaulcon, "what news have you, general?"

"That will his Excellency the Governor of Ayuthia here tell."

"My lord," said De Fourbin, "a formidable rebellion, headed by Petraxa, is brewing, and if I mistake not will soon break forth."

" Count," replied Phaulcon thoughtfully, deliberately, " I am not surprised, but how know *you* this ?  Have you proofs—proofs I mean sufficient to authorize me to order his instant arrest ? "

" Of that shall you judge for yourself; but first permit me to ask a question, Is it true that the king is sick nigh unto death ? "

" He is."

" Then listen.  The prince, taking advantage of his opportunities of entering the palace of Ayuthia, has taken impressions of the royal seals, and of these he has made quick service ; for he has used them to obtain from the keepers of the arsenals, arms, powder, and other munitions of war."

" But the rascal keepers have not delivered them ? " said Phaulcon.

" How could they refuse aught demanded by a personage so high, and under the royal seals ?  Moreover, well bribed by the prince, they *say* they believed them to be for the king's own immediate use."

" The dogs ! the traitors ! " exclaimed Phaulcon.  " But, count," he added, " suspect you when the outbreak is intended ? "

" The instant the breath hath left the king's body."

" Then, by mine honour, we will be beforehand with the rogues.  General, as you are true to your own sovereign and the cause which his majesty has so much at heart, get thee on the instant back to Bangkok, and with all haste bring the troops to Ayuthia ; in the meantime, I will take other means that shall ensure them a successful reception and a speedy victory."

" My Lord Phaulcon, your command shall be obeyed ; but once and for ever this turbulent scum must be cleared from the kingdom, and the people be placed out of all danger of a renewal of these panics at every death and succession of a king."

" Would that such an end could be reached ; but how ?  Who can command the future ?"

" My lord," said the general, " I will speak plainly.  You are pledged to my master, the King of France, to christianize this land; that can never be accomplished while the reigning sovereign remains a pagan ; promise me, then, that the breath once out of the king's body, his successor shall be a Christian."

" General," said Phaulcon, biting his nether lip, under the influence of an indignation he did not dare show, " you demand an impossibility ; who shall control the conscience of an Asiatic prince ? who shall beard the numerous and influential priests of Buddha by whom he is surrounded ?  No, no ; time, patience may do all this, but not coercion."

" My lord," replied Des Farges, " must I speak even more plainly ?  Then, in the name of the great Louis, I ask of thee, in return for the support of the French troops, one promise."

" What ?" exclaimed Phaulcon, starting, as the Frenchman's meaning flashed through his mind.

" To give Siam a Greek for a king, and the fathers of holy Church for its priests."

" Do you dare to propose to me such treason, treachery ?" exclaimed our hero, indignantly ; but remembering the imminent danger in which he would stand if he alienated the goodwill of the French officer, he added, " but I cry your pardon, for I know you *mean* well to me and the good cause, yet, general, while the crown is in danger of falling into the lap of Petraxa, it is scarcely meet to provide for its ultimate bestowal."

" That danger will pass away with the coming of my regiments into Ayuthia ; meanwhile, my lord, forget not my proposal," replied the general, who then took his leave.

"De Fourbin, my friend," asked Phaulcon, when the other Frenchman had taken his departure, "go you to Bangkok?"

"I do, my lord, but to return speedily to Ayuthia, second in command to Des Farges."

"It is well," replied our hero, "for I mistrust that man's love for me."

"Nay, nay," replied the Frenchman, "the general is rough, but honest."

"May it prove so," murmured Phaulcon, as De Fourbin left him.

From that hour Phaulcon could know no peace of mind until he had discovered every warp and woof of the net which he now knew Petraxa was weaving about him. To attempt open violence against that prince and his party would be imprudent in the extreme, for he had but a mere handful of European troops in Louvo, and he dared not trust to the native troops. It was a perplexing position, the game to be played difficult, and the stakes high; being no less, indeed, than his own life and fortune, the security of the royal family, the French occupation, and the Christian religion. Could he by a ruse seize the person of Petraxa, the conspiracy would, in all probability, be at once crushed. But the wary prince now kept aloof from all but his immediate followers and friends. The king could render him no assistance, for he was too ill to act. No, Phaulcon had but one hope, the coming of Des Farges' regiments, and for that he looked forward with an anxiety almost unbearable. Each hour two of his spies brought him news of the growth, the gradual spreading of the conspiracy; yet three, four, five days elapsed, and the French came not; at length, upon the evening of the sixth day, the Count De Fourbin entered his presence in hot haste.

"The regiments, count, the regiments! thank God they have arrived at last," exclaimed Phaulcon.

"Alas, my lord, no. There has been treachery at work."

"Man," cried our hero, seizing the count's arm, "what mean you? Hath Des Farges proved coward and traitor at my last need?"

"The Frenchman lives not who is a coward," replied the count. "Four days since we left Bangkok with one thousand picked troops, but, upon reaching Ayuthia, the general received information from Louvo that the king was dead, thyself deposed, though not placed in durance, and that Petraxa, being master of everything, had proclaimed himself regent."

"Dolt! idiot! not to have foreseen this," exclaimed Phaulcon. "But this general," he added scornfully, "who is so easy of belief, where is he? At Ayuthia? If so, return and tell him after what manner he has been played upon, and bid him come with what speed he may, for that the king is alive, and Phaulcon still in power."

"Alas! my lord," replied the count, "the general, I fear me, was willingly deceived, hence the reason of my bringing his message. It is, that 'Petraxa being master, he dares not risk the loss of Bangkok, thus he has returned thither. But he begs that the Lord Phaulcon, with his family, will hasten to that fortress, where they will be safe beneath the flag of France.'"

"Coward and rascal! Does he think me base as himself?"

"My lord," said De Fourbin, "I entreat that you will accept this offer, if not for thine own sake, for that of thy family; for neither Louvo nor Ayuthia are any longer safe places for them."

"Silence, De Fourbin, or I shall deem thee but little less base than thy general.  What thinkest thou has come to Phaulcon, that he should forget the interests of his religion, or be ingrate enough to abandon the king his master and kind friend to the mercy of his enemies?  Shall *I* seek safety in flight, and leave it to my foes to say, that I erected that fortress of Bangkok, and brought French troops there, less for the good of religion and the nation, than that in case of necessity I might have a place of refuge?  Not so, count.  Stay thou or go, for my own part I will perish rather than leave the king in the hour of his illness and tribulation."

"By St. Denis, my lord, it is a noble choice, and one worthy of a gentleman.  In honour you could not choose otherwise, and the Count de Fourbin will remain by you to victory over these traitors, or death."

"Well spoken, dear count," said Phaulcon; "and whether for good or bad, we shall have done our devoirs like soldiers. So now get you back to Ayuthia, and bring with all speed every man that may with safety be spared of the troops in garrison."

The defection, if defection it was, of Des Farges, was a terrible blow to Phaulcon, leaving him but little hope of maintaining his power in the event of the king's death.  True, he was on terms of intimate friendship with his majesty's two brothers, one of whom, under ordinary circumstances, would have succeeded to the throne; but then, not only were these princes detested by the king, but unpopular with the nation.  It was the knowledge of this dislike of king and people to the princes, and the extreme improbability that the Siamese would endure the succession of the latter, coupled with his great popularity

with the Buddhist priesthood and the old nobility, that induced
the cunning and ambitious Petraxa to regard his succession to
the throne with certainty, if only the French would take no
part in the matter. Thus, it was upon the troops under Des
Farges, that both Phaulcon and Petraxa had based their hopes
of victory. With what prudence the former could now rely
upon the general, we have seen. Phaulcon had, in fact, cast
French aid from his thoughts, and after De Fourbin's departure
he sat for some time in deep contemplation. At length he resolved
upon one effort by which there was a possibility of his checkmating
Petraxa; a faint one indeed, as it would, he knew, be strenuously
opposed by the king. It was, however, his only remaining chance;
thus, that same night, he sought an audience of the sick monarch.
His address is thus given by the Père d'Orleans.

"Sire," said he, "it is impossible to hide from your majesty,
that your long illness is causing factions in the land; cabals
are forming in your court which may cause great troubles hereafter. Whilst you were in health, nothing could escape your
acute penetration; but a prince on his bed is not like one on
his throne, or at the head of his troops. Courtiers, naturally
attentive to their own interests, think that an invalid king may
die, and attach themselves to that pretender to the crown from
whom they think to reap the most advantage. This is occurring
among the nobles of your court at this very moment. I have
perceived it, and found the evil sufficiently pressing to hasten
the remedy. I know but one which I can suggest to your
majesty. Your nobles are divided—compel them to unite themselves to one whom you will attach to yourself by appointing
him your successor. It being for your glory that the crown
should remain in your illustrious family, you cannot do other-

Y

wise than choose one of your brothers. It may be painful, sire, but it is unavoidable, unless you are determined to sacrifice your greatest interests to useless resentment."

Notwithstanding the force of Phaulcon's argument, adds the father, he could only obtain the half of what he requested. All the king would do to show his deference for the wise counsels of his minister was, to appoint his daughter his successor, with power to choose for husband one of her uncles. But this was sufficient for our hero's purpose. For when once it became known to the people that the princess had, at the desire of the king, chosen a husband who was to reign, not alone, but jointly with her, their affection for their good king would lead them to give their allegiance to his successor, even though it might be Monfit, the most unpopular of the royal brothers.

Thus one important step was gained. The next would be the sudden arrest of Petraxa himself, a scheme in which he was warmly seconded by the Count de Fourbin, who, the day following Phaulcon's audience with the king, brought fifty picked troops to our hero's palace ; and the same evening it was arranged that the seizure of Petraxa should be attempted the next morning.

## CHAPTER XXIII.

MISFORTUNE.

CONFIDENT in himself, and placing every reliance upon the bravery and support of his small body of Frenchmen, Phaulcon had but little doubt that his scheme for the seizure of his dire enemy, Petraxa, would prove successful. Thus he slept soundly the night preceding its attempt, and in the morning, therefore, he felt as much pleasure as surprise when his chamberlain awakened him, to say that the Count de Fourbin and the Father Thomas desired an immediate audience.

"By my faith, count, thou art to thy time," he said, as he entered the room were the twain were waiting. But, observing their rueful countenances, he added in alarm—

"Why, how now, my good friends? what mishap hath chanced to cloud your faces in such midnight gloom at the very turning point of our fortunes, nay, at the very hour which is to prove whether it is Petraxa or Phaulcon who is to rule in Siam?"

"My Lord Barcalon, the wheel of our fortunes, either for good or bad, has taken a quicker turn than we anticipated; at this present moment our very lives depend upon our swords and strong right arms," replied the count.

"Petraxa," said the priest, "having gained intelligence that you intended to attempt his arrest this morning, hath at once opened the rebellion. During the night he assembled his retainers and friends, and by their aid made himself master of the palace and the king's person."

A thunderbolt had fallen at Phaulcon's feet; he was as if stricken dumb with astonishment. Speedily, however, recovering his presence of mind, he said, as he placed his hand upon the count's shoulder—

"This is indeed sorry news; nevertheless, while the Prince Monfit,* the betrothed husband of the princess and brother of his majesty, is at liberty, even this daring act of rebellion will avail Petraxa but little, for he dares not cause himself to be proclaimed king; so get thee to Ayuthia at once, and from me, from the king, charge the Prince Monfit to fly to Des Farges at Bangkok."

"My lord, in this you have been outwitted. Petraxa, knowing that, after the king, Monfit would be the best card in either of your hands, 'has, by his emissaries, succeeded in corrupting the guards, who have themselves carried the prince to him. Thus is he master of the whole royal family."

"Then, indeed, is there nothing left to us but prayer and a choice of death," exclaimed Phaulcon dejectedly.

"My son," said the priest, "for the present *only* fortune is against us; fly while there is yet time; seek refuge under the French flag, till at least the first fury of these traitors has subsided; the next turn of the wheel perhaps may be in our favour."

"Count," replied Phaulcon, after a minute's thought, "we resolved to arrest Petraxa this morning, it may yet be done; the better, as, elated with success, he will be taken by surprise. There are hundreds within the palace who will join us if

* This prince had been for some time kept in durance at the palace of Ayuthia, by order of the king, his brother.

we but once gain the inner court. Art still in the same mind?"

"Madness, sheer madness to make the attempt," interposed the priest; but the count replied—

"It is the course I would have counselled; and this I wager, that if we never get back again, it will go hard indeed if fifty Frenchmen cannot hew their way through a host of such dusky rapscallions as surround Petraxa."

"Then so be it. No longer than it will take to arm will it be ere I join thee in the court-yard. In the meanwhile, summon all those of the native soldiers who are yet willing to strike a blow for their king."

"It is a rash, most desperate venture, yet may Heaven reward thee with success, my son, for it is in a holy cause," said the father; but, with minds bent upon the coming fray, both the count and Phaulcon left the apartment, the former to obey orders, the latter to seek his wife.

Monica was in the private chapel of the palace, and in fervent prayer, her eyes brimming with tears. Phaulcon watched her, then, when she had concluded, he said—

"We meet in a fitting spot, dearest, for that which I have to tell thee."

"Dear Phaulcon," she replied, "I know a portion—the success of Petraxa, I can imagine what will follow."

"But thou knowest not that they have counselled me to fly, to take refuge in Bangkok, and thus, cowardlike, leave the king, my friend and benefactor, in the hour of his sore distress," he replied.

"Phaulcon, dear husband, such counsel must have fallen upon dull ears; thou couldst not do it; death were better

than dishonour; yes," she added, earnestly, " even *I* should
scorn thee, couldst thou be guilty of such coward baseness;"
and, perceiving her husband's emotion, she continued, "nay,
speak not, dearest, the words would choke thee; let me give
utterance to thy thoughts. They are that this present moment
may be the last we may pass together upon earth. Well, even
so, I repine not, for it is the will of Heaven; come, join me,
dear Phaulcon, let us pray that it may be otherwise," and they
knelt before the altar, their mingling thoughts giving utterance
to the same prayerful words.

Then rising, Monica, now reconciled to the parting, with
a bright smile upon her countenance and in a brave tone,
said, "Hark! there is a tumult in the street; go, Phaulcon, .
go, for 'tis thy duty to God, thy king and thyself, and may
victory attend thy footsteps."

"Monica," replied our hero, embracing her, "should I fall,
get thee on the instant to Bangkok, and seek the protection of
the French flag. God take thee in his keeping," and so upon
this momentous occasion did husband and wife part.

*　　*　　*　　*　　*　　*

As Phaulcon for the last few days had kept the guard
attached to his palace under arms, the soldierlike De Fourbin
very speedily "turned them out," and forming them into two
separate columns, he added to the van of each one half of his
Frenchmen, and to the rear a mounted native officer, whose office
it was, according to the military custom of the Siamese, to
stimulate the faint-hearted with the point of his spear, and
it must be admitted that, in this instance, it was highly
necessary, for when, in a short address, the count told them
the expedition upon which they were proceeding, they openly

THE PARTING

declared their disappointment. Then marching the two columns
without the walls of the court-yard into the open streets, he found
the people in tumult, and, with the fickleness of the masses,
crying aloud the praises of Petraxa, and shouting abusive epithets
against the foreign Barcalon and his French allies. Thus revolt
and mutiny seemed imminent. As, however, in the midst of the
uproar, Phaulcon rode from the court-yard and placed himself at the head of one of the columns, the people, as if
suddenly remembering the good he had done for them and their
country, greeted him with cheers.

"With these slaves," muttered our hero, "to be out of sight
is to be out of mind;" but openly noticing neither cheers nor
groans, he harangued the native soldiers, begging of them to
bear in mind not only the benefits they had already received,
but that their fidelity would be highly rewarded; further, he
exhorted them, on their manhood and loyalty, to strike a blow for
the great king whose life had been spent in the service of his
country and for the welfare of them all. The effect was electrical;
loud were their cheers, and many the declarations that they would
hew the head of the traitorous Petraxa from his body, or lay
down their lives in the attempt; and having worked them up to
this pitch of enthusiasm, Phaulcon ordered the advance.

"By my faith it will be an easy victory," said the Barcalon,
as, approaching the royal palace, they saw that the gates of the
outer court-yard were open and unguarded.

"Nay, my lord," replied the count, "this may be but
a trap, for doubtless the inner courts are filled with men; at
least," he added, "it shall be my duty to be the first to
enter."

"Not so, De Fourbin, we will enter together; but let it be

with your gallant Frenchmen, who are fitted to support the brunt of a sudden attack; the natives can follow in support."

"Hast faith in these fellows? Fear you not that they may fall short, leaving us in the hands of the Philistines?"

"I've faith in them as a rear-guard; besides, they have eaten my bread, partaken of my wealth, and it is to their interest to be faithful."

The count then forming his own men into a compact column, the two leaders dismounted, and at one bold dash led them through the gateway.

Once within the court-yard, they saw that their work was cut out for them, for they were confronted by a treble column of Petraxa's troops. Prepared for this, Phaulcon ordered the French to fire a volley. The discharge was well directed and telling; the enemy fell upon all sides. In the midst of the confusion caused by the falling of the dying and wounded, he ordered them to charge with their pikes, and thus, by main force, make a way through to the king's apartments.

Nobly was the order obeyed; the native ranks were thinned by the terrible fire, and the leader, sword in hand, and the men with their pikes, had literally hewn their passage through into the third and last court. As, however, they entered the latter, a cry arose among the Europeans that the native guard had thrown down their arms and deserted.

"The cowardly villains; onward!" exclaimed Phaulcon; but at that moment fresh bodies of the enemy poured forth from the avenues, passages, and doorways of the court, and the day was lost, for a demi-god could not have withstood such odds. Nevertheless, Phaulcon and his allies fought heroically, keeping the advancing masses at bay, until three parts of the attacking party were lying either dead or wounded. As for our hero, he now fought with desperation, and as if madly seeking death in every direction; but this he found impossible. The Siamese had been commanded by Petraxa to take him, the foreign Barcalon, alive; and, with slavish fidelity, they permitted themselves to be hacked to pieces rather than strike a blow that would deprive their anticipated prize of life. At length, however, a blow in the sword-arm, and a sudden pressure, and Phaulcon was disarmed and a prisoner. De Fourbin, now seeing that to attempt the rescue of our hero would be but to offer himself and his few men a useless sacrifice, suffered the Siamese to take him; and it was the wisest course, for he knew that Petraxa would fear to take the life of a French officer of rank, while a general, with a large force of his countrymen, held possession of the two chief fortresses in the kingdom. He hoped, also, that a bribe would speedily obtain for him his liberty.

# CHAPTER XXIV.

"ALAS, alas! the Lord Barcalon, our noble master, hath been slain!"

Thus abruptly was the failure of her husband's enterprise brought to Monica, by an affrighted slave who had escaped the conflict. For an instant she stood as if petrified; but recovering her presence of mind, she would not, could not, realize the idea of his death.

"Man," she cried, "this is not so! No, no! wounded, a prisoner, not dead."

"Alas, lady, that I live to say it."

"Stay," she exclaimed; "didst see him stricken?"

"Noble lady, I did; he fell encompassed by hosts."

"Slave," she cried almost fiercely, "again I say this is not so. My noble lord still lives. Get thee gone, for thine own coward fears have magnified the evil. But stay," she added, "tell my women that I would quit the palace on the instant, and afoot;" and the brave wife purposed to go herself to the palace. But as she spoke there was a tumult in the courtyard.

"They come! they come! my boy, my boy!" she exclaimed; and now trembling with fear for her son's safety, she fled toward his apartment; but the mother and son met midway;

for, alarmed at the noise, the boy had been hastening to her apartment, and to the latter they now proceeded together, reaching it only in time to receive one of Petraxa's mandarins.

"Lady," said the officer, but seeing that, as he approached her, she stood before the child, like a lioness at bay and in fear for the safety of its young, and as if, forsooth, her feeble strength would be all-sufficient to defend the boy against a host, he stopped, and bowing respectfully, added—

"Lady, be not terrified, no harm is intended either thee or thy son. The noble Prince Petraxa is too generous to make war upon women and children."

Taking courage at these words, Monica threw herself upon her knees before the officer.

"Tell me, oh noble mandarin," she cried, "of my husband! Say it is not true that he has been slain, but that he is a prisoner."

"Lady," replied the Mandarin, much moved at her agony, "of thy husband I may say naught; such is the command of the dread Regent and most high Prince and Mandarin Petraxa."

"Thank God, then, he lives," she exclaimed, and as the mandarin bowed an assent, the noble-hearted woman, who had been tearless upon hearing of his death, swooned from joy.

"Tell me," she said, when she revived, "is he wounded?" But the officer making no reply, she added, "It is well, it is well; you have intimated that my noble husband lives."

"Better, lady, that he had been slain in the fight, for terrible is the vengeance of the regent."

"No, no!" she exclaimed, "Petraxa may deprive my husband of rank, power, wealth, but he dares not attempt the life of the friend of the great French king. But," she added, "tell me, I implore thee, where they have confined him; aid me to reach and comfort him, and my life shall answer for thy safety; the very wealth of this palace shall be at thy disposal."

"Lady," replied the mandarin, "I may pity, deeply pity, yet cannot aid thee; already, by admitting that the noble Phaulcon lives, have I done that which, were it known to the regent, would cost me my life."

"True, true," she replied bitterly, "there are those to whom thy safety is as dear as their own lives, and it is criminal of the wretched Monica to demand of thee to risk it." Then, retiring to her oratory, she knelt, and having prayed that her husband might be speedily delivered from the hands of his enemies, registered a vow that, if on earth, she would search him out; and from that moment she devoted her whole mind to the discovery of the place of his imprisonment; but for many many days her efforts were unavailing, neither in her distress had she the consoling company of the Father Thomas.

Then it became bruited about among the populace that Phaulcon had been put to a cruel death. This report reaching his unhappy wife, she would have resigned herself to hopeless despair, but for the possession of her son. Then her dread that the tyrant's vengeance might yet even reach the boy, so occupied her mind with schemes by which she might elude the vigilance of the guard placed over her by Petraxa, and flee to Bangkok, that she almost forgot her misery.

One morning, while thus pondering upon a plan of escape, she was pleasingly surprised to receive a visit from the Jesuit.

"Father," she exclaimed, seizing him by both hands, "what news of my husband? Say, in Heaven's name, say that this hideous report is untrue. The tyrant has not dared to slay one so dear to the French."

"Console thyself with that thought, my daughter, for the tyrant, even all-powerful as he is, must fear to take the life of the noble Phaulcon while the French troops remain in Siam," replied the Jesuit.

"Heaven bless thee, father, for that assurance;" but she added, "has not the French general yet, upon the part of his own sovereign, demanded my husband's release?"

"My daughter," replied the Jesuit, "every effort has been made by the General des Farges, as a Christian and a European. As the friend of the French king, the general hath formally demanded that the noble Phaulcon should be set at liberty."

"The tyrant has refused!"

"He *has*, lady, but there is hope yet."

"Then," she replied warmly, "why has not this false Frenchman marched at once upon Louvo, to save from the claws of the tiger the noble-hearted man who has done so much in Siam for his countrymen? But," she added in tones of anguish, "this thing will he never do; the man who failed to bring his men to Ayuthia, who broke his plighted word with my noble husband, is a coward, and hath the heart of a mouse."

"My daughter, such a course would be to fly in the face of Providence. It is by milder means that our end must be attained, for the numbers of the French in Siam are insignificant, and this Petraxa is most powerful; all men have submitted to his yoke—the talapoins, because they regard him as the restorer of their religion; the great nobles, as they see in him the man whom they believe faithful to his country and a hater of foreigners; and the fickle masses because they love novelty. But listen, and thou wilt no longer charge the noble Des Farges either with cowardice or as being lukewarm in thine husband's interest.

"Petraxa," continued the father, "hath recently declared himself no enemy to the Christians, nay, that he will leave them for the future unmolested; further, that he desires to maintain the French alliance, hence he commanded my attendance at the palace, when, having told me his intentions, he desired that I would at once repair to Bangkok and request the French general to visit him at Louvo, as he wished to confer with him on the part of the sick king. 'Tell the general,' he added, 'that if he comes not on the instant he will excite suspicion as to his intentions against the Siamese people, and do a serious injury to the alliance between the two nations.'"

"Surely, oh my father!" said Monica, "you did not comply; or if so, the chief of the French in Siam is too wise to let himself be thus easily entrapped by the wily tiger who, ruling in the name of his sovereign, still keeps his majesty a close prisoner?"

"My daughter, had the general refused compliance simply out of fear for his own safety, he would, indeed, have merited the epithets of false and coward; for, at the same time that Petraxa sent this message, he intimated that a refusal would but immediately precede the execution of thy husband, the French—indeed all the Europeans within his power."

"Has the general arrived?" she asked nervously.

"He has, and is to have an audience to-morrow."

"Then Heaven alone can help us," she replied despondingly, adding, "for never will he return, at least, with the permission of

Petraxa.  Oh my good father!" she continued, "is it possible that ye men, wise priests and brave warriors, could have been so witless as not to see through the fraudulent schemes of this man?"

"Daughter," replied the priest solemnly, "if we have erred, it has been the fault of circumstances, and, at least, for the benefit of thee and thine; if we fail—then God's will be done."

"Good father," she replied, "pardon me if my great misery hath made me too bold.  But," she added, "in the name of Heaven, tell me, if thou canst, in what part of the palace my husband is confined?"

"Daughter, for some reason his prison hath been kept a secret, yet will I use all means to discover him.  Heaven take thee in its keeping till we meet again," and the father arose to depart; but, taking his hand, she said—

"If you discover his prison the gratitude of Monica will end only with her life.  But, father," she added, "canst obtain me an interview with the French general this night, for I would see and converse with him before the audience of to-morrow?"

"It is but a slight request, my daughter; doubtlessly, upon hearing thy desire, he will attend thee.  But be cautious of thy speech with him, for the spies of Petraxa have long ears, and, moreover, they are numerous in this palace of thine;" so saying, the Jesuit departed, and within an hour Des Farges was closeted with her.  The result, however, of their long converse we shall see by the proceedings of the next day, when the new ruler of Siam received the French general and his suite.

About an hour before sundown the next day, the Regent Petraxa was seated in the king's audience-chamber, just beneath the throne (he had not yet dared to occupy the seat of royalty) with four naked sabres by his side, and surrounded by the great mandarins of his party.  On his right was his son Soyaton, on his left the Prince of Macassar, now reinstated in his old offices and dignities.  Around the room, armed to the teeth and headed by the traitor D'Aguilar (whose sentence of death Phaulcon had been persuaded to commute to perpetual imprisonment), was a European guard, composed chiefly of the mutinous Portuguese, who, upon the success of the regent, had at once offered their services against their old commander.

A profound silence reigned in the court of the high mandarin (for at that time he had assumed no greater title) until the chamberlain announced that the general of the Frenchmen *humbly* and upon his knees craved to be admitted to crawl at the feet of his highness.  The gait and bearing, however, of Des Farges, as he entered the hall, did not by any means verify the chamberlain's assertion; on the contrary, as he approached the magnate's seat, he bowed scarcely so low as if he had been in the presence of one of his native princes.

"Does the Farang know in whose presence he stands?" exclaimed the regent haughtily; but no less haughtily answered Des Farges—

"I am in the presence of the Prince Petraxa, and demand to know for what purpose I have been thus hastily summoned."

Concealing his indignation, Petraxa then said—

"The chief of the Farangs is summoned here by order of the king of Siam, whose regent I am, to make it known for what reason, and with what design, he and his countrymen have entered the realm of Siam, to the disturbance of the peace of the people."

"The Prince Petraxa's question is unreasonable, for he knows that the French came to Siam by the desire of the king, and under a treaty settled between the two sovereigns of this country and France," was the reply.

"That treaty was part of the dog Phaulcon's plot to subjugate the nation to his own ambition, and the rule of the Farang king; but it no longer exists. Yet," he added, "if the French will be our good friends and serve us, the regent of the kingdom, as faithfully as they have the Greek, will we keep to the terms of that treaty, and give them honourable employment."

"As the French entered Siam with honest intentions, and for the good of the kingdom alone, it matters but little under what government they serve; thus, without doubt, their sovereign, the great Louis, will permit them to remain," replied Des Farges, evasively.

"This is well," replied the regent; but, he added, "it is necessary that we have the guarantee of more than one Farang chief; it is therefore the will of the king, that on the instant you send an order to the captain left in charge at Bangkok, to repair to our presence with all speed."

The blood mounted to the temples of Des Farges, as it flashed through his mind that the regent only desired to entrap the chief officers of the French into his power, but he answered—

"I will this night ride to Bangkok, and despatch hither the lieutenant."

"Not so," replied the regent; "thou art our honourable guest, and we would put no such menial office upon thee;" and so determinately was this spoken, that Des Farges, remembering that he and the officers with him were entirely in the

regent's power, and moreover thàt he had a great purpose to
serve, replied readily, as if without the most remote suspicion
of the prince's treacherous intentions—

"Be it so, my lord.  But," he added, "if the Prince Petraxa
be desirous of keeping in amity with the sovereign of France,
how is it that he does not fear to put to death the Lord Phaulcon,
who is a Christian, and the friend of the great Louis?"

"Farang, many have been the demands that thou hast made
that this Greek dog should be delivered into thy hands, and as
many have been our refusals.  Again, we say, that this traitor, this
man who has misled the King of Siam, is doomed.  Know then,
that with this affair, neither thee nor thy king can have aught
to do; but after to-morrow's sundown you will trouble us no
more, for before that hour he will have paid the penalty of
his crimes against the kingdom."

A shudder ran through the veins of the Europeans present
as they heard this sentence; but Des Farges, affecting to accept
it as a matter of course, said—

"After these words it is not my province to ask for his life.
Yet, oh prince! it is not possible that your highness, who has
been so long celebrated as a devotee to the gods of Siam, should
refuse the miserable Phaulcon the consolation of being attended
during his last moments by a priest of his own faith."

The regent hesitated, but the Mahomedan Prince of Macassar,
coming forward, said—

"In thy wisdom, great Petraxa, grant this thing; for it is
not fitting that a man should die unattended by a priest of his
religion."

"The Prince of Macassar is right; and as he himself hath
suffered much at the hands of this dog, he hath the right to

speak, therefore, let it be even so. But," he added, turning to D'Aguilar, "the prisoner is in thy care, thou who hast long sworn his destruction; be it, therefore, thy care to introduce the priest into his prison; but leave them not for an instant alone."

"Prince," said D'Aguilar, "thy will shall be done, and well your highness knows that you could trust no better man. But *the* priest?" he added, interrogatively, to Des Farges.

"A monk of the Franciscan house established by the Lord Phaulcon. I will bring the holy man to thee ere nightfall," replied the general.

The regent then rising and retiring through the doorway at the back of the throne, the audience was at an end.

# CHAPTER XXV.

### THE FLIGHT.

UNTIL nearly midnight, D'Aguilar sat in his private quarters attached to the guard-room of the palace, awaiting the coming of the priest, whom Des Farges had promised to bring, to console the last hours of the condemned prisoner.

"A murrain on this French general, that he comes not with his priest!" exclaimed the Portuguese, jumping from his chair and pacing the room impatiently.

"The General Des Farges, colonel," said an orderly, entering the room almost simultaneously; and, without reply, the colonel— for to that rank the Portuguese had been raised by Petraxa— followed the soldier to an anteroom, where he found the general and the promised monk, the latter with his cowl drawn over the greater part of his face.

"Your pardon, Monsieur *le Colonel*," said Des Farges, emphasizing the rank, "for having kept you waiting, but the holy father was absent from his monastery on a work of charity, or we should have been here before. May it please you," he added, "to conduct us to the Lord Phaulcon's prison."

"I cry you mercy; not só, sir general, for no man but the holy priest may be admitted to the Greek traitor," replied D'Aguilar.

"You are complimentary in your over-caution, Monsieur le Colonel," replied the general ironically; "for surely the Portuguese

guard and the native troops of the regent must estimate highly
the valour of Frenchmen, to fear that but one, aided by a poor
monk, could sprite away your prisoner."

"*Fear!*" repeated the Portuguese scornfully; "but," he continued in softer tones, "none should better know than the general
Des Farges, that it is a soldier's duty to obey orders: mine are
that none, saving myself and the priest, visit the prisoner
Phaulcon."

Then, beckoning to the monk to follow, he led him across the
two court-yards, which, with the exception of a European sentry
placed at intervals, were deserted, to the inner palace, or apartments
of the king. Entering this building by a low portal, he proceeded
along a narrow passage, till they arrived at a small door, strongly
plated with iron. The latter being opened by D'Aguilar, they
descended a flight of stone steps a depth of some twenty feet
beneath the basement of the palace, when they came to a cavernous
opening, lighted by a small glimmering lantern, at the farther
end of which was another strong door. As he placed the key
in the lock—the same which had served for the opening of the
doors above—D'Aguilar said—

"I will crave thy patience, holy father, while I prepare the
prisoner for thy coming;" so saying, he passed within. We will
follow him.

It was a small stone apartment, scarcely nine feet square, the
walls humid and slimy, the flooring of earth, and half-covered with
water; an oil-lamp hung from the centre, by the light of which
could be seen the haggard features and gaunt form of the once
handsome Phaulcon, as he lay stretched upon the floor, secured
to the wall by one chain, his hands and feet being bound together
by two others, and all being fastened by iron padlocks. Our hero's

incarceration had not been of long duration, yet sufficiently so, in such a place, with but a scanty supply of rice and water, to have had its effects upon his once powerful frame.

"May thy servant be pardoned his intrusion at this late hour, my Lord Barcalon," said the Portuguese, with mock humility and a glance that bespoke the savage satisfaction he felt at the plight of the fallen minister.

"D'Aguilar," replied Phaulcon, coolly, "thou wert ever a villain, but since I have been here, thou hast proved thyself a cowardly dog."

"Dog," repeated the Portuguese scornfully, adding, "well, every dog has its day; you had yours while you kept me so long in durance. Now, my Lord Barcalon, *I* have *mine.*"

"Coward, do thy best, or worst, I can yet scorn and spurn thee; yet mark the words of, perhaps, a doomed man. As I now am, so ere long wilt thou be."

"My Lord Phaulcon has turned prophet," and as he spoke he contemptuously struck the prostrate man with his foot, adding, "but can he foretell the hour, nay day, when he will die the death of a traitor?" But, finding our hero answered him not, he continued, "scorning, hating thee, and longing as I do to witness thy last agonies, by which alone my revenge can be quenched, yet as a good Catholic would I now counsel thee to prepare for another world, for the fiat has gone forth. To-morrow thou diest in the forest of Thale Phutsun."

"That this is true, I believe from the savage satisfaction in your eyes, pitiful coward," replied Phaulcon; adding, "but be present as you have promised, and at your own last moments with agony you will remember how easily he can die who never of his own will wronged a fellow-being."

"But man, dost not desire the consolation of a priest?" asked the Portuguese, astounded that he should so coolly receive the news of his death sentence.

"Aye, as a Christian, that would I ask even of such as you, did I not know that its refusal would give you pleasure."

"Heaven and our Lady forbid!" exclaimed the Portuguese, who, like the rest of his countrymen in those days, did not, in the midst of the greatest crimes, forget the usages of his religion. Yet, like them again, not losing an opportunity of turning even religion to a profitable account, he said, as he pulled forth from his vest an inkhorn, pen and paper, "it is a favour to be paid for."

"Avaricious wretch," exclaimed Phaulcon, "yet," he added, "in my position I cannot blame thee for worshipping thy only god, pelf; unlock these fetters, set my right hand free, and for but two hours of the company of a monk, I will give thee an order upon my treasurer for a hundred crowns of gold."

Without another word D'Aguilar took a key from his vest, and unlocked the fetters upon his prisoner's wrists; Phaulcon then writing the desired order, placed it in the hand of the Portuguese, saying—

"Now, as you regard the welfare of your own soul, fail me not in this."

"Fear not, Greek, for it is the only favour that thou couldst ask me that I would grant, nay, that as a good Catholic I dare not refuse. The monk shall attend thee right quickly;" so saying, he reopened the door, and, to the astonishment of Phaulcon, the ecclesiastic entered the chamber, but with his head bent forward, and muttering a prayer, in which the name of the prisoner was distinct.

"Holy man," exclaimed our hero, "canst tell me how it fares with my wife, my child? Answer as thou art man as well as priest;" and tears trickled down his cheeks, as the sight of the father brought vividly before him the hour when he should be parted from those dear ones for ever, at least in this world.

"My son," replied the monk, in a thick yet tremulous voice, which startled Phaulcon, "they are safe, and well as their terrible misfortunes will permit; but the lady thy wife is happy in her knowledge that her husband lives." But, as he approached nearer to the prisoner, D'Aguilar, suddenly remembering that he had not replaced the fetters upon the prisoner's wrists, stepped between them and knelt down to replace them—at the same moment the monk threw back his cowl, Phaulcon started, but quickly withdrew his hands, and on the instant they clutched the throat of the Portuguese, who now, in the place of the monk he had himself introduced into the dungeon, saw the lady Monica.

"Rascal, but a single word and you die," said our hero, keeping one hand upon his foe's throat, while with the other he grasped a pistol his wife had taken from beneath her robes, and held close to the face of the prisoner.

In the astonishment of the moment, D'Aguilar had let fall the key of the fetters; losing no time in picking this up, Monica had in another minute set her husband free, at least from chains.

"Now, dog, put forth thy wrists," said Phaulcon, still retaining his clutch upon his prisoner's throat, and holding the pistol to his head; "you, Monica, pass the fetters round."

This being accomplished, Phaulcon gave the weapon to his wife, telling her to fire if D'Aguilar either spoke or resisted; and the key being turned, the rogue was speedily in the same position as his late prisoner, with the addition that he was gagged, so that he could not speak.

"Neatly done, dear wife," said Phaulcon, when the changes had been thus cleverly and speedily rung; "now iugrate and robber, in the name of holy Church, my prophecy is fulfilled, for I leave thee to a worse fate than you had hoped for me; as, however," he continued, "we are of about the same bulk and inches, I will borrow some portion of your habiliments."

Then, by the aid of Monica, having removed his helmet, sword, cloak and boots, the husband and wife passed through the passages and court-yards of the palace, without exciting the least suspicion that they were other than the colonel and monk, who, but a short time before, had been seen going towards the prison. A feat, by the way, they would have found impossible during the light of day.

Once without the walls of the palace, they soon reached the forest country between the cities of Louvo and Ayuthia; and less in fear of wild beasts than of their fellow-humanity, they resolved to pursue their journey by land, within sight of, but not on the river. For three hours they journeyed, till, foot-sore, weary, and fearing that the light of day which was now breaking might discover them to any of Petraxa's people, they entered the jungle, there to rest until night again should come, agreeing to watch and sleep by turns. Here they remained till dusk, when they resumed their journey. Scarcely, however, had they entered the path, than, hearing the trampling of horses' feet, Phaulcon exclaimed, "Dearest, our flight has been discovered; we are pursued—yet, no!" he added, as he listened to the sounds, "there is not a horse in Siam can run at that pace, they are at full gallop; rise and follow."

They returned to the thick jungle, but only a few feet within its cover, so that Phaulcon might catch a sight of the horsemen.

"We are safe, it is the French !" he exclaimed, joyfully ; and in a few minutes, Des Farges, De Fourbin, and two other officers had reined in their steeds.

"By my faith, lady, you have accomplished a brave deed," said Des Farges. "But we are pursued by these rascal Moors; dismount De Fourbin, and get behind me. Haste, my friends, haste ; there are half a hundred armed Moors at our heels ;" and in a minute, De Fourbin had obeyed the general, and Phaulcon and his wife were seated on his saddle.

"Straight for Ayuthia," shouted Des Farges ; and away they galloped. But three miles brought them to a jungle so dense that it was impassable for horses.

"A pest on the country—we are lost !" cried Des Farges.

"We will die sword in hand," said Phaulcon.

"Neither, by St. Denis," exclaimed De Fourbin. "See," he added, pointing to a large barge full of talapoins, just then setting out upon their matutinal begging expedition.

"By my honour, it is lucky that one of their friends seems to be keeping them waiting," said Des Farges. Then so quickly, yet quietly, did they dismount, and so suddenly did they fall upon the priests, who were too deeply engaged in conversation to notice the approach of the Europeans, that they were all hoisted or driven from their barge a minute after the former had reached its sides. Our party then, taking their seats in the middle of the vessel, commanded the rowers to work with all speed or their lives would be the forfeit.

"I would give a hundred gold pieces for cord enough to lash these fellows to their seats," said Phaulcon.

"True," replied De Fourbin, "they swim like water-rats, and may quit us without notice; scarcely, however, without a dagger blow or two, so look you my men," he added to the rowers, "no tricks upon travellers, or perchance they may be your last;" and such an impression did this threat apparently have upon the men, and so hard did they toil at their oars, that even Phaulcon put faith in their honesty, and could quietly and at his ease listen to Monica's account of her plan with Des Farges for his rescue from the dungeon. Then having praised his heroic wife for her bravery and coolness, he cried, "Foul shame upon me, general, for ever having doubted your good faith and honour."

"Tut, tut," replied the general, "a French soldier and gentleman could not have done otherwise; shame, I cry, upon me, for having permitted myself to be entrapped by that cunning rogue Petraxa;" and then he told them that although well treated by the regent, and having easily obtained the release of De Fourbin, that he and his officers were in reality prisoners under the guise of guests; indeed, that they were not even permitted to ride out without a guard of Moors. The very first time, however, the latter gentry accompanied them, they put their horses upon their mettle, and speedily left their guard behind; "And by my faith," concluded the general, "it was a lucky chance for thee and thy fair wife that we succeeded in escaping the rogues."

"Heaven, be thanked!" exclaimed Monica; and then, the darkness being now so dense that they could scarcely see each other, our party of fugitives, one and all, became silent, each communing with himself, and lulled almost to sleep by the regular and musical flashing of the oars. But suddenly the silence was broken by a shrill whistle from one of the boatmen, and the barge trembled violently, nearly to the capsizing of the whole party.

Monica shrieked—the men were breathless with astonishment. "What ho there, Des Farges! the villains have duped us," exclaimed De Fourbin. He was right; at the signal whistle, the whole of the eight rowers, four upon each side, had leaped from their seats into the river.

"Seize the oars or they will be overboard," cried Phaulcon; and at once the whole party, including Monica, obeyed, and began to pull for their lives, for they knew that the moment the Siamese reached the shores they would arouse the peasants, and although there were now but six instead of eight oars, the collective physique was so much greater that the speed became doubled.

By daylight, however, their strength had become spent, and they resolved to land and pursue their journey on foot. But this was no small difficulty, for the dispossessed talapoins had fled before them, giving the alarm that thieves, who had robbed and maltreated them, were, for some nefarious purpose, rowing towards Ayuthia; consequently they were met by troops of peasants, who shouted at them as thieves and robbers. A couple of pistol shots, however, drove the affrighted Siamese off, and our party succeeded shortly afterwards in reaching a wood near the capital, where they hoped to hide effectually from their pursuers.

Having entered what at first appeared to be a thicket, but which proved a kind of natural paling of jungle surrounding a large piece of green sward, one of the French officers, throwing himself upon the grass, said, "Here let us remain, or die if need be, it is impossible to proceed farther without food or rest.

"So be it," replied Des Farges, "but as I am less wearied than any among you, I will at once go farther in the wood and forage. In the meantime rest you all."

"General, this is a generous offer, and for my wife's sake I thank you; but for her I would accompany you."

"Nay, remain for her protection;" and the general then leaving them, they all threw themselves upon the sward, and even hungered as they were, were soon buried in sleep.

Phaulcon was the first to awake, as he thought at the return of Des Farges, for a man was heard entering the thicket; but no, it was the leader of some twenty Moors, who, rushing in, made the whole party prisoners ere they were fully awake. The Mahomedans, who had been directed to the hiding-place by the peasants, having secured their prisoners roughly, cruelly bound them with cords, and lost no time in taking them back to Louvo. The Frenchmen muttered military oaths; our hero and heroine spoke not, their hearts were too full of grief. Phaulcon resigned all hope, naught could now save him from an immediate death; Monica, that a life, a short one perhaps, of misery was before her. A less pious woman would have prayed for death as a relief, not so the wife of Phaulcon; like many a heroine of her race and kindred, she resolved to bear womanfully those ills which it had pleased Heaven to inflict upon her.

Upon reaching Louvo, the prisoners were very differently disposed of. The French were permitted to be at large within the palace. Phaulcon was taken to his old prison, but this time literally loaded with chains. Monica implored of the regent to be permitted to share her husband's incarceration, aye, even in chains like him, so that they would not part them. This the tyrant sternly refused. But, with a moderation unusual with Asiatic conquerors, he gave orders that she should be set at liberty, and allowed to reside in her palace unmolested. This was but a sorry consolation at first, yet, upon further consideration, she accepted it gratefully, for at least she might make some other attempt to obtain her husband's liberty. What, however, was her grief upon reaching her home to hear that her son, her only child, had been seized by the tyrant's soldiers, while on his way to Bangkok. At once she repaired again to the regent's presence, and implored of him to give her back her boy. Petraxa, who had caused the child to be taken as a hostage, assuming to admire her many virtues, ordered the boy to be restored to his mother, and even condescended to declare that it was by no command of his, but by a mistake of the soldiers that he had been seized.

# CHAPTER XXVI.

## THE SORROWS OF MONICA.

Busy as was her brain, and concentrated her whole mind in concocting some means for her husband's rescue, weeks passed and no step had been taken. The tyrant had this time been too wary. Great was Monica's misery, but then the news came, brought by the good Mandarin Pronawi, who, the better to serve the family of the unhappy Greek, had taken service with Petraxa, that the tyrant, to make a show of justice, had resolved to put Phaulcon upon his trial; but that first, to make him confess the crimes with which he was charged, had put him to torture by burning the soles of his feet, and having his forehead bound by an iron hoop. But at length came a blow which threatened to bring a speedy termination to the heroic wife's miseries. She was in her oratory, with the Father Antoine, when they were interrupted in their devotions by the Mandarin Prenawi, who, with haggard features and the tears streaming down his face, fell at her feet, then clutching the hem of her garment, he looked upwards in her face, but remained silent.

There was a spasm at her heart, but pressing her hands upon her bosom as if to suppress its agony, and looking firmly in that face which bespoke the intelligence its owner dared not utter she said—

"Speak, man; I can bear all. They have slain him!"

"Alas, lady! alas! It is true, the Lord Phaulcon is dead; slain by the orders of Petraxa."

Monica had miscalculated her forbearance; one terrible shriek, and she fell senseless in the arms of the Jesuit. It was not, however for long, and on coming to, her first words were—

"My husband, my lord! Thou who came into this ungrateful land as its protecting angel, what canst thou have done to deserve this fate? Why should they have slain thee like a vile criminal?"

"Alas! alas!" cried Prenawi, "the Lord Phaulcon's only crime was his goodness, his wisdom."

Fearing that the violence of her grief might affect her reason, the father summoned her attendants, and Monica was led to her chamber, and the company of the living Phaulcon, her son.

The news of the death of Phaulcon being bruited about, several of the Jesuits then in Louvo came to offer consolation to the widow. "They did all in their power," says the Père d'Orleans, "although they could scarcely console themselves, the loss to them being almost as great as to the wife; for in him they had lost their best friend and most zealous patron."

For weeks the unhappy lady was left to her solitude and the soothing condolence of the Father Thomas. During this time she had been left unmolested, untroubled by Petraxa's people, and, what she most dreaded, the presence of the Prince Soyaton; aware, however, that her safety and that of her son depended but upon the mere breath of an Asiatic tyrant, she had meditated some plan of fleeing to the protection of the French at Bangkok. Such a course soon became her only hope, for the king had died, it was rumoured by poison, and, moreover, that to secure the succession for himself, Petraxa had caused his majesty's two brothers to be tied up in velvet sacks, and to be beaten to death with sandal-wood clubs—a mode of execution considered so honourable in Siam, that it is only awarded to princes of the blood.

With the death of this king, Christianity lost its best friend; for no sooner did Petraxa assume the purple, than he gave orders for its uprooting from the land; and then a series of persecutions began, to be paralleled alone by those which took place some years earlier in Japan. We have now, however, to see in what manner the accession of the new sovereign affected the fortunes of Monica.

Upon the third day after the proclamation of king Petraxa, Monica was startled — nay, terrified — by the announcement that Soyaton, now heir-apparent, was at her gates, and desired admittance to her presence. That the prince should ask *permission* to visit one who was surrounded by his own creatures, she knew to be a mockery of courtesy, veiling some deeper design; still, although with trembling heart, she resolved to meet him as befitted a woman who had been Phaulcon's wife. Thus, as he entered her apartment, she said—

"What can the Prince Soyaton desire of the unhappy Monica, that, forgetful of his high rank, he should seek her at her own house?"

"Ah! beautiful Monica—more beautiful even in thy weeds—there is a feeling pervading the very existence of the miserable Soyaton that levels all ranks."

It was what she had expected; yet the words sent the indignant blood to her temples, and, rising from her seat, she said, "Prince, I will not affect to misunderstand thy meaning; but away—get thee gone; no more of this. On thy manhood—thy princely rank—I charge thee, persecute me no more!"

A A

"Lovely Japanese," he replied, "neither will *I* affect to mis-understand thee; but listen, for the time is past that Soyaton need fear to speak his thoughts—to proclaim his will. Lady," he continued, "in Siam, the marriage contract is sacred, but thou no longer canst seek its shield : thou art a widow, free to enter into a second union—nay, for the protection of thyself and son, it is necessary; or the hapless boy will be exposed to the vengeance of his father's enemies. I ask thee, then, to become my wife, the chief of my wives, my princess, and future queen."

For an instant she wrung her hands in agony, knowing as she did but too well the influence the man before her possessed over the fates of herself and son; but remembering Phaulcon, she replied :

"Is it possible that Soyaton has forgotten who I am? Does he not know that I am a Christian, and that my religion forbids so monstrous a marriage? Is he ignorant how I have lived? How dares he make such a proposition to a woman who loved her husband, and who has ever maintained a reputation for per-forming her duty !"

"Thy *son*, lady—thy *son*. The beasts of the field will sacrifice their lives for those of their offspring, wouldst thou be less?" said Soyaton.

"Man," she answered firmly, "Monica has known how to love, she knows how to suffer ; let that be my answer. As for the future of myself and son, it is in the hands of God ; but it shall never be said that the wife and child of the noble Phaulcon purchased even their lives by so shameful a proceeding as that which you desire." So saying, and turning a deaf ear to Soyaton's supplications that she would remain and hear all he had to say, she quitted the room.

Finding his overtures rejected, the mortified prince returned to his palace. It was, however, but to concoct fresh schemes for the attainment of his object. Monica's refusal did but serve to inflame his passion; then again and again he repeated his solicitations, and finding them unavailing he placed people about her who were charged, at every opportunity, to persuade her not to refuse the only means by which her son's safety could be secured. "Moreover, he made her promises which would have flattered the ambition of a less noble woman, and, as a pledge for his fidelity, ordered her to be left more at liberty than before; nevertheless, he forbade her any intercourse with the Jesuits, as he had been told that the fathers, by their advice, strengthened her opposition to his will.

"By continued refusals, Monica hoped to turn the prince's love into hate; but the tyrant, not to be turned aside from his purpose, resolved to seize her by force: thus one night he caused her to be conveyed to his apartments in the royal palace. But herein Soyaton made a false step, for finding to what place she had been taken, so great were her screams, that they reached the ears of the king, who, discovering the cause, at once commanded his son, whose irregularities he detested, to have her sent back to her own palace.

"Being defeated, the prince bethought himself of appealing to his father's cupidity. Thus, he told him that the wealth contained within Phaulcon's palace was enormous, and properly belonged to the State; and to a certain extent it answered his end, for the king sent two mandarins to demand from Monica her husband's official seals, arms, and papers. These men sealed all the boxes, took the keys, and, by the order of Soyaton, placed a strong guard before her dwelling and a sentinel at the door of her room."

"Hitherto," says the Père d'Orleans, "nothing had shaken her equanimity, but this last insult so confounded her, that she could not help complaining.

"'What,' she exclaimed, weeping, 'what have *I* done to be treated like a criminal?'

"This, however, was the only complaint drawn by adversity from this noble Christian lady during the whole course of her trials. Even this emotion of weakness, so honourable in a woman of two-and-twenty who had hitherto known nothing of misfortune, was quickly repaired, for two Jesuits who had succeeded in reaching her presence, and were with her at the time of the last outrage, having mildly represented to her that Christians, who have their treasures in heaven, and who regard it as their country, should not afflict themselves like pagans for the loss of wealth and freedom—

"'It is true,' said she, recovering her tranquillity; 'I was wrong, my fathers. God gave all; He takes all away; may His holy name be praised!'"

Scarcely two days had elapsed after the placing of the seals upon the boxes, when a mandarin, followed by a hundred men, came to break them by order of Petraxa, and carried off all the money, furniture, and jewels, he found in the apartments of the palace. But, in the direst extremity, Monica sustained her greatness of soul. She herself conducted him through the palace, pointing out the places where the most valuable articles were kept. After his departure, turning to the father, she said—

"Now God alone remains to us! but none can separate us from Him."

Having thus, by the plunder of her house, reduced her to a

state of extreme poverty, the wretch Soyaton believed that Monica would most assuredly become his prey. But no ; she resisted his overtures as firmly as ever. Almost maddened at her obstinacy, the barbarian then sent one of his physicians to her, who told her, that if she still continued to refuse to become Soyaton's wife, both mother and son should be put to death.

"Then be it so," she replied. "My trust is in God, and death is better than dishonour."

When the physician reported this reply to his master, the latter, greatly infuriated, determined to make use of the law against her. Thus she was speedily seized, and, being taken before a judge, was charged with having hidden a large portion of her husband's treasures ; but so clear were her answers to this charge, that in open court this official could proceed no further in the matter. But being in the prince's pay, he, the same night, sought her in her own house, telling her that if she did not conform to the wishes of Soyaton, and become his wife within three days, that he was resolved to condemn her to receive one hundred blows with a cane, and that in spite of his own wish he should be obliged to see the punishment put in force.

"This, oh my lord ! is not possible," she replied. "Knowing my innocence, you would not dare commit an act of such injustice."

"Lady," he replied, "build not thine hopes upon so feeble a foundation. If you obey not within three days, the sentence must be carried out, or I am a lost man."

"My duty to God, myself, and my husband's memory, is plain," she replied. "So be it." Then, when the judge had departed, she took counsel with an old relation, who, although a Christian, was greatly venerated by all parties for her extreme age of ninety years.

"Let no fear of him, nor torture, my daughter," said the aged lady, "induce thee to forget thy duty to God. Remember that thou art of the blood of martyrs, and that martyrdom is honourable." Thus Monica devoted the next two days to preparing herself for another life, for she doubted not it was Soyaton's intention to slay her.

Upon the day he had named the judge came, attended by his satellites, and made a demand that she should give up the hidden treasure. But let the Père d'Orleans describe the scene that followed.

"'I have nothing hidden,' she answered; 'if you doubt my word, you can look. You are the master here, and everything is open.'

"So temperate a reply appeared to irritate the ruffian. 'I will not seek,' said he, 'but, without stirring from this spot, I will compel you to bring me what I ask, or have you scourged to death.'

"So saying, the wretch gave the signal to the executioners, who came forward with cords to bind, and thick rattans to scourge her. These preparations at first bewildered the unhappy lady, thus abandoned to the fury of a ferocious brute. She uttered a loud cry, and throwing herself at his feet said, with a look that might have touched the hardest heart—

"'Have pity on me.'

"But this barbarian answered, with his accustomed fierceness, that he would have no mercy on her, ordering her to be taken and tied to the door of her room, and having her arms, hands, and fingers cruelly beaten.

THE TORTURE.

W. DICKES

"At this sad spectacle, her aged relative, son, and servants, uttered cries which would have roused any one but this hardened wretch. The whole of the unhappy family cast themselves at his feet, and touching the ground with their foreheads, implored mercy; but in vain. He continued to torture her from seven till nine o'clock; and not having been able to gain anything, he carried her off to the palace of Soyaton, at Ayuthia."

# CHAPTER XXVII.

Now the Mahomedans who had pursued Des Farges and his officers were so delighted at the unexpected capture of Phaulcon, a personage of much greater importance in their eyes, that they gave up all further pursuit, and thus the French chief, by a fortunate accident, ultimately succeeded in reaching his head-quarters at Bangkok. The general's escape, however, so greatly enraged Petraxa, that he determined to throw off the mask, and at once make known his intentions respecting foreigners in Siam. Thus he immediately ordered large bodies of troops to march upon the French garrisons, and to proclaim throughout the land that it was his (the king's) determination to drive the foreigners from Siam. Further, he sent several ships of war to the mouth of the river to entrap into his power any strange ships which might arrive. But, hating the French as he did, there is yet one anecdote in connexion with the first outbreak of hostilities worthy of being recorded here, inasmuch that it proves there was light as well as shade in the usurper's character. It is as follows :—

Two of the sons of Des Farges having been seized by the followers of Petraxa, the latter, before the beginning of hostilities, compelled the youths to write to their father, telling him that if he did not immediately surrender Bangkok he would have them put to a cruel death.

' "Tell the boys," said the brave Frenchman, "that I feel deeply for their situation, and could I save their lives by sacrificing my own I would do so on the instant. But to accede to this proposition would be to tarnish my honour and fair fame, and neglect my duty to my king. Let them therefore prepare for the worst, regarding it as a glory to suffer in the cause of God and their sovereign. At the same time, let them have this consolation—their deaths shall be avenged."

This reply, instead of irritating the king, so excited his admiration, that he at once released the two lads; but, as another expedient, he sent word to their father, that if he and his men did not immediately quit the fortress he would destroy every missionary and Christian in the kingdom at the mouth of the cannon. To parry this terrible threat, which the general had but too much reason to fear would be carried out to the letter, he set on foot a negotiation by which he agreed that he and the rest of the Frenchmen should quit the kingdom as soon as they had received certain sums of money, and ships sufficient to bear them away to the French settlement at Pondicherry. To this the king agreed, but when provided, the vessels proved to be in such wretched condition that Des Farges would not embark his men. Hence fresh negotiations were commenced.

One day, while the latter were pending, a large ship which had some months before been sent by Phaulcon to Batavia, was standing towards the bar of the river. Her captain, St. Cyr, glass in hand, was upon the quarter-deck, looking at the Siamese blockading ships. By his side stood a tall, deeply bronzed Englishman, seemingly as much interested as the Gaul in the appearance of the two vessels.

. "By my faith, but I should like to know the reason of those

old war tubs being placed at the very mouth of the river?" said
St. Cyr. "What think you, my friend?"

"They are blockading, but against whom? Not the Dutch, or
we should have heard of that at Batavia," replied the Englishman,
who, in fact, was no other than Blake Taunton.

"By my honour, but it may be, though, for, did he think it
necessary, the Greek is not the man to wait until war had been
declared," replied St. Cyr.

"Phaulcon is *not the man* to do aught that is dishonourable,"
replied the other, sharply.

"Nay, nay, I meant not that; nor would such a course be un-
fair, for it is the custom among the barbarian Asiatics the Barcalon
so wisely rules," replied the Frenchman; "but," he added, as he
saw two boats coming towards the ship, "we shall find out from
these fellows."

When two mandarins, accompanied by some fifty men, came
on board all courteous and smiling, and bearing, according to their
custom, refreshments, St. Cyr desired news of the Lord Barcalon
Phaulcon.

"The great and wise Lord Phaulcon," replied the chief of the
two officials, "has long been awaiting, at Tabanque, the coming
of the French captain, but yesterday urgent business compelled
him to return to the Court at Louvo. Thus he commanded his
servants to tell the noble Farang that his lordship anxiously
awaits his arrival, for the king is at war both by sea and land with
the people of Cambogia, and desires the aid of all his good friends
the French."

"Ay, this then accounts for the blockade," said St. Cyr; but
he added, "Look you, my friends, more than one half my crew are
disabled, for we have encountered much sickness and foul weather,

and I shall be glad if you can spare me a score of your fellows here; otherwise, we shall not reach Louvo for the next two months."

"It is well; the noble Farang shall have men sufficient when the ship has crossed the bar. In the mean time, the sailors who are with me shall aid in working the ship," replied the mandarin; and making a signal to the Siamese, they fell to work among the crew, good humouredly taking any part assigned to them by the over-worked sick Frenchmen.

In a few hours the ship had crossed the bar, and was running between the two blockading vessels, one of which hailed to her to stand to. With reluctance the French captain complied, for suddenly a suspicion flashed through his mind that all was not right, and this was speedily confirmed, for simultaneously a boat's crew of armed men from each ship came on board, and then the chief mandarin, approaching St. Cyr, said:

"It is the will of the king that the Farang captain should quit his vessel here, and proceed at once in yon ship"—as he spoke he pointed to a large armed junk, bearing the royal ensign—"to Louvo."

"We are betrayed! What treachery is this? Draw, my friend!"

"Stay!" cried Blake, clutching the hot-headed Frenchman's arm, "violence cannot serve us; we must submit, and," he added, in French, "await our opportunity."

"You are right," replied St. Cyr; then to the Siamese he said, "We accept the king's invitation; signal to the junk."

"The noble Farang is displeased," replied the mandarin. "But it is without reason; no personal harm is intended; the king is desirous only to see him in Louvo. His friend," he added, as he bowed to Blake, "may accompany him, if it so please him."

"What say you to this, Captain Taunton?" asked St. Cyr, as if he doubted the willingness of the latter to accept the invitation.

"That I am rejoiced," was the reply; and, as soon as the junk came alongside, they went on board, and as passengers, and with the liberty of passengers, they were treated during the passage. When, however, they approached Bangkok, and St. Cyr asked permission to go ashore and report his arrival to the governor, the mandarin said, "It is not possible, the Farang general is in rebellion against the king," and almost as he spoke there came the booming of great guns, and large shot struck the side of the vessel.

In an instant the fiery Frenchman's sword flew from its scabbard. "Dog!" he exclaimed to the mandarin, "you have betrayed us." But at a signal from the latter, the native sailors surrounded and, seizing the two Europeans, led them to separate cabins below. They were, however, only kept in durance for four or five hours, for upon the junk's arrival at Louvo they were summoned upon deck, and formally delivered over to the chief mandarin of the river, whose barge had come alongside to receive them.

"What, are we prisoners to my old friend, the Lord Prenawi Consit?" said Blake, as in the official before him he recognised the worthy mandarin.

"The brave Farang, Captain Taunton!" exclaimed the no less astonished Prenawi; but as he warmly shook the Englishman's hands, tears rolled down his cheeks, and he glanced timidly around at the native sailors and their officer.

"'Tis a fortunate meeting," said Blake; "but how is this? What can have happened that the Lord Phaulcon should have suffered or ordered an officer of his good allies, the French, and his friend and almost brother, to be entrapped at the mouth of the river, and to be brought hither like pirates?"

For a moment, Prenawi hesitated to reply; but then, with a meaning glance at Blake, he said for the listening ears of his fellow-countrymen, every one of whom was a spy upon the words and actions of any man who was known to have once enjoyed the friendship of the deposed minister—

"Has the noble Farang come from another world, that he knows not that the King Narai is dead; the great Petraxa rules in his place; and that the traitor Phaulcon has expiated his crime?"

"Ah! what say you?" exclaimed Blake; and a cold shudder ran through his veins, for those few words told the ruin, perhaps death, of his old friend.

But again Prenawi gave a significant look, and replied, "The name of the Greek is forbidden to pass the lips of honest men."

"Whew," whistled the Frenchman; "there has been a revolution, this Petraxa has been successful, war has broken out against the French, and we are prisoners."

"The noble Farang is wrong. He is not a prisoner, but will be detained in Louvo only until his countrymen are provided with ships in which to quit Siam. Until those ships are ready, the king has willed that no foreigner shall pass up the river without the company of his own officers. Moreover," Prenawi added, politely, "I am commanded by the king to entertain you in Louvo, until the ships are ready for sea."

"But," said St. Cyr, "this vessel was fired upon by the French garrison at Bangkok, and my countrymen attack not those with whom they are at peace."

"The noble Farang will find those in Louvo who may answer his question," replied Prenawi, evasively. "In the meantime," he added, "he will remain his mean servant's honoured guest."

"Well, guests or prisoners, and the two words have the same

meaning, we must submit," replied St. Cyr, as he sulkily followed
the mandarin into the barge. When, however, in about an hour,
they landed before the palace of the latter, Prenawi, addressing
the Frenchman, said—

"The Farang captain doubted his servant's honesty; he was
wrong. Let him now choose whether he will stay my honoured
guest, or seek the residence of some of his fellow-countrymen
who are now in Louvo. If the latter, he shall be conducted to
their house at once."

"Your pardon, noble Siamese; but since I have the choice, I
must join my countrymen," replied. St. Cyr; whereupon, without
a word of objection, the mandarin ordered a slave to attend him.

"Tell me, oh noble Prenawi!" said Blake, as soon as he found
himself alone with the worthy man, "is it possible that they can
have murdered Phaulcon? But, alas! it is an end I ever feared."

"It *is* even so," replied Prenawi. "The great Lord Phaulcon,
the noble minister, the good friend, has passed away, and I fear
by means of a death as cruel as it was secret, for insatiable was
the hatred of his enemies."

"But his wife?"

"Alas! she languishes beneath a load of persecution and
wretchedness. But enough of this for the present."

"Nay," cried Blake, "one more question: Is the lady in the
power of the tyrant?"

"Hush!" whispered the mandarin, looking around in alarm;
"walls have ears." Then, in the same low tone, he added: "For
some time past the Lady Monica has lodged with the wives of
the Prince Soyaton, until the latter shall have completed a separate
suite of apartments for her reception. A few days since, however,
news being conveyed to her that her aged and nearest female

relation was dying, she prayed to be permitted to attend her bed-side. This the prince dared not refuse, and thus she is now beneath her relative's roof."

"This is welcome intelligence. I must see her, Prenawi," said Blake.

"My elder brother shall have his wish. It cannot, however, be accomplished till the city is hushed in sleep. No slave or servant must know the lady has spoken with a Farang—least of all, with her late husband's friend."

"Stay, noble Prenawi, another question," said Blake, as the mandarin arose to quit the room. "Know you aught of the Father Antoine Thomas? I would have speech with the good man."

"Then must my elder brother at once hasten to Bangkok, for in that city the good priest but now awaits the ship that is to take him from Siam."

"Say you so. This is, indeed, unfortunate, for to seek out the father was the main object of my present voyage to the East," said Blake.

"Let not my friend repine, since fate may have directed him to the aid of those whom the Lord Phaulcon loved dearer than his life," said Prenawi.

"You are right, noble Prenawi. I *should* rejoice at the chance that hath brought me here at this present time. But get thee to the lady, and beseech of her to see me with all speed."

"Let my elder brother bridle his impatience till midnight," replied Prenawi; and he left the room.

At the time appointed, however, he returned, and led him to the lady's residence, where, in a secret chamber, he remained during the night.

## CHAPTER XXVIII.

### MONICA'S FLIGHT.

"BLESSED be the name of the Most High, who hath raised to the widow and the orphan a friend at their utmost need!" exclaimed Monica, as, at the entrance of Blake and Prenawi, she arose from beside the couch of her sick relative.

"Would, lady," replied Blake, as he took her hand, "that my power to aid thee were equal to my will; but, alas! I am myself but little less than a prisoner in this city."

"It *is* within thy power, for but yesterday the treaty was signed by which ships are to be supplied to take the French troops from this land of misery. All foreigners may now take their departure from Louvo unquestioned," said Prenawi.

Falling upon her knees, and clasping her hands, Monica exclaimed, joyfully—

"Said I not that Heaven had sent us aid in the hour of our utmost need? Then," she added, clasping Blake's knees, "thou, oh noble Englishman! my husband's oldest and dearest friend, wilt protect his wife and son? Take us, I beseech of thee, to the protection of the great king's flag at Bangkok."

"Lady," replied Blake, raising her from her kneeling position, "thou art right; I will save thee and thy child with my life. Some means must be found by which we may quit this city."

"Think well, oh my beloved daughter! of this thing you

propose," said the invalid lady; "reflect upon the perils of so hazardous an attempt. Should you be overtaken in your flight—and the river and roads to Bangkok are crowded with the creatures of the usurper—your ruin, and that of thy son, would be certain."

"Long, Oh! my dear mother," she replied, "have I pondered upon a means of escape, and well do I know the perils to be encountered; but the latter are as grains of sand compared with the horrors of remaining in this city, where my honour, and the religion of myself and son, are in hourly danger from the machinations of the brutal Soyaton. Nay, there is not an hour to be lost, for but yesterday the prince sent a messenger telling me that the apartments he has been so long preparing are ready for my reception." Then, again throwing herself upon her knees, she took Blake's hand, saying:

"Blake Taunton, as an angel sent from Heaven for my preservation do I regard thee; you were ever the friend of my noble husband; by his memory, I conjure thee to preserve the honour of his wife, the religion of his son. Look upon my wretched position, compelled either to fly or be shut up for ever in a place more terrible to me than a prison or the grave. Yes," she concluded, "I know—I see that in you we shall find our liberator; you *will* convey us to Bangkok."

"Lady," replied Blake, "I beseech of thee to rise; it is unfitting that the widow of Phaulcon should kneel to Phaulcon's friend. It *shall* be as you desire; from this moment I devote myself to your service."

"Pray Heaven that you may not fail in this perilous attempt, for then better had you be in your grave than in the power of Soyaton," said the invalid.

At these words, as if stricken with a sudden thought, Monica clutched Blake's arm, and, with a look of determination, said:

"Blake Taunton, on thy honour, by thy memory of Phaulcon, I crave—nay, demand, one promise."

"It is granted ere asked," said Blake; but imagine his astonishment when she added:

"That, should we be overtaken, and again about to fall into the power of Soyaton, you will throw both mother and son into the river."

"Lady," replied Blake, moved almost to tears by her earnestness, "while I live you shall not fall into the tyrant's power. I can say no more."

"This is well," said Prenawi, as he arose to depart. "Let my elder brother then remain hidden here, and thou, Oh, lady, prepare all things for thy departure during the dark hours, when I will return."

At midnight, the mandarin again came, and then conducted Monica, her son, and Blake, through a labyrinth of houses on the poorest side of the city to the river, where they found awaiting them a small barge, manned by twelve of Prenawi's most devoted slaves. In this they took their departure from Louvo; and although Bangkok was at least twenty leagues distant, and the river and its banks were crowded with the usurper's people, they succeeded in reaching the fortress late the following day.

Once beneath the flag of France, the mourning widow, in the midst of her great grief, felt consoled; her boy was safe, and she herself free from the persecution of Soyaton. She now awaited but to hear the confirmation of her safety from the lips of the governor; but although she received congratulatory visits from many of the chief officers who had known and loved her husband,

three days passed without bringing an invitation from Des Farges.
It was mysterious; it was cruel.

Each day had Blake gone to beg of Des Farges to give the
widow of Phaulcon an audience, but on each occasion he had met
with some excuse for postponing the interview. Upon the fourth,
he returned, looking sad, yet flushed with anger.

"Say, Oh! my friend, that you have this time succeeded—that
Des Farges will receive us!" she cried, as he entered her presence.

"Dear lady," he replied, "be prepared for the worst."

"The worst," she said, interrupting him; "what can be worse
than the persecutions of Soyaton?"

"Wife of Phaulcon, be thyself; let not my sad news overwhelm
you. An agent of the King Petraxa is in Bangkok. This man
demands, as the price of the ratification of the treaty of peace, that
you should be sent back to Louvo."

"And the governor, this Des Farges?" she cried, with bated
breath.

"Was too craven-hearted to refuse."

For a moment, the poor lady stood utterly confounded; then
she exclaimed:

"Is this possible? What, under the flag of France, the asylum
for all who are unfortunate, is the widow of Phaulcon to be the
only one not to find a refuge? No, no; I will not believe even if
you swear it;" and, falling upon her knees, she offered up a prayer
to God to protect her son. "Oh! Phaulcon, my lord, my beloved,
was it for such men as these that thy dear life was offered up
a sacrifice?"

"Dear lady, there are brave men among these Frenchmen—nay,
those who have told the governor that it would be foul shame
to deliver thee to thine enemies, that it would disgrace the flag

of France if there were one among them who would not die
to serve thee in this need."

"Then there is yet hope ? " she exclaimed, eagerly.

"Yes; that Des Farges, fearing the disgust of his officers,
may evade Petraxa's demand;" and with this gleam of hope
Monica that night comforted herself. But Blake was wrong in
his conjecture; for Des Farges, dreading a fresh rupture with the
usurper, had resolved to send her back to Louvo. To perform
this harsh task with at least a show of politeness, he, the next
day, sent a French priest to persuade her to return of her own
free will.

"Lady," said the ecclesiastic, "your remaining with the
French will endanger the peace of two nations, and the safety
of our holy religion in Siam. Is it possible, then, that one so
gentle and religious should desire to incur so much evil for the
mere gratification of a visit to France ? "

"Visit to France," she replied. "I desire it not; take me to
Goa, to Macao, anywhere that my honour and my son's religion
may be preserved."

"Lady," he replied, "your desires are commendable, and
natural; yet if, for the sake of Christianity in Siam, and
the French garrison here, it be necessary you should return to
Louvo, and you can do so without fear of danger, it is your
duty as a Christian woman to obey cheerfully."

"Do you hope to dazzle me with words like these ? " she ex-
claimed. "The king will persecute none on my account. What
Christians are there at the present time who would fear him ?
His own subjects — I know them not. The Portuguese have
been his friends ! As for the French, believe me, father,—
Petraxa will attack them no more; he fears the vengeance of

the Great King too much. No, no, father; I will never return
to Louvo of my own free will. I ought not, will not, sacrifice
to any other interest my reputation nor my son's religion. Who
—who in Louvo is capable of protecting me against the brutal
Soyaton ?"

"Lady," replied the priest, "these objections are unreasonable ;
thy fears are groundless, or at least exaggerated. The Prince
Soyaton will no longer be suffered by the king to persecute
thee. Yet," he added, "there is one means by which the
remotest fear of persecution from this prince may be stayed."

"Impossible !" she cried; adding with a look of astonishment, "But name them."

"By giving thy hand to the Portuguese Captain, D'Aguilar.
Thus would an impenetrable barrier be placed to the passion
of Soyaton, for the veriest heathen in this land holds sacred
the marriage tie." The priest remained silent for a minute to
watch the effect of this proposition. Her face and neck were
suffused with crimson, her eyes flashed with indignation, her
face streamed with tears, but she spoke not. Encouraged by
her silence, he continued : "Agree to this, lady, and as a further
protection against the prince, the Governor Des Farges will
insist that a clause be inserted in the treaty now soon to be
signed, by which thou shalt be placed beneath the paternal
care of the seminary of holy fathers, which the king agrees
to permit to remain in Siam."

But Monica, having recovered her self-possession, replied :

"The wife of Phaulcon has, indeed, fallen low. This to *me*,
and from *you*—a priest, a Christian, a Frenchman; while I
mourn my noble husband's death—ay, not even certain of that
death—you propose a second marriage. Tell me," she added,

passionately, "were I a thing so vile, what would be thought
in France of the woman who, being the widow of one whom
the king had raised to the highest dignities in the realm, could
stoop to marriage with an unknown · Portuguese, her husband's
direst enemy ? "

"Lady—"

"Nay, hear me out. You tell me that the Siamese respect
the marriage tie. Has Soyaton respected them in the persons
of Christian wōmen whom he has carried off from their husbands ?
You offer me the protection of the seminary. It cannot protect
itself. No; since I am refused the protection of the French
flag, go, priest, tell thy general that no living man shall make
me accept the alternative. My trust is now in God alone. Des
Farges may slay me and my son; my life is of little value, but
my honour is too dear for me willingly to expose myself again
to perils which I alone can fully comprehend. Now, father,"
she concluded, "you have my answer; it is irrevocable—go ! "

"Lady," replied the priest, as he took his departure, "painful
as my duty is, it must be performed ; you have refused all
overtures. Prepare, then, for thy return to Louvo, for to-morrow,
at sunrise, you will be taken on board one of king Petraxa's ships."

In an agony of suspense, Monica awaited the return of Blake,
who had been absent the whole of that day. It was late in
the evening before he came. Then she told him all that had
passed between her and the priest. Blake, having listened
attentively, replied :

"Lady, fear not, I have good news : our dear Phaulcon's friend,
the Count de Fourbin, has just arrived in Bangkok. I have seen
and told him of thy sad strait, and, like a noble gentleman,
he has sworn to release you. Even now I go to arrange with

him the means ; so I pray you trust in heaven. Even should this Des Farges deliver thee to the Siamese mandarin ere I can return, go willingly—ay, cheerfully—for help will be at hand."

"I believe thee," she replied joyfully ; and patiently, hopefully, she awaited his return : but as the hours passed away, dismal thoughts took possession of her mind. Des Farges might have received some intimation of the scheme for her rescue, and have caused him to be seized ; still, with heroic courage she carried out Blake's instruction, for the next morning, when Des Farges' aide-de-camp came, accompanied by a Siamese mandarin and the chief of Jesuits, who had been greatly befriended by Phaulcon, she protested to the officer against the violence shown her beneath the flag of France ; then, turning to the chief of the Jesuits, she warmly expressed her thanks for the constant friendship she had experienced from the fathers of that company, adding :

"You, Oh ! my father, loved Phaulcon in good and evil fortune ; you have felt the misfortune of his family. God and thine own conscience will reward you."

Having thus spoken, Monica, with great dignity, and leading her son by the hand, followed the Siamese to the river side, where the barge was awaiting that was to convey her on board the native vessel. Seeing, however, that it was not manned by natives, she exclaimed, bitterly :

"Is it possible, then, that so many Frenchmen could be found to deliver over to her enemies the widow of the man who loved and benefited them at the cost of his own life ?" and she took her seat, weeping at this last insult. How anxiously she gazed around for the promised aid ! Would it come when she had been taken on board the native vessel ? No, it was at hand ; for suddenly the Siamese mandarin sprang from his seat, crying aloud that he had been betrayed, for they had run the barge in an opposite direction from the native vessel, and towards a large French ship.

"Not another word, as you value your life!" cried one of the rowers, as the barge grazed the side of the French vessel. It was the Count de Fourbin, who, with Blake, had disguised himself as a seaman.

In a few minutes more Monica and her son trod the deck.

"Kneel, boy," she cried, in an ecstasy of joy, "kneel, and thank God that we are at length delivered from the hands of our enemies."

Having stood with doffed caps while the lady offered up her gratitude to heaven, the count, taking her hand, said:

"Lady, heroic is your courage; martyr-like your resignation in misery; can you as bravely bear great joy?" and he whispered a sentence in her ear. It caused her whole frame to vibrate. "Oh, joy incredible; my husband alive!" she cried. At the same moment Phaulcon came forth from the deck cabin, and, embracing her, she swooned in his arms.

"My wife, my dear wife! my boy! this is indeed a blessed moment! De Fourbin, nobly have you redeemed your promise; and you, too, Blake, old friend," he said. "Oh, this moment, indeed, is enough to redeem the miseries of a life!"

But we will draw a veil over this happy reunion, and proceed to relate how it came about that Phaulcon was still alive, and on board that ship.

## CHAPTER XXIX.

As we have seen, it was generally believed throughout Siam that Phaulcon had been put to death shortly after his recapture. This rumour, however, had been set afloat by the command of Petraxa, who, while he feared that, if it were known our hero was still alive, the French would insist upon his life and liberty being made one important article in a treaty of peace, at the same time determined that his sufferings should be prolonged. Thus, he had caused him to be confined in his former dungeon, but laden with chains so heavy that his strength was barely sufficient to bear them. Moreover, both the king and Soyaton took a pleasure in daily visiting their prisoner, and taunting him with his crimes (for so they called them). In time, however, the most savage animals become tired of torturing their prey; so the king at length commanded that he should be put to death under the eye of Soyaton. One favour, however, was granted the unhappy man, and that was the attendance of a Christian priest, viz. the Father Antoine Thomas, who happened about that time to have come from Bangkok to Louvo, on some matter concerning the pending treaty.

The day appointed for the execution having arrived, Phaulcon was mounted upon an elephant; and well guarded by a body of Malays, under the command of the Prince of Macassar, was led into the forest of Thale-Phutson, as if the tyrant had chosen the horrors of solitude to bury in oblivion an unjust and cruel deed.

"Those who conducted him," says the Père d'Orleans, "remarked, that during the whole way he appeared perfectly calm, praying earnestly, and often repeating aloud the names of Jesus and of Mary."

When they reached the place of execution, he was ordered to dismount, and told that he must prepare to die. The approach of death did not alarm him; he regarded it then, as he had at a distance, with intrepidity. He asked of Soyaton only a few minutes to pray with the father, which he did kneeling, with so touching an air, that these heathens were moved by it. His prayer concluded, he lifted his hands towards heaven, and, protesting his innocence, declared that he died willingly; having the testimony of his conscience, that, as a minister, he had acted solely for the glory of the true God, the service of the king, and the welfare of the state; that he forgave his enemies, as he hoped himself to be forgiven by God.

"For the rest," he said to Soyaton, "were I as guilty as my enemies declare, my wife and son are innocent. I commend them to the protection of the king, asking neither wealth nor position, only their lives and liberty." Then turning to the father, as if to address him, "But—"

"Enough!" exclaimed the impatient Soyaton, at the same time beckoning to the executioner to advance. But as the man came forward, sword in hand, the Macassar prince rode forward.

"Prince, I pray thee let the Greek confer with the priest—we war not with the dying."

"What words are these? Who dares step between Soyaton and his vengeance?" cried the king's son, savagely; but observing the fierce looks of the wild Malays, and knowing full well that at the slightest show of insult to their prince they would not improbably slay him then and there, he added, in a subdued sulky tone:

"Be it so!"

During the conference between Phaulcon and the father, the Prince Abdullah continued to gaze anxious and expectantly into the thick wood around, at intervals exchanging glances with the prince. The conference was long; Soyaton was chafing with impatience, when, suddenly, he placed his hand upon his sword. It was at the shrill ringing cries of some fifty French seamen, who came forcing their way through the trees.

At a signal from Abdullah, the Malays prepared to receive the new comers.

"We are betrayed—treason!" exclaimed Soyaton, putting himself in a position of defence. To the terror of the latter, however, at the very first onset, the Malays gave way, all but their prince fleeing into the forest, closely followed by Soyaton.

"Phaulcon, my friend, thank God, we are in time; we have saved you; you are free! Let us, however, lose no time, lest the rogue Soyaton may return with a host."

But, for a minute, Phaulcon stood amazed at seeing Abdullah sitting upon his horse, and looking upon the French, his enemies, as pacifically as if in the midst of his own men; then, again, the Malays, habitually brave and devoted troops, had fled at the first attack.

"Is it possible," he exclaimed at length, "that God can have changed the heart of Abdullah—that my once implacable foe can have become my friend?"

"But for this prince," said De Fourbin, "no aid of ours could have saved you."

"It *is* possible—it *is* true," replied the prince. "Allah," he continued, "has removed the film from before his servant's eyes. Greek, you preserved to my children the life of their father when it was fairly forfeited. A prince of Macassar forgets neither an injury nor a kindness. But enough of words. It is a life for a life; a heavy debt has been paid now," he added. "Get thee hence, with these Franks, and not a word to living soul in Siam, that Abdullah saved thee from the vengeance of the king's son, or it may chance that the blow intended for thee may fall upon my neck. Now, farewell! Allah preserve thee!" So saying, without waiting to hear a reply, the prince turned his horse's head, and galloped after his men.

"A miracle!" said De Fourbin.

"Nay, God never made a man without some good in his heart," replied Phaulcon.

"My son, every instant is fraught with danger; let us to the river," said the father; and speedily the party had reached the barge, and were on their way to the French ship at Bangkok.

"How, Oh! my father! came about this most providential escape?" asked Phaulcon.

"Through the Macassar prince alone," replied the father. "It was he who told me that the rumour of your death was false, of your sufferings in the dungeon, and, lastly, of the day and place appointed for your execution. Knowing his long hatred to you, Petraxa fearlessly placed you in the hands of Abdoul and his men; but having sworn to repay the debt he owed you, he sought me out, promising that, if I could get some of thé French who were about quitting Louvo to make a feint of attacking his men at the very spot of execution, the latter should retreat; and nothing could be more fortunate than this proposition, for the same day the count here had arranged to take me with him to Bangkok."

"My friend, next to Providence, you have saved me. How shall I ever repay thee?"

"By saying no more about it," said De Fourbin, warmly grasping his hand. "Our joy at finding you yet in the land of the living is reward sufficient."

"This is generous," said Phaulcon, returning the grasp. "But my wife—my son?"

"Safe in Bangkok; at least, so I hope; for they have succeeded in quitting Louvo," replied the father.

"The great God be thanked for His many mercies!" exclaimed Phaulcon, piously. But sad were his feelings, and many his cries for vengeance, as, during the journey, he listened to the story of his wife's sufferings. "My friends," said he, at the conclusion of the recital, "on our arrival at Bangkok, not a minute will I rest until I have searched every nook and cranny of the town for my beloved son and most suffering wife."

"Nay," replied De Fourbin, "you must remain hidden on board ship. To show yourself in Bangkok would be madness, for you would be claimed by the Siamese chief now there; and Des Farges would not dare refuse, for by so doing he would risk the destruction of all the French in Siam. No," he added, "rest you content; and if your lady and son be in the town, heaven and earth shall be moved ere I fail to discover and bring them to your arms."

"De Fourbin, my friend," replied Phaulcon, "it is hard to delegate such a duty, but I feel you are right, and I dare not imperil the safety of all. Be it as you will." And from the following morning, when the count commenced the search, he rested not until he had brought about the event related in the last chapter.

## CHAPTER XXX.

### DEPARTURE FROM THE EAST.

THE next day the good ship was flitting before a stiff breeze in the Gulf of Siam. Her chief passengers were seated in the deck cabin, asking and answering questions of each other.

"Blake, my friend, it overjoys me that it fared well with the good captain and his daughter when you left England; but didst discover aught satisfactorily as to your birth, for if my memory fails not, that was the chief purpose of your voyage to the old country?"

"It was; and the result rendered it necessary for me to return to Siam to seek out the good father here," replied Blake, pointing to the Jesuit, Antoine Thomas, who sat near him.

"To seek me?" exclaimed the priest, with surprise.

"Ay; but listen." Blake, then, having repeated the story he had told Phaulcon many years before about the death of his mother at the siege of St. Heliers, and by what accident he had become the adopted son of Captain West, the priest, lifting his hands, exclaimed, "The ways of God are indeed wonderful!" then, taking him by both hands, and closely scanning his features, he said:

"Thou art, indeed, the son of that unfortunate couple. When we first met in the seas of Cochin China, the likeness seemed familiar to my mind; yet, still, I dreamt not that thou couldst be their son."

"Father," exclaimed Blake, "this is indeed fortunate; for the object of my voyage is attained. With thine aid, I shall no longer be nameless. One day," he continued, "about three years since, a man advanced in years, but from his apparel well to do in the world, sought and obtained an interview with my adopted father. "'I am an old soldier,' said he, 'of the cavalier army. Dost bear in thy memory, captain, the siege of the castle of St. Heliers?'

"'Right well; but why this question, my man?' replied the captain.

"'When you roundheads sacked the place, didst not find the body of a lady, who had been slain by a stray bullet, and a boy by her side?'

"'Right well, again,' cried the captain; adding joyfully, 'Hast news, man, to tell of that lady and the birth of that boy, my own adopted son, Blake Taunton?'

"'That boy, or man now, is Sir Herbert Carteret, the nephew of my late master, Sir George, once Governor of St. Heliers.'

"'Who died at St. Malo soon after the siege?' said the captain.

"'Who was *thought* to have died at that time and place; but who only departed this life six months since, in a Spanish monastery, to which he retired after the apparently total defeat of the royal cause. With his dying breath Sir George bade me seek one Captain West, and tell him that the boy he had so long protected was his brother's son, and thus his own heir; while living he had sworn never to disclose the secret, but dying he forgave the past. "Tell the captain," said my dying master, "that there is but one man living who is cognisant of the painful past of my family, and who may help the boy to his name and inheritance, and he is a Jesuit father."

" Where is the priest to be found ?   What is his name ?" said the Captain, joyfully.   But at this question the man's countenance became blank.   "Alas !" he replied, " ere my poor master could utter another word his soul had taken flight."

" But his papers ?   mayhap some clue may be discovered among them."

" They still remain at the monastery, the monks declining to give them to any but an official."

"Thus," said Blake, " the whereabouts, nay, even the name of the only person who could help me to my birthright was still wanted ; however, the Captain at once wrote to me to return to England ; I complied with all speed, but upon my arrival guess my chagrin to hear that these papers having been obtained from the Spanish monks at the instance of the English minister, the name of the priest proved to be Father Antoine Thomas—his whereabouts, Siam."

" My son," replied the father, "it is fortunate for thee that Heaven has been pleased to save my life, for it is *indeed* true, that if Sir George be dead, I alone in the world can establish thy identity.   The Baronet and his brother Herbert," he added, " were born of a house, none of whom had ever forsaken the faith of their forefathers, and up to manhood both adhered to it firmly.   Unfortunately, Herbert became passionately attached to a beautiful, but heretic lady ; he married her according to the rites both of the Protestant and Romish Church ; at the latter I officiated.   This marriage caused an estrangement between the brothers, which, however, might have been healed by time, but alas ! the fratricidal war between king and Parliament broke out, and Herbert left both Church and king to become a heretic and

c c

a roundhead ; at this apostasy the Catholic cavalier elder brother became so enraged, for he regarded his house as being for ever dishonoured, that it was most providential they never again met. By a curious accident, during the siege of St. Helier's I was taken prisoner by the Parliamentarians ; the soldiers, maddened at the sight of a priest of Rome, would have slain me on the spot ; but a fortunate chance brought Captain Carteret to my rescue.    He did more ; he kept me in his lodgings as an honoured guest ; but alas ! one day they brought him to his quarters mortally wounded.    Dying, he besought me to convey his wife and child to the beleaguered castle, and tell Sir George that his brother's dying request was, that he would take the widow and orphan under his protection ; with these words he placed in my hands the certificates of his double marriage, believing they would be safer under my charge than in the care of his lady. I at once sought the Parliamentary chief, and entreated permission to set out immediately for the castle ; the noble Blake complied, and generously gave liberty to a cavalier officer, that he might escort us at night.    The latter obtained us an entry into the fortress ; and the next morning we were to have an interview with Sir George. It is not true that the lady and her brother-in-law met on the night of our admittance, nor, alas ! did they ever meet, for on the following day the castle fell into the hands of the roundheads. Neither did I ever see the lady or her child after that night, for in the encounter I was wounded even to being bereft of my senses, and in that state carried by the cavalier soldiers to St. Malo.    On recovering from my wound, I went to Sir George to inquire about the lady and her son ; the former he said was dead, the latter he believed to be in safe hands.    Then I begged of him as the uncle, as in fact the only relative of the boy, to send for him. But he sternly replied that he would have naught to do with, or own as a member of his house, the offspring of a traitor and a heretic. Soon after this, Sir George entered a monastery in Spain. For many months, being near this religious house, I frequently saw and conversed with him, but never could I discover the whereabouts of the boy. Still, with an indefinite hope—a presentiment that I should again see him, I kept the marriage papers of the unfortunate couple, unwilling that they should be in the possession of one who in some wild moment might be tempted to destroy them."

"Father," cried Blake, "how can I sufficiently thank you?" but not noticing the interruption, the priest continued—

"Well, I took them with me to Siam; but some five years since, believing, or rather hoping that time might have softened the heart of this stern man, I wrote, telling him I was in possession of the proofs of his brother's marriage, and begging that he would do justice to his nephew and legal heir; but the letter must have fallen short of its mark—I received no reply."

"Nevertheless," said Blake, "that epistle performed its mission. It was the means by which your whereabouts was discovered."

"The hand of God is visible in all this," replied the father.

"Blake, or Sir Herbert, I heartily congratulate you upon your good fortune," cried Phaulcon, grasping his friend's hand; "but, Zillah West," he added, "how fares it with the gentle girl? are you reconciled to her, and the Captain, my dear old friend and patron?"

"Zillah West no longer, Phaulcon, she is my wife, my kind loving wife! Aye," he added, with a smile, "in spite of the transient affection she once entertained for a certain person who shall be nameless."

"Was it so, indeed?" said Phaulcon, thoughtfully. "My poor friend, how can I ever atone for the years of trouble I then unconsciously brought upon you?"

"By forgetting all about it," replied Blake, warmly; adding, "by coming to our house; by witnessing our happiness; and that too of the good old Captain, who never lays his head upon his pillow without offering up a prayer for your welfare. By— and pardon me—accepting a portion of that fortune which is doubly valuable in my eyes since it may benefit you and yours."

"A generous offer, dear friend, and for which I am deeply grateful," replied Phaulcon; "but," he added, "I need it not; having while in power, and in the enjoyment of wealth, at the suggestion of my wife, who foresaw the possibility of evil days, transmitted to Europe a sum amply sufficient for the modest requirements of a simple gentleman of my native isle."

"Is it then possible," said Blake, "that Phaulcon, whose entire life has been one continued effort to climb the very heights of fortune, can forego activity, ambition?"

"Activity, my friend! No! for it is a necessity to man's happiness; but that may be found in the humblest sphere. Ambition; yes! except it be that of perfecting the happiness of a devoted wife, and the training of my son to become a better man than his father."

"May he be no worse," replied Monica, affectionately, "and my life, end when it may, will not have been spent in vain."


THE END.

---

LONDON: R. CLAY, SON, AND TAYLOR, PRINTERS, BREAD STREET HILL.